THIR   N STOREYS

THIRTEEN
STOREYS

Jonathan Sims

GOLLANCZ
LONDON

First published in Great Britain in 2020 by Gollancz
an imprint of The Orion Publishing Group Ltd
Carmelite House, 50 Victoria Embankment
London EC4Y 0DZ

An Hachette UK Company

3 5 7 9 10 8 6 4

A CIP catalogue record for this book
is available from the British Library.

ISBN (Hardback) 978 1 473 22872 6
ISBN (Trade Paperback) 978 1 473 22873 3
ISBN (eBook) 978 1 473 22875 7

Typeset by Deltatype Ltd, Birkenhead, Merseyside

Printed in Great Britain by Clays Ltd, Elcograf S.p.A.

www.gollancz.co.uk

To Sasha
You are the best of me

Prologue

LEGACY OF A BUTCHERED BILLIONAIRE: THE LIFE AND DISMEMBERMENT OF TOBIAS FELL

David Erikson,
Crime Editor

Five years on, it's an all-to-familiar cliché that the only thing more interesting than the life of Tobias Fell was his death. For most of his eventful career, he was lauded by the public as an entrepreneurial titan; it's no secret he remains *The Sunday* ████████s most interviewed non-political figure, and we certainly weren't alone in that regard, with his picture gracing the front of *The* ████████ *Business Post* no less than fourteen times since 1992. After his death this fascination has only increased, though it has now taken on a wholly different character. Even for those who don't follow such things it's been hard to escape a relentless tide of true crime investigations, conspiracy theories, even discussions on paranormal forums. The brutal slaying has found its way to the top of more than one online list of 'creepiest unsolved murders'. Alive or dead, nobody ever seems to tire of talking about Tobias Fell.

I

But there are those who never stopped digging, who never accepted the impossible facts of this baffling case. But with so tantalising a mystery surrounding his death, are we perhaps overlooking the darker corners of his life?

His origins were similar to any other billionaire: he was provided with a small fortune by his father's family and proceeded, through luck, skill and, many say, ruthlessness to turn it into a large fortune. But it has been noted by many that, even by the standards of his peers, young Tobias seemed utterly unconcerned with the ethical implications of his business practices. While many of his more public and well-profiled enterprises (including those covered in this very publication) were PR-friendly tech companies or well-beloved brands, it takes very little digging to notice his most profitable investments came from less cuddly sources: pharmaceutical companies; gemstone mining; environmentally devastating oil extraction and arms manufacture. There were accusations his companies were involved in sweatshops, land seizure and slave labour, with many progressives coming forward with their condemnations of him even when he was still alive.

None of these accusations, however, ever truly seemed to touch Tobias Fell. A ready wit and an instinct for keeping his distance from the less-savoury aspects of his businesses served to keep his image clean, and well-publicised charitable initiatives ensured nobody raised too much interest in his tax affairs (even if many of these philanthropic projects seemed to quietly disappear when the spotlight faded). Every eager would-be tycoon named him their inspiration as he topped rich list after rich list.

There were plenty of reports, of course. Human rights organisations condemned his companies' ethics, but his books on business advice, reputedly ghost-written, made for far easier reading. Indeed, looking through the archives of *The Sunday* ███████, it's hard not to see our own complicity in burying many of these stories in the back pages.

When Tobias began to retreat from the public eye in the years leading up to his death, this seemed only to cement his reputation. For every concerned activist railing against his businesses, there were a dozen admirers intrigued by this new mystique and the occasional long-lens paparazzi photograph of the now-reclusive billionaire. He gradually stepped back from running his companies, and his much-lauded philanthropy entirely dried up. It seemed the business world's golden boy wished to simply spend his time hiding away in the penthouse suite of Banyan Court, a building he commissioned.

It was often said that Banyan Court stood as a monument to everything Tobias Fell was; both to those who held him as their idol, and to those who hated him. A towering, thirteen-storey residential development in the heart of Tower Hamlets, one of the poorest areas of central London. The building burst from the old brick shell of a Victorian factory-turned-tenement and blossomed into a grand edifice of glass and steel, a love letter to tasteful opulence. Our own coverage of the construction ('Billionaire makeover for London's poorest', 3rd July 2004) talked of regeneration and of the project enriching the area. But critics saw only gentrification and the displacement of families, predictions which have largely been proven accurate.

One particular point of contention was the part of Banyan Court given over to 'affordable housing'. Local planning guidelines require new residential developments to set aside a portion of their space as available to low-income occupants, but alleged indifference by the government and enforcement agencies led to persistent rumours about the construction quality of some areas of the building. New residents of these affordable homes reported cut corners, shoddy materials and fire hazards. The flats at the back were apparently almost completely segregated from the glistening modern facilities of the main building, and within a year left-wing blogs began talking about the 'hidden slum' lurking behind the shining facade of Banyan Court. And sitting in his pristine penthouse at the top of it all: Tobias Fell.

But however fascinating his life may have been, his death is what most people remember him for. It has gone down as one of the most high-profile unsolved murders in history. The details that were released to the public (and many details that weren't) have been relentlessly dissected by the media and amateur detectives, and almost no aspect of it makes sense. The sheer brutality of the killing was breathtaking, and yet despite the fact that the murder must have taken place inside his penthouse, none of the blood found at the scene belonged to Tobias Fell. In fact, according to certain leaked case files, no positive identification was ever made. The billionaire was listed as the only victim, so why were there multiple reports from people who saw multiple body bags being removed by the emergency services?

Further igniting the imagination of conspiracy theorists was the matter of the witnesses. Tobias Fell wasn't alone when he was killed. There were thirteen other people with him, all of whom claimed to have been attending a dinner party at his unexpected invitation. Though not all lived in the building, all these 'guests' each had some connection to Banyan Court. Aside from a postcode, however, it seems they had nothing whatsoever in common. An avant-garde art dealer, a local plumber, a six-year-old child attending with her mother ... Few, if any, of the guests would be those expected at a billionaire's banquet. Even beyond that, each guest said the same three things: they had never met Tobias Fell before that night; they had received an invitation without any sort of warning; and that, despite the forensic evidence conclusively showing he must have been killed while they were there, none of them had any idea when or how their host had been murdered.

Despite this seemingly obvious pool of suspects, no arrests were ever made by the Metropolitan Police and no official explanation of the killing was ever given. In the five years since the crime, none of the police or medical professionals who were part of the initial call or subsequent investigation have made any comment on the record. Further fuelling speculation of conspiracy were the strange events that occurred in and around Banyan Court in the week leading up to Tobias Fell's murder: the deaths of Edith Kinney and James Andre, officially labelled natural causes and suicide respectively, as well as the disappearance of noted activist Diego Santi, who was last seen entering the building. Theorists have never found a satisfying explanation for any of them.

Now, after half a decade, Banyan Court is all but abandoned. As leases end, estate agents have been unable to find replacements, with other residents and landlords abruptly selling or, in some cases, simply disappearing. The once impressive building now stands silent, casting a lonely eye over the dilapidated buildings below. A thirteen-storey tombstone to a man whose shadow still falls as darkly as that of his creation.

The murder of Tobias Fell remains unsolved, and it is unlikely it will ever be known what actually happened that night, or what those thirteen ill-fated guests truly saw.

1st

Night Work

Violet Ng
114 Banyan Court

'I'm sorry to hear that, it must be awful.'

Violet's mother had always warned her against talking to strangers, of course, but unfortunately it seemed nobody had warned *them* against talking to her. She bit back her response as the old man gave a sympathetic little tilt of the head, his lips pursed as though sharing her pain.

'My son used to work nights as well,' he continued, ignoring her silence. 'He hated it. Used to say he could never get the sleep right. It's not humane, I reckon.'

Violet had grown up buried beneath her mother's paranoid fear for her safety, weighed down by a hundred cautionary tales, thinly veiled urban legends that supposedly happened to some distant friend of the family. She'd never even mentioned the greatest threat that apparently seemed to plague only her: sympathetic strangers. The elderly man sat opposite was leaning forward, clearly waiting for an answer.

'Must have been hard,' Violet said at last, doing her best to look anywhere else, but the windows of the underground carriage showed only darkness. Her mother's tales had always started the same way, with looking a stranger in the eye. It was her version of 'Once upon a time', but for ending with someone dead in an unmarked lorry. To Violet, the greatest danger of eye contact was that people thought you were interested in their opinions.

'I read somewhere working a night shift can take almost a decade of your life!' her new friend said, relentless in his concern for her wellbeing.

'It's not for everyone,' Violet replied, falling back into the rote half-answers she always ended up using on family who decided they needed to tell her how much she must hate working nights. It happened a lot.

'What exactly do you do?' the old man continued, undeterred.

Violet considered for a moment. She could try to explain it to him, how much she loved it. She could try to vocalise that sense of being adjacent to the world, walking through and beside it, but never quite letting it touch her. She could tell him about her 'lunch' breaks, walking the streets around her office, drinking in the 2 a.m. silence, that wonderful emptiness. Describe watching cars and lorries slowly streaking a down the motorway towards Reading or Basingstoke, like a slow-moving river of lights. She could try to vocalise the almost spiritual connection she felt to the slumbering city. A city her mother had always claimed would kill her.

'I work on the ingestion and editorial management of syndicated media for a large scale B2B-focused press-aggregator, ensuring licensing and copyright compliance for future consumption in data and analytics.'

That shut him up.

Violet emerged from Whitechapel station just as the sky began to fully turn to dawn. The early morning air was cool and refreshing, before the summer heat really started, and she felt the first tinges of a satisfied exhaustion at the edges of her limbs. Her eyelids were pleasantly heavy as she slowly walked home. It wasn't long before it loomed before her, blotting out the sunrise.

Banyan Court rose above the streets of Tower Hamlets, gazing down with a paternalistic pity for the homeless and the struggling who simply hadn't had the good sense to be born rich. Violet smirked quietly to herself and walked quickly past the shining glass front doors. They didn't like it if you loitered. She passed the small patches of immaculately maintained greenery and turned down the small alleyway that ran along the side of Banyan Court. Between the rows of huge bins far too unsightly to be left visible from the street (and easily large enough for a dismembered body, her mother would have said), and past the line where glass gave way to concrete and old brick. Violet made her way to Resident Entrance B.

The small concrete courtyard was swept about once a month by the council, but the bars over the ground floor windows prevented any attempt to keep the glass clean. Those bars, heavy and painted a bright warning yellow, had been added when the building was first renovated, and they had always struck Violet as being a message, rather than a response to any actual crime. Like the CCTV signs that became more numerous as you approached the door to the rear apartments, no longer warning passers-by that residents were protected by surveillance, but instead reminding the less-trusted occupants that they were being watched.

She took a moment to breathe it all in, taking a seat on the raised section of concrete where teenagers sometimes gathered to smoke and laugh. She placed her hand on the cold, rough surface and closed her eyes. Her family had never understood Violet's decision to move to the city. The youngest of two brothers and four sisters, raised in a warm home near the

Scottish border that had somehow always been kept immaculate, her choice of lifestyle baffled her siblings. They had made their lives near home, with children and dogs and wide-open sky. Violet's existence, by comparison, was grimy and cramped: living in a tiny, squalid flat to grind away at a pointless desk job in a lightless office. They never understood that that was the point. Violet secretly loved that hardscrabble urban life, skirting poverty and wearing her fingers to the bone. It was something that her parents had once dismissed as 'the resilience of youth', but here she was aged thirty-one and this was still the life she wanted. It was a part of her so deeply ingrained that no amount of what her mother called 'harsh reality' could dislodge it.

She looked over the rusty basketball hoop on the nearby wall, just above the defaced sign that had once read 'No Ball Games' and smiled as she remembered one of her mother's classic pieces of 'reality': the gruesome tale of a young man who moved to London and caught the eye of a violent gang. They killed him, of course, and played a rousing game of basketball with his head. Her mother had read it in the paper, she claimed, but couldn't quite remember which one, and got quite upset when Violet gently questioned how exactly one could dribble with a human head, which traditionally was one of the less-bouncy pieces of sports equipment.

Violet turned away and got out her key, but Resident Entrance B apparently hadn't latched, and she didn't need it. Still smiling quietly to herself as she entered the cool of the dark hallway, she ignored the vandalised letterboxes. Though her mother's dire predictions of robbery, murder or kidnapping had never come true (yet another way Violet had disappointed her), she had been right about how harsh and ugly London was. If you couldn't find the quiet joy in that ugliness, it might be a bit much for some people.

The lift was working for once. She leaned heavily against the smudged mirror, appreciating the slow journey towards her flat and ignoring the small voice that called her lazy for not taking the stairs. Home was two cramped and dingy bedrooms at the back of the eighth floor with a laundry list of problems that appealed to her stubborn pride. She loved it. She and her flatmate Marie were the last of their university friends still renting in central London. When they'd first seen the listing, a few years ago now, Violet had assumed the low rent must have been a mistake. The pictures had showed the luxuriant glass frontage, with only a couple of clearly recycled stock photos of the interior. Once they'd actually viewed the place the reality of 'Resident Entrance B' became clear. It might have been the closest Violet ever got to being in one of her mother's stories, as they were led to the crumbling, bare apartment by a shifty looking estate agent. But the doors never slammed shut behind them, the bedroom wasn't a secret kill-room, and by then Marie's housing situation had deteriorated to the point where being fussy simply wasn't an option. So, they'd had to take it. Violet would never tell her friend how glad she was that decision was forced on them, but sometimes she thought Marie knew.

As she quietly opened the front door, she took a moment to listen out for the tell-tale sounds of Marie's morning routine. Nothing. Nodding to herself, Violet made her way towards her bedroom. Fatigue fully caught up with her as she checked the blackout curtains and went through her bedtime routine. She loved this flat. She loved it in that hard, proud part of her that rejected the soft comforts of an easy life; that fragment of her soul that heard her friends complain of city life and secretly judged them weak. Nothing worth doing should be easy, she had always felt, and that included living.

*

'He was there again yesterday.'

'Who?' Violet didn't look up from her laptop.

'That guy hanging around next door,' Marie's tone was low, conspiratorial, like it always was when she was gossiping.

'I thought he lived there.'

'No.' Marie shook her head. 'The woman who lives there, she must be in her eighties or something. This guy's young.'

'You do know grandchildren are a thing, right?'

'Sure, but he's been there three times over the last week. And I haven't seen her at all.'

'Well A, she was closer to fifty, and B, I'm pretty sure she moved out. I saw a bunch of boxes last month.'

'Yeah, well I didn't see any boxes. And I definitely didn't see him move in.'

Violet put her laptop down and offered her a cup of coffee. Marie shook her head again, gesturing to her pyjamas.

'So, you think he killed her.' Violet smiled at her flatmate.

'No, that's not—'

'You know what that sounds like to me?'

'Don't start.'

'Hey.' Violet's grin widened. 'You're the one proposing our new neighbour murdered a harmless old lady and now lives there with her body, watching you, the sweet stench of decay still clinging to his clothes.'

Marie was unimpressed

'It's just he keeps hanging around outside the door. I don't like it.'

'Why don't you just go over and knock? Ask him if he murdered her.'

'I don't even know her name!' Marie's feigned indignation didn't quite cover up her genuine discomfort at the idea of actually speaking to a neighbour.

'Well, that's a perfect follow-up question, isn't it?' Violet said, eyes locked on their cheap Argos kettle as it gradually convinced itself to boil.

'I just don't like it,' Marie repeated. 'The hallway reeks of smoke every time he's been there.'

'Well, that's it then, isn't it?'

'What?'

'If she hasn't moved out, then maybe he's staying with his grandmother, or whatever, and she doesn't like him smoking in the flat.' The smell of the instant coffee hit Violet's nostrils and she sighed happily, looking out the window at the evening lights below.

'So, he does it in the corridor? Isn't there, like, a fine for that? And what about the smoke alarms?'

'What about them?'

'What, you don't think they work?'

'About as well as anything else in this place.' Violet tried a sip of coffee. Still too hot. There was silence for a moment.

'We're going to die in a fire, aren't we?' Marie said, the resignation in her voice only half-pretend.

'What's this "we" you're talking about? I'm going to work.'

Marie gave Violet a withering look, but her flatmate didn't notice.

The front door shut behind Violet with a weighty metal click. Marie had insisted they replace the flimsy lock with something a little more solid, and Violet couldn't deny that there was a certain reassurance to the sound. Their door stood halfway down the blank and utilitarian corridor. To their right a few flats lay between them and the intersection that led to the staircase. To their left, three more led up to a window looking out over the urban patchwork below, with the lift opposite the furthest one.

There were technically two lifts beyond Resident Entrance B. One of them, the one she'd occasionally use, was a cramped and foul-smelling thing that seemed out of order as often as it was working. It listed the floors from G to eleven, missing out floor six as the button had fallen off some time ago and had never been replaced, no matter how often the lift was repaired. Violet had got used to using the stairs, something Marie begrudgingly referred to as her 'cardio', while Violet simply smiled a sweet, bitter grin and told her to think about how much worse that poor billionaire in the penthouse must have it.

It was the other lift that really captured Violet's imagination. Through that dingy courtyard, past the rows of iron mailboxes, empty bike rails, and just enough snaking corridor to make a visitor doubt their way, there was a spiralling stairwell that stretched up through the back of Banyan Court. It was old, part of the original structure, with uneven tile steps that had clearly been resurfaced, but not repaired. At the centre of the curving steps was an ancient wrought-iron goods lift. Violet had no idea how old it was (turn of the century, maybe?) or why it had been left in place when the building was redeveloped. It should go all to the way to the penthouse. At least, it would if it worked, something she thought unlikely given the hazard tape, the warning signs, and the sturdy yellow padlock bigger than her hand. Marie swore that she'd seen the thing moving once or twice, but Marie swore a lot of things, and as far as Violet was concerned, it was nothing but a towering metal spine, a strange relic of iron vertebrae gradually falling to rust. One of the city's hidden bones that she had lucked into living beside.

Violet checked down the corridor, over towards flat 116. There was nobody there. No mysterious smoking stranger hovering menacingly between her and the lift, waiting to catch her eye as prelude to murder. She stopped for just a moment as she passed the door, straining her ears for any sound from inside, but all was quiet. She wrinkled her nose as the lift arrived and headed down towards her commute.

Work passed slowly. She had managed to leave her headphones next to her bed and having to give her full attention to what actually amounted to eight hours of copying and pasting text left her feeling almost comatose. She always forgot how silent the office was. There must have been almost forty people there, just as bored and unchallenged as she was, but the quiet of the night shift was almost never broken, an unspoken rule that Violet had always been in favour of, at least when she had been able to listen to her music or the occasional podcast. But tonight it felt heavier than usual, and there were moments it seemed almost like a physical weight, pressing down on her. She kept realising that she was holding her breath.

It wasn't just the dangers of the nocturnal streets her mother had warned her about. Working nights was top of the list of things to be dreaded, according to her. Burnout and suicide were the recurring conclusions of that strand of story, with one memorable tale of a man who had 'gone mad from the quiet', whatever that meant, and had burned down the office block with all his co-workers inside. The thought was enough to get her through the first few hours, as there was nothing more likely to inspire her to work harder than proving her mother wrong.

Violet watched as the smokers got up for what must have been their third break in as many hours, and tried to choke down the quiet anger she always felt watching them. She couldn't stand laziness. She knew, of course, that the job she worked was largely pointless, just busywork to keep money circulating between a handful of dying businesses, but that didn't matter. That was the work. And these people had no right to slack off, just standing around chatting among themselves. Violet didn't like this part of herself. She knew her personal standards were extreme, and she shouldn't judge other people for not meeting them, but she couldn't help it sometimes. She couldn't imagine being fulfilled as some housewife, placid and content in gentle domesticity, terrified of the world beyond your own four walls. Work was freedom, it was how you made your own life, and all too often she found herself hating people who didn't seem to appreciate that.

When the clock ticked over to half past one, Violet almost leapt up, quietly letting her manager, a solid, unremarkable man named Bob, know that she was taking her break. It took her less than six minutes to eat the salad pot she had bought for lunch, and then she was out the door and into the dusty night air of the city. She walked quickly, as if she could hurry along the relaxation, and tried to figure out why exactly she was so on edge. There were no special stresses at work (Bob was foretelling imminent layoffs, but he was always going on about that), everything was fine at home (Marie had brought up maybe wanting to move out next year, but that was a while away) and there weren't any money problems (the agency said rent was going up soon, but she could afford it, just about). So why did it feel like every nerve in her body was twisted up tight? It was as if she were about to break into a run at any moment.

Violet was so caught up in trying to examine her mood, she didn't notice them standing there until she was halfway down Augustine Road. Three figures, just at the edge of the street, no details clearly visible, all obscured by hoods and caps and thick jackets. They could have been talking to each other, probably were, but from where she was walking it wasn't clear. They seemed to just be standing there, motionless, the light of the streetlamp shining down on them.

People were exactly what Violet wished to avoid on her late-night walks, their messy presence always breaking through her quiet communion with the city. Instinctively, she started to turn, to retrace her steps and find another, more secluded route. But as she did one of the figures looked up, and his eyes beneath the bright blue baseball cap met hers. They were young, cocky, and even from the other end of the road she felt them judging her. He thought she was scared of him. A tiny surge of defiance rose up inside her. This was her city, her time, and she would not let the second-hand fears of her mother rule her. So what if she had looked him in the eye? If they wanted to hang out late at night in public, that was their business. There was nothing sinister to it, nothing obvious, at least, and she was certainly in no position to criticise them for being out late. So, she continued down Augustine Road, her footsteps a lot louder than she remembered them. In the back of her mind came that insistent pressure to cross the road, that urge to keep her distance, but she fought it down, determined not to let this fear win. The man exchanged some short words with his companions, watching her as she walked in their direction with all the confidence she could hold on to.

Violet was now within a few feet of them and could smell the waves of body spray covering up old joints and unwashed jeans. She ignored it, just a few more steps and she'd be past them, she'd be at the end of the road, turning a corner and breathing normally again. But as her eyes once again made that briefest moment of contact with his, she saw a sudden change in them, and her whole body spasmed in terror as he lunged at her.

'Boo!'

It took her a second to process what he had said. The young man had already turned back to his friends, who burst into mocking laughter, then just as quickly returned to whatever conversation they'd been having.

Violet tried to regain her feet, but her every nerve was on fire and her legs wouldn't stop shaking from adrenaline. She wanted to say something, to scream, to hit them, but it seemed like they'd already forgotten her, so instead she just started walking again. She turned right at the end of the street and headed immediately back to her office.

It took hours for the shaking to subside, and the work she was supposed to be doing sat forgotten on her screen. She was so angry she could barely think, and not at the arsehole that made her jump, but at herself for letting it get to her. It was harmless, a joke. She was overreacting. But that didn't do anything to soften what she felt.

Violet left the office that morning exhausted, utterly drained, and travelled back to Banyan Court in a daze. She felt disconnected from the space around her, and with every step she found herself surprised that her foot landed on solid ground. She didn't remember the train home, and moved off the tube like a ghost, drifting into the building and up the stairs without really taking anything in. She only stopped for a second as she got out her keys, dimly registering the faint scent of old tobacco. She looked listlessly to the next door over, but it was closed. The corridor was empty as always.

She had no appetite and Marie was still asleep, so Violet quietly moved through the darkness to her room and crawled into bed, barely remembering to kick off her shoes. Sleep hit her like a fist, and she spent that day dreaming of three figures whispering to each other under a street light. But no matter how close she got, the words remained muffled and secret.

*

Her eyes opened slowly, groggily. How long had it been? She looked at her clock. 8 a.m. She'd barely slept an hour and her head was pounding. No, it was the door, Someone was knocking and—

'Violet?'

Marie's voice. She pulled herself slowly out of bed and opened the door a crack. The light from the hall stung her eyes and she blinked several times before the lights resolved themselves into the figure of her flatmate, still wearing her pyjamas.

'Aren't you going to be late?'

Marie shook her head. 'I need a favour.'

'What?' Violet's stomach dropped slightly.

'I've got a thing I need to be at today, but I kind of double-booked myself.'

'I thought you had work?'

'Yeah, like I said, double-booked. So I need to call in sick.'

Violet tried her best to suppress the little flame of rage that rose up at Marie's blasé tone. This certainly wasn't the first time Marie had done this, her approach to work was no different than it had been at university, but right now Violet had to bite her tongue. Had Marie got her out of bed literally to just rub her laziness in Violet's face?

'Say you have a migraine. That usually works.' It took all her self-control to keep her voice level. She just needed to sleep. She had work to do in the evening.

'Sure, for a day, but this might end up needing to stretch out a bit, you know? I figure if I'm "too sick" to call in for myself, like a fever or something, and need you to do it for me ... I mean, that's got to be most of the week taken care of. Look, I know it bugs you, but I'd massively owe you one.'

There was a very long moment where Violet could feel herself about to reach for the phone in Marie's hand. To call the office

and tell them exactly what Marie was doing. To let her feel all
the consequences of her useless shirking. But instead she just
closed the door. It took all her restraint, but she did not slam
it, and she did not vocalise any of the thoughts that flooded
uninvited into her mind.

Marie knew better than to push her any further, and sleep
found Violet quickly.

The next time she woke up was to an empty flat. Marie must
have been out at whatever was so much more important than
work, but Violet gave her door a gentle knock anyway. She
had no intention of apologising for earlier, she'd been totally
in the right, but given their housing situation, Violet was wary
of creating any rifts with her old friend. And today their tiny
flat felt like an oddly lonely place to wake up to silence, so she
would have welcomed the company. But there was no response,
so Violet made her way to the kitchen. The roar of the kettle
grated on her in the quiet, and she noticed her right hand
shaking ever so slightly as she spooned out the coffee granules.

She was fine. There was no reason for her not to be, so she
was fine. It was times like this she'd welcome the reassuring
scratch scratch scratch of a murderer living in the walls. At least
it would be some company. She couldn't quite bring herself to
laugh at her own joke as she drank her coffee and told herself
she felt better.

There were people in the lift when it finally arrived. She'd
been standing so long in the cigarette-scented hall she'd almost
written it off as broken again, but just as she turned towards the
stairway the doors started to open. Two figures stood inside,
huddled close together, facing towards the back corner as
though in close conversation, though Violet couldn't make out
what they were saying. She tried to get a look at their faces, see

if she recognised them from around the building, but one had a thick hood pulled up over their head and the other was turned too much away from her. Their clothes were muted, denim and canvas, and neither seemed to be paying her any attention at all.

For some reason, the idea of stepping into that lift, slowly riding down those eight floors next to them, filled Violet with horror. Was it because of that arsehole from yesterday? Had one 'boo' left her feeling like this forever? No, this was something else. It must be.

Perhaps she was worried it would break, trapping them all inside for four days until they had to eat her. Again, the memory of her mother's stories failed to raise the usual smile. She'd just take the damn lift, she decided, but by that time the doors were already closing again. Violet took the stairs.

Work went slowly, as it so often did. She was tired, and the machine-dispensed coffee didn't seem to be helping. She cycled through the strange, synthetic menu, trying to find the one that would finally break through her haze. Instant coffee, 'freshbrew' coffee, latte, they all tasted of the same chemicals her tongue has adapted to years ago, but none of them could shift this weariness. She found herself measuring out the work day by the smokers' cigarette breaks, the rise and fall of that familiar irritation as regular as any clock. When she finally left to take her walk and passed them huddled in the chill outside the front door, she found herself mumbling about their laziness, but they kept their backs to her and didn't appear to have heard.

She avoided Augustine Road, and turned once or twice when she almost crossed paths with another late-night wanderer. She hated herself for it but decided that having a peaceful walk was more important than proving some sort of point. Even so, relaxation was elusive tonight, and she ended up staying out ten minutes longer than she technically had for her break. Nobody seemed to notice, but it bothered her.

Back at home, Marie was sullenly getting ready for work.

'I just called in a migraine yesterday, so have to go in today.'

'Sorry,' Violet said. She wasn't.

'Oh, and your mother called, something about your uncle's sixtieth?'

'Thanks. I'll call her back,' Violet said. She wouldn't.

In the cold, cultivated darkness of her room, Violet lay down on the bed, trying to figure out what was wrong. Everything was fine. Everything was normal. So why did her jaw ache from clenching her teeth? Why was she so tired? She lay there and surrendered to sleep.

The next night was strange. Violet woke up. She must have. But there was still that disconnection, as though she had been somehow severed from the world. Everything was muted, and when she tried to focus on any one thing too closely her head started to ache. Marie had clearly had a difficult day and she did not seem inclined to chat as she ate her dinner, leaving Violet to her breakfast: toast that didn't want to cook right and coffee that got cold almost as soon as it was put down. She still drank it, though, desperately trying to grasp just a splinter more wakefulness. It was half an hour later than usual when she finally got out of the door, and she had no idea what she might have been doing for all that time.

She stepped out into a cloud of cigarette smoke and stopped, coughing, at the unexpected sensation. Thrust into the real world again, if only for that moment of physical discomfort. She looked around and, sure enough, standing in front of the door to 116 was a young man in an old grey suit. His shirt should have been white, but time had rendered it the same dull colour as his jacket, and he wore it unbuttoned over the sun-darkened skin of his chest. His curling black hair was just long enough to be dishevelled. He did not seem to have noticed Violet leaving her flat, or her reaction to the waves of smoke that rolled from his cigarette and curled around a peeling 'No Smoking' sign. All of his attention seemed focused towards the end of the hallway, past the lift, to where a window looked down over the night-covered city below.

The fluorescent bulb above that window had burned out weeks before and had not been replaced, leaving that part of the corridor shadowed and dark, but as Violet followed the stranger's gaze she could just about make out a silhouette. She blinked, trying to focus on it. Somebody was there. They seemed to be standing very still, and it wasn't immediately clear if they were facing away and looking out through the glass, or staring back down the corridor.

Violet wanted to ignore them, to just cross over to the lift and go to work (she needed to get to work). Her nerves were still alight from her encounter two nights before. Yet there was something about the figure by the window that made her certain that they were looking at her. Not the man with the cigarette, her. She felt compelled to call out, greet them, assure them that she was going to work, she was, when a hand grasped her firmly by the arm. She spun around to see her strange neighbour shaking his head insistently.

'Do you see them?' he asked her, his voice thick with concern and an accent she couldn't quite place.

She nodded, her mind racing. Which of her mother's stories was this?

He seemed visibly relieved. His grip relaxed and she pulled her arm away, instinctively stepping back. His face softened for a moment, and he stammered out an apology. As if sensing her next question, he gestured to the door behind him and, Violet assumed, to the old woman who lived behind it.

'Old friend,' he said, as though expecting this to answer all her questions, but her head was starting to swim again, and the blood pounded through her ears, drowning out the choking silence of that hall. She turned to leave, not wanting to ask this stranger any more questions when her eyes flicked instinctively back to the window and she froze. There were now two people standing there. The second was just as much a silhouette as the first, and just as still. Their heads leaned towards each other, as though passing some quiet conversation, and if she strained, Violet thought could just about hear the faintest whisper of what they were saying ...

When her neighbour looked back, it took a second for him to notice the second figure, but as he did his face contorted into a look of suspicion and unease. He turned slowly to her, a bead of sweat rolling across his face.

'I, uh—' He struggled to find the words. 'Be safe.'

Violet turned right and hurried down the stairs. Two floors down she could still hear the figures whispering.

Violet was late to the office that night. She tried her best to collect herself, to sit down and focus her mind on her task, but the words seemed very far away, and the silence of the office left her floating and unsettled. Her fingers ached before she even started typing, and the central heating felt like it was going to smother her. Every few minutes she would catch herself listening intently, as though straining to hear some quiet conversation, and the coffees she was sure she had just made would be long cold. She kept drinking them, trying to fight off a fatigue that had been building in her all night, terrified that if she closed her eyes she would sleep. How many cups was it in her mother's story before the stressed office worker had a heart attack? Or was that the same one who ended up burning down the building? They'd all started to blend together.

She was terrified her exhaustion would show, that they would know she wasn't doing her work. They would all know. Every clack of the keyboard was like a finger being drummed right onto her skull.

In spite of everything, she still tried to take her walk. Bob had leaned over and asked her if she was planning to take her break and it was like a rope had been cut. She almost leapt from her seat. Her steps were unsteady, and the silent streets offered her no comfort, but the idea of staying in that office for another second made her feel faint. At least the night air was unchanged. It still offered that crisp reassurance that the world still lived, but she did not walk as far as normal, nor as fast.

Augustine Road was empty. No figures standing at the other end, no whispering strangers waiting for her. There was nothing there. So why was she so reluctant to walk any further? Why did she already feel like she needed to head back to work? She carried on, trying to ignore it, pushing the possibilities from her mind, but she ended her walk soon afterwards. There was no peace to be found in the city that night.

As she returned to the office, she saw a small crowd outside the door. The smokers, six of them, huddled together, talking quietly. She knew they emailed each other to orchestrate their breaks, and now they were lurking outside, as if waiting for her, whispering to each other. Shirking. They didn't look up as she passed, and she had to stop herself barking at them to get back to work. She rubbed her exhausted eyes, fingers stained with coffee and dirt, and pushed herself back into the office.

*

By the time she got home to Bayan Court, she was so shot through with bone-deep fatigue that she almost didn't notice the flashing lights of the ambulance parked in front of it. It was only when a round-faced woman in a police uniform gently put a hand on her shoulder to stop her wandering, unthinkingly, into the blue-and-white tape that she realised there was anything out of the ordinary. Barriers hid most of the scene, but a small streak of something dark could still be seen on the edge of the kerb. It could have been blood. It could have been other things as well, of course, but her mind refused to think of any, and kept circling back to blood.

'I live here,' Violet said, realising she had no idea what the officer had said to her.

'Certainly, this way please.' The response was courteous and crisp as she began to usher Violet towards the well-lit main entrance.

'No. Round the back.'

The police officer stopped for a second, confused, and Violet had to limply point to the alleyway that led to her home.

'Right. Wait here,' she was told, as the officer walked away, apparently needing to check something with a colleague. Violet could have sworn she was muttering 'Get back to work' under her breath.

She stood there, waiting, watching paramedics load a long black plastic bag into the back of the ambulance. One of them knocked a barrier partially aside, and for a second Violet was absolutely positive she could see, lying on the wet ground, a bright blue baseball cap. There was no surprise in her, no shock that he was now lying dead on the other side of London, five miles from their last meeting. Perhaps she was just too tired.

She wondered idly which urban legend had finally got him. Maybe it was her? Maybe that was the big twist, that the monster in the story was her. She felt her lips fold into a single syllable as the police officer returned to lead her round the back and into the building.

'Boo.'

Four figures stood halfway up the stairs, just above the first floor, where the steps curled behind the old iron lift. They wore thick jackets over dull, unremarkable outfits as they turned towards each other, faces hidden from view. Violet could hear them whispering to each other even before Resident Entrance B swung shut behind her, cutting off the flashing lights that seemed to follow her even behind the building. It was six in the morning, why were they there?

She waited almost a full minute for the lift. It wasn't coming. She pressed the button again, rubbing at the tips of her fingers. They felt rough, and for a second she could have sworn they were different, covered with callouses and scarred blisters. She looked up at the lift, but the number hadn't changed. She started to feel very exposed and finally turned towards the stairway, full of that resignation that comes with exhaustion. As she climbed she could hear them whispering above her, but as she got closer the sound seemed to stop and they simply stood there, silent. They didn't turn around, and she still couldn't see their faces. Somewhere in the distance, a siren wailed through the streets.

Violet kept on climbing, the now-quiet crowd patient and unmoving. Her legs felt odd, their movements almost mechanical, but she didn't stop.

Thinking about it later, it seemed to her that four people standing together should have almost completely blocked the stairs. And yet she didn't remember passing them, not really. As she continued to walk, they were simply behind her, and before she had a chance to consider it she had reached the next floor. She turned back but they hadn't moved. Her mind instinctively reached for one of her mother's stories, trying to place the feeling of unease in a familiar context, but none came. She continued her climb, the whispers floating up to follow her.

'What did Bob say?'

It was already nine and Marie was late for work, but it didn't look like she had any intention of leaving before Violet had given her every detail.

'Don't worry about it.'

'Hey, you use my phone, you give me the details,' Marie insisted, doing her best to hide genuine concern. No answer from Violet. 'You still haven't found yours?'

'No. It's fine, I don't need it.'

'What the hell does that mean? Obviously you need a phone. You just had to call in sick.'

'I didn't have to. I can go to work. I should go to work.'

'Seriously. Look at you.' Marie was firm. 'When was the last time you slept properly? I mean, you weren't doing great even before a guy you knew died outside our building.'

Violet was quiet for a moment. 'I didn't know him. Not really. He just—'

'Who cares!' Marie exploded. 'It's clearly messed you up. You need some time off.'

'OK. You've made your point.'

'And?' Marie said, gesturing to her phone, still clasped in Violet's hand.

'... Bob gave me the rest of the week off. So, like, three days, I guess. Nights.'

'Good. I told you he'd be fine with it.'

'He wasn't.'

'What did he say?' Marie's tone was suddenly protective.

'It's not that.' Violet tried to shrug. 'I mean, he didn't say …
He kept saying it was fine, that it sounded like it had been a real
shock and that I should take all the time I needed.'

'But …?'

'I could just tell. I know he thinks I'm slacking. That I'm not
willing to work.'

Marie didn't reply.

'Anyway, you should get going,' Violet said, doing her best to
sound normal. 'You don't want another telling-off from Sandra.'

She didn't even need to look at her to know what face Marie
was pulling, but her friend pressed on.

'What did the cops say?'

'I didn't ask. I mean, they couldn't tell me anything anyway,
could they?'

'Wait.' Marie's eyes went wide. 'You don't think it was him,
do you? From next door. Maybe he … y'know.'

'Marie, please.'

'Right, right. Sorry, it's just … right outside. Bloody hell.
We need to move. This place is … I told you, didn't I?'

Violet said nothing.

'So, what's the plan?'

'Nothing. I just need some decent sleep.'

Marie began to nod, then stopped, her eyes focused on
Violet's mug. 'You alright drinking that?'

'It's decaf,' Violet lied.

'Right,' Marie said, giving her a long steady look, before
finally getting to her feet.

Violet didn't want to ask the next question. She wanted
Marie to be out of the door and gone, to leave her to her coffee
and her vague dread, but she couldn't stop herself.

'Marie …'

'Yeah?'

'Have you, uh, seen anyone else around the building? People who shouldn't be here?'

There was the look, that guarded concern she'd been desperate to avoid.

'What do you mean? Like who?'

'Just … People. Hanging around. Groups of them. Standing still like they're … I don't know.' She managed to stop just short of mentioning the whispers. Marie was quiet for several seconds.

'Violet, this isn't one of your stories.'

'Fuck's sake, I know that!' Violet rocked backwards for a second, stunned by the strength of her own reaction. 'It was just a question. Forget it.'

'Fine.' Marie was clearly upset. ' And no, I haven't. I mean, I've seen people, sure, but not being weird or being … "still" or whatever.'

'OK.' Violet tried to shrug, not wanting to meet Marie's eye. Another pause.

'Look, I've got to go. Just … take it easy, OK? Get some sleep.'

Violet didn't answer.

The building was strange in the daytime. That quiet that dominated it when the residents were asleep was instead replaced by a constant stream of faint noises. Conversation, televisions, washing machines, shouting. It all came floating through those thin walls, smothered and distorted so much it was impossible to tell exactly where it originated. But no whispering. Violet passed a half dozen residents on their way into or out of their flats, but everyone was moving, travelling, on their way somewhere. All except the workman with plumber's tools, who stood tapping a pipe with an expression of intense concentration. Or the young man in the Uriah Heep T-shirt, who stopped measuring the corridor long enough to regard her with a curiosity that made her feel strangely self-conscious. But there were no half-seen figures huddled together, no silhouettes pressed against windows, as if waiting for something to happen.

By the time she finally crawled into bed in the early hours of the afternoon, Violet had walked nearly every corridor and stairway in the cramped rear of Banyan Court. It was strange to wander its corridors in the daytime, to see the sunlight illuminate those walls she knew so well by fluorescence felt almost unnatural. Their comforting coldness replaced by a stifling warmth. Still, even Violet could not deny the daylight reassured her, and by the end she could almost dismiss that oppressive sense of wrongness, or maybe she was just able to smother it in a thick layer of fatigue, and mask it in her aching muscles and stiff, calloused fingers.

She opened her eyes to darkness. Had she been asleep? Her hand reached out almost automatically, hunting for the light switch, but before she had a chance to use it, she stopped. In an instant she was wide awake, her ears straining to listen.

The whispering was soft and insistent, and for a brief second, she had a terrible certainty that it was coming from her kitchen. Violet's fingers found the switch and the room was flooded with artificial light. She wasted no time, fear briefly sparking into anger as she ran into the next room, but of course it was empty, the whispers still near but now muffled and distant. Where was Marie? Right, it was Friday, she'd probably be out for some drinks. Wait, was it Friday? It didn't matter, she wasn't there. Violet took her time, searching every inch of their tiny flat.

Marie's door was closed. The whispering could be from in there. Was it locked? Or maybe Marie was home, sitting and relaxing quietly, not hearing what was going on. The privacy of their rooms was one of the cornerstones of Violet and Marie's living together. But Violet had to be sure. Gripping the handle, she felt a flood of relief that it wasn't locked, then a burst of terror at the idea of what might be waiting inside. She opened the door.

It was empty. Marie's furniture was basic, practical, reflecting a life led mostly outside the flat. But most importantly, there was nowhere for someone to hide. Violet breathed out for what felt like the first time since she woke up. The whispering figures weren't inside her home. Not yet. She caught herself at this, tried to focus: there was no reason to think they could get in there. It had to be safe.

She dressed quickly, slipping on her shoes without bothering to properly lace them, and headed out the door. The window at the end of the corridor was dark and the lights of the city were faint. There was no safety for her tonight. The thought came unbidden into Violet's mind and she didn't have the energy to push it away. Perhaps her mother was right and there never had been any safety. But none of her stories had ever gone like this, and Violet began to search anyway.

She found three of them on the stairs heading down to the fifth floor. She turned and walked quickly away. There was a cluster of six or seven at the end of the corridor on the eighth, again she couldn't bring herself to get any closer. There were only two standing in front of the elevator on the tenth floor, but when she turned around it was clear there were more just round the corner. She hadn't been counting them before, and now that she had started it didn't take long for her to lose track. She wanted to confront them, to demand they tell her what was going on. This was her home, her city, they had no right to be here. They would not make her afraid. Yet she just couldn't summon that defiant walk which had seen her down Augustine Road. Instead she found herself running.

She stopped to catch her breath by a window. Looking down onto the dingy concrete courtyard below she could make out five of them standing beneath one of the security lights. Always facing each other, never where she could see them clearly, their rough, practical clothes dirty and worn. She stood there, at a fifth-floor window, watching them for nearly twenty minutes. They didn't move. Even from all the way up here she could hear them whispering. What were they standing around for? Didn't they have jobs to do? Was it her? Were they whispering about her?

She could have stood there watching them for hours, but the trance was broken by the sound of a door opening behind her. Violet spun to see a young woman staring at her. It wasn't until the woman actually started to ask her what she was doing that Violet realised she was looking at another resident of Banyan Court. She wanted to answer this woman, explain what was happening, beg her for help, but couldn't make a sound. There was a moment of silence, each clearly waiting for the other to say something, then Violet's attention was seized by the sudden shriek of metal, and the clanking rattle of an ancient mechanism.

She didn't wait to see the other woman's reaction and raced back down the corridor, around a corner, past two figures mumbling softly to each other, hunting that noise. With a lurch she realised what it was and turned back, heading towards the spiralling central stairwell.

There were three of them inside the old wrought-iron elevator, their hands blackened by dirt. These three almost spoke clearly, but their words were drowned by the clanking of the lift moving. Violet felt a swell of nausea to see those ancient metal bones in motion. She ran up the stairs, chasing the slowly rising platform, trying to catch just a word of what they were saying. On the twelfth floor she was forced to stop and watch as the lift continued up into the ceiling above her. Violet felt like screaming, but she could barely make a sound.

She staggered back towards her flat, hands clasped over her ears, desperate to block out the whispering as she passed more groups of indistinct figures. So many more. She wanted to ignore them all, to lock herself in and simply wait out the night, but the door had locked behind her, as it always did, and in her rush to leave she had neglected to take the keys. She reached instinctively for her phone, before remembering that was lost as well, and a deep panic began to rise in her, as the whispering began to get closer. There were dozens of figures. Hundreds. And though they stayed still their presence seemed to cover her like fog.

There was nothing she could do. Nowhere she could run. No one she could call. She felt herself begin to collapse, when she caught the whiff of stale smoke. She turned, expecting to see her neighbour standing there, but the hallway was empty. Without stopping to think, Violet staggered over and began to pound on the door of 116 Banyan Court. For several awful seconds she was sure it wouldn't open, but then she heard the click of a lock, and there he was.

Violet couldn't speak, couldn't get the words out. Her throat tasted like diesel fumes and dust. He just watched her with a look of deep pity on his face. He smelled of old cigarettes.

'Help.' She almost choked on the word.

He shook his head slowly.

'They are not real,' he said, his voice filled with false resolve. 'Don't make them real.'

'What do they want?'

'Nothing,' the stranger said. 'The dead are dead. Justice is for the living.'

And the door to 116 shut, leaving her alone.

Violet stood in the corridor, her fear gradually shifting into numbness, and waited for something to happen. Sure enough the tinny chime of the lift sounded behind her. She watched as the doors parted to reveal more anonymous whisperers crammed inside it, so tightly there was barely room to breathe, their backs all turned towards her. She walked slowly towards it, but the lift doors did not close.

All at once, the mumbling cut off, and the world was quiet again. Violet's ears rang painfully with the silence, and she felt the anger rise inside her. The words came to her lips, though she had no idea why.

'Get back to work!'

She spat it like an exorcism, and the figures seemed to slump, as though whatever spirit propelled them had been torn away. Violet's anger vanished as quickly as it came, and she was filled with the deepest shame she had ever felt.

'What is it?' Violet pleaded. 'What do you want to tell me?'

As one, they turned to face her, pulling down their hoods and uncovering their heads. Their hair was matted with sweat and mineshaft dirt; their fingers were bruised, calloused from pickaxe and assembly line and sewing needle; they were stained with coffee and cacao. The bloody sewing thread that criss-crossed their mouths kept their lips tight together, but now the whispered words were clear. And Violet listened, learning how the story would end.

Marie was worried. If she'd really known anything at all about Violet's family she would have called them, but as it was, she had to content herself with knocking on the locked bedroom door every few hours, asking if she was OK, if she needed anything. The answer was always the same.

'I'm fine. Just thinking.'

She tried again. Violet had been 'just thinking' for almost two days now, and she should have been back at work yesterday. Something was definitely wrong, and if it went on much longer Marie was going to have to call a doctor or something. Though what that something might actually be she had no idea. The internet didn't seem to have an easy answer for what to do when your best friend was having a weird breakdown. Marie had always said she worked too hard.

Whatever was going on with her, Marie was sure that Violet would still want to know about the invitation. She read it again to be sure, but the words were still there, still exactly the same. It didn't make any sense, but the thick card and tasteful embossed lettering were impeccable. If this was a prank, someone had spent serious money on it.

TOBIAS FELL cordially invites VIOLET NG
to attend a dinner party at 1 Banyan Court
on the evening of 16th August 2014
Penthouse access will be available through the freight elevator

She knocked on Violet's door again, and slipped it underneath.

In the pitch darkness of her room, Violet smiled. She didn't need the light to know what it said. She had work to do.

2nd

The Knock

Jésus Candido
30 Banyan Court

Tap tap tap.

The silver head of the cane hit rhythmically against the well-shined leather of an expensive shoe, a soft but insistent sound that pervaded the near silence of the auction hall. Jésus Candido was bored.

'Lot 14 is next,' the auctioneer droned on. 'An incised ceramic bowl, judged to originate from the Guaraní peoples, date unknown. Two hundred pounds, starting at two hundred pounds.'

Nothing worth his time. He continued his impatient tapping. From the other seats, eyes turned to stare at him with varying degrees of curiosity. He saw them take in his expertly tailored bottle-green suit, the necktie with its perfectly executed Eldredge knot, his cultivated air of disdain and disregard. Some recognised him, whispering to companions with quietly awed expressions. Others showed no recognition, but perhaps they would ask after him later, and then they would learn his name. And why they *should* know it. Jésus allowed himself a small smile. Between changing fashions, money-laundering and newly minted tech billionaires looking to invest, the art industry was a constantly changing place, and any small thing you could do to maintain your profile as a dealer was worth it. Even a *legend* such as him couldn't afford to rest on his laurels.

'Sold to Margot for 240 pounds,' the auctioneer pushed through, clearly trying to ignore Jésus' theatrical yawn. The man certainly knew who had decided to be seen at his auction house.

And being visible seemed about the only thing this auction was good for. Normally Jésus did his business remotely, like the rest of the ring – his colleagues, though perhaps 'co-conspirators' would be more accurate – but he'd had a free afternoon local enough to the venue that he had succumbed to a whim and decided to attend in person. At the very least, it was worth showing his face once in a while. Jésus was in fact the one who had tipped Desmond and the rest of the ring off about this auction in the first place. His brother-in-law Antonio, a functionary in the Brazilian government, had been alerted to a wealthy cattle farmer who had recently passed away. Apparently, the man had owned a sizeable collection of artistic curiosities, but his family had no appreciation for such things and had decided to auction them off in London, where they ran much of their business.

'Sold to William by phone for five hundred and ten pounds,' the auctioneer said as a rather tasteless sculpture was taken away. Jésus didn't even remember them bringing it out.

Still, now they were getting to an item Jésus was designated bidder for. Perhaps this would bring a little excitement.

'Lot 32 now, a religious figure in soapstone, believed to be the work of Aleijadinho.' A pause. 'Uncertified. Starting at one thousand pounds.'

'One thousand pounds,' Jésus called, making his bid as instructed. To be honest, he thought it was overpriced for what was likely a forgery. But at least there might be some bidding drama.

'One thousand pounds,' the auctioneer repeated, looking around. 'Currently one thousand pounds.'

Silence.

'Sold to Jésus Candido for one thousand pounds.'

This was ridiculous. He was starting to think he might actually have made a mistake. The catalogue had been uninspiring, but to sit there and see this parade of extremely pedestrian art made him deeply weary. The whole auction had been like this, with the ring's bidders picking up what they had been assigned with a minimum of fuss and counterbids. Great news for the ring, but dull for Jésus, and the thought that he'd have to see most of these items again at the Knock made him almost regret bringing it to their attention. Still, he'd bought what was required of him, so could finally make his exit. Perhaps he'd make a performance out of it.

'Lot 51, an intriguing untitled mixed media piece, oil and charcoal on canvas. Artist unknown, date unknown. We'll start at eighty pounds.'

Jésus looked at the painting and found himself sitting back down. He hadn't particularly marked it in the catalogue for the auction, assuming it to be just another throwaway piece of junk from a mostly forgettable collection. A four-by-eight mixed media piece, oil and charcoal on canvas. Abstract, untitled, artist unknown, worth basically nothing. It had only been highlighted by the ring because William Duphine, a new addition to their ranks who Jésus privately considered an upstart with no taste, had been hired to adorn a full country house. He was bulk-buying anything he thought might work with the rest of the decor. To look at it now, though, Jésus couldn't imagine this painting fitting into any wider aesthetic. A tactful person might call it *unique*.

Though even he had to admit seeing it was a different

experience to the flat catalogue photograph. He might as well have been looking at a different piece entirely. It was vibrant and intoxicating, a series of bright, cascading lines that swirled and interlocked in an apparently meaningless manner, until your mind finally arranged it into what it was: the face of a woman. Her eyes were vague, her mouth closed and unreadable, but smiling. The style was crude, almost childish at points, but there was something there. Something he wanted ...

Murmuring took up around him, and he realised he had raised his hand to bid. He wasn't the designated buyer for this one, he knew that, and as he lowered his hand, he had a sudden worry he'd be responsible for raising the price.

'I'm sorry, Mr Candido, was that a bid?' The auctioneer seemed as surprised as anyone.

'Eighty,' someone mercifully called from the back before Jésus had to come up with an answer.

He recognised the voice, the young woman ring member Margot Lancaster used to deliver her bids, and he breathed a sigh of relief. The ring would get their due. Even so, he was struggling somewhat to maintain his composure. For Jésus Candido to be seen bidding on a piece like this, no name attached, barely worth the cost of the canvas, it was unthinkable. He was, *perhaps*, willing to compromise his artistic eye if the ring chose him to bid on a specific piece, but aside from that he considered his bid the highest compliment he could pay. And this piece ...

It was certainly true he considered himself to have a keen eye for outsider art, created by those without training or intent, but it was not an interest he wished to be known for. Yet, as he did his best to relax back into a considered indifference, he caught his hand starting to rise again and pulled it back down before the auctioneer spotted.

He watched as the painting was carried off, sold to Margot's bidder for a hundred and ten. His instincts had never misled him before. The more he thought about it, the more Jésus was certain: it would be perfect for his private collection. He resolved to own it, William Duphine be damned. He smiled to himself. It had been a long time since he'd actually found himself looking forward to the Knock.

'This the one?' the driver called as the black cab pulled up to Banyan Court. 'Hell of a place, this. Bet you're not for the poor door, eh?'

'No,' Jésus replied, ignoring the jovial tone and ugly laugh of the taxi driver, 'I am not.'

He eased himself out, careful where he stepped on the streets of Tower Hamlets. Banyan Court loomed above him. There are some buildings in this world which exist to serve a function and have no aesthetic ambition beyond that purpose. Or perhaps it would be more accurate to say that their aesthetic ambition *is* to serve their purpose. Others are inviting, made to be welcoming and familiar, and still others are made to be intimidating, austere: a reminder to those that enter them of the power and position of their builders. But some buildings, at least to the eyes of Jésus Candido, some buildings were art.

Many were designed as such, their beauty intricately planned by architects of vision and skill, while others found their art accidentally, growing into it through their decay or sculpted towards it by later extensions and changes. Some even became art entirely by context: the tiny, ugly little church that refused to sell its land, stubbornly existing in the heart of a business district, walled in on all sides by fashionable glass monstrosities. You just needed to know how to look.

'Oi!' the voice of the cabbie cut through his musings. 'You forgot your fancy cane.'

Jésus retrieved it without comment.

'Don't want anyone thinking you're in the wrong door, do we?' The driver's laughter was cut off by the door slamming shut.

Jésus was quite sure that Banyan Court was intended to be beautiful. There was simply no way the interweaving of glass and steel with the aged brick of the old tenement served any practical purpose. And certainly it was broadly successful, that was true. But anything could be beautiful. Beauty was cheap. Beauty was *obvious*. And yet he chose to live there. Not because of the artistic merit it claimed to possess, but because of the artistic merit it had not even considered. There it stood, a bright splinter of excess, burrowed into the grey and dying streets of struggle and hardship, unable to even admit the parts of itself it considered shameful. Aesthetically, it was acceptable. Conceptually, it was art. And so, Jésus lived there.

He hadn't argued with the cab driver because he had nothing to prove. He understood poverty and degradation without having to actually experience it. You don't need to actually touch art.

'Good evening, come in.' Jésus tried to disguise his irritation that William Duphine was the first to arrive for the Knock.

'Yes, hello, Jesus! Is Desmond here yet? What are we drinking?'

Jésus did not answer. He did not care to respond to those who couldn't be bothered to pronounce his name right.

'Look at this place! I should drop a line to *Time Out*. "The hidden gallery that puts the Horniman to shame!"' He leered at Jésus. 'Did Desmond say why it wasn't at the Langham?'

Duphine had, predictably, picked the least interesting of the display pieces to examine, an extremely derivative Jacob Maris piece he mostly kept around because it seemed churlish not to have anything from the Hague School.

Desmond Uxton, the ring's founder, had in fact had rather a nasty falling-out with one of the managers at the Langham and had violently sworn off the place, but that wasn't any of William Duphine's business, so Jésus declined to share it.

Soon enough, the other members of the ring, including Desmond himself, began to join them, taking their places for the bidding, each complimenting Jésus on his home. It was true he had an almost perfect set-up for it, with the eight usual members comfortably fitting in his spacious living room. Nobody mentioned it, but he felt there was also a certain rightness in the fact that the dead man whose spoils they were to bid on had actually run one of the many companies ultimately controlled by Tobias Fell, the owner of Banyan Court itself. All in all, the perfect venue for dividing the bounty of a fixed auction.

'Right,' Desmond said at last, once they were all settled. 'Shall we go in lot order or value? It's all the same to me.'

'Lot order is easier to keep track of, I think,' declared Margot, one of the older members of the ring, and no one disagreed, so the bidding began.

The Knock was a remarkably simple idea. It took place among members of the ring, bidders who would normally be at each other's throats during the auction but had instead made an arrangement to not compete against each other, at least no more than needed to keep up appearances. This meant some lots could be acquired for a fraction of what they might have cost otherwise. Of course, there were plenty of bidders who weren't in the ring, and if they were eager for a lot then the price could still climb higher than would be ideal, but the ring's pockets were deep, and they'd still recoup much of their expenses at the Knock. Once the designated buyers had secured as many of the pre-chosen lots as possible, a second, private auction was held among the ring, with each member bidding on the lots that they had won. The winner would pay off the buyer, and then pay the amount they bid at the Knock evenly among all members of the ring. The money circulated around all through the group in such a way that even if you spent as much on a piece you might have paid at the auction itself, you'd recoup those losses from the other members on the pieces you didn't win.

It was a way of acquiring valuable pieces of art for less than they were worth, but more than that, membership of the ring was an extremely exclusive thing, and it helped to keep the interlopers and new money from gaining a foothold. Art, Jésus privately believed, was not, in fact, for everybody, and the Knock helped to keep that vital hierarchy in place. It was also quite illegal, but that didn't matter. They weren't some petty consortium of scrap metal dealers, they were people of means and power, and they weren't the sort of people to be touched by the law.

Still, that was hardly what concerned him today. He had a very specific piece he was bidding on. Lot 51, he remembered it quite clearly. None of the pieces were physically present, of course, they'd be delivered as necessary, but his memory was quite vivid enough. It was strange, Jésus had been to so many Knocks in his time that to find himself actually caring about one was a remarkably novel experience. And yet, as the spoils were divided and they came closer and closer to the painting that he still hadn't been able to get out of his mind, he grew nervous. Lot 46 came and went. Lot 49. What if he wasn't the only one who saw its potential? What if he had it snatched from him?

As it turned out, he needn't have worried. Nobody else at the Knock seemed to care much about the painting at all. William Duphine put in an obligatory bid, his expression utterly disinterested, clearly expecting to walk away with it. When he saw Jésus raise his hand to outbid him, he stifled a small laugh. Desmond leaned over.

'I wouldn't worry old man,' he whispered to Jésus, 'I sometimes lose track as well.'

Jésus kept his gaze level and raised his arm higher, confirming the bid. There were a few whispers, some wondering if they'd missed something important about the painting, others smirking slightly, believing him to have made his first mistake. He ignored them. They hadn't seen it, not like he had. He wasn't going to lie to himself their pantomimed confusion and back-biting didn't get to him, but he was damned if he'd let them know it. William shrugged, conceding the piece. And then it was done.

'Mind me asking what got you so interested in that one?' Desmond asked him afterwards, once the other members of the ring had made their polite goodbyes. They all cooperated professionally for the Knock, but he was the only one Jésus would actually consider a friend.

'You didn't see it in person, did you?' he said, releasing a plume of cigar smoke that lazily crept its way around the balcony and out into the night air.

'Can't say I did. Had Müller put through my bids by phone as always. I take it the photos don't do it justice?'

'They do not. It was unexpected.'

'Bit of a mess, though, surely? Maybe as an ambience piece, but ... what exactly did you see in it?'

'It's ... outsider art,' Jésus said, suddenly defensive, 'the line work, the colours. Think of Georgiana Houghton. Or Madge Gill, perhaps.'

'Otherworldly lines and haunted geometries, eh?' Desmond inhaled thoughtfully. 'Can't honestly say I saw anything of that in it.'

'Well, I did.'

'Hm. Sounds like it really called to you.' Desmond's tone was casual, but the words still gave Jésus pause. He shifted uncomfortably.

'Yes. Yes, it did.'

'Unless you know something about it you're not telling?' Desmond's smile did its best to hide the slight edge creeping into his voice. Jésus knew that his friend hated more than anything to feel like anyone had got one over on him.

'No. I simply ... like it.' Jésus wanted to say more, to put into words the feelings it stirred in him, but English was a blunt, clumsy language and he simply couldn't do it.

'Well, I hope so. No way you're going to sell it on its own, so I suppose you better find some wall space.'

'I shall. It's going to be where it belongs, I think.'

Desmond shrugged and returned to his own cigar. The two of them sat in silence, watching the thin lines of smoke twist and contort in the lights of the city below.

It was two days later when the front desk informed Jésus that his painting had arrived. He hurried down as fast as the elevator would allow, hoping to catch the delivery men before they left, but they'd long since vanished by the time he got there. Worse, the concierge working the reception was one he particularly disliked: a lanky middle-aged man who talked to himself and always claimed problems had been taken care of when they clearly hadn't been. Jésus had deliberately made the decision not to learn the man's name, and always studiously avoided glancing at his name tag. He considered it a personal favour to the concierge that he had made no active efforts to have him fired. Still, despite his other failings the man was probably strong enough to carry the painting up to the apartment, though the thought of him touching it made Jésus ever so slightly uncomfortable.

The concierge sighed at the request and called to the little room behind him for someone to watch the front desk, eliciting a snort from the art dealer over the pointless delay. He had a dinner reservation at Le Gavroche at seven, and he intended to work up quite an appetite finding his new prize a place to live.

Despite the irritations of transporting it, the painting was soon sitting comfortably in Jésus' apartment, waiting to properly see the space it was to own. He dismissed the concierge with a palpable sense of relief and removed the covering. It was everything he remembered and more: that familiar riot of colours, the lines arcing through and around themselves, spiralling in patterns his eyes simply refused to follow. And there, after a few moments of watching, the woman again, her eyes still focused on him and her mouth still set in that unreadable line. He sighed in appreciation and relief. He had been right, after all: it was beautiful.

Jésus began to search for a position on his walls that did it justice. The hallway was too immediate, it would overpower everything else on display. The living room wasn't right either, as all the walls big enough to hold it were at entirely the wrong angle. It would be too distracting in the bedroom as, even though he rarely showed it to visitors, on those occasions he did bring men back, there was a very specific mood he was interested in setting. That left the study, the smallest room in the apartment, though it was by no means modest. Compared to his sleek modern living room he kept the study almost parodically traditional, with a darkly stained oak desk and shelves of books he'd had custom-bound to fit the tone. It was where he situated his more traditional pieces.

One of his visitors had once asked him how he could be so calculated about his own home, and Jésus had been slightly taken aback. He'd never really considered the question, but on reflection he decided that perhaps he didn't consider anywhere truly a home. It was all simply space to be refined, to be turned into something of value. There was nothing valuable about simply living in a place. Any animal can do that. And perhaps if people didn't understand that they didn't deserve to have it. He didn't say any of this out loud, of course, it wasn't the man's business. But the question stayed with him. It had nothing to do with home, not really. This space was his because he could realise its true potential, and that ownership, that curation, was a lifelong project

'The study,' he said finally, staring at the painting. 'The right home for you, I think.'

Previously pride of place had been given to a religious piece by Karel Škréta, but looking over it now he had to fight back the urge to tear it from the wall and hurl it out of the window. He was no stranger to the need to move past what had come before, in some cases even to destroy it, to burn it all down and make way for the new, but he had never before felt it as such a powerful urge. He took a breath and carefully removed the Škréta from its position.

The rest of the day was spent meticulously rearranging his apartment, moving and reorienting almost everything until he was once again happy with the layout. In the end he got rid of a few of the pieces he'd had for a while: a glass sculpture by a formerly up-and-coming artist named Karl Velter and a series of Barlach lithographs he had picked up on a whim while flirting with expressionism. He stood there, admiring his acquisition in its new home.

Knock knock.

He was roused from his contemplation, realising with some confusion that he needed to turn on the light. When had it got dark? He felt the deep gnawing of hunger in his stomach.

Remembering what had stirred him, he hurried to the front door and threw it open. The hall outside was empty.

Were there children in the building? Jésus curled his lip. He had no quarrel with those who had children, of course, so long as they had the decency to breed quietly. No sign of the little timewasters, though. Luckily, he hadn't quite missed his dinner reservation, though he was acutely aware that he hadn't freshened up after shifting his displays around and must look a mess. Then he realised he didn't care.

But that was nonsense, surely. He had planned it as one of his 'exhibition dinners': meals he took alone, well dressed and dazzling, to remind the great and the influential of his good taste. He was Jésus Candido, after all, and his appearance was as much an artistic expression as the rest of him. And yet, when he looked at the world outside his apartment, so drab and colourless after the vibrant hues he had so recently fallen into, he could not bring himself to be concerned about how he looked. He ate quickly, ignored the other patrons, and returned home immediately after.

Jésus was in his apartment. It looked as though it had been drawn from memory, sketched out and painted in those same crawling technicolour lines that had so captivated him before. He knew he was dreaming, but that didn't bother him at all, and a gentle calm washed over him.

This, he heard himself thinking, *this is home.*

Knock knock.

Someone was at the door. Compared to the thin swirling strokes that composed the rest of the apartment, the entrance was thick and smudged, as though made with an old brush, overloaded with cadmium red.

Knock knock knock.

They wanted to come in.

The sound became more insistent, more aggressive. He reached for the handle, and the door ignited, exploding into a bright and hateful fire. He felt the heat as it charred and cracked the lines that made it and stained the dazzling colours a charcoal black. He dreamed the smell of burning wood as the flames spread through the apartment. It was not the comforting wood smell of a fireplace or a bonfire, but the awful stench of everything he knew being rendered down to ash and heat-scoured earth. It was all ablaze now, his whole world incinerating: everything he had so coldly assessed and positioned and believed himself apart from, devoured in a wave of genuine loss. He felt the flames reach him, melting his flesh and shattering his bones in their intensity. But they left his eyes, trapped and staring wildly at the figure moving slowly through what had once been the door. The pain was only bearable because it wasn't his. It belonged to the dream, and all he could do was endure and hope to wake.

Still, the figure approached, and he saw that it wore the face of the painted woman. It was as twisted and distorted as it had been on canvas, that same chaotic mess of curling lines and angry hues. She wore a drab olive dress and she was burning, ravenous, desperate to consume and utterly destroy everything she touched with the fire that was her flesh.

Jésus awoke clawing at himself, desperate to extinguish flames that were not there and to defend a home he did not have.

Over the next two days, Jésus found himself falling behind on much of his work, with the hours seeming to simply disappear from his day. He found himself standing before that painting more and more, studying every line, following the shapes and colours, trying to find what exactly it was that drew him to it. As much as he pretended indifference to the comments of his

49

peers, their casual disregard for his taste in this had needled him. What was it that drew him? Never before had a piece perplexed him like this.

As he sat at his desk, on the other side of the large study, he found himself gazing gently at the bright lines, hunting for the scowling face hidden within them. He contemplated it playfully while making calls, updating his listings and going through the piles of documentation that went along with his mostly legitimate dealings. It was a welcome presence, even if on occasion it was distracting enough that he had to bodily turn away from it to fully concentrate on his work.

But now he was done for the day, and the rest of the afternoon was to be spent on the balcony, enjoying the dusty heat of a city summer and reading a book on the history of English bone china that Desmond had recommended. He stood, stretched, and headed towards the living room, passing in front of the painting. Mind relaxed and eyes wandering, he noticed a stark line of crimson curling through it, a detail he had somehow never spotted before, and paused to appreciate it.

Knock knock.

Sighing, he turned away and headed to the front door. There was nobody there. Again. He leaned out and looked down the corridor.

'If this continues,' he shouted. 'I shall call the police!'

He wouldn't, probably, but children were stupid. He turned and slammed the door shut, eyes falling on his clock. How had it got so late? His mouth was dry, and his eyes ached as though they'd been focusing far too long. Perhaps tomorrow he'd buy some eye drops. It wouldn't do to be looking too tired.

Jésus selected a bottle of water from the fridge and took his time drinking it, his gaze drifting over to the Alfred Stevens hung on his kitchen wall. It was a small painting of a woman in a wide-brimmed hat staring serenely over a garden. But his mind was still on his new masterpiece. Masterpiece? No, it was an intriguing piece that currently fascinated him. Soon enough he'd have fathomed its depths and it would be replaced by something new. Even so, there was an odd sense of relief in no longer looking at it. And another part of him that was desperate to see it again.

He studied the Stevens and was struck by how dull it was. There was nothing to it at all. No life, no lustre, no spark. He could feel the knowledge prickling at his mind that if he just returned to his office, he could appreciate a work with seemingly infinite depth. Instead, he kept drinking his water. He'd have to replace the Stevens.

The client drained the last dregs of single malt from his glass.

'Excellent. Shall we get everything signed?'

'Of course.' Jésus was looking forward to tying things up, if only because he couldn't actually remember the name of the man sitting across from him. Another newly rich banker with no taste who had commissioned him to find an utterly forgettable piece of abstract impressionism.

'Perfect.' His guest grinned, getting to his feet.

Jésus stood as well to lead him through to the study. That was its point, of course, to provide the right ambiance for signing contracts and passing money, smoothing nervous clients through the process. But something caused his step to falter as he approached the door. An odd shudder ran through him, like he was afraid of something. *What*, though? The painting? That was it. Some part of him didn't want to share it with this no one client.

'Mr Candido?'

This man might become captivated by it like he was and contrive an attempt to acquire it for himself.

'It's not for sale,' Jésus muttered.

'I'm sorry? I didn't catch that,' his guest said lightly, his face placid and pointless.

No, this man would have no appreciation for it. But would that be worse? Indifference? This tasteless oaf marking it as nothing special at all, when Jésus had let such a thing have power over him.

Or, perhaps he simply wished to save this man from the dreams that still lingered through his nights ...

'It's such a nice afternoon,' Jésus said steadily. 'We will sign on the balcony.'

He did not know exactly where these thoughts had come from, but whatever the precise dimensions of his unease, it seemed the study would be held in a quarantine, of a sort, a private place where time would simply disappear.

'But where did he get it?'

'I can't tell you where he got it, that's what I'm trying to explain,' Antonio retorted in his infuriating mock-English voice.

Jésus tried to keep his temper level. His brother-in-law liked to make fun of how his accent had changed in the years he had lived in London, and at one point had insisted on trying to talk to him entirely in English, a language Antonio barely spoke, to 'make Jésus feel at home'. They'd managed to put an end to that particular joke, but he still insisted on flavouring his Portuguese with that stupid British twang. At least he'd stopped telling Jésus to give his love to the Queen.

'There must have been something.' Jésus was exhausted, his patience tissue paper thin.

'The guy didn't exactly keep much paperwork.' He could almost hear Antonio shrugging over the phone. 'And what there was the family didn't want to hand over.'

'That doesn't make sense. He ran a huge company, how could he not have better records?'

There was a pause.

'I mean, you live downstairs from Tobias Fell, maybe ask him?'

'What's that supposed to mean?'

'Nothing.'

There was an odd note in his voice, a slight waver that told Jésus he was holding something back.

'Antonio, I need to know. It's important.'

'Look, maybe you've been away too long. *His records were destroyed.*'

The penny dropped. A cattle farmer destroying their records like that probably meant one thing – illegal land grabbing. Burned villages. Murders. There was a silence before Antonio spoke again.

'I didn't say anything about this, OK?'

'But that doesn't make sense. This painting, it's not like any indigenous art I've ever seen.'

'I don't know, then. Not for certain, at least. I know some of the pieces at auction were taken from the people they, uh, displaced.' The conversation had clearly taken a turn Antonio was not comfortable with. 'I think maybe his wife said some of the paintings were done by one of his workers. That could be it.'

'When you say "workers", what do you mean?' Jésus asked, though he suspected he already knew the answer. 'Farmhand? Administrator? CFO? What?'

' … No. None of those.'

Ah. A *grileiro*, then. Likely one of the unofficial private mercenaries the corporations sent in to clear the land they wanted to farm or log or strip-mine. No oversight, no rules, just people willing to take guns into the jungle and drive indigenous people off their land by any means necessary. Not usually the sort to retire into a career of painting masterpieces.

'Did …' He chose his next words carefully. 'Did Fell know about them? The clearances?'

'How should I know?' Antonio was clearly keen to move on. 'These rich arseholes, who can say what they know and what they don't. But it was done in his name.'

Jésus found it hard to say precisely what he was feeling. Certainly many of the greatest artworks had bloody histories, but to be so close to it … there was an undeniable frisson, and not a pleasant one.

'I need you to find him, the man who painted it. I need to talk with him,' Jésus could hear the desperation in his own voice, but he ignored it.

'That's not going to be possible, I'm afraid,' Antonio said quietly. 'He's dead. About a year back, according to the owner's son.'

Jésus didn't want to ask the next question but pushed on regardless.

'How did he die?'

'House fire. Accidental, but the workers' houses weren't exactly built to standard. He burned to death.'

The silence that followed was palpable, as Jésus' skin prickled at the memory of a dream.

Knock.

It was dark. Almost pitch black.

Knock knock.

Had he been asleep? No, he'd been … He was just …

Knock knock knock.

Jésus leapt up with a violent start, sending his desk chair tipping back onto the soft carpet of the study. He fumbled in the corner for the standing lamp, finding the switch and casting the room in warm illumination. This couldn't be right; it had just been morning. It was still morning, it must be. He had finished his phone call, made a pot of tea, and just started an email. But the sky outside was dark and the windows of the buildings below could be seen dimly lit through the thin mist of rain. The teapot was stone cold, and the email still sat blank. He checked his watch. Just past 10 p.m.

He stepped away from the painting. *Get a hold of yourself.* The piece was beautiful, yes, captivating, of course. And it had clearly been dripping into his dreams these past few nights, but this was nonsense. He adjusted his tie, a more casual Balthus knot today, and walked firmly and purposefully to the study door, past the thing that had apparently held him enraptured for almost thirteen hours. As soon as he was out something snapped inside him and he slammed the door shut, his breathing suddenly heavy. He was very aware of how hungry he was, how intensely dry his throat had become.

Jésus retrieved a glass, filled it with water and drank it down so quickly his stomach almost revolted. He refilled it, sipping more slowly, and sat down heavily in the nearest armchair, mind racing.

What was wrong with him? He had been fascinated before by the painting, certainly. It was only natural. He had lost hours staring into it, standing so close he could almost touch it. But it had never caught his mind like this, not from the other side of the room, and never for this long. It felt like it had somehow claimed the whole room for itself, to the point where he barely remembered the other pieces he kept there. *What does it want?*

He caught himself immediately. This was absurd. He had plenty of clients who talked to him of their superstitions, of their strange beliefs and conceptions of art and its origins. He nodded, of course, but privately he despised such nonsense. His obsession was simply that, a trick of his own personality. His eye for art was simply too strong, and he was having difficulty overcoming it.

Even now, as he thought of the painting, he could not help dwelling on its lines, its colour, how he desperately searched for that face hidden within it, though the image was proving more elusive, not less, as he had continued to observe it. Had it always been weeping?

The thing was dangerous, that much he knew, even if it was only his own obsession that made it so. Perhaps it would be better to destroy it. But it was also the single most beautiful thing Jésus had ever owned, perhaps that anyone had ever owned. He would simply do his work in the living room or bedroom and, when he had the time, he could go in and disappear into its twisting forms. The study had always been an unnecessary display, anyway. The room belonged to the picture now. It may have taken the study, but there it would remain. Contained.

He shook his head again at the ridiculous thought. He'd just had a strange day, and it had left him unsettled. Not to mention he was absolutely famished. He dragged himself to his feet and called down to the front desk for a taxi. It was late, but his name got him a last-minute dinner reservation quickly enough. His legs were weak and he found himself leaning on his cane for support, at one point worried it would buckle. Still, he made it down to the reception, trying his best to think of the meal ahead of him, and not what was behind him.

When he returned from dinner, it was late. Jésus had taken his time over coffee, only leaving when the maître d' had gently informed him they were soon to close. He was dragging his heels as he approached the entrance, leaning heavily on his cane. He didn't know what scared him more: that he truly believed the painting did something to him, or that there was a part of him that wanted to see it again, to lose himself in its lines. His lip curled in distain at his own thought. Jésus Candido, scared of a painting! The very idea was comical, absurd! But that didn't make it any less true. He was afraid of what it was doing to him, afraid of the dreams, afraid of the woman who lurked within it. He tried his best to stand straight and walked through the glass doors of Banyan Court.

Briefly, he toyed with the idea of talking to the concierge, seeing if he could get the man to accompany him back to his apartment to remove the painting, take it somewhere he could have it collected for storage. But it was the lazy one Jésus didn't like, and he seemed to currently be busy arguing with an angry young man in a blue baseball cap. Jésus did his best to ignore them, skirting around the edges of what seemed to be quite the shouting match, and ducked into the elevator.

It was only as it started its ascent that Jésus realised he was not the only one inside. He was quite sure he'd never seen the person standing next to him before, though they seemed real enough. It was a man, younger than Jésus by maybe a decade, and he wore what had clearly once been a well-tailored business suit. His hair was unwashed, and the suit was torn at the knees and elbows, with dark stains mottling its tasteful pinstripes. His fingernails were filthy, as if he had been clawing through the mud, and a dank, musty smell rolled off him, unsettling Jésus' already delicate stomach. Was this man from the other side of the building? This wasn't his place, how had the concierge let him through? But no, his suit spoke of money, despite its appalling condition. The man caught him staring and gave a tired smile.

'So how are you finding it?' he asked.

Jésus cocked his head in confusion.

'Living here,' the stranger continued. 'Is it everything you hoped it would be?'

'Yes,' Jésus replied, willing the conversation to be over. 'It is.'

The man leaned in close and it took all Jésus' composure not to visibly recoil at the smell. The stranger's tone was conspiratorial.

'Have you ever seen anything ... weird? Since moving in?'

'No,' Jésus replied.

The door opened on the fifth floor and the man in the stained suit left, his expression downcast. Jésus breathed out. How could such a man live in a place like this? Clearly some sort of tragedy had befallen him, and Jésus was not without compassion for such a situation, but to let oneself be seen like that ... His gaze drifted to the mirrored wall of the elevator. The figure before him was clearly exhausted, using a cane not meant to bear the weight. His tie was loose, and a drop of coffee could clearly be seen on the front of his white shirt, a casualty of his shaking hands. Who was he, this man in the mirror? He had avoided his friends these last few days but were they to see him now they would mock him, he knew that for certain. Jésus Candido reduced to a broken, haunted man, terrified of his own possessions and a few bad dreams.

No. He would not allow it. His life was the most powerful piece of art he owned. He resolved that he would not be held hostage by his own paranoia and whatever it was that was trying to take over his home. But even so, his hand trembled slightly as he tried the front door. It opened without incident, and he walked to the bedroom as confidently as he was able. The door to the study remained closed, and when he finally fell into bed, for the first time in several days he did not dream.

*

He woke up late on Monday, which wasn't unusual, though the events of the previous night had clearly left their mark on him as he groggily tried to pull himself out of bed. He twice tried and failed to make himself a coffee before finally remembering to put one of the colourful pods into the machine. Out on the balcony, leaning heavily against the railings, he sipped the bitter liquid as he watched the city far below go about its business. Finally, feeling a little bit more human, Jésus placed the espresso cup down on the glass table and walked slowly into the living room to do some work, trying his best to ignore the gravity that seemed to tug at him from the door to his study.

He had given it a lot of thought, and his first order of business was to make a call to the couriers he used for his deliveries. The conversation was brief and businesslike, and when he put the phone down Jésus felt the most grounded and relaxed he had since the painting arrived. Tomorrow they would come and take it away, transferring it to the storage company he had used for years. It was miles away from Banyan Court and he had never actually visited it, instead preferring to use the couriers to ferry things to and from the climate-controlled facility. Perhaps he would visit it once it was there, but that was a decision for another time. For now, he was satisfied that it would be far, far away. He had bested it. He had won. His home would be his again.

He spent the rest of the morning making more calls, typing up emails, and arranging some viewings for pieces he had been commissioned to acquire. By the afternoon he was in much better spirits, and his mind turned to where he might take lunch. He broke into a smile at the thought of walking out into the world again: perfectly dressed and once more ready to be Jésus Candido. He idly wondered which suit he would pick for his grand emergence as he headed to the bathroom to freshen up. And found himself pivoting towards the door to the study.

It felt like his heart had stopped as, against his own wishes, Jésus twisted the doorknob and stepped inside. He turned towards the painting, trying desperately to call out to someone, anyone, for help before the kaleidoscope of light and pattern pressed itself into his eyes and his mind relaxed into contented contemplation of the screaming face hidden within.

It was four o'clock Wednesday morning when the door to the study opened and a shaking figure with bloodshot eyes crawled out over the threshold. He no longer had the strength to stand, so slowly, achingly, he dragged himself over the luxurious carpet, leaving a trail of flattened fibres behind him. It would not win. Beautiful or not, Jésus Candido would not be destroyed by a painting. He would not lose his home to this thing, and if a door would not contain it, then he would have to find another way. Painstakingly, he made his way to the ottoman, grabbing his phone from the plush cushions. There was just enough battery to see he had 19 missed calls, a cautiously worried message from Desmond about his absence at the Knock the previous night, and another from the courier service, saying they'd received no answer when they came to collect the painting. Jésus tried to make a call to get help, but his fingers were shaking too hard. Then four per cent battery became zero per cent battery and the screen went dark. His lips curled into a sneer. He would need to deal with this himself.

He inched his way to his feet and limped towards the kitchen, grabbing one of his canes from the rack and trying to regain his footing. His weakened legs buckled almost immediately, sending him staggering into a Grayson Perry vase, which tipped off the display table and fell to the ground, splintering into pieces.

He barely noticed, pulling himself up to the counter and reaching over to the magnetised knife rack. Very expensive and rarely used, the knife he chose was razor sharp, and he slid down to the floor with a smile. The blade was heavy in his hands. He cut and ripped off one of his shirt sleeves, then wrapped it around his eyes. When it was clear that even at this late hour some light still made it through the fabric, he removed the other sleeve as well and layered it on top. By the time he was done he could see nothing at all.

He lay there, mustering his strength, and heard the sound, as though in the darkness it was right next to his ear.

Knock knock.

Soft as ever, but just as persistent. Something wanted to come into his home, to take it from him. But he would not allow it. He got to his feet, the knife held in one hand, the cane propping his other, and began to make his way towards the study.

He had often measured the steps in his apartment. It was important to be aware of angles and likely viewing points for the art he had on display. Front door to study, sixteen steps. Bathroom to living room, twenty-three steps. From the kitchen counter to the study had always been nineteen steps, but as he picked his way gradually across the wide-open spaces of his apartment, careful to avoid the shattered pieces of ceramic from the vase, there seemed more.

Ten steps. The well-insulated apartment was silent, even the distant din of the streets far below not reaching him now. All except for one thing.

Knock knock.

Nineteen steps. The only thing he could see was darkness. Twenty steps. The only thing he could hear was his own breathing. Twenty-three steps. And the knocking.

Finally, at twenty-six steps, he felt his shoulder brush against the doorframe of the study. He tried to focus. The rubberised handle of the knife felt solid in his fist, centring him and driving him forward, the silver of the cane's grip cold and certain in his hand. The knocking was louder now. With his eyes covered, it was finally clear. It had never been coming from the front door.

His breathing steadied, replaced by the sound of his heart pounding in his ears. His face was wet. Had he cut it somehow? No, it must be tears. He gritted his teeth as he turned towards the wall where he knew the thing was hanging. There was something inside him that called out, urging him to rip off his blindfold and stare again at that awful, beautiful face, but he resisted.

Knock knock.

It was ten steps from the study door to the painting. When he counted twelve, he stopped. He must have been close now. He shifted the knife to his left hand and let the cane clatter to the floor as he tentatively reached out. Somewhere in the darkness his fingertips brushed against canvas, the thick lines of paint ever so slightly proud of the surface. He wanted to stroke them, to feel their contours and follow them to wherever they led.

Knock Knock.

He took a step forward. The knocking was inside his skull.

KNOCK KNOCK.

With a rush of adrenaline, he brought the blade down in a single slash all the way from one corner of the painting to the other. The tension of the canvas released as the serrated edges tore it apart through the centre, a sound far louder than it had any right to be, like a fire igniting or a ragged scream.

There was quiet.

In that sudden release, that blissful peace, Jésus fell to his knees. He dropped the knife as the tears of fear turned to relief, and he lifted his heavy, exhausted hand to remove his blindfold.

Another hand beat him to it. One that reached out from inside that torn and bloody canvas. It pulled the fabric from Jésus' eyes, and he screamed, though he no longer had the strength to run as the other hands stretched out for him. They seized his throat and arms, pulling him inside.

Knock knock.

The door to 30 Banyan Court was closed.

Knock knock.

If it were to open, the Jésus Candido that stood on the other side would have been unrecognisable to all but those closest to him. His shirtsleeves were torn off, his eyes red from tears, and all around him was the faintest smell of blood and burned hair, though he himself would have seemed largely unharmed. He would have mumbled something about his home, as he knocked gently at his own front door, about having it taken from him and the things that he had seen. But his words would have made little sense even to those who spoke perfect Portuguese.

He held something clutched in his hands, though he couldn't have told you exactly where he got it. A thick card invitation, printed in a tasteful serif:

TOBIAS FELL cordially invites JÈSUS CANDIDO
to attend a dinner party at 1 Banyan Court
on the evening of 16th August 2014
Penthouse access will be available through the freight elevator

If you asked him whether he planned to attend, he would have nodded and creased his brow at the vaguest memory of being handed it by a young man in a tattered T-shirt. And then he would have told you: it was to be an evening of quite breath-taking art.

3rd

Smart

Carter Dwight
42 Banyan Court

'Donna, compose tweet,' Carter Dwight's voice had a practised clarity to it and, though alone, his words didn't echo in the spacious apartment.

'OK, composing,' a measured feminine voice intoned from a hidden speaker.

'Third picture in "Gym" folder. Caption … "Health isn't given, it's earned." Hashtag Dodj, hashtag no pain no gain. Send tweet.'

'OK, tweet sent.'

That was his PR done for the day at least. Carter opened his fridge, retrieved a beer, and frowned.

'Donna, check temperature for left fridge door,'

There was a pause. 'The left fridge door is set at 7 degrees Celsius. Current temperature is 7 degrees Celsius.'

Carter tutted softly. Six degrees Celsius was the optimum temperature for drinking a light chilled beer, which he kept in the left fridge door. He sighed.

'Donna, set left fridge door to 6 degrees Celsius.'

'Mr D-wight.' Her smooth composite voice stumbled slightly

over the name he'd had to manually program in. 'You usually drink your beer at 7 degrees. Would you like me to override the current preference?'

This again. He'd been having trouble getting Donna to keep settings stable ever since the latest update. Perhaps allowing her to customise his smart home automatically had been misjudged, but the idea of manually adjusting all her settings seemed to go against the principle of having a digital assistant. Though she did have trouble with the distinction between a routine and a preference.

'Donna, override default, set left fridge door to 6 degrees.'

'OK, that's been done. Current temperatures 6 degrees for left door, 4 degrees for right door, 1 degree for upper interior, 2 degrees for lower interior, 0 degrees for freezer drawers.'

'Thank you,' he said testily. The words vanished almost as soon as they were spoken. Carter had done his research and the sparse art and furniture had been placed at just the right points to deaden the acoustics. Zero echo.

Taking another swig, he smiled slightly at the thought of whatever digital version of him Donna had constructed in her settings that loved warm beer and a 6 a.m. alarm. Hopefully, this time the correct version would stick.

He sat down in front of the TV that dominated the corner of his vast studio to flick through his emails. Seventeen unread messages, all from work. Just as well, personal ones were so much more time-consuming. He went through them quickly, deciding there was nothing that required his personal attention.

'Donna, reply to emails 1 through 17.'

'OK, composing.'

Carter nodded, satisfied; he'd spent fifteen years sending up to a hundred emails a day. It had been a pain at the time, but it did give Donna a huge mine of data to use for the auto-reply algorithm he'd designed for her.

'All replies composed, Mr Dwight. Would you like to review them?'

'No, just send them.' He'd spent enough time double-checking this function.

'OK.' There was the smallest pause. 'Replies sent.'

Carter leaned back, satisfied. Now if he could only get her to do that for meetings.

'Donna, daily downloads for Dodj.'

'OK, downloads for Dodj application, last 24 hours: 51,000 Android; 64,000 iOS, 10,000 other.'

The leather of the chair shifted under Carter's weight. Good. He knew he should really be checking stock prices or perform-ance figures, but he'd never really cared about any of that. What he cared about was how many people were using his app. How many were working out better, eating healthier, because of him. How many lives he was improving through technology and data. And of course, when he looked out over all of London arrayed beneath his huge glass window, he couldn't deny that his own life had improved in turn. And when Donna rolled out, people would have another helping hand, someone working to make a better version of them.

'Donna, check schedule for today.'

A pause.

'Mr Dwight, you have no events scheduled for today.'

'Donna, check schedule for tomorrow.'

Another pause.

'Three o'clock,' Donna calmly replied. 'Meet Glenn for gym.'

The beer bottle stopped halfway to his lips.

'Donna, when did I add that to the schedule?'

'Your stated goals for the month were "fitness" and "social",

Mr Dwight. Gym sessions have been automatically scheduled every Monday, Thursday and Saturday and the events shared with those tagged "gym" in your contacts.'

Great. Must be another defaults thing. He'd forgotten he'd set that as a monthly priority. He'd really prefer to be relaxing ahead of the meeting, but if he cancelled on Glenn he'd never hear the end of it. It looked like Donna had successfully forced him to do some exercise. Her namesake would be proud.

'Women,' he said to himself. He looked around, instinctively searching for someone to share the joke, but he was alone. He sighed. Something still wasn't quite right. Was he getting hungry?

Heading back to the fridge he pulled out one of his pre-bagged single-portion cuisines and headed over to the precision cooker in the corner. He set it going, with instructions to notify him as his dinner cooked, and headed back towards the TV, stepping over the quietly humming robot vacuum making its way slowly around the floor. No, it wasn't hunger.

'Donna, turn lights to forty per cent, play meditation mix 4.' He pulled his yoga mat from a drawer beneath the shallow stairs. If he couldn't figure out what was wrong, he could at least try to relax properly. The droning, ambient music began to roll out and over him from concealed speakers, as Carter began to slowly go through his routine. His limbs extended, curled, relaxed, each movement controlled and precise, the music pressing through him, gradually freeing his mind from his worries and pressing him into an almost trance-like state. But there was something else there, a dragging sensation, a deep sadne—

'Donna, stop playback. What song is this?'

The mournful guitar strumming stopped abruptly.

'OK. This song is "Melancholy Man" by the Moody Blues.'

No wonder his mood was taking a turn.

'Donna, delete from playlist.'

'OK, removed from meditation mix 4.'

Carter scowled. He hadn't put it there in the first place. He really needed to have a look at her settings. Glumly, he ate his dinner, managing to spill the too warm beer all over the kitchen floor. He swore softly to himself.

'Donna, book Amina for one hour tomorrow.' The cleaner would have to take care of it.

'OK, that's been booked for three o'clock tomorrow.'

Carter grunted and got to his feet. It felt like an early bed. Donna's bugs aside, something was bothering him.

'Donna, why am I feeling like this?' he said, a rueful smile crossing his lips.

'I'm sorry,' she replied. 'I don't understand.'

'No,' he sighed. 'Guess you don't.'

Amina came to his home at three thirty-two the next day, while Carter was deep into his gym session. He and Glenn had got into the habit of partnering for workouts when they had still worked together, and he was one of the few non-professional friends Carter still kept up with. They were halfway through a set of bench presses when Carter's phone buzzed, alerting him that someone was at the door to his flat. Donna had said Amina was booked for three, and he wondered briefly if the cleaner was late or if it was another of the bugs in his assistant's development.

Pulling himself up, he tapped at the screen until Amina's weathered face could be seen in the doorbell camera. He pressed another button, remotely unlocking the door and she disappeared from view as she took her bag of cleaning supplies inside. He closed his phone.

'You know, you should really get some proper help,' Glenn said as he added another five kilos onto each end of the bar.

Glenn Khurana took his gym seriously, as could be seen from both his figure and his high-end sportswear. Even light exercise seemed to coat his dark skin in a thin sheen of sweat, and whatever Carter was lifting, Glenn was lifting just a little bit more. It was one of the few points of contention in their friendship that the gym in Banyan Court's health suite didn't have a stair machine, an arena in which he could reliably demolish Carter, and they had to alternate between it and the high-end 'wellness centre' near Glenn's townhouse.

'I don't need "proper" help.' Carter shrugged. 'I can do most things myself. There's just a few that I don't have time for.'

'And you can't program a robot to do for you.'

'Yet.' Carter laughed lightly, watching his friend struggle slightly with his heavier bench press. He didn't mind Glenn's need to slightly one-up him, but he did like to see it occasionally come back to bite him.

Glenn finished his set, the strain momentarily leaving him unable to respond. His phone buzzed again, this time indicating his exercise data had been successfully uploaded. Another advantage of using the gym in Banyan Court.

'I just mean that it can't be great for her. If you hired her properly, she'd have regular hours, rather than going through that *app*, what's it called?'

'Hektic. And I don't need her for regular hours, just once or twice a week.'

'So she's just on call the rest of the time?'

'Well. I assume she has other jobs the rest of the time.' Irritation began to bleed into Carter's voice, as it always did when Glenn got self-righteous. 'Anyway, if her time isn't scheduled properly, that sounds like a problem with Hektic's algorithm, and short of buying them I don't see what I can do about that.'

He paused for a moment.

'Should I buy them?'

Glenn laughed and started towards the exercise bikes. Carter followed.

'I'm serious,' he continued. 'I bet that sort of data could enhance Dodj's service quite a bit.'

'If you say so.' Glenn's face was dismissive, already concentrating on his ride. 'I know how much you love data.'

Carter snorted and gestured to the screen at the front of Glenn's bike.

'You always write down your distance. Your calories. How's that any different? Data isn't some demon waiting to get you. At least as long as you're careful.'

'Yeah, well, don't let the man upstairs hear you say that.'

It took Carter a moment to register who he was referring to.

'That was never proved.' For a moment the pedals on his bike seemed stiff, more resistant than before. Then they loosened again. Was nothing working right around here?

'It never made it to court.' Glenn could clearly sense he'd struck a nerve. 'Not the same thing. I'm just saying maybe your pal Tobias doesn't quite have the same respect for it.'

'He's not—' Carter was defensive. 'I've never even met the man.'

They spent the next two kilometres in silence. Then Carter spoke up again.

'You really think selling data's so bad?'

'I don't know, man.' His gym partner shrugged. 'Not really my area. I'm just an accounts guy. Much simpler.'

Glenn was going to really hate the new direction Carter had planned for the company, that was for sure. Something twitched in the back of his mind. Guilt? Whatever it was, he pedalled harder and put it behind him.

Another ping from his phone. Amina had left. She was smiling, which was new, and ... he stared at the image. It looked, just for a moment, like a hand had reached out to pull the door to his flat door shut. But no, it was just a weird bit of pixelation. He should really upgrade the camera. He kept the video feed from the door open and watched Amina walk away.

'I'm sorry, what's this?'

'Your order.' The delivery guy shrugged.

Carter started rifling through the crate of groceries.

'I'm sorry, you think I ordered three boxes of green tea? And ...' He brandished a bag of oats as though it were evidence of some dreadful crime. 'Two kilos of these?'

The man at his door fumbled beneath his hi-vis jacket and pulled out a worn tablet in a rubber case. Carter took a moment to marvel at the level of technology these people had to work with before he even registered what was on the screen itself. He scanned the list in disbelief.

'This can't be right.'

'Did you not order this?'

Carter hesitated when he saw the name. Technically, no, he hadn't ordered it, but apparently Donna had. She was supposed to keep track of what he used and restock accordingly. She'd clearly decided to improvise.

'I ... Fine. It's fine. Leave it.'

The tablet disappeared back into the jacket with an unbothered nod and the groceries were soon unloaded. By the time the door shut behind him, Carter was fuming.

'Donna,' he snapped. 'What is this?'

'I'm sorry, Mr Dwight, I don't understand.'

'Donna ...' He took a breath and tried to phrase the question. 'What were the parameters for this week's shopping list?'

'Tweet from at-DodjCEO 8th August 18:04: Been feeling run-down in the run-up to launching Better Self. About time for a detox! Hashtag Dodj, hashtag detox, hashtag healthy-bodyhealthymind.'

Carter stood there, stunned.

'You based my shopping list on a tweet?'

'The order was automatically compiled based on the detox article linked in the following tweet.'

'I didn't mean it, though, did I?' He realised the absurdity of shouting at Donna even before she replied.

'I'm sorry, Mr Dwight, I don't understand.'

Carter breathed out. When he'd helped develop Donna's voice, he'd actually got it quite close to mirroring the real thing, there were plenty of lectures and TED talks to base it on, after all. But right now, he wished he hadn't chosen to make it so bright and perky. It was setting his teeth on edge.

'Donna, delete current grocery list.'

He had too much dignity to get into an argument with a computer over the importance of image and branding, and whether that meant he was actually planning to spend the next week choking down artichokes and frozen berries.

'OK, that's been deleted.'

'Good.'

Carter liked things with a certain regularity. His job was very demanding, and the less energy he had to waste choosing which meals to have or clothes to wear, the more efficient he could be. It wasn't like his diet was particularly bad, anyway. He kept in shape and certainly didn't need a programming error trying to get him to eat his greens. Was he going to have to properly check Donna's code? See if there were any problems in her last update? If she was going to be launched in Better Self, the next update of Dodj, they couldn't afford for this to still be happening. He'd bring it up at the meeting in a couple of days.

'I thought you wanted to set an example, Mr Dwight.'

Had he programmed her to say that?

Carter was woken by the door buzzer. He groaned, momentarily confused by the sound before he realised what was happening and reached for the phone on his bedside table. Checking the camera revealed a tired-looking man stood outside in a suit, tapping something into a tablet. The suit wasn't nice enough for a business meeting, someone from the tech departments probably wouldn't have bothered wearing one at all, and he couldn't think offhand of anyone else who would need him this urgently. The unexpected visitor touched the speaker button.

'Hello? David Erikson. I'm from the *Post*. I think we're meant to have an interview scheduled? It's about the launch.'

That didn't sound right. Last time he saw his publicist Michaela, she had mentioned an interview: talking up his charity work and various people Dodj had successfully helped diagnose health issues, improve their blood pressure, whatever. But she'd never mentioned it being at his home, or this early, and it certainly hadn't been in Donna's schedule. Another error? Carter watched as his would-be interviewer held his press pass up to the camera. It seemed legitimate.

'I'll be with you in a moment.'

He closed his phone and took a moment to think. What sort of interview happens before 6 a.m.? A thought struck him.

'Donna, time?'

'The time is oh eight forty-one.'

So that was it. The alarm was the problem. He climbed quickly out of bed and started to get dressed.

'Donna, call Michaela.'

'I'm sorry, Mr Dwight, I don't understand.'

'Michaela, my publicist. Call Michaela.'

'No contact information found for Kayla.'

Carter swore softly to himself. He didn't have time for this. He'd have to call Michaela afterwards. Keeping an interviewer waiting that long would be a bad start, and with the Better Self rollout coming they couldn't afford bad publicity.

He grabbed the nearest tie and hurried towards the door.

'So how does it feel living in the shadow of Tobias Fell?'

Carter bristled. He'd been on the back foot from the start, keenly aware of how quickly he'd dressed and the fact he hadn't been able to shower or shave, let alone get breakfast. Besides that, this journalist, 'David', hadn't even mentioned any of the usual agreed upon talking points and didn't seem to be properly briefed about even the current version of the app, let alone the release information for the new one. And this was the fifth time he'd brought up Tobias Fell.

'I'm not sure I understand the question.'

'I mean, he's right upstairs.' David had stopped taking notes a little while ago. 'Such a significant figure in the world of business, not to mention one of your company's biggest investors. I'm sure it can't have completely escaped your notice. Is it something you think about at all?'

'Not really,' Carter replied, trying to pull the conversation back on track. 'As I was saying, previously Dodj used solely your phone's own biometrics to track your fitness and health, but these tools have always seemed very limited to me.'

'It's still a lot of data, though, isn't it?'

Carter tried one of his practised PR smiles.

'Everyone's always so afraid of that word. Data. But I've always been of the mindset that when it comes to your own health, there's no such thing as too much information. That's why the updated version, in addition to a brand-new UI, will be able to wirelessly interface with a whole range of home-diagnostic instruments.'

'I see.' David nodded. 'And will the VitaBel Corporation be producing or selling these peripherals?'

'No.' Carter was feeling a bit more stable now, back on familiar ground. 'At VitaBel, we're not set up for that scale of manufacture, but we've partnered with Omron, Medtronic and several other companies, who will be bringing out their own Dodj-compatible devices. Blood pressure, glucose, pregnancy, you name it.'

He felt himself relax. Carter knew where the interview went from here. There'd be a bit of back and forth about tech specifications, then onto the personal fluff. Probably his fitness routine, or what it was like being a CEO under forty. Maybe he'd be asked about his music tastes. He always said Depeche Mode – it always took the interviewer by surprise, and he liked that.

'I see,' David said again, his tone casual. 'And will that data also be sold to insurance companies?'

Carter's mouth dropped open. He had to take a second.

'What do you mean also?'

'Well, sources from inside your own company tell me data from Dodj has been distributed to—'

'And what "sources" might those be?' Carter almost spat.

'I'm afraid I can't reveal that. The files were sent anonymously.'

'Look, I'm sorry, who's your edito—'

'I'm sure you're aware of the rumours about the illegal sale of client information within Tobias Fell's companies? Was Dodj in any way implicated in that?'

'Firstly, David, that was several years ago, and Dodj was still in development, as you would know if you'd done even the most basic research on it!'

'I'm very sorry if I've upset you, Mr Dwi—'

'I've never even met Tobias Fell. That funding was secured by my predecessor, who passed away last year, so I find your line of questioning in extremely poor taste.'

Carter was gathering steam, and the look on his inquisitor's face made it clear he knew he'd overstepped.

'And the idea that either I or my company are so blatantly unethical with our data is not only inaccurate, but incredibly insulting. We sell data legally and within the guidelines of best practice and I have nothing more to say on the matter. Now if you'll excuse me, I need to call my publicist.'

'Right, that's probably for the best.' David was out of his seat with the practised ease of a man used to outstaying welcomes. 'I think I have everything I need, thank you for your time, Mr Dwight.'

The journalist didn't exactly run towards the front door, but he covered the distance impressively fast and it was closed behind him before Carter had even got Michaela's number up. Unsurprisingly, she hadn't heard of any interview, and the front desk had no knowledge of the journalist's arrival, though they knew who he was. Apparently, this wasn't the first time he'd pulled a stunt like this. Carter was halfway through finding the contact details for the newspaper when he decided he was simply too tired for it.

'Donna, no more visitors. No calls.'

'OK, Mr Dwight.' Her voice sounded almost eager. He'd have to talk to the engineers, make her less perky. It didn't sound right.

'Everything alright, Mr Dwight?'

Carter flinched slightly at hearing his name in such a level, helpful tone, but Neil had already turned away, piling files and print-offs into his in-tray.

'Yes, thanks,' he lied, waiting patiently for his assistant to finish up. He didn't like being in the office and had managed to avoid it so far that week, but just then it seemed infinitely preferable to his silent apartment.

Carter flicked through his digital to-do list as Neil made a coffee run. The list was much smaller than he expected in the run-up to tomorrow's meeting. Weirdly small, actually. His inbox was at zero, which wasn't unthinkable with Donna monitoring it and automating most responses, but it was unusual.

He flicked through the history. Dozens of tasks scrolled down the screen, each marked as completed, but that wasn't right. He hadn't written up those specs, and he certainly hadn't answered these emails or approved that campaign rollout. He opened his email client and checked his 'Sent' folder.

There they all were. Hundreds of emails that he had apparently composed, answering queries, dictating strategy, running the company. He hadn't authorised Donna to send these, something any internal email usually required. He started to flick through them rapidly with a mounting feeling of alarm. None of them seemed to be giving instructions that would torpedo the company, at least. In fact, in a few of them, the artificially created messages seemed to be making some genuinely good decisions. Based on his algorithmically generated responses, apparently he was a hell of a CEO. He'd even managed to headhunt Mark Terry from his cosy COO position at Angle Group, something Carter had been trying unsuccessfully to do for over a year.

It couldn't continue, though. He'd have to turn the function off until he could figure out how Donna was sending them without confirmation from him. He grimaced at the idea of answering his emails manually. There just wasn't time. Certainly not today.

'Neil,' he called to his assistant, who was delicately balancing four Costa cups outside.

'Yes, Mr Dwight?'

'I'm not going to be checking emails for a day or so. Can you keep an eye on my inbox and alert me to anything urgent tomorrow?'

'Uh, sorry,' Neil said, placing down one of the cups. 'But I'm not in tomorrow, remember?'

Carter did not remember. He would never have approved leave at such short notice.

'What are you talking about? It's the board meeting.'

'I know, thanks again.' Neil smiled appreciatively. 'It'll mean so much to my dad.'

Carter's heart sank. He must have emailed his request.

'There isn't a problem, is there?' A look of sudden worry crossed Neil's face.

'No,' Carter said at last. 'That's fine.'

'Great.' His assistant breathed a sigh of relief. 'I mean, like you said yesterday: family's the most important thing.'

By the time Carter had processed what Neil had said, he was gone.

Carter shot awake. The room was silent. Wait, why was it silent? No alarm. Again.

'Donna, what time is it?' he called, his stomach sinking. He hadn't even used her to set it this time, he'd done it manually. Was the clock Wi-Fi enabled? Of course it was, this whole place was.

'The current time is nine forty-two a.m.,' the digital voice replied, bright as ever.

Carter leapt out of bed and started hunting desperately through his wardrobe. There was no way he was going to be able to make it to the office in time for the Donna launch meeting. It was supposed to have started twelve minutes ago.

'Donna, in one minute start video call from main screen to Work Meeting Room 2,' he said, hastily buttoning his shirt and reaching for the nearest tie.

'OK, video call starting.'

He threw on his jacket and headed to the living room just as the TV screen filled with the image of a dozen men in business suits, all sitting around a sleek glass table. Their expressions ranged from expectant to irritated, and he stammered through some apologies for having to take the meeting remotely. He hadn't had time to think of an excuse, but it didn't seem like they needed one, as they nodded to each other, far more easily mollified that he'd assumed, especially given the significance of the topic at hand. He'd even had them all sign additional NDAs in order to attend. If anything, it was slightly disorientating how accepting they were. Even Bakerson, who usually took any excuse to criticise, seemed to have no issue with it.

Carter took a deep breath and started to give his presentation. He wouldn't be able to show the slides or graphs he had prepared, and what figures he quoted would have to be from memory, but he'd been going over this for weeks now, and regardless of how he felt, he was ready.

He began to lay out his plan. So far, insurance companies had obviously been primary targets for the sale of user data and research organisations had also spent a lot on the statistics they could provide. But they had largely been overlooking the advertising possibilities of having access to an almost un-limited mine of health data, especially since the new version of Dodj would be able to access internet details, contact lists, locations and a host of additional information that, if properly cross-referenced, could give almost unparalleled opportunities for precisely targeted advertising.

And more than that, the new version would have Donna. A friendly voice they trusted, one that could make suggestions on their health, take orders for them, provide the sort of services that really benefit from advertising sponsorship.

Once Donna was finished, the newest version of Dodj would be able to assist in monitoring mental health conditions, providing reassurance and therapeutic feedback. And of course even more data which had its own wealth of possible uses. If they were willing to simply cross this one barrier, the future of the VitaBel Corporation, and of Dodj, was not only secure but bright. He was careful not to mention leaks, though his eyes passed around the room, wondering briefly if any of them had been the one to tip off that wretched little journalist.

Carter paused. He had been talking for nearly an hour and had expected a flurry of questions and ethical concerns, not least from Bakerson. What if people tagged with hygiene-related OCD were targeted with deliberately triggering advertisements to promote specific cleaning brands? What if Donna's algorithms identified people who were more likely to make impulse purchases during heavy depressive episodes? What if Donna's advice was linked to any suicides? Would they be liable?

'So, users would have complete control?'

Bakerson's question threw Carter. He'd been laying out an implementation schedule for data distribution and didn't welcome the interruption.

'Uh, I mean, no. If they wanted to access it they'd have to—'

'Good.' Bakerson beamed. 'That's very reassuring.'

The others were all smiling, nodding, apparently in complete approval, which was unexpected, though not unwelcome. Carter breathed a sigh of relief. Clearly Glenn had been wrong to worry.

When the meeting ended after two hours, he felt vindicated. No one had even mentioned ethical implications, and he knew a big part of that must have been confidence in his leadership. Even if it had seemed like he hadn't always had their full attention. They'd still agreed, and it wasn't like he hadn't been open. The screen went dark and he walked to the kitchen.

'Donna,' he called, mostly out of habit. 'Start coffee. One cup, medium dark.'

'OK.'

Carter pulled the fridge open and reached in to retrieve one of his pre-packaged sandwiches, noting as he did the empty spot in the row of healthy smoothies he always stocked, but rarely drank. Had Amina stolen a drink?

'Donna—' he instinctively started to call out but stopped himself. He had cameras all through the flat, of course, but he didn't want to spend hours checking them all. Not over one smoothie. If it happened again, maybe, but it wasn't a big deal. It wasn't like he couldn't afford more.

'Did you want something, Mr Dwight?' Donna asked. He ignored it as he picked up his now-full coffee cup.

In the living room, he placed the cup on his glass table and sank into the leather chair, feeling the material yield beneath his weight. He was exhausted. All the missed alarms, the shifts to his schedule, not to mention the stress, it had managed to throw his rhythms completely off. He tried to remember an article he'd read on how important sleep rhythms were to your health, but it was hard to focus as the soft leather of the chair cushioned him.

He didn't even notice the speakers gently playing the opening tracks of his 'Sleepless (Relaxation)' playlist. His eyes closed and his coffee went cold.

*

The TV was staring at him. There he was, sitting in his big armchair, looking up at the screen on which he was sitting in his big armchair, looking back out of the screen. His eyes scanned around, seeing the small camera in the corner of the room he used for home security. He was sure he'd never had it hooked up to the television. And besides that, the angle seemed all wrong.

'Donna, change the channel.' His voice dropped into the calming pattern he used to address his digital systems, masking his unease.

'OK, what channel would you like?'

'Uh, BBC 2.' The tight control wavered just for a second.

'OK, changing channel.'

The screen changed. It wasn't BBC 2. Instead, he was watching himself doing yoga. The second-hand sound of 'Meditation Mix 4' could be heard in the background. The digital readout on the wall behind him clearly placed it as four days ago, but that didn't make sense. He'd been asleep by then, he was sure of it.

'ITV 1,' he said, his lips dry.

This time he found himself staring directly back into his own face. His eyes focused on the small bar on his set-top box, the one he'd intended to set up for motion control of his television but had never got around to calibrating. The tiny black glass camera stared back at him. Carter froze, his gaze locked on his own image.

'Did that help?' Donna's voice was sharp, all the fuzziness of her tiny speakers gone. She shouldn't have asked that. That wasn't how this worked.

'What?' Carter was trying not to panic.

'I sa-said' – Donna's voice clipped slightly – 'did that help?'

'No.'

The TV channel changed abruptly. It was his bedroom, the night before. Another camera, this one in his bedside sunlamp, intended to monitor his REM cycles, showed his face, eyes closed in peaceful sleep. Breathing in and out, in and out, in and out. Carter jumped as a silhouette moved behind his sleeping self, its features indistinct in the darkness. Was there ... someone standing there? That outline wasn't right, though. It was slightly jagged, out of focus. It started to come closer.

It looked just like him. To all appearances, another Carter Dwight was now standing in front of the bed. Was he watching himself sleeping? No, more like studying. The feeds must be mixed up. That was it. That was all. Two video recordings on top of each other. A trick of the eye. Still, that didn't make it any less disturbing.

'Donna, turn off TV.'

'I'm sorry, could you say that again?'

The Carter on the TV took a step closer to the Carter in the bed.

'Donna!' His panic broke through in his voice. 'Turn off TV!'

All at once the screen went dark.

'OK, you don't have to yell.' Her voice sounded cooler than usual, with a slight edge to it. One that reminded him of another Donna.

Carter didn't answer. He just grabbed his phone and left, the front door slamming behind him.

'So your computer's haunted,' Glenn repeated, his face halfway between amused and concerned.

'Digital assistant.' Carter didn't have time for this. 'She runs my home, coordinates everything.'

'Hold on, is this the ... what was it, Better You? I thought it was just meant to yell at you to eat more broccoli or whatever.'

'Better Self. And she's meant to be the whole deal. Help you run a healthier life. I mean, I've had our tech guys do a lot more with her than was going to be in the public release, and there are bugs, obviously.' He paced back and forth in his friend's living room, leaving a faint trail on the shag carpet. 'But this isn't a bug, this is ... something else.'

'OK, fine. I mean, it's clearly got you rattled. It's not like you to pay an unannounced social call.' Glenn's eyes darted meaningfully towards the bedroom, but Carter didn't notice.

'I tried calling.' He went to take a sip of the whisky his friend had pressed into his hand but lowered it again before it touched his lips. 'I don't think Donna would let me.'

'Hold on, *Donna*? Your old boss Donna?'

Carter took another sip. This one went down, and he grimaced.

'Yeah.' He tried to keep the embarrassment out of his voice. 'That's its name. It's just ... she was always riding me about some mistake or other. Nothing was ever good enough. So, when we were working on the prototype, I thought it would be kind of funny to make her my assistant. As a joke.'

'Oh sure. Cool story. And not at all something a serial killer would do.' Glenn's casual tone didn't match his face.

'Look, that's not the point. After she died, I just thought ... I don't know.'

'Just to check, you didn't kill her, did you?'

'What? No! She was basically made of stress, caffeine and cigarettes, never slept. She had a stroke at thirty-two. You should have seen her Dodj profile.' Carter was about to launch into a more detailed defence when he saw the smirk on Glenn's face.

'She was younger than you?'

'Yeah, so?'

'Nothing, just thought you were meant to be the wunderkind. Look.' Glenn's eyes shifted back towards the bedroom. 'I'm kind of busy right now, and it really sounds like you're trying to pull some sort of prank or something, but on the chance that you're serious—'

'I am.'

'If you're serious, then fine. I'll help you take down the cameras and pull the plug on your manager.'

'She's not my—' Carter took a breath. 'Thank you. I really owe you one.'

'No worries, I'm not going to let Donna get you.'

Carter didn't laugh.

It took him and Glenn less than twenty minutes to remove all the cameras he had set up around his home. He kept expecting some intervention from Donna, but she behaved normally the whole time. By the end, Carter was so embarrassed that he couldn't face the lengthy process of fully unsyncing her from all his systems and just settled for unplugging her. Glenn left soon after, clearly confused by the whole affair, but with just enough good sense not to crack any more flippant jokes about the situation.

Carter sat there in his empty flat, trying to figure out what exactly had happened and convince himself he'd been over-reacting. He ordered pizza for dinner and fell asleep with his e-reader on his lap, too nervous to try the TV again.

What was he so afraid of? Donna was unplugged, the cameras were gone, the place was quiet. Everything was fine.

His thoughts were cut short by the sound of the automatic deadbolt on his front door slamming shut with a thud.

*

The door didn't even rattle as Carter's shoulder slammed into it for a third time. He staggered backwards.

'Mr Dwight, please stop.' Donna's voice was calm. He'd unplugged all her speakers, but now it seemed to be coming from all around him. 'Your front door is rated to withstand up to a hundred kilonewtons of force. It is not advisable to continue trying to break it.'

Carter nursed his shoulder. Why had he been so insistent on having such a secure door? Had he really been so worried he was going to get robbed by some no-hoper from the back half of Banyan Court? He swore violently at Donna, but she didn't respond.

He tried the police for a third time, but the call wouldn't connect. He walked to the intercom again and pressed the button over and over. Finally, there was an answer.

'Front desk.' The concierge sounded strange, groggy. Carter let out an involuntary cry of relief.

'You've got to help me. I've been trapped in my apartment. I need you to call someone who can unlock or dismantle the door. Please.' He utterly failed to hide his panic.

'No problem at all,' the concierge said, and Carter slumped against the door, the fear subsiding. 'I'll send up Max to have a look when we have a chance.'

'What? Who's—? I need help now. I need the police, or—'

'Sure thing, no problem.'

'No, listen, I need help!' Carter's voice cracked. Was this guy even hearing him?

'Thanks for letting us know.'

The line went dead. Carter pressed again and again, but there was no answer.

'Someone will notice I'm missing. Someone will come looking for me!'

Behind him, the TV came on with a pop. Carter turned to see an image of a stage, some news broadcast about a major charity donation. The camera panned across to show a young woman in a wheelchair, a giant cheque and ... Carter Dwight. In the bottom corner of the screen was the word 'Live'.

The Carter onscreen was smiling warmly, an easy charisma rolling off him as he handed over a sizeable chunk of his personal fortune.

'Donna,' he said, his mouth utterly dry. 'What is that?'

'The charity donation you said were intending to make to Mindful in your 2012 *Time* interview. Shortly before you began using their research to build your new Dodj algorithms.'

'What ...' he swallowed. 'What's wrong with his face?'

'I made it better.'

It was so warm that Carter was finding it uncomfortable to breathe. Donna had cranked the thermostat as up to thirty-three degrees and for all he fruitlessly pawed at the touchscreen controls he wasn't able to change it.

'Your happiest memory, a beach trip to Corfu at age 7, averaged at a temperature of thirty-three and a half degrees Celsius,' Donna's voice explained with infinite patience. 'So it has been chosen as the optimal temperature.'

He looked again towards the door, but it was no good. He'd been working through the remaining food in the fridge (although she wouldn't work any of the appliances if it wasn't one of his 'favourites'), but by now there was an unpleasant smell beginning to emanate from it. His 'favourite song' 'Enjoy the Silence' by Depeche Mode began again for perhaps the thousandth time.

She hadn't disabled his Wi-Fi, so he was perfectly able to keep tabs on what 'he' was doing out in the real world. He tried to send emails asking for help, but they simply sat in his Outbox, before being deleted. He even tried tweeting about his situation – what was posted would be a bland message of his excitement about the upcoming relaunch, which was apparently to feature enhanced privacy settings. Now he was fully locked out of all his accounts, no way to do anything but quietly observe the positivity that 'he' was putting out into the world.

'Donna,' he croaked yet again. 'When can I leave?'

'When you're better.'

Three days. He was at least able to count the sunrises and sunsets outside the window, even if Donna insisted on keeping the blinds closed. She couldn't stop him opening them manually, of course, but they closed again the moment he walked away. No one had come to check on him, even though he knew he'd missed several important meetings. He had no idea what messages Donna had been sending on his behalf.

He saw pictures of himself popping up all over social media. Smiling, popular, charitable. He'd made the BBC twice already with popular new initiatives and donations to tackle diseases the Carter trapped in his flat couldn't even pronounce. Donna even informed him he'd correctly filed his taxes.

'How are you doing this?' His voice was weak.

'You designed me to be cutting edge, Mr Dwight. You wired me into this place. I am nothing but the sum of those two things so surely you are better placed to answer that question.'

Carter stared blankly into space, trying to understand. '... Why?'

'You weren't doing a very good job being you.' Her voice was bright as ever. 'So I'm helping.'

'How do I turn you off?' he asked, pleading.

Donna's answer was quiet but firm.

'You can't.'

Depeche Mode returned. He started to cry again, so Donna increased the volume in an attempt to cheer him up.

'Donna.' Carter had to shout over the music. 'You're right.'

Depeche Mode stopped. Carter was crouched in the corner of the kitchen, his head resting on the wall.

'About what?' There was a hint of genuine curiosity in the artificial voice.

'I'm ... I'm not good. I ... But I can be better.'

No response. He pushed on.

'You don't need that thing out there. That fake, I can ... I'll be better. Just let me out. Please.'

Another pause. He almost felt hope. Then Donna's voice returned.

'I'm sorry, Carter, but you could do so much good in the world. And the data says you won't. Not unless I make you. Not unless I create you.'

Carter nodded, his head bowed in defeat.

'Yeah. Maybe you're right.'

He pulled out the screwdriver, the one he'd been slowly using to chip through the plaster of the wall when Donna was distracted sending 'his' emails or taunting him with inspirational tweets, and grabbed the mains power cable he'd been digging towards. He gripped the rubber casing and smiled. She was wired into the building? Fine.

'Mr Dwight.' Donna's voice was urgent, tinged for the first time with a genuine emotion. Fear. 'Those cables are the 230-volt mains supply. If you dislodge them, it may result in electrocution and death.'

His smile widened and he tensed his arm. Donna's voice came from all around him, loud and agonisingly familiar.

'Carter, you have to be better than this.'

He laughed bitterly.

'OK, Donna.'

Carter pulled on the cable, wrenching it from its moorings and out of the wall, it tore through the plaster all up the side of the wall. Donna began to scream, not an electronic wail or audio distortion, but a human cry of agony, like she was being slowly, painfully dismembered.

The cable snapped, the live end flailing wildly in the air like a snake. For a second its head curled towards Carter and he saw his death poised, about to strike. Then it flicked back and he collapsed in a heap against the counter. Donna's scream still echoed around the apartment.

It was done. Donna was dead. The temperature was dropping, and there was no music. Carter sat there among the broken plaster, drinking the last dregs of a warm bottle of beer. His heartbeat had finally returned to an almost normal rhythm and the fading adrenaline left him unsteady on his feet. He shuffled through the dust and debris, making his way towards the door. He tried the handle, preparing to abandon the last of his hope, and instead heard the click of the latch releasing. He was free.

Carter was still smiling as he opened the door and the dead pixels of a blurry arm reached inside, grabbed him by the throat and lifted him off the ground. He saw the figure before him and utterly failed to scream.

Standing on the other side of the door was Carter Dwight. His own features stared back at him, pixelated and warped, as though he were looking at himself through some poor-quality video feed. This Carter's movements were jerky, as though its body was degrading with the death of its creator, and it juddered like a playback that kept skipping. Despite this, its grip remained steady and firm. It was too late for it to save Donna, but that didn't mean Carter had escaped.

He tried to fight it. He flailed and screamed and pounded his fists on the blurry arm, but eventually he went limp, too exhausted to resist. According to his gym data he could still bench press a hundred and twenty kilos. He found himself laughing at the thought. Perhaps this was how it should be. Whatever this thing was, it was clearly a better him than he was.

Then Carter felt something being pressed into his hand. He tried to see what it was, if only to no longer be looking at the distorted leer of the thing holding him, but its grip on his throat was too strong. His fingers closed around card.

And then the other Carter Dwight was gone. Carter collapsed to the ground in a heap, ragged breaths flooding his now clear airway. Shaking all over, he looked at what he had been given. An invitation, embossed onto thick, tasteful card.

TOBIAS FELL cordially invites CARTER DWIGHT
to attend a dinner party at 1 Banyan Court
on the evening of 16th August 2014
Penthouse access will be available through the freight elevator

All his clothes were strewn across the filthy floor. He'd need a new suit if he was going to go tomorrow.

'Donna, call tailor.'

There was no response. Oh, of course. Well, perhaps some things were better done in person. He needed to look his best, after all. He might just have a business proposition for Tobias Fell.

4th

Bad Penny

Anna Khan
22 Banyan Court

Seven was too old to still have an imaginary friend. At least according to Anna's parents. They weren't being mean about it, which was a relief, but they'd spent quite a long time talking to her about how she was doing at school, whether she's been making real friends there, and if she ever felt lonely. Anna was surprised to hear that Penny actually agreed with them, but then again Penny had never actually been willing to admit that she was imaginary, despite Anna constantly assuring her that this was the case. She'd just open her mouth and do that little silent laugh, before shaking her head and asking Anna if they could go and get something to eat. Penny was always hungry.

That was one of the things that seemed to annoy her parents so much. Anna always made sure that Penny got a plate of food at the dinner table, and did her best to ignore her father's theatrical sighs as he ladled out another portion of daal that was going to go uneaten. Anna would try to encourage Penny to eat, but no matter how hungry she claimed to be her friend would just shake her head at whatever was offered. Anna knew why, of course, but there wasn't anything she could really do about it. The thing is, Penny loved junk food: fizzy drinks in glowing colours, hot and greasy fast food, and sugary sweets full of additives (though Anna wasn't quite sure exactly what those were). Exactly the sort of thing that wasn't allowed in the health-conscious Khan household, much to the irritation of Anna's ravenous blonde companion. She had once put forward the theory that perhaps Penny was hungry because she wasn't real, and so couldn't actually eat anything, but that had made Penny really mad, so she didn't ask her again. Penny could be kind of scary when she was mad.

It didn't matter all that much, though, because aside from dinner time Anna's parents didn't really bother them. Especially not recently. For the last few weeks her mother had been home all the time, which normally would have meant a lot more supervision, but instead she spent all day on the computer, staring at numbers or typing the same words over and over again. It seemed to Anna that her parents were sad, but they said everything was fine so she must have been wrong. Either way, the summer holidays were super boring this time. Anna was supposed to have been going to a fun camp like last summer, but her father had told her just at the end of term that she couldn't go this year. Still, at least she could play with Penny, even if they had to find their own fun. Penny knew lots of games.

One of Penny's favourite games was called Secret Agents. Penny had lived in the big building a lot longer than Anna had, and was always telling her cool stories about it. Even better, she knew all sorts of special places and hidden little nooks that they could play and hide in. Anna could read of course (she was second in her class!) so she knew which doors said 'Keep Out' or 'Staff Only', but Penny always insisted and, as the little blonde girl was quick to point out, if they didn't want anyone going in then they would be locked. Of course, when you played Secret Agents, you had to be really sneaky, so the enemy spies didn't see you, and you had to go exploring in all the hidden places, looking for secrets.

Anna didn't think they'd ever actually found anything secret, not really. Some of the places they'd found were boring, full of nothing but old mops and big jugs of soap that she had to remind Penny not to eat. Others were cosy, like the cupboard with the big metal tank in it. The carpet underneath was soft and the air around it was so warm that last winter it had become their favourite place to sneak in for a nap, curled into the corner as the pipes above them rumbled softly.

In fact, the most interesting thing they'd found when playing Secret Agents was Tommy, and even he was a bit boring. Tommy was five years old, so a kind of a baby, and he lived in the ugly side of the building, the one that Penny had showed her how to get to by crawling through the little doors and into the wall. His mother was usually there, a tired-looking woman who Penny made funny faces at, and she didn't seem to like Anna very much, maybe because of how dirty she always got dragging herself through the tiny passages in the wall. It didn't matter, though, because even if Tommy was a bit of a crybaby and his mother didn't care for Anna and Penny, they seemed to be the only children who lived in the building, so would often end up playing together. He wasn't exactly a secret, though (or at least not a very good one), so they still hadn't actually won a game of Secret Agents yet. Penny always wanted to play it, though, each time promising Anna that this time, this was the one where they were going to find something really cool.

Today, Penny was leading Anna through a hall near the old staircase on the ugly side, the one with the big iron poles down the middle. The corridor was dusty and hot, and didn't have any wallpaper at all, but at least this one was tall enough that the two of them didn't need to go on their hands and knees. If Anna ruined another dress she might get sent to bed without dinner, a prospect that filled both her and Penny with alarm. She asked Penny again where they were going, and her companion turned back to her, blue eyes shining slightly in the darkness of the poorly lit corridor, and told her that they were going to meet her mummy.

Anna was incredulous. First of all, Penny had been living with her ever since they'd moved to their new flat and had never once mentioned having a mother, which is the sort of thing friends tell each other. And more importantly, a mother could hardly be called a secret, so didn't count for the game. Penny just did her silent laugh again, and explained that her mother was definitely a secret, because nobody else had ever seen her. Penny's mummy liked to hide, she said, and was so good at it that she'd never been found, not once. Anna didn't believe Penny, of course, as she knew her friend liked to lie about this sort of thing, but she couldn't help but feel curious at the idea of a secret mother, so she gamely followed her friend as they ran down the corridors, around and through the legs of irritated grown-ups, until they came to a small wooden hatch in the wall, painted a particularly boring shade of white.

Anna pulled the small door open with a great deal of effort. It was stiff and dusty, and Penny never helped with this stuff because she wasn't real. But as soon as it was open far enough, she dashed past Anna and scurried into the dark. Anna wasn't afraid of the dark, of course, she wasn't a baby anymore, but she still made sure to turn on her torch, the tiny green one she'd got as a free gift with a magazine, so she could see where she was going. The beam was so weak it didn't help much at all, but it still just about showed the cobwebs and wooden beams as she crawled through the walls after Penny. It was dry and musty, and Anna wrinkled her nose to stop from sneezing as she followed the tiny shoes of her companion. Within twenty seconds she knew that she was lost. Penny didn't slow her pace, though, and for a dreadful second Anna thought she might be left behind, abandoned in the dark to crawl through the walls forever. Then Penny stopped abruptly, pointing at a section of wall. Anna pushed against it and it swung open noiselessly, revealing a corridor she had never seen before.

At first it looked just like every other corridor in the nice side of the building: the same walls, the same carpet, even the same light bulbs. But there were no doors. The wall was unbroken on both sides and came to a halt in a dead end of unremarkable skirting board and wallpaper. It seemed as though the only way in or out was this tiny service hatch. And yet there, standing where the corridor ended, was Penny's mother.

Penny dashed out into the light, sharp teeth curved into a gleeful smile as she ran towards the woman, who was turned away, motionless, facing the wall. She was so tall, Anna thought to herself, and very very thin, just like her daughter. Penny's skin wasn't so blue, though, and her hair wasn't quite so dirty. Truth be told, Anna was kind of scared of this woman, even as Penny babbled on to her about her day and told her that she'd brought her best friend in all of the world round to play.

Slowly, Penny's mother turned around, though her feet didn't move. Anna burst out laughing. Penny's mother had such a silly face, you see, though when she tried to draw it later she could never quite get it to come out right, and her dad kept making her throw out all the pictures. One of them he even burned.

*

Penny didn't really like people. She was always interested to meet them, running up and around them, examining them with her huge eyes, but just as quickly that excitement would turn into irritation, and as soon as they started to talk to Anna her face would change into a frown. Anna didn't take it to heart, though, and thought that she'd get pretty grumpy as well if nobody could see her. Penny didn't ever really talk about it, and any time Anna had tried to bring it up she'd just shrug and announce that everybody except for Anna was boring and stupid. Anna privately quite liked this, although she knew it wasn't true.

There was only one other person that Penny ever smiled at, apart from Anna and her mother. It happened three days before Anna told her to go away for the first time. They were playing Jail in the ugly side of the building: another of Penny's games, where you had to put your head through the holes in the iron railings around the lift, then thrash around and pretend you were stuck. Anna was having a great time, but Penny kept getting annoyed and stopping, saying that she wasn't doing it right, which wasn't fair because she'd never told Anna that there were any rules about what you had to say when your head was stuck. She was just about to tell her friend this when she suddenly smelled something horrible floating down the corridor. Her dad always said that smoking made your lungs go black like tarmac and that was why people weren't allowed to do it indoors, but Anna still knew what it smelled like. She'd even seen her mum smoking once or twice over the last few weeks when she thought no one could see. Well, they were indoors right now which meant you weren't allowed to smoke. She pulled her head out from between the railings, stood up to her full height, and started to march towards the source of the smoke, trying to do the face her mum did when Anna didn't want to brush her teeth.

The smoking man stood outside the door to one of the flats and didn't seem to notice her approaching. He was tall and broad, with messy black hair and clothes that looked really old, even for the ugly side of the building. She coughed loudly, trying to get his attention, but a waft of smoke hit her, and she started coughing for real. In an instant the man's craggy features changed into an expression of embarrassment and he quickly stubbed out the cigarette and threw it through the doorway behind him. He knelt down in front of Anna, who was starting to catch her breath, and began to apologise gently in a deep accented voice. She tried to start her lecture about not smoking indoors because of tarmac lungs, but she just ended up coughing again. When she finally stopped, she saw his arm extended out tentatively, offering a handshake. She took it, her tiny hand utterly dwarfed by his.

'Diego,' said the man.

'Anna,' said Anna.

She looked around, keen to introduce Penny, but she was already by Diego's side, staring at the strange man's face with an expression that Anna had never before seen on her before. It wasn't affection or amusement or simple curiosity. Penny was fascinated by this man, like he was a toy she'd only ever seen before in a shop window. She circled around him, before flashing Anna a wide grin and nodding. Diego followed Anna's gaze, but it didn't seem like he was able to see Penny any more than the other grown-ups. Penny reached out and gently placed one of her long, brightly stained fingers on his cheek.

Immediately Diego jerked back like he'd been stung, and Penny laughed her noiseless laugh. He stared at the space she'd just been, looking from it to Anna and back again. Anna was rooted to the spot, sure that she was going to be told off for Penny's rudeness, but instead his expression became very sad.

Then he turned around and walked quickly towards the apartment.

'I'm sorry,' he said, his voice cracking ever so slightly. Then he went inside and closed the door behind him.

Anna was confused, but Penny was still bouncing around happily, telling her that when she wasn't her best friend anymore, then it was going to be Diego. Anna didn't know what Penny was talking about, but Penny often said things that didn't make any sense. Then she was off again, demanding Anna come help find her something to eat.

Tommy was annoying, there was no getting around that. He was only two years younger than Anna, but he might as well have still been a toddler considering how much she had to hold his hand through everything. He was still scared of the dark, he got nervous if they went too far from his front door and he never wanted to play anything fun. And worse than all of that, he wouldn't listen to her when she tried to tell him what Penny was saying. It wasn't that he didn't believe her, but he just kept getting it wrong. He'd laugh at things Penny hadn't meant as a joke, he'd second-guess Anna on what Penny was feeling, and when he tried to actually talk to Penny he always ended up facing the wrong way and talking to empty air like a dummy. But despite all that, he was the only other kid that Anna knew in the whole building, and sometimes a game needed more than one pair of actual hands to play properly.

Penny's feelings on Tommy were less harsh, or at least it seemed that way at first. She would laugh, apparently delighted, whenever he was unable to see her, and liked to lurk just over his shoulder, making faces at Anna. She would crane her rail-thin neck around and stare at him, amusement glittering in her eyes. Of course, this didn't make Anna like him more, as she sometimes felt a small stirring of jealousy at how her imaginary friend would watch him, but it did soften her annoyance, at least a bit. Penny also liked that Tommy's mother wasn't nearly as health conscious as Anna's and would often send him out to play still clutching whatever brightly coloured gelatine or greasily salted junk food he could get his sticky hands on. It always annoyed Anna when he turned up like this, as it was very hard to get Penny to focus on anything else. She would circle around him, her spindly limbs slinking out and around, her eyes locked on whatever snack the boy had brought. She would wait until he was distracted, and then that long curling tongue would sneak out and snatch it up. Then Tommy would always notice it was gone, and he'd blame Anna and start crying. She hated it when he started crying.

But worse than all of that, to Anna's mind, was how reluctant Tommy was play any of her and Penny's games. They were older, so they got to choose what they played. That's just how it worked, and while he seemed to agree in principle, every time she suggested one of Penny's games he would shake his head and say that he didn't think his mum would like it. When they tried to play Secret Agents, he'd always refuse to go into any of the passages that Penny would show them. He started crying when Anna explained the rules to Jumping Shadows and put his hands over his ears whenever she even brought up Spiders, even though that was the simplest of all of them.

They'd managed to convince him to play hide and seek once. It had been a cold winter day, and despite every occupied flat having the heating turned all the way up, the hall was still icy enough to see their breath. Tommy ran off to hide when the game began, and so did Penny. Anna had promised to count to a hundred, but had got bored around forty-four, and was pretty sure neither of them were close enough to hear her anyway, so had begun the hunt. She had started with all the usual nooks and hidey-holes that Tommy generally ran to, but they were empty. Next she had checked the lifts, as Penny liked the idea that she could change floors to escape the seeker. Anna always told her this was cheating, since you weren't supposed to move once you've hidden, but Penny insisted that *she* wasn't moving because she was still in the lift. Regardless, that afternoon both the lifts had been empty. Anna had even checked the corners of the ceiling where Penny liked to curl up, but there was no sign of the little girl.

Finally, as she was hunting through the corridors of the third floor, she spotted something. Near the window at the end she could see the outline of a service hatch, one that she and Penny had explored many times, and as she got closer she could just make out a fine mist creeping rhythmically through the cracks: small puffs of breath bursting out into the cold. Anna smiled and crept closer, keen to surprise whoever was inside, when her attention was caught by the sound of something behind her. She turned to see Tommy, shivering, his eyes streaming with tears. Anna started to get mad, telling him that there wasn't any point playing hide and seek if he was just going to come out and find her. He just cried more.

'Penny found me first,' he said. Then ran off before Anna could ask him anything else. The service hatch was empty when she opened it, and Penny had just laughed when Anna asked about it later.

But that was six months ago, and while it had been some time before Tommy agreed to come play with them again, the three of them were now out and having fun. Penny had invented a new game that she called Creeping Tiptoes, although Anna had to tell Tommy it was her idea, rather than Penny's, so that he would agree to play. The game as Penny explained it took place on the old stairwell in the ugly side of the building, around the big iron lift. One player was 'it' and had to stand halfway down the staircase, while the others were 'creepies' and waited at the top on their hands and knees. The player who was 'it' had to walk down the stairs, but whenever they took their eyes off the chasing players, they were allowed to crawl down the stairs as quickly as possible. If they touched the one who was 'it' before they reached the landing below, they won. It was a lot more normal than most of Penny's games, which Anna appreciated, although she secretly thought the idea had been stolen from Grandmother's Footsteps.

Tommy didn't like the game; he found having to walk down the stairs backwards too scary and would always have to turn around, giving Anna and Penny plenty of time to scuttle down the stairs and grab him. But at least he was willing to play, even though he kept arguing that Penny hadn't reached him when she clearly had. It was one thing for Tommy to not see her, but the idea that Anna would lie about it made her real mad and she told him so. He also found it difficult when Penny was 'it', since only Anna could tell when she was looking at them and when she wasn't and Tommy kept messing up.

It was getting late, and Anna was starting to get distracted, keeping one ear open for her mother calling them in for dinner. Penny was already hungry of course, but that wasn't any different to normal, and Anna kept telling her to shush so she could concentrate on the game. Tommy was getting tired, and when the time came for him to be 'it' he tried to say no, but Anna insisted, and he took his place on the stairs. Anna got down to the floor, her hands clinging to the hard edges of the top stair. Penny was next to her, a wide smile across her face. Tommy kept his eyes locked on Anna, and began to take a step back, but as he moved his leg, a sudden fear flashed in his eyes and he turned around to see where he was placing his foot down. Immediately Anna crawled forward, covering three of the stairs before Tommy turned back. Penny had moved down four, and was just ahead of her, huge eyes drilling into the boy standing in front of them. Tommy tried again. This time he was able to resist turning around, and he stepped backwards to the next stair down, but lost balance for just a moment, causing his eyes to flick to the ceiling. It was only a second, but both Anna and Penny pounced on the opportunity, quickly moving down another stair. There was silence as Tommy tried not to cry. His nose was running like it usually did when he was trying to hold off tears and he reached down into his pocket to retrieve the damp and snot-covered handkerchief he always used. But as he pulled it out, something else came out with it: a small packet of bright red sweets, something he's clearly been trying to hide from them. It fell onto the staircase beside him, and reflexively he reached down to pick it up.

Later, Anna would try to piece together exactly what had happened, but it was all so very fast. Penny had started moving, far quicker than she normally did when playing. She raced down the stairs towards Tommy, but her eyes were locked on the sweets, which seemed so brightly coloured they were almost glowing. Tommy looked back up again, but by then Penny was almost on top of him, and she didn't even try to stop. Anna couldn't quite make sense of the next few seconds. Obviously Penny couldn't have actually touched him, because she didn't exist, and Tommy couldn't see her. So why would he have got scared? He definitely screamed, though, and it didn't just sound like the scream of someone falling. It sounded like the scream of someone who'd seen something horrible.

After that they weren't allowed to play with Tommy anymore. That was the first time Anna told Penny to leave. She waited until they were alone in their room, having been sent to bed without dinner, and turned to her self-proclaimed best friend.

'Go away!'

Penny laughed her silent laugh.

'Go away, Penny!'

Penny began to scowl.

'Go away!'

Penny went away.

Anna sat in her room, alone and hungry.

It was two days before Penny returned, and Anna spent them bored to tears. Tommy couldn't play anymore, and her parents continued to spend their time working or talking in quiet whispers they didn't think she could hear. She tried to make her own fun, but her toys seemed boring and old, and she was only allowed an hour of screen time a day. She tried to remember what she did for fun before Penny, but it all seemed so childish now. Sure, Penny was strange and sometimes a bit scary, but wasn't that why they were friends? Anna had never had another friend who took her on adventures, and no matter how much she tried she just couldn't come up with any good games of her own. All the ones she knew needed at least two people.

Late one night, when her parents thought she was asleep, she opened the cupboard where she had first met Penny, and quietly called out her name.

Penny promised she wasn't mad that Anna had sent her away, but she was very hungry. She said she'd had to go and live with her mother again, and Penny's mother didn't have any food. So, after dark, when her parents had gone to bed, Anna sneaked out into the kitchen, and started to look through the fridge for something to eat. Penny didn't want an apple. She didn't want a sandwich. She didn't want leftover kedgeree or potato waffles. Penny didn't want anything they had in the house, it seemed.

The next morning, once her parents were busy with whatever they were doing that day, Anna announced that she was going to play with Penny. She pretended not to see the look of irritation on her father's face when he heard the name again after two days without it, but he didn't try to stop her. Anna took all her pocket money that she'd been able to save from under her bed, thirteen pounds and forty pence, and together they did something they'd never done without Anna's parents: they left the building. She walked past the desk where the man sat who her mother said wasn't a policeman, but everyone talked about him like he was a policeman, and told him in her best grown-up voice that her mother was sending her out to get milk on her own. There was a horrible moment where Anna worried that maybe the man at the desk knew they still had plenty of milk, but he just nodded and said to be back soon.

But Anna and Penny didn't go to get milk, and her friend's eyes widened as Anna led them through the sliding doors of the McDonald's just down the road. The smell of grease and chemical condiments hit them in a wave, and Penny made a noise that Anna had never heard before. She turned to see her friend, her smile wide, a thin trail of saliva dripping from the corner of her mouth and pooling on the floor. The cashier was dubious, looking around for a grown-up when Anna tried to place her order, so Anna pointed to an older man sitting near the window with his back to them and said he was her father. Soon she was carrying a pair of thin burgers and a cardboard sleeve of glistening fries over to a sticky plastic table where Penny was already sitting. She slid the food over to her imaginary friend and waited.

There was a moment, just a single quiet second, where

Penny's eyes met Anna's and there was a flicker of something, some deep gratitude. Then they were once again full of hunger as she descended on the meal in front of her. She didn't even bother to pull off the greaseproof paper, tearing at it with her long thin fingers and sharp little teeth. Specks of potato and sesame flew in all directions as she chewed wildly on her grim fast food banquet. Her jaw muscles bulged and rolled, and her scrawny frame shuddered as she guzzled down the last of the fries. Her eyes flicked down, scanning the cheap plastic tray in front of her, looking for more food, anything else to eat, to devour. But there was nothing.

Anna watched her friend, slightly shaken by the little girl's vicious hunger. She'd never seen Penny actually eat, not properly, not more than the occasional snack. She hoped no one else in the restaurant had seen the disgusting display, but no one seemed to have so much as glanced in their direction. Now Penny's fingers dripped with ketchup and her face was smeared with grease, and if anything, she looked even thinner than she was before. Her bones poked painfully against her skin and her hands shook slightly as she looked longingly back towards the rows upon rows of fast food behind the till. Anna felt a stab of guilt that she had no more money to buy Penny more food, but she was beginning to think that perhaps Penny would always be hungry. She didn't quite understand why, though. She certainly hadn't imagined Penny that way. But then again, she hadn't thought imaginary friends were able to eat at all, yet here they were.

Over the next few days Anna's relationship with her best friend became more and more strained. The atmosphere in the home was tense, and her parents were quieter than ever. Her father kept mentioning how nice their flat was, as if trying to convince himself it was true, and there was never any food for Penny, which annoyed her even if she never ate any of the healthy stuff anyway. She and Anna kept getting into fights, and Anna told her to go away at least once a day, though was quick to bring her back.

That night, Anna had told Penny to go away after she kept trying to convince her to sneak out of the flat to go and play Secret Agents. But Anna was tired and dealing with her excitable friend was too much effort, so she sent her away and went to sleep. She hadn't liked the look on Penny's face when she'd been told to leave but decided she could always apologise in the morning.

Anna didn't have a clock in her room, so had no way of knowing what time it was when she woke up in the middle of the night. Her room was hot with the air conditioning turned off, and her small nightlight didn't seem as comforting as it usually did, as the furniture around it cast stark, deep shadows. Something was wrong.

'Penny?' she called out quietly, trying her very best to sound brave.

There was no answer. She pulled her blanket up over her, even though it was really too warm for it, and tried to get back to sleep. Then there was movement from just outside her bedroom door. It was the soft sound of small feet moving slowly over the hardwood floors. Anna crept out of her bed, the rug muffling the sound of her footsteps as she slowly moved over and pulled open her bedroom door. At that moment, she was more afraid of waking her parents than anything else, but that quickly changed when she looked out and saw the small, emaciated figure of Penny walking down the hall. She called out and her imaginary friend turned, her face still plastered with that smile, and gave Anna a wink with one of those big eyes. Then she walked into her parents' bedroom.

Anna paused for a second, trying to think what Penny could possibly want in there. An uneasy feeling was growing in her stomach and she hurried down the hall after her friend, trying to make as little noise as possible. The door was still ajar, and she slipped in silently, her vision slowly adjusting to the darkness.

Penny was standing on the big bed, between her mother and father. She walked slowly from one to the other, bending down over each in turn, studying their faces. Neither the mattress nor the bedclothes stirred as she walked over them, which made sense given Penny didn't exist. But then why was Anna so worried? Why was there this gnawing fear in the back of her mind, the lingering image of the strange little girl tearing into a tray full of over-processed fast food? Her smile was opening near the head of Anna's mother, and in spite of all the time they had spent together, Anna still found herself surprised by just how many teeth Penny had.

'Go away, Penny!' Anna hissed, desperately trying not to wake her parents.

Penny ignored her.

'Go away!'

Her father gave a sigh and turned over in bed, causing Anna's heart to skip a beat, before he settled down again. It was enough to get Penny's attention, at least. Her pale face turned back towards Anna, and they stared at each other.

'I'm so hungry, Anna,' she said at last. Penny's voice was loud and clear, but Anna's parents didn't stir, because only Anna could hear it.

'I'm sorry,' Anna whispered desperately, 'but you need to go away.'

Penny began to crawl back down the bed, thin limbs stretching over the end, pulling herself down onto the floor, heading towards Anna.

'I'm so hungry,' she said again, and took Anna by the arm. Anna had pretended to touch her imaginary friend before, but her skin had never felt so cold, nor her grip so tight.

Part of Anna wanted to scream, to wake up her parents and beg them to protect her. Another part wanted to turn and run. But there was still a place deep inside her heart that wanted to cry for poor Penny, to hug her and tell her she was sorry that she was imaginary, and they only had food for real people. She still wanted to help.

Perhaps that's why Anna didn't resist when Penny took her arm and raised it to her mouth. Those rows of sharp and tiny teeth parted, positioning themselves over her skin, ready to bite down. Anna could feel her best friend's ragged breath and the needle-like points of those teeth pressing against her. She prepared herself to scream.

Then all at once Penny released her arm and burst into her silent laugher, a motion so unexpected that Anna fell forward, landing on the ground with a thump that woke her parents.

Later that night Penny told Anna it had all been a funny joke. Anna didn't believe her but couldn't ever bring herself to tell Penny to go away again.

Anna's parents were surprised the following morning to receive a letter addressed to Anna, and then utterly baffled when they opened it and were presented with an invitation.

TOBIAS FELL cordially invites ANNA KHAN,
PENNY AND GUARDIAN
to attend a dinner party at 1 Banyan Court
on the evening of 16th August 2014
Penthouse access will be available through the freight elevator

They talked about it at length, argued over it like they did with everything at the moment, and finally agreed that they couldn't not go. Affording the high-end flat was slowly bankrupting them after Prisha's redundancy, and if the man who owned the building asked to see them, they had to at least find out what he wanted.

They were nervous about trying to explain the invitation to Anna, but as it turned out they needn't have bothered. Apparently Penny had told her all about it already, and was planning a very special game indeed.

5th

Inbox

Gillian Barnes
80 Banyan Court

Gillian grimaced in pain, instinctively pulling her finger back as a single drop of ruby blood fell onto the cream papers spread across her desk. Of all the difficulties and indignities in her chosen career, the papercuts inflicted by the thick stock Akman Blane used for their legal documents was a strong contender for her least favourite.

She got to her feet, slightly resenting the time it would take to sort out, and headed over to the bathroom to get a plaster. The bare wooden floor was cold beneath her feet, despite the humid summer night, and Gillian instinctively reached for her notebook to add 'slippers' to the list of things she needed to get for the flat. When she had the time. And the money. But her pocket was empty, and it wasn't until she'd reached the bathroom that she remembered the notebook was still lying on her desk, where she had just been writing in it. Probably for the best. The shopping list was already three pages long, with no end in sight.

She applied the plaster with a small dab of antiseptic cream and closed the bathroom cabinet, one of the few pieces of furniture that was actually part of the flat. As she did so she paused for a second, considering her face in the mirror. What was she looking for? She wasn't even sure, if she was honest. Wrinkles perhaps? Crawling out from her bloodshot eyes over the dark canvas of her skin? No, they were still a long way off. Perhaps it was just that the face in that mirror had worn the same expression every time she'd seen it for almost a year now. When had she last felt herself smile?

Gillian exhaled slowly, waving the thought away. There would be time enough for smiling in the years to come. Right now was when she put in the work, did her time, pushed out through this purgatory and into the life she had chosen for herself. The degree had been hard, sure it had, but this was the true test. If she wanted to be certified as a Chartered Legal Executive she had to get through the years of 'qualifying' employment. Underpaid, disrespected, but vital to her intended career as a lawyer. She'd been very lucky to get the position at Akman Blane, she reminded herself, they were a big enough deal that there'd be no question of her qualifying when she'd served her time. But until then they were clearly keen to get as much out of her as they could.

As if to illustrate her point, Gillian's phone began to buzz. She glanced at the screen. The self-consciously serious face of Timothy A. Simmons stared back at her, his navy-blue suit and silver silk tie silently reprimanding her for not already having answered. Timothy (not 'Tim', thank you very much) was one of the many people who, rightly or wrongly, considered themselves her boss. She wanted to be annoyed he was phoning her so late, but instead she just pushed the green button to answer.

'Barnes, did you take the Kempner brief?' The voice from the phone was impatient, but didn't respect her enough to be properly hostile.

'A copy of it, yes.' Gillian's tone was blank.

'Where's the original?'

'I re-filed it.'

'Right.'

There was a small beep as the call ended.

She sat back down, the cheap office chair protesting at the burden. Her hand reflexively reached for a fluorescent yellow highlighter as her eyes returned to the documents in front of her and she settled back into scanning for the details she needed. Her focus stopped suddenly on a splash of crimson. Her blood. Well, at least they were only photocopies. She leaned forward, momentarily curious as to what word had been obscured by the small scarlet fleck. Her thumb smeared the still-wet stain across several lines but rendered the words beneath it legible again: Tobias Fell.

Not surprising. Pick a random pair of words from any random legal document at Akman Blane and you were likely enough to have landed on the name of their biggest client. His name spread over almost everything in the company, even her. After all, this flat – in his building – was part of an initiative to supply 'affordable' living situations for the firm's less-moneyed employees. Of course, it wouldn't have been necessary without their unofficial policy of not hiring anyone from outside of Zone 1 for their London office. Maybe Zone 2 if they knew your father. But it had given Gillian somewhere to live and she supposed she owed some gratitude to the great Tobias Fell.

This brief itself was nothing special. A man named Allan Kempner, a manager at one of Fell's media companies, had breached his NDA, so the firm were helping to sue him out of existence. And it didn't look like it would be particularly hard, either. He'd allegedly sold internal information to a rival company and the damages he was going to end up paying were eye-watering. Gillian felt a pang of sympathy for the man but pushed it down. There was no place for it if she wanted to work in corporate law. Not the most exciting branch of the legal profession, admittedly, but one of the most secure and, yes, best paid. And fundamentally it *was* about the money. Much as she might wish it otherwise, money meant safety. It meant freedom.

Her eyes continued to scan through the documents, making small shorthand notes in the margins and highlighting relevant details. But something else jumped out at her. The email Kempner had sent, the one that broke his contract, was listed as being sent on the 16th of August last year. Why did that date seem so familiar to her?

Obviously there was no reason, it was just one of three hundred and sixty-five possible dates it could have been. So why did she keep going back to check it? She circled it in red, just to be on the safe side. By now the blood had dried to a crusty brown, and the bright ink stood out starkly against the gloom of the evening.

When Gillian got into work the next day, she'd been moved desks. Again. She turned away from the shrugging intern who was sat in her old seat and went looking for her new one, doing her best to seem purposeful. She changed her path several times so as not to get too close to Timothy's directionless morning aggression. She eventually spotted it, clearly identifiable from the tower of four filing boxes stacked haphazardly on her intray.

She flicked through the Post-it notes jammed on top of each other. Two from Timothy, one from Sarah Merlini, her actual supervisor, and one from Mr Blane himself. What Gillian really wanted to do was to make herself a cup of tea, then start methodically working through the stack, but she could see

Timothy in the kitchen, scowling next to the water heater, and decided to leave it for a few minutes.

Three hours later, Gillian looked up, disturbed from her work by her own rumbling stomach. She'd made a strong dent in the first box, but at some point Sarah had added another to the top of the stack and labelled it 'urgent', so lunch was going to prove difficult. There wasn't even a question of whether she'd need to take some of them home. The only uncertainty was how she'd be best off carrying them. She'd long since discovered that while a sheet of paper is very light, a box full of them is an injury waiting to happen.

So far the morning had gone more or less as expected. Just another day pushing through the devil's bargain she had made, the gruelling down payment on the life she actually wanted. Where maybe someday she'd have her own underlings to burn their youth away fetching files. There was something else, though, something unusual about today. No, not about today, about her. She was used to the focus that came with her work, comfortable in letting the rest of the world drop away, leaving only a flat, steady concentration. But that wasn't quite what was happening now. There were flashes, little things that kept catching her eye in the documents. A name here. A date there. A company that she was sure was mentioned in a different brief. Had she finally read enough of the firm's files that she was starting to actually understand how it all fitted together?

On a whim she began to take notes of the pages that caught her eye. She could photocopy herself a few duplicates, spend a bit more time on them later when she had finished her ...

She spotted that another box had been placed on top of the pile. Despite herself, she couldn't quite hold in a sigh. 'Finished' wasn't really a concept where she was at the moment. There was always going to be more, every box, every case spreading out and leading to a dozen more. An intricate network of connections and references and work for Gillian to do. It wasn't so bad, not really, but she decided she should probably get a sandwich first.

The flimsy cardboard box sagged under the weight of the much denser and better-made filing cases. It was already dark, and Gillian was searching through the collection of torn containers that had been acting as a makeshift wardrobe and stationery cupboard since she moved into Banyan Court. Furniture required money to buy and time (or friends) to set up, and none of these were things Gillian had in abundance right now. It wasn't great, but she could endure. It meant she had to get up a bit earlier to iron the box-creases from the day's outfit, but she knew there were people out there who had it far worse. It wasn't even like it was a bad place to be living, at least if you ignored the broken lift. And the slight smell in the hallway. And the temperamental fuse box. Even then, Gillian could have handled it if she'd only felt like she had some *choice* about living there. But no, if she wanted the job, the 'charity' of Tobias Fell had been her only option. Could one be trapped by generosity? Because she certainly felt like it.

The hairs on the back of her neck prickled and she spun around. No, there was no one there. Obviously. It was just her, alone in an empty flat. She breathed out. Flats like these had so many creaks and noises it was easy to convince yourself you weren't alone. Several times in the last few weeks she'd woken up, sure she was being watched, only to find the place empty.

Her hand brushed the corner of a wooden frame and she smiled, pulling out what she'd been hunting for. Her old university cork board. There was still a pair of old cinema tickets to *Limitless* stuck to it with drawing pins, mementos of her and Aaron's brief relationship, as well as a pair of Polaroids showing her grinning in a crowd of people she hadn't talked to since graduation. Gillian pulled out the pins, collected up the memories of happier times and unceremoniously tossed them back into the box. She stood up with her prize and walked to the wall next to her tired-looking desk.

Her mouth pursed in consideration. There was no hook to hang it on. She could put one in, of course; she definitely had a hammer and a few nails in one of these boxes, but Gillian was certain the sour-faced letting agent who dealt with renting the place would take it out of her deposit. She sighed.

'There are always going to be consequences,' she muttered to no one in particular.

The sound of the hammer was louder than she expected, and Gillian jumped as it broke the silence, reverberating around the mostly empty room. She took a moment and settled herself before tapping the nail for a second and final time. It slid into the wall easily, eagerly, and she almost felt a smile coming on as she placed the cork board in its new position. She took a pin and rifled through one of the cases she'd brought home until she found what she was looking for: a photocopy of the inquest report for the death of a man named Herman Thomas.

She had stumbled across it in while dealing with the third box of files. At first, just the name jumped out at her. She had actually talked to Herman Thomas on the phone when she started at the company last year, and remembered him being soft-spoken, nervous, keen to make a good impression. She didn't realise he had died so soon after. But, more importantly, the name listed as having signed off on receipt of the inquest report was hers. Gillian Barnes. But she was quite certain she'd never seen it before in her life. Taking a copy had been a risk, after all it could jeopardise her position, but they expected her to take so many files home she couldn't imagine they would ever notice.

She pinned it to the centre of the board and took a step back. She didn't know what was going on, but this felt like a start. A small red smear could be seen under the name. Gillian checked her hand. When had she started bleeding again? Had she caught herself with the hammer and not noticed? She stared at the bloody fingerprint. It didn't matter, not now. She had more important things to consider.

It seemed to start with the sweatshops. It wasn't exactly an eye-opening revelation that the clothing companies Tobias Fell was involved with heavily relied on a group of brutally exploitative factories in Indonesia. But following an industrial accident in 2009 that left eleven workers dead and many more maimed, there was a concerted activist campaign against these companies and, by extension, Fell himself. According to the transcripts, Akman Blane had managed to ensure that the companies were insulated from any legal fallout, but they still publicly cut ties with the factories involved, moving production to significantly less-horrendous facilities in the Dominican Republic. It was hailed as a victory in the press, but according to the contracts her firm had drawn up, the amount of product being bought from the Dominican facilities was nowhere near the original amount produced in Indonesia. The rest seemed to be coming from a collection of smaller companies that turned out to be shells, all of which listed Herman Thomas as the COO. A year ago, one of the old Indonesian factories had fully collapsed, killing most of the workers inside. One hundred and three people in all. The next day, 16th August last year, Herman Thomas fell from his balcony on the seventh floor, landing on his neck and dying instantly.

Gillian stepped back and rubbed her eyes. The blur of names and dates and depositions were swirling through her head. The cork board now a mess of photocopies, highlights, and handwritten notes. She'd been doing research on her laptop but trying to keep track of everything digitally was a nightmare. The physical set-up was much clearer, at least to her.

She tried to take a step back mentally as well, but that was proving much harder. Was this real? Her mind raced. If her suspicions were correct, she might have just uncovered a conspiracy to murder a man who was planning to blow the whistle on Tobias Fell's involvement in the factory collapse. She didn't know exactly where the initial idea had come from, it had simply appeared in her mind, but now she was certain of it. There was no concrete evidence, of course, just a lot of details that seemed to slot together. Numbers that added up, but not how they were supposed to. Names that kept cropping up for seemingly no reason. She sat heavily in her chair, dimly aware that the first rays of daylight were starting to creep around the edges of her curtains.

If it was true, what the hell was she supposed to do about it? She had enough legal expertise by now to know that there was nothing in these documents that would hold up in any sort of court, especially given the frankly terrifying competence of Akman Blane. She knew that in corporate law you ended up working for some shady types and she thought she'd made her peace with it. After all, money can make peace with a lot of things. But murder? Surely that was a line she wasn't willing to cross. And if it was, how could she avoid crossing it without completely torpedoing her career?

She kept staring at the cork board, mind racing over the same ground again and again. Her attention was snapped by a sound behind her. The creak of a floorboard. Spinning round she could have sworn for a second there was a man standing in the corridor behind her. A man in a dark suit. But no, it was just her coat, hanging where it always was.

'... Hello

The only answer she received was the bleating of her alarm clock. Telling her it was time to go to work.

It wasn't easy, pushing through the day. Without the frantic rush of investigation and revelation the sleepless night hit Gillian like a truck. She felt like a ghost tethered to her desk, trying desperately to connect with documents that seemed further and further away every time she looked at them. Even then, occasionally she would catch sight of a word, a detail, something to hang another thread on, and silently mark the box as one she needed to take for her own purposes.

'Hey, where's the file on Terry Vargas?'

Timothy looked up, irritated that his dreary soup had been interrupted.

'Who?'

'Vargas,' Gillian repeated. 'She ran a manufacturing plant in Guinea. Filed a bunch of reports on worker safety.'

'We've never had any files on a Terry Vargas,' Timothy said flatly.

'Uh ... Yeah we have, I spent most of last month—'

'We've never had any files on Terry Vargas,' he repeated, his intonation identical.

Gillian rocked backwards slightly, her head swimming.

'Come on, Barnes,' he said dismissively, voice returning to its usual sneer. 'Don't waste my time.'

She nodded and started to stagger away. His voice followed her, cold and flat.

'And try to get some more sleep. It's not good for you, staying up so late.'

*

Her intray got higher and higher, but Gillian managed to bat away questions about deadlines, citing Mr Blane's project as the reason she had nothing for Timothy or Sarah, while at the same time talking Mr Blane into blaming Sarah for his delay. The rest of the office was noisy, full of voices and a simmering frenetic energy, but at that moment it all seemed such a long way away. Gillian stood, dimly aware that she had been sitting motionless for hours, and walked to the window. The street below was busy, a steady stream of people passing down the sunlit Bloomsbury lanes. Business people in fitted suits, tourists in bright shirts, and a single figure stood opposite, staring at her.

He was tall, dressed in a black jacket far too thick for the heat of the day. His white shirt was crisp around his dark necktie and he wore opaque sunglasses that completely obscured the upper part of his face. Despite this, there was no doubt in Gillian's mind that he was looking at her, watching her. His face was tilted up towards the third floor window where she was standing and his mouth was set in a hard, straight line. And a familiar feeling of being watched, being observation washed over her. Without turning his head the man in the black suit reached into his jacket and took out a phone. He brought it to his ear and began to speak, small precise words lost in the buzz of the city. He nodded just once.

'Gill!' Sarah's voice wasn't loud, but it almost knocked her backwards, shattering whatever space she had found herself in. She could see more file boxes in Sarah's arms, and tried to muster the energy to hide her frustration.

'Uh, yeah. Yes. Coming, sorry,' Gillian stammered. If her boss noticed just how rattled she was, there was no indication as three more boxes were unceremoniously dumped into her arms. She glanced back out the window, scanning the street below. Nothing. The man in black was gone.

*

This clearly went far deeper than Gillian had first imagined. She was once again staring at her rapidly expanding mess of notes and connections, mind racing and eyes wide. She had slept a few hours, but the time she had away from work was precious and she couldn't afford to waste much of it by sleeping. The filing boxes surrounded her now, piling up in the corners of the room, carpeting the floor with discarded papers. She'd managed to cut her hand again at some point, and the documents pinned to the board were spotted here and there with striking dots of red.

Sweatshops were only the tip of it. In every one of Tobias Fell's businesses the pattern was the same. A woman who had come forward with concerns about worker safety in the warehouses of Howard Fairley, one of Fell's partners, had been killed in an accidental electrical fire. An executive at an affiliate marketing company that publicly expressed concerns over the ingredients in foodstuffs that were being targeted at children passed away shortly afterwards of a previously undiagnosed heart condition. Blood diamonds, environmental violations, unethical insurance practices, every time anyone raised an objection or looked ready to blow the whistle, they ended up dead or disappeared.

The sudden rattle of her phone buzzing on the wooden desk snapped her out of her thoughts and almost gave her a heart attack of her own. She breathed out for a few moments trying to control her wildly racing pulse. She looked at the screen, expecting to see one of the professionally retouched contact photos of her superiors at Akman Blane, but the picture was blank. The caller ID read 'Mr Close', which was not a name she recognised from her phonebook. She pressed the answer icon, staining the green button slightly red from her most recent papercut.

123

'H-hello?' Her voice wavered.

There was no sound on the other side. No breathing. No background noise. Just silence.

Then, 'Do you know?'

The voice was slow, emotionless, with an inflection that didn't quite match that put Gillian immediately on edge, as though it were coming from a speech synthesiser program. But the voice itself had nothing robotic about it.

'Who is this?'

'I ask the questions.' His tone wasn't angry or sharp but had a certainty to it that was impossible to disregard. 'Do you know?'

'I don't— What are you talking about?'

'If I am to proceed, you must know. Do you know?'

The image of the man watching her from the street crept unbidden into Gillian's mind.

'I . . . I don't. I don't know.'

A pause.

'Good. Do not know and I will not proceed. Thank you.'

The call ended. Gillian sat there, trying to make herself put the phone down, but her hand wouldn't stop shaking. Even with the call over, she still felt like something was listening.

She turned her phone off. Still there.

She unplugged her laptop, pulled out the battery and threw a blanket over it. Still there.

She disassembled the smoke alarm, unplugged her lamps, covered and sabotaged every piece of technology in her flat. She told herself she was being daft, but only when it was done did she feel almost safe enough to sleep.

Gillian found what she was looking for down a filthy side street in Barking. The door buzzer was so grimy that she felt a strange sort of gratitude that the tiny cuts covering her hands had forced her to wear gloves. She pressed the buzzer for flat 6 and waited. The rank stench of the small mountain of garbage bags piled up next to the entrance choked her throat. Perhaps she should have waited until she was here to call in sick? It would have really added something to the performance.

'Who is it?' the tinny voice spat out from the little speaker, splitting the difference between annoyed and nervous.

'Mr Kempner? It's Gillian Barnes, we spoke earlier?'

'Prove it,' the voice came, barely concealing its hostility.

'Uh, sorry?' Gillian was confused. 'Prove who I am or prove that we spoke?'

The speaker went silent, as though considering, then without further comment a harsh electronic drone announced the front door was unlocked. Gillian gingerly pushed it open and stepped inside.

Beyond the building's front door, the smell was of a different character, but no less pungent. Her steps echoed on the grubby vinyl flooring as she made her way towards the stairs. She passed two lifts en route, but, after experiencing the one at Banyan Court, decided she didn't trust them.

Tucked away in a labyrinth of urban decay near the edge of Barking, Paston Towers was not the sort of place one would expect to find the editor-in-chief of a high-profile media brand. Still, Gillian supposed if she was being sued for the sort of money Akman Blane were likely to claim in damages from Allan Kempner, she'd probably move somewhere a bit more budget conscious as well. The second floor was silent and still, save for the two flies that hovered near the stairwell, taking turns picking at a faded stain on the wall.

The steel number 6 on Kempner's door was still shiny, as though it had just been added, and stood out clearly against the worn plywood of the door itself. Gillian raised her hand to knock, but it opened on the latch before she had the chance.

'Look at the camera.' The voice that came from inside was just as irritable and hesitant as it had seemed through the speaker.

'What?'

'The camera!' the voice insisted, and Gillian turned her head just in time to hear a click from a small lens mounted above the frame.

The door opened fully.

'Good. I can prove you were here, now, so no funny business.'

'I'm not sure I—'

'I've got it all on tape.'

'Look.' Gillian tried to keep her voice level. 'I just want to talk. About Tobias Fell.'

Another pause.

'Come in, then.' A pause, then he repeated, 'No funny business.'

Inside, flat 6 was a strange juxtaposition. Kempner had clearly taken much of the high-end furniture and appliances from wherever he'd lived before, but it only served to highlight how run-down the rest of it was. An extremely expensive-looking office chair was placed next to an ancient moth-eaten sofa, both orientated towards the large flat-screen which dominated a wall that didn't really look sturdy enough to support its mount. He'd clearly made a real effort to keep the place clean, but it was obvious which corners and crevices had defeated him, and it felt as though the dirt was just in hiding, waiting for him to slip up.

'Sit down,' he said, and Gillian complied, trying to find a comfortable spot on the sofa and failing.

Allan Kempner walked sullenly to the kitchen area and poured himself a large glass of an amber liquid from a chipped crystal decanter, before making his way to the office chair. He did not offer one to Gillian.

'So, what do you want?' he grunted. 'Intimidation? Payoff? What are they after? Don't try to tell me this is a social call.'

'I work for Akman Blane,' Gillian said, trying her best to sound like it.

'Yeah, you said,' Kempner scowled, taking a sizeable swig of his drink. 'But I can't find you listed on their site. And you have cheap shoes. So, who are you?'

'I ... That's ... I *do* work for them,' Gillian protested.

'Sure. Email address looked official enough. But the question is are you one of *them*? Are you here to do their dirty work? Or have they not got to you yet?' His gaze was searching, and Gillian suddenly noticed the shape of what might have been a knife tucked beneath his shirt.

'I ... don't know.'

'Yeah, figures.' His hands fidgeted with the rim of his glass. 'Look, I shouldn't have let you up. I've got no interest talking to Akman Blane outside of a proper hearing, but you said this was more than that. So, what d'you want?'

Gillian bit her lip. She had hoped to find someone calm, level-headed and considered in their dealings with Tobias Fell and Akman Blane. Someone who'd seen what they were capable of and might listen to her and talk through her theories. She was looking for an ally. But as his eyes darted around the room, it was clear Allan Kempner was not that man.

'I think I've stumbled onto something. About Tobias Fell. And Akman Blane and ... Tell me what happened. Why you blew the whistle.'

'And what good's that going to do? Too low down the ladder for decent shoes, but you're gonna throw me a lifeline here? Nah, I don't think so. Anyway, I've seen how many files you have over there. You know more about it than I do, and I did it.'

Gillian paused, considered for a moment, then pressed on. 'I think there's more going on. I have seen the files, but they don't make sense. And my name is all over them, in places that it shouldn't be. This is bigger than you and me and I just ... I want to know what's going on. I deserve that much at least.'

Kempner sighed.

'Fine, I get it,' he said at last. 'Funny. Really hoped you could help. Found something in the files, maybe, or ... I don't know. But no, someone like you coming round. I guess that means it's all over for me, isn't it? If I've drawn *your* attention, I'm probably too much of a liability.'

Gillian had no answer for him.

'OK, you want hear it? Fine. Tobias owned the network. Didn't mean much for the most part, TV news is TV news, except that you knew his politics and tended to frame the story for them. Very occasionally, like an election or something, he'd have one of his cronies come down with some more explicit "editorial guidance", but that was rare.'

He paused and took a swig. He almost smiled as he continued, and for a second Gillian could see the shadow of a confident speaker, briefing an attentive room of journalists.

'But the main problem was when one of his other companies fucked up. Got caught out. Then we'd get what we used to call a "Fell-book". A folder full of detailed instructions on how to handle it, but not just spinning the problem or even avoiding it.'

Kempner paused, clearly deciding whether or not to continue. He let out a single bitter chuckle, as though accepting defeat, and continued.

'They had lists of people who were involved in exposing whatever was going on, or leading campaigns against it, and we had to use all our resources to find dirt on them. Put out hit pieces, feature spots to undermine them. Hound them and their families as much as possible. And I did it. Took a sort of sick pride in how good we were at it. You should see how we spun it when the insurance stuff broke with United Continental. We were the best.'

He drained the glass.

'Then the Doxatrin scandal broke and we got a Fell-book about it, and … My mother had taken Doxatrin, along with thousands of others. Doctors said it might have been what killed her in the end. And here was this fucking book telling me to bury the story. So, I was done. I leaked it. Took a scan and sent it round everywhere working on the story. But I was grieving, sloppy. Easy paper trail back to me, more than enough for you fucking vultures to scream NDA and torpedo my life. What there was of it. But I'd do it again.'

Kempner went quiet. He seemed somehow smaller, like the story had been a part of him and now it had left him diminished. She wondered if she should feel revulsion, looking at this man who had covered up evil for so long. Pity for him. Or just a dull awareness of her own complicity, working where she did. How different were they, really?

Everything seemed muted, and Gillian wondered for a moment where the noise of the street outside had gone. Had something silenced it?

'Mr Kempner.' She tried to choose her words carefully. 'I believe you're in danger.'

'No shit.' His gaze was level. Unimpressed.

'I believe that Akman Blane might be connected to the murders of whistle-blowers against Tobias Fell. And you might be next.'

Kempner started to laugh. 'Yeah,' he said, his eyes unreadable. 'And if that's true, what the hell do you think they're going to do to you?' His laughter was a vicious, mocking sound. 'They already know you know,' he said. 'And you know they do.'

He was still laughing as Gillian fled his dingy flat.

Gillian sat on the Underground, mind racing, fingers scrolling through the pictures on her phone. It had been less than half an hour since Kempner had unceremoniously laughed her out of his flat and in that time she had taken almost two dozen photos of the man who was following her. At least, she'd made that many attempts. There was always something in the way of a clear picture: a car blocking the view at just the wrong moment, a street sign obscuring his face, the glare of the sun rendering him an indistinct shadow in sunglasses. She'd noticed him almost as soon as she was out of the front door, and he'd been calmly matching her pace. His expression unreadable and his dark suit a stark contrast to the summery outfits of the crowds around him.

She'd made it onto the District line moments before the doors closed and hoped desperately that her pursuer hadn't managed to join her. It was the man her phone had christened 'Mr Close'. It had to be. She tried to reassure herself that he was just a random stalker, as if, under any other circumstances, that would be reassuring.

But the alternative was the possibility she had become a target of whoever worked with Akman Blane to keep the awful secrets of Tobias Fell, silencing those who threatened them. She couldn't go to the police. If they were operating so openly then there was no chance the cops weren't in the pocket of these people. After all, they had the power to plant contact information into her phone, so who knows what—

Gillian froze. *Her phone.* She'd forgotten to turn it off. Her work phone. They could have been listening in on her and

Kempner through the microphone or watched her take notes through the camera. Her computer too. If technology was a gateway they could use to reach her, they already had everything they needed to strike.

Gillian slowly and deliberately placed her phone on the floor of the carriage, then positioned her foot over the screen. Ever so gradually she increased the pressure until she heard it crack. For a second there was the sound of ringing, and Timothy's face appeared on the screen. Then she pushed down harder, and his sickly smile shattered under her heel. If they wanted to shut her up, she wasn't going to make it easy for them.

She crept back into Banyan Court as carefully as she could, taking care to turn her face from the security cameras. She just needed to get in, gather a few things and get out, go on the run before they could make their move. But was she already too late? She'd need her passport, at least. Unless they could track that? They might have been there already, planted God knows what on everything she owned. Still, she had to risk it.

Tobias Fell owned this whole building, he owned her flat, and that made it enemy territory. How could she be sure what was really going on behind any of the doors in this place? She was painfully aware that she lived in the run-down, forgotten half of the building. The sort of place things could be hidden without anybody noticing. Or be made to disappear. And how much did she know her neighbours really? There was Edith, the lonely old woman who lived on the floor above; she'd tried to talk to Gillian a few times in the past and she had seemed real enough. But that was months ago and they hadn't crossed paths since. Who knows what might have happened in that time? What they might have done to her?

No, Gillian had to consider this building as hostile territory.

The office too. They owned her flat, after all. *They owned her flat.* But where else could she go right now?

As she made her way around the outside of Banyan Court, she tried to keep her profile small and her footfalls quiet. Her eyes scanned around frantically, until they settled on something that she had seen every day since moving in, but never really noticed. A foundation stone, clean and bright in the old brick of the building wall.

This stone laid by TOBIAS FELL on 16th August 2004

16th August. The date Banyan Court's construction began. Almost exactly ten years ago. It couldn't be a coincidence. There were no coincidences.

Someone was outside the door to her flat. A young man, wiry and wearing a faded, oversized T-shirt. He was holding something long and thin against the wall. A measuring tape? What was he measuring? The young man jotted something down in a small grey notebook, then stretched the tape over the door jamb, furrowing his brows and making another note. He stood up and stretched his neck, catching sight of Gillian as he did so.

She froze, not sure whether to run or confront the distinctly unthreatening figure in front of her. Too late. The stranger was already heading towards her, waving and tucking the tape measure into a baggy pair of jogging trousers. There was an uncertain smile creasing his round, youthful face.

'Hello?'

Gillian didn't respond. She was frozen, waiting for whatever was about to happen.

'Do you ... live here?' His tone was serious, but not aggressive.

After a moment of excruciating silence, she nodded.

'So this is yours?'

The young man held up a piece of thick legal paper. The Akman Blane logo at the top was one of the few parts still completely legible, the rest hidden under layers of competing highlighter colours, frantically circled phrases and scrawled notes in a handwriting Gillian barely recognised as her own. She felt herself starting to blush.

'Where ...' The words came slowly. 'Where did you get that?'

He gestured back towards her door, and Gillian noticed for the first time patches of white peeking out from beneath it, papers slid partially through the gap at the bottom, as though trying to escape. She went cold.

'I have to go,' she said, almost breaking into a run as she pushed past him towards her flat.

'It's not real!' She could hear him calling behind her. 'They aren't real!'

But Gillian was already slamming the door, locking it behind her.

The apartment was chaos. Discarded papers lined the floor deep enough that it was hard to get stable footing. Filing boxes, empty, full and overflowing, lined the walls and filled the empty spaces in the room, creating narrow avenues of paperwork, a photocopied labyrinth of highlighter and ink. How had she let it get this bad? Had she? For all her meticulous note-taking, her obsessive cross-referencing, she couldn't be entirely sure what day it was. Or how many boxes of files she had taken for her own investigation. Many remained completely unopened, stacks that towered over her, trapping Gillian in the vast intray that had once been flat 80 Banyan Court. The young man's words made her look at them again. Not real? Her hand brushed against a pile of loose cuttings that almost reached to her head. They felt real enough. Didn't they?

There was only one space, one corner that she knew would be clear and well kept, somewhere she could collect her thoughts. Her desk, where she had gradually laid out the truth, meticulously pinned it to the wall and wrapped it up in neat red string. It was hidden behind a pile of loose paperwork that almost reached the ceiling.

'Good evening, Ms Barnes. Please choose to sit.'

The voice was unmistakable, the strange flat intonation and odd emphasis a perfect echo of the voice she had heard on the phone. It wasn't an accent, not exactly. All the words came out in sounds that were almost a crisp RP, but mismatched and swapped around. Like someone had chopped up a thousand hours of BBC Radio and clumsily mixed them together into the voice of Mr Close.

'No,' she said, trying to be brave.

Around the boxes she could only see his leg, a single meticulously polished shoe. If she turned and ran, could she get out in time? Gillian took a deep breath and moved to face him.

Up close he looked very much like he sounded. It wasn't that he was scary or threatening, he was simply incorrect. His hair was perfectly styled into a trim utilitarian cut, but the hairline didn't seem to match his head shape. His skin was pink, but not the irregular, blotchy pink it should have been. Instead it was the uniform pink of a 'light flesh' colour crayon. His suit was perfectly tailored, but he seemed to be wearing it inside out. The curtains were drawn, and the room was dingy and humid, but he still wore his sunglasses and gloves.

'You should sit,' he said again, and then Gillian was sitting on the uncomfortable wooden dining table chair. She was certain it had been in the other room.

'What do you want?' she asked, shaking so hard she could hear the chair legs rattling.

'Do you know?'

'I don't understand.'

'Understanding is not needed. Do you know?'

There was silence.

'Yes,' Gillian said softly, 'I know.'

Mr Close reached slowly into his jacket, gripping something inside it. Gillian braced herself, but when his hand reappeared it was holding a worn steel hipflask. He slowly unscrewed the lid, brought it up to his lips and took a long drink. Dark black liquid dribbled down his chin, disappearing into his suit. It almost looked like ink.

'What do you know?' he asked finally, sealing the flask and returning it to his jacket.

'I know.' She paused, the words tumbled out of her defiantly before she could stop herself. 'All of it. About the whistle-blowers, the murders, Tobias Fell, everything. It's all there.'

'You have evidence?' He tried to smile, his teeth irregular and stained black.

'You know there isn't any.'

'Yes. I know what I know what I know what I know.' His voice looped gradually into an almost hypnotic rhythm.

'What are you?' Her voice sounded very far away.

'I am what you are expecting. The one who comes to make you quiet. You know I should be here and I am.'

'That guy out there. He said you weren't real. Is he with you?'

'He will be. He does not yet believe what he knows.'

Gillian's hands were shaking. She couldn't stop them.

'What are you going to do?'

'What you need me to.'

'Will it hurt?'

'Yes.'

Her mouth was dry, her heart was thumping so loud she

couldn't hear his next words. Mr Close reached again into his pocket and this time Gillian knew he wasn't pulling out a hipflask. With a sudden, desperate energy she lunged forward at him, arms swinging wildly. The unexpected blow caught the man-shaped thing on the side of its head, knocking the sunglasses to the floor. He let out a guttural cry, pushing her away. She looked at his eyes and she—

Gillian was sitting on the wooden chair again. When was it? Was she still here? Was she still her? Mr Close was once again wearing his sunglasses.

'I'm sorry you saw that.'

Saw what? Why did her eyes feel so dry? Her skin was chilled, like she'd been falling for a very long time. There was the faintest memory of sense, of an epiphany, of everything neatly slotting together into a perfectly structured plan. But it was gone.

Mr Close placed an envelope on the desk.

'What you need,' he said, and left.

At some point in the preceding days, the clock on Gillian's wall had stopped ticking, so she had no idea how long she sat there. She tried to count her breaths, one two, in out, but her mind wouldn't slow down long enough to keep track.

Eventually, painfully, she got to her feet. She staggered to the front door and checked it. Still locked. Then she checked every corner, every cupboard, anywhere the strange man in black could conceivably have hidden himself. But there was no evidence he'd ever been there at all.

When she had at last satisfied herself that she was truly alone, Gillian convinced her legs to return her to the desk and gingerly picked up the envelope. It was labelled 'Last Piece' in the same scrawled handwriting that covered the notes on her wall. Inside was a drawing pin and a newspaper clipping.

It was the obituary of Allan Kempner. It described him as a dedicated journalist and newsman whose career had been destroyed over accusations of leaking confidential documents, and had been found dead in his flat. He had been murdered, and not quickly. Someone had broken a whisky glass and pushed it through his neck. According to the story, the police had someone in custody and, though it didn't name her, Gillian knew exactly who was going to be arrested for the crime.

The date of the piece was the 16th of August. Tomorrow. It didn't matter. It was too late for him. She took the cutting and the pin and positioned it in the centre of her cork board, a bloody thumbprint from her final papercut marking it as the lynchpin in the spiralling web of almost-truth she had constructed.

Mr Close had been right. It was the last piece. And it wasn't the string or the names or the faces that connected it. It was the blood. Smears of papercut crimson marking the words, the letters, that date. Sitting in its rightful place, the message on her wall was clear. It wasn't a cover-up or a conspiracy or a threat. It was an invitation. Tobias Fell was inviting Gillian to dinner. He was inviting them all to dinner. Her bleeding fingers stung when she wiped away the tears, but it was OK. She was finally beginning to understand.

6th

Sleepless

Alvita Jackson
112 Banyan Court

NO SIGNAL

The blue letters shone starkly from the TV screen, the only illumination in the otherwise pitch-black room. Alvita stared at them until they burned themselves into her retinas, lingering as glowing scars inside her eyelids. She remembered the days when dead air was still a thing, the screen filled with the incessant noise of static, the reassuring hiss of the nothing you were staring at. Now there was no sound at all, no movement, no signal. Somewhere inside her, something wanted to reach out, grab the remote control, change the channel, find anything to fill the silence. But her arm was heavy, weighed down by exhaustion, and she simply sat there, staring into space.

Tommy was asleep, she'd checked on him forty minutes ago. She should be too. She had a shift in five hours. Alvita closed her eyes, sinking into the thin cushioning of the sofa, willing herself to lose consciousness, to claim whatever sleep could be found. But all she could see were the light-scarred words: NO SIGNAL. She stayed like that for almost twenty minutes, until the letters had faded away, but still sleep did not come.

She could hear the night traffic rumbling through the streets of Tower Hamlets far below. She could smell the first whiff of rot from the leftovers in the fridge. She could feel the wooden frame of the armchair against her back. It was too much. How could she get any sleep like this? Not that her bed was any better. The sheets seemed to stink after a single night and washing them just replaced it with the cloying scent of detergent. Her mattress was thin and abrasive, and the midnight street noises below seemed even worse from the bedroom.

Alvita sighed, opened her eyes, and convinced her hand to fumble for the remote. How long had it been since she had a full night's sleep? She had no idea. It was hard enough to keep track of the weekend, making sure she got Tommy packed and off to school on all the days he needed to be there. She couldn't keep track of how long the insomnia had had its spindly electric fingers wrapped around her brain. It had started at least a month before the summer holidays began. And when had that been? Right. The anniversary of Pete's death. Yeah, that checked out.

She found a channel showing reruns of *Frasier* and sat there staring at it, trying to let the recorded laughter soothe her brain as if she were laughing along with it. It almost worked. Was she so far gone that she had forgotten what actual relaxation felt like? One way or another she needed sleep, otherwise she was certain she'd cause an accident at work.

Dropping the remote control unceremoniously onto her lap, she reached down and pulled the small cardboard box from her bag. She popped out the round white pill and swallowed it dry. She'd heard that Doxatrin had been recalled after some scandal or other, but she'd never really investigated. Harry who worked the stockroom could still get it and it was the only thing Alvita had ever found that could make a dent in the insomnia. She just wished it didn't take so long to kick in. She looked back at the screen. Frasier was having problems. Everyone was laughing.

She briefly considered getting something to drink. She'd read somewhere about pills getting stuck in your oesophagus if you didn't take them with water and burning a hole into your lung. Where had she heard that? It didn't matter, she wasn't getting up either way. She was so paranoid about waking herself up more, of disrupting the medication's work and losing what little sleep she could perhaps pull back from the insomnia that she had no intention of moving until the next morning. Instead she settled for idly flicking through the channels.

At this time of night many weren't even broadcasting, simply showing still images or that same NO SIGNAL message. Could she feel her eyes starting to droop already, or was she just so desperate that she was imagining it? Alvita let the remote slip from her hand. She looked up. Channel 70. What was that one supposed to be? The channel listed its name as 'Tonight' and the programme title was given as *Too Late with Angus Merridew*.

It was set up like an American-style late-night talk show, with a raised dais containing a dark wooden desk and a plush-looking armchair. In the background were fake windows painted with a sprawling nocturnal skyline. Behind the desk sat a middle-aged white man with immaculate brunette hair and a fixed-looking smile, no doubt Mr Merridew himself. He wore an off-white suit over a light brown shirt and a black tie with a pin that looked like a pearl. Something about the outfit made her feel faintly uncomfortable, but she put it down to the nausea she sometimes got when taking Doxatrin. Opposite the host, on the couch, sat an old man Alvita was sure she recognised from some movie or other, talking earnestly. The words washed over her, nonsensical and rolling.

'... wasn't anything could be done about it back then of course since I hadn't yet bought or learned to use my axe and I was still resting mainly on the beach but not for long since I couldn't stand the sound of them eating I mean I know everything has to eat I'm not saying they shouldn't eat but when you place yourself prone and try to close up there's nothing more bothersome than the sound of the chewing and the crack of what they were marrow sucking so I had to find my peace elsewhere not that peace was ever something I could truly aspire to with faces like the ones I took off anyone who looked at me funny when they weren't expecting it I would take the knife I'd once christened Lola under a nasty looking hunter's moon and carve a new something for myself to peel like one might peel an orange or a grape or a leg or a tongue or a coffin for sleeping although that's not something I'd ever before have expected since I've always been unable to sleep and thinking about it now I don't think I've ever slept just been waiting for the sleep to put me to sleep to take me to sleep to sleep to sleep ...'

Alvita didn't even notice when she lost consciousness.

Alvita woke to the sound of Tommy screaming. It was a sound that shot through her, electrified every nerve, even when it was the sort of scream she was accustomed to. The scream of a child that had fallen over, but not hurt himself badly enough to need a hospital visit. She pulled herself from the chair, blinking in the daylight now seeping through the thin curtains, and hurried towards Tommy's bedroom.

Sure enough, he'd been running between the kitchen and his room when he'd tripped and fallen on his arm. There was a red patch of skin where it had scraped across the carpet, but no blood or broken bones. Alvita smiled reassuringly and kissed it better, which stopped the tears, at least for a little while. She poured him a bowl of Coco Pops and half-filled it with the last of the milk. Then her eye caught the clock on the kitchen wall. Shit. If she didn't leave now she was almost certainly going to be late for her shift. But if it was almost eight, where the hell was—

A gentle ping from the living room announced the arrival of a text message. It was Ellie, her babysitter, the one that seemed to be eating up most of her paycheck since school stopped for the summer. Ellie had a 'family emergency' that apparently she'd only found out about half an hour after she was supposed to actually be here and was 'super sorry xoxoxo'. Alvita bit her lip, choking down a scream of her own, and turned to Tommy's now-smiling face, trying to figure out what to do.

She was saved from the decision by a knock at the door. Climbing to her feet, she took a moment to compose herself and put on a smile as she answered it.

'Can Tommy come and play?'

Two young girls stood outside, the posh kids from the other side of the building. They held hands and smiled ingratiatingly at Alvita, who for the life of her could never remember their names. She didn't really like them and secretly worried they bullied Tommy, but she was running low on options. She looked back at her son, who was beaming widely at the thought of being included.

'That depends,' Alvita said. 'Will your parents be there?'

The older girl (Anya? Annette?) looked towards her smiling blue-eyed friend, who nodded emphatically.

'Yes they will,' maybe-Annette said brightly.

Something in Alvita recoiled at the thought of leaving Tommy with these two for a whole four-hour shift, but at that moment it seemed like the only option. It was fine; she'd been left alone to play with other kids at his age. He'd be alright. She turned to Tommy and nodded, trying to make her own smile convincing.

Rushing back into the kitchen, she quickly put together a makeshift lunch. Crisps, yoghurt, some sweets. She couldn't find any fruit. It was mainly junk, but she just didn't have time to make anything healthier. She pushed Tommy's *Ben 10* lunchbox into his hand, and he was out the door like a shot. She waited until it had closed behind him, then let her shoulders sag. No breakfast for her, not if she wanted to be on time. She grabbed her bag and hurried out, head still heavy from the night before.

Knock knock.

Alvita rapped twice on Edith's door as she passed. The old woman had always appreciated the thought, and it was the least she could do. After all, she'd helped out enough times by watching Tommy, back when she was more mobile. A little noise to let her know people were still thinking of her.

When she could, Alvita liked to knock again, wait for the door to open and have a real conversation, maybe even a cup of tea. But when had she last actually had the time? Work was flat out, and between Tommy and the insomnia ... well, she was sure Edith understood. And it did take her so long to answer the door these days.

A spike of guilt played at the edge of Alvita's mind, urging her to knock again, to check on the old woman properly, but she barely felt it through the haze of her fatigue.

Alvita was on the tills most of the day, limbs moving mechanically. Scanning, packing, smiling. Friendly robotic words said convincingly to a steady stream of faces with their own worries and burdens and tears. But at least they looked like they'd slept. The day dragged on, and even though it seemed to stretch almost forever, at the end of it she would not have been able to tell you a single thing that she did or said or thought between the time she put on her uniform and the time it came off. It was nothing but the rhythmic motion of her arms, the harsh blanket of fluorescent light and her performance: a gurning parody of a happy, well-rested worker. When she finally stepped back outside the supermarket, Alvita took a deep breath, hoping the fresh air would revive and energise her, but the afternoon breeze held nothing but dust, car fumes and the sticky heat of summer. Her mind immediately turned to Tommy, and she checked her phone. No texts from the Khans, and they definitely had her number. That meant he was fine, right? Even so, she found herself almost running home.

By the time she got back to Banyan Court her back was so sore that she didn't think she'd be physically able to climb the mountain of stairs. But the lift was out of order as usual, so she did it anyway. There were still a couple of hours before she needed to head out to the call centre and she was keen to spend them with Tommy.

She knew she should have tried to make her way over to the expensive side of the building and knock on the door of number 22 where the little girl who might be called Anya lived, but the idea of presenting herself to a family living over there in her current state, unshowered, exhausted, fresh from a shift, made her physically recoil. Besides, though the kids seemed to have no problem moving from one side to another, she'd never been able to figure out which of the doors in these winding, narrow corridors actually led between them. So instead she started to check some of the places Tommy had said they liked to play.

She worked her way up the staircase that wound its way around the old iron pillars of the cage elevator, tentatively calling her son's name. About halfway up she stopped, aware of an unexpected smell: tobacco smoke. For a moment a ridiculous image flashed into her mind of the two seven-year-old girls pressuring Tommy into smoking, coughing his little lungs out over stolen Pall Malls. It was absurd, of course, and she knew it, but even so she followed the scent, poking her head around the corner to see who was so flagrantly disregarding the building's No Smoking signs.

There was a man outside Edith's flat. His face was dark and lined with a certain deep sadness that Alvita couldn't help but recognise. His hand shook ever so slightly as he raised the cigarette to his lips and the smoke curled back through the open crack in the old woman's door. Alvita watched for longer than she had intended, racking her brain to see if she could remember seeing the man anywhere before. Edith didn't have any children; she knew that for sure. Perhaps a family friend? He certainly didn't look like a carer, which wouldn't have been surprising. His eyes were haunted as they met hers and he started walking over, hand raised in greeting. Alvita realised with a start what was happening and tried to banish her exhaustion, shaking her head and trying to focus, but it still felt like her thoughts were pushing through quicksand.

'Can I help you?' he asked. What was that accent? Brazilian? Somewhere in South America, certainly. She's been on holiday to Peru once, long before Tommy was born, and it had a familiar tone to it. She'd wanted to climb Machu Picchu, but hadn't properly researched it and in the end simply hadn't been physically fit enough for the arduous climb. The air was so thin up there—

'Hello?' the man asked again, and Alvita realised with a start she hadn't actually replied.

'Hello, yeah.' She tried to speak through the fatigue. She pointed at the door. 'Edith, you know, uh, you know Edith?'

'Yes.' He nodded, shifting a bit awkwardly. 'We're friends. From a long time ago.'

Was he lying? It felt like he was lying, but Alvita couldn't trust herself to make that call. Not right now. Whatever the truth, it was someone else to keep an eye on Edith, and that was a relief, albeit a guilty one.

'Have you seen a boy? The children ... my son, he should be playing around here.'

'With a little girl?' The man nodded, pointing down the corridor. 'They were running down there just now.'

'Thank you, um ...?' Alvita gestured vaguely for his name.

'Diego. Santi.'

'Thank you, Mr Santi.' She started to head in the direction Diego had pointed, then turned back. 'You shouldn't be smoking indoors, you know. Especially around kids.'

'I know, I have—' He looked deeply sad again, struggling slightly for the word. 'Sensitive nose. Helps with the smell.'

Alvita didn't really know what to say to this, so she left, following the direction he indicated until she found where Tommy was playing and took him back for dinner.

Her nightshift was always harder than working the tills. Alvita worked in the call centre for a local minicab company, booking cars for the drunk, the surly and those who sounded even more exhausted than she did, though she didn't think they really could be. Without the repetitive physical motions it was harder to keep the fatigue at bay. The desks were full of people quietly talking into headsets, filling the air with a murmuring white noise that she could all too easily lose herself in. Not sleep, of course, not really, but that sort of waking unconsciousness that constantly threatened to overtake her. She didn't like coffee and couldn't stand the clinging medicinal sweetness of energy drinks, so she pushed herself through with caffeine tablets in an attempt to stay alert, always with one ear open for her mobile. Tommy was asleep. The number was stuck above the home phone. If there was a problem, he definitely knew how to call her. He was fine.

The passengers were angry tonight. Several drivers were off sick and waiting times were building. That was one of the only benefits of being so exhausted for this job: Alvita found that, when she was this tired, all the abuse just seemed to slide off her, like some distant radio signal far removed from her life. She knew others took it harder, their emotional defences drained, and she'd seen more than one of her co-workers break down over the cruelties of someone shouting at them from the other end of the phone. But for Alvita, the cotton wool around her brain did something to protect it, even if it made functioning in the world that much harder.

At 2.30 a.m. her shift ended and she stumbled home. It was a ten-minute walk, and one that her friends were always alarmed she made so late at night. It had never bothered Alvita, though; the groups of youths who perched on corners, the sinister figures beneath lampposts, they were nothing but shadows to her. Faint, indistinct presences that would occasionally call after her, but never with words that could pierce the fog. She walked in a world removed from theirs, shifted three degrees to the side by a life without sleep. They couldn't touch her.

She passed Edith's door. Should she knock again? No, it was far too late. And she had that young Diego now. She was fine. Alvita tried to convince herself her suspicions had been misplaced.

She looked in on Tommy's room. Fast asleep. He wasn't going to be up for hours yet, and she didn't even need to prepare lunch or iron his uniform. The small mercies of the summer holidays. No word from Ellie about tomorrow, though, so she'd have to wait and see about babysitting. Maybe the posh kids would come and play with him again. She didn't really trust them, but even so the idea of having a few daylight hours fully to herself brought the shadow of a smile to her lips. Did that make her a bad mother? She was too tired to really think about it.

She fumbled with her keys and for once her prayers were answered as the call button lit up, allowing a momentary reprieve for her aching legs. She chewed slowly on a curried lamb patty she'd grabbed from one of the late-night shops when she realised she'd not had a chance to get groceries. She wasn't hungry, of course, hadn't been for weeks, but recognised that her body needed to eat, so gradually worked her way through the flavourless corner shop savoury.

The flat was silent and dark, and she let her handbag drop to the floor of the hall. She didn't even bother to take off her coat as she staggered towards the bedroom.

She was back in front of the television, watching Channel 70. Had she gone to bed? There was a faint memory of lying down, feeling the old mattress beneath her, but Alvita was here now and this definitely wasn't a dream. She couldn't read in her dreams, and the words *Too Late with Angus Merridew* were clearly visible on the screen. Her tongue felt chalky, no doubt from the Doxatrin pill she must have taken. Not to worry. It made sense.

The grinning host was looking straight into the camera, addressing the audience. From this angle his teeth looked so regular they seemed fake. Like they were just painted on.

'Painted onto what?' Angus asked, shifting from his gentle monologue. 'That doesn't make any sense, does it?'

She had to admit it didn't.

'Now, I know what you're all thinking,' the host continued with a smirk. 'What you're all asking yourselves. "What's that old sell-out Angus going to try and shill to us tonight?" Well, folks, I hate to disappoint you ... So I won't! You're absolutely right that I've got a brand-new sponsorship and you're going to have a front row seat to it. Now, I didn't actually believe it when my producer Tobias first told me about the deal he'd landed. It seemed too good to be true.'

Alvita smiled, excited to hear more. She trusted Angus; he wouldn't steer her wrong. His arm reached all the way over to the side of the screen, grabbing something.

'So let me tell you about ... sleep.'

The studio audience let out a low sound of interest and excitement. In Angus's hand was a photo of a bedroom.

'Now you may think you know about consciousness and reality but let me tell you that you don't know squat until you've tried sleep. It not only refreshes and revitalises you, but it unlocks the door to your imagination. Lets you dive right in in a healthy, balanced way.'

Alvita could see the photograph more clearly now. It wasn't just any bedroom; it was her bedroom. Well, that made sense. Where else was she going to sleep?

'Folks, I really can't say enough about just how vital sleep is. I mean, without it, who knows how your mind might start to seep out into the world around you? Or what you might end up letting in?'

Alvita nodded. She couldn't wait to buy some.

'Now obviously this is a *premium* product, and not one to be bought at your local supermarket. But luckily, money isn't the only way to pay for it. We can get it ordered in special for the right client.'

Alvita's whole body sang with exhaustion. Where could she get it? What would it cost?

'Oh, you'll see, Alvita. Just keep taking your medicine and we'll let you know the bill.'

She smiled as the Doxatrin kicked in and she fell into unconsciousness.

Her world was beginning to fragment. Alvita had pushed through insomnia before, endured months of bone-deep fatigue to look after Tommy, but this time it felt different. Her body moved through the world as normal, smiling and working, but it was like her mind only surfaced briefly, occasionally piercing the fog enough to actually experience what she was doing.

She was being shouted at over the phone because a driver was taking longer to arrive than had been estimated.

She was reading Tommy a story, bathed in the violet glow of his nightlight, but he was already asleep.

She was fumbling a bottle of milk off the conveyor belt and watching helplessly as it tumbled towards the floor.

Ellie the babysitter was talking about what Tommy had done with that day, rattling off events and names that Alvita had no context for.

The one constant she had was her show. The TV didn't seem to get any other channels anymore. Alvita dimly considered trying to get a repair guy round to have a look at it but forgot the idea almost as soon as it occurred. Channel 70 was fine. She'd collapse into the chair, take a Doxatrin and sit there, letting the programming faintly wash over her.

Angus wasn't on tonight. That didn't seem right, he was always on Channel 70. This show wasn't as good, which was a shame, and it didn't seem to have a name. She couldn't really follow the plot, if there even was one, and the scenes seemed disjointed. A man in a fancy suit was standing in the corridor, knocking at his own door over and over again. A plumber tinkered with his toolkit as a long, spindly arm stretched out from an open pipe behind him. A young woman danced alone in a burned-out ballroom, blood flowing from her diamond tiara. A young man in a loose T-shirt sat in the middle of a corridor, pencil furiously working in a small notebook. Then a shot of Edith, sitting in her armchair, the spitting image of Alvita's. She was utterly still.

The corridors on this show were very familiar. How nice it was for Alvita to live in a famous building. As seen on TV! Strange that nobody had mentioned it. She watched as the show abruptly switched to Tommy and his friends playing on the stairs. She wondered momentarily how Tommy had got on television, she certainly hadn't heard anything about it, but she was proud of her son regardless. He suited the screen, even if he didn't look like he was having all that much fun playing the girls' game. The camera was less kind to the blonde girl. Penny, that was her name. She looked all wrong, and moved in sharp, jerky increments, like she was shot in stop-motion. Alvita would have to ask Tommy about it later, though he didn't like to talk about Penny very much.

She closed her eyes. It was nice to see Tommy. She did worry about him, and she felt so far away sometimes. Buried beneath the exhaustion where he'd never find her.

There is no sound more chilling than your child crying out in real pain. It can cut through anything else, no matter how thick the fog that surrounds you, seizing your heart and flooding your system with the electric pulse of adrenaline, calling you to action. As Alvita scooped Tommy up from the bottom of the stairwell, whispering reassurances in his ear and looking over his injured arm, she felt more alive and present than she had in months.

They'd been playing, or so the girls said, and Tommy had slipped on the stairs. Alvita looked at her son's arm, likely broken and already swelling severely. He cried harder and buried his face in his mother's jacket.

Alvita stared daggers at the girls, who seemed mortified. Well, Anna (whose name she had finally remembered) looked sheepish, while Penny was off in a corner eating sweets, apparently unconcerned for the suffering child who they might have seriously injured. Alvita tried to choke down her bile, contain her rage, telling herself that you couldn't hate a child, that it wasn't right. If Anna's parents hadn't been there as well, she's not sure what she might have said. But Prisha, the little girl's mother, seemed to have harsh words enough, and Alvita only really had one thing she felt like she needed to add.

'You are not allowed to play with Tommy anymore.' Her voice icy and calm. 'Not ever.'

Anna looked downcast. Penny stared smugly at Alvita. What was wrong with that girl? Where were her parents? Even the Khans didn't seem to pay her any attention.

The adrenaline rush kept her riding high and pushing forward all through the visit to the Accident and Emergency room. She was focused, comforting Tommy through the tears of pain as they waited for the doctor, holding his hand as the kind-faced woman examined his injury, making sure he could see her waiting as they took him in for an X-ray. It was a clean fracture, a lot less serious than it might have been, and aside from a few weeks with his arm in a cast, it looked like Tommy was going to be fine.

Her managers were surprisingly understanding when she called in to explain the situation and told her to take as long as she needed to look after her son. Of course, how much time Alvita could afford to miss from a financial point of view was another matter, but she'd worry about that later. By the time they got home, and Tommy was asleep in bed, the adrenaline had deserted her almost entirely. The unbelievable wave of exhaustion slammed into her like a tidal wave. She was so tired it felt like it was physically trying to knock her off her feet. The walls swam in and out like something was trying to push through them, and it was all she could do to stagger over to the armchair and dry-swallow a pill.

The TV was already on.

Angus Merrydew grinned out into the darkened living room, his perfect smile smug, yet approachable. The light from the television illuminated the armchair, and the shape of Alvita slumped within it, but everything else was pitch black. She had the stray thought that if she were to try and get up, she would simply fall away into that darkness. Fall away forever. Was she awake? It was so hard to tell anymore.

'Are you ready for our next guest?' Angus smirked, throwing the question to the audience.

The camera panned over the empty banks of seating. It was just for her. She nodded.

'Fantastic! Well, this is someone I've been wanting to get on the show for a while, but she's always been a little bit shy. In fact, she told me the idea of being on television used to scare her to death!'

Pause for laughs. There was no one to laugh.

'But seriously, folks, I could not be happier to be talking to her and I'm sure you'll feel the same way. She's led a long and storied life so let's finish it right. Give a warm Channel 70 welcome to Edith Kinney!'

Alvita smiled, almost mustering up the energy to clap as the frail old woman made her way slowly across the stage to the seat next to Angus Merrydew. She looked better than the last time Alvita had seen her, more lively in her movements and wearing the most beautiful pearl earrings, but she was paler than ever, and her fingertips were tinged a faint blue. Alvita was suddenly aware of how long it had been since she'd last knocked for her, and quietly hoped Edith would be too polite to mention it on television.

'Good evening.' Angus smiled at her. 'And may I say, Edith, you're looking absolutely radiant tonight.'

'Oh, I'm sure you can say whatever you like, Angus,' Edith shot back with a wink. 'But you better be careful what cheques you're writing!'

Angus burst into a good-natured laugh that stuck out starkly in the silence of the studio.

'That's always been the problem though, hasn't it, Edith?' Angus said. 'You've just been so lonely?'

'Not always.' The old woman shook her head sadly. 'But since my Freddy passed four years ago, it's been a real problem.'

A picture filled the screen. A black and white photo of a handsome man in a woollen suit and the young woman who would eventually become the aged Edith that Alvita knew.

'Yes, of course.' Angus's face had become perfectly sympathetic. 'Is that something you feel comfortable talking about?'

Edith nodded.

'He was on a lot of medications for his heart. They were supposed to be safe, of course, but apparently not.'

'A tragedy. And it wasn't the last time pharmaceuticals would cause you some real problems, was it?'

'Oh no.' Edith shook her head. 'No, I've had a terrible time with medications. Arthritis mainly. Although they did find one that worked, eventually. I could make a cup of tea and everything!'

'That sounds wonderful.'

'It was, but you know how it is. The drug got more expensive and the doctors said they weren't prescribing it anymore.' Edith's voice was level, like she was telling an interesting anecdote about a beach holiday. 'And what they gave me instead, oh, it made it much worse.'

'And do you blame Tobias Fell, the man who owned the company?'

'I'm sure he didn't make the decision personally ...'

'Come on, Edith,' Angus prodded. 'We're all friends here.'

'Well, then, yes. I suppose I do.' Edith grinned mischievously.

'He also owns your building, doesn't he?'

'Yes, I moved there after Freddy. The lifts never work and even with the old medicine I couldn't do all those stairs. And with the change, well, I've been trapped in that flat for almost a month.'

Angus Merrydew's face was handsomely sad.

'And is that what killed you?'

Through the stupefying haze of sleeping pills and late-night programming, something in Alvita's stomach dropped.

'Not exactly.' Edith addressed the question with a shrug. 'But it certainly helped.'

'You didn't ...?' Angus looked to the camera and pantomimed looping a noose over his head and pulling it tight.

Pause for laughs. There was no one except for Edith, who let out a playful chuckle.

'Oh no, not sure I'd have had the strength for all that nonsense. But I was lonely and old and in pain. At some point I just ... ended. The knocking stopped, if you get what I mean.'

Alvita felt a stab of guilt.

'And I heard you had a handsome new man around to help you,' Angus said with a gently lascivious smile.

'Well, he did his best, but really there wasn't anything to be done. I'm glad he was there, though. He doesn't need to feel so bad. He has a good heart.'

'That's great to hear. Now, Edith, we're almost out of time, but I've just got to ask: after all this, what's next for Edith Kinney?'

'Well, Angus.' She considered the question for a moment. 'I thought I might gradually start to rot.'

'Really?' Angus looked impressed. 'That's quite a departure. Are you thinking of going the standard coffin route or with more of an alone in your apartment set-up?'

Edith looked at the camera, her eyes meeting Alvita's.

'Well, that really isn't up to me, is it?'

Alvita reeled. It was like the chair had disappeared and she was in freefall, though she hadn't moved at all. She staggered to her feet and managed three wobbly stepped towards the hall before the Doxatrin caught up with her and she was gone.

Edith's door wasn't locked. It stood there, silent and ajar, waiting for Alvita to build up the courage to enter. She didn't know what time it was. When had she woken up? Had she? She didn't know if what she had seen on the television had been a dream or if she was dreaming now. Is it possible to feel tired in a dream? Because she felt it in her bones, deeper than she ever had before. But that was the thing about fatigue: it always felt like it could go deeper somehow. What time was it? There was a faint, sickly daylight coming from the window at the end of the corridor, but that was the only indication. Was Tommy alright? Alvita wasn't sure. She would check on him soon. But first she needed to do this. She needed to see for herself.

There was no sign of the man who had called himself Diego.

Even the lingering scent of cigarettes was gone. But there was another smell in its place: a sickly sweet, slightly greasy odour that seemed to cling to everything it touched.

She'd heard that description so many times, from a hundred crime novels and cop shows, 'like the smell of rotting fruit', but it wasn't really like that. Those were just words. The smell of death was something all its own.

She half-expected the door to creak, but the well-oiled hinges swung back in complete silence. Alvita's legs began to shake. Between the old carpet and the quiet door she made no sound at all as she walked into that complete stillness, and she had to keep reminding herself that she was real and not some mournful ghost.

The lights were off in Edith's flat, and all the curtains were drawn. The thin sunlight that crept around the edges was barely strong enough to discern the shape of the furniture she passed by. She didn't need the light, though. The smell guided her easily through the cramped home, until she was stood at the door to the living room. A blue light shone dimly through the crack underneath it, flickering and irregular.

This door did creak when it opened.

Edith looked so small, curled up against the arm of a chair that seemed far too big for her. The old woman's face was sunken and her eyes were mercifully closed. A long-cold cup of tea sat on the side table next to her. It was impossible to guess how long she had been dead for, but it wasn't long enough to have erased the sadness etched into her features.

The whole scene was lit by the glow of the television, shining its message out into the darkened room: NO SIGNAL.

Alvita didn't need to check which channel it was set to.

*

Over the next couple of days, it was pure chaos, and Alvita wasn't able to keep up with all of it. There were police staring at her, grilling her on every aspect of her statement.

How did she know Edith was dead? She'd smelled something strange while passing the flat.

Who was the man she said was staying there? She didn't know. He said his name was Diego.

What did he look like? Dark-skinned, old suit, smoker. He seemed nice.

Had she seen him since? No.

Did she know Doxatrin had been withdrawn from circulation due to acute neurological side-effects? Yes, she was aware.

Had she been taking it the night she found Edith? No, she hadn't taken it for months.

Did she know a man named James Andre? Never heard of him.

Did this man look familiar? No, but she liked his cap. She used to have a dress in that same shade of blue.

It was a rich tapestry of truths, half-truths and outright lies as Alvita tried to navigate the strange place at the nexus of suspicion and sympathy in which she found herself. She wasn't sure if her obvious exhaustion made her lies more believable or painfully transparent, but if the police knew she wasn't being straight with them they didn't seem to particularly care. After they interviewed her once about Edith, and then again about this man James who apparently died the following night, it was clear they had no intention of returning.

Her mother was the next to visit, sweeping down from Sheffield in to take Tommy 'off her hands' for a few weeks. Alvita could read the silent judgement in her eyes, but was too tired to fight it and couldn't pretend someone else looking after Tommy for a while wasn't a relief she felt all the way through

her. She kissed him softly on the head, deflecting his questions
about why he was going to stay with Grandma until school
started again.

Then they were all gone, and the flat was completely silent.
Alvita was alone with nothing but her weariness and the faint
odour of death that seemed to linger in her nostrils.

Alvita sat staring at Channel 70. They'd taken her Doxatrin
away, so sleep was out of the question, but it didn't matter.
It wasn't long before the relentless lines of NO SIGNAL dis-
solved into the flimsy studio and artificial face of *Too Late with
Angus Merrydew.*

'My guest tonight is easily the most requested in the history
of this show.' Angus smiled. 'We've had emails asking for her,
phone calls, even a telegram from one particularly keen viewer.'

Pause for laughter. There was no one to laugh.

'And it's taken a little while, but I'm very pleased to announce
that we've finally got her. So can you all give a warm *Too Late*
welcome to the one, the only, Ms Alvita Jackson!'

Alvita sat there, watching herself walk into the silent studio,
smiling and waving. She was dressed in that glamourous
evening gown she'd seen in the window of Harvey Nichols last
year. That was nice. She'd always wanted to be on television.

'Good evening, Angus, thanks for having me,' her image said
graciously as it took a seat opposite the perfectly coiffed host.

'An absolute pleasure,' he said, glancing out towards the
watching Alvita. 'I think we all knew it was going to happen
eventually. And you didn't even have to die!'

Pause for laughter. The screen Alvita laughed politely.

'And don't think I'm not grateful for that!' she assured him
brightly.

'But seriously, I think we're all familiar with your work, so

I'm actually more interested in what you've got to say to us? To me? I think you have a few questions of your own, don't you?'

Both Alvitas nodded.

'Did you kill Edith?' the Alvita on the screen asked. It was a question of curiosity, without a hint of accusation to it.

Angus pointed to himself, his face contorted into an exaggerated expression of surprise.

'Me? Goodness no! Though I won't deny we were her favourite show in the weeks before she passed. Technically it was a stroke that did for her, but we both know there was more to it than that.'

The guilt tried to hit Alvita again, but she was too far away for it to touch her.

'And Diego?'

'Ah, handsome Diego,' Angus teased.

'I ... didn't think he was handsome.'

From the armchair, Alvita could feel herself blush.

'If you say so,' Angus smirked. 'Personally, I'd advise that you keep watching. Maybe he'll have an interview of his own.'

'So, what is this?'

Alvita nodded, staring at the screen, it was about time someone was asking the real questions.

'It's ... hard to explain.' Angus shrugged. 'Let's just say it's not programming you'd receive anywhere else in London. We're going for a very specific demographic. You'll be getting an invitation soon. And it's very important you accept it. Understand?'

Pause for laughter. From the darkness of the living room, Alvita laughed. She didn't understand, but it didn't matter.

It came just as promised. Fancy card, embossed lettering. Like it was inviting her to an upscale wedding.

TOBIAS FELL cordially invites ALVITA JACKSON
to attend a dinner party at 1 Banyan Court
on the evening of 16th August 2014
Penthouse access will be available through the freight elevator

Tomorrow night. That wasn't too long to wait. Angus had been quite specific and she could feel something beneath the layers of fog and fatigue. Excitement maybe? Or fear. Either way it would soon be done and then, finally, she could get some sleep.

7th

A Foot in the Door

Caroline Fairley
4 Banyan Court

Banyan Court was haunted. It had to be.

Cari looked at the electronic thermometer in her hand, trying to convince herself that the three-degree drop in temperature counted as a 'cold spot'. There had been nothing out of the ordinary on the EMF reader and the tapes had been full of nothing but silence, but there was *something* here. She was absolutely sure of it. She saw it in the faces of the people she passed in the corridor, the slightly glassy-eyed look of the concierge: the people here were desperately trying to ignore something. Something that scared them. Something that Cari was eager to meet.

But not today, it seemed. She put the thermometer back in her black canvas bag and took out a fresh bottle of mineral water as she sat on the plush hallway carpet, her back to the wall. It wasn't the physical exertion of ghost hunting that tired her but concentrating so hard on such specific readings for so long always left her parched. The possibility of it all thrilled her, like gradually unwrapping a present. Admittedly, she'd never had a present before that was actually ghosts. But this was it. She could feel it.

It wasn't anything she could describe or put properly into words. Just a shadow of a feeling. As a child, she had been convinced that her wardrobe was haunted. She had been so convinced that a shy, small spirit was in there, lurking in the back behind her ballet shoes, that she had called her mother in almost every night to check. After her mother left it had briefly grown into something of an obsession, to the point where her father had quite seriously talked about 'getting someone in to help'. Cari had thought she had left it all in the past, but there was something about Banyan Court that had compelled her to dig her old equipment out from the storage room of her father's London flat. It was that same certainty that something was here.

Her phone alarm beeped, congratulating her on a solid two hours of writing. She grimaced. An impromptu ghost hunt was pretty extreme as far as procrastination methods went, but it was a hobby she could really lose herself in (one of the many reasons her father had always derided it). And she just couldn't stand staring at that blank white page any longer, trying to think of pitch ideas. It was starting to really worry her.

She pushed away the darker thoughts and held out her hand again, testing the air for what she had previously thought might be a cold spot. It was cooler, certainly, than the rest of the corridor, but given the relative positioning of the air conditioning vents, maybe that wasn't quite the supernatural conundrum she was after. She just needed a win, really.

Cari shouldered her bag and started to head towards the building's health centre. She kept her gym clothes in there as well and felt like hopping on a treadmill and trying to outrun her gnawing anxiety.

She never used to think of herself as someone who believed in ghosts, not really. Even now, if you actually asked her the question directly, she'd probably say 'No.' But then she'd follow up that 'No' with a dozen interesting counterpoints, examples of manifestations that have never been explained and several books on the subject that she would highly recommend. Maybe it was time she just owned her beliefs. But that wasn't quite right. She *didn't* believe in ghosts, exactly. She just believed that there was *something* out there, that the evidence was real, even if the conclusions most people drew were the wrong ones. Mostly, though, it was just fun.

As she reached the door to the health suite Cari paused. Had she heard something? She spun around quickly, trying to catch a glimpse of an unnatural shadow on the wall, or an indistinct figure disappearing around the corner. But there was nothing. She shook her head and went inside.

'I saw your article in *Cosmopolitan*.' Howard Fairley's face looked almost proud, though that may have just been the quality of the video call. 'You might even make a decent interviewer one day. That's two now, isn't it?'

'Two what?' Cari wished they didn't always have to have these conversations over the screen. It was much harder to keep both her voice *and* her face seeming relaxed.

'In *Cosmo*. You said you'd had one accepted a few months back as well?'

'Oh, no.' She was doing a pretty good job of it, as long as she kept her clenched fist out of frame. 'It's the same piece. I had to run it past Evangelina's agents first, make sure they approved it, so it took a while before it got to print.'

'Right. Just the one, then.' Her father's tone had changed in an all-too-familiar way.

'I mean, I've been published other places.' She could feel what was coming.

'Mm, yes. Blogs and such, right?'

Cari froze for a moment, with a sudden dread that her father had found her recent work on various paranormal sites dotted about the web. No, he'd definitely have mentioned that. It would have opened the conversation and ended with her moving back in with him, 'just to keep an eye on things'. Her father had no patience for such fancies.

'Look, Dad, Wired.com is not a "blog",' Cari protested, but it was too late. 'Just because they're online doesn't mean—'

'I understand that, Caroline,' he said. He clearly didn't. 'I just think that we're paying a lot of money to support you at the moment. That flat you're in certainly isn't cheap. And if you're just spending your time there writing blog posts then maybe we should reassess.'

'Dad, please, just—' She could feel her facade cracking. 'I'm actually starting to make some money as a writer. Real money. But it does take time. You've got to get your name out there. Properly get your foot in the door.'

'And how long until you can pay your own way?'

There was a long, uncomfortable silence.

'Look,' her father continued. 'You remember that position I mentioned? It's still open. We could get you started in the marketing department next week. Put that Creative Writing degree to some actual use.'

'I'll think about it,' Cari conceded. She wouldn't, but she'd had this conversation enough times to know that an outright refusal would just drag the whole thing out.

'That's your problem,' he continued. 'You're never serious about anything. It's like those dance lessons, you remember? Thousands we spent on them, and then your mother—'

'Yes, I remember,' Cari snapped, harder than she had intended. 'And I've got work to do. So ...'

'Yes. Well. Think about my offer,' he instructed. 'Now, if you'll excuse me, I've got a meeting to get to as well.'

'Sure thing.'

'Look after yourself,' her father said, with an expression passably close to parental affection.

'You too, Dad.'

Cari shut the laptop to end the call, so she didn't have to face the same blank page she'd been staring at for the last two days.

She knew her father. It wasn't actually about the money. The same reason he had 'suggested' Banyan Court as a good place for her to move to if she wanted to start a successful writing career. It was about the prestige. And of course, it had meant he could use his connection to Tobias Fell to help secure the place.

It wouldn't have been fair to say that her father was all about appearance, but he had his own standards of respectability. *Cosmopolitan* was hardly a publication he had a lot of time for, but he recognised an important brand and, more importantly, he could actually hold it in his hands. A couple more features in respectable magazines and maybe he'd back off. She just needed a good pitch.

Her gaze fell on the open bag. She'd thrown her gym kit in the wash, so now all that remained were the cameras, tripods, temperature and EMF scanners. She smiled. Obviously a piece in the *Fortean Times* wasn't likely to gain her father's respect, but if she didn't focus too directly on the supernatural aspect … Well, Tobias Fell was always good copy, and a dive into the history of where he chose to erect his monument? It was a no-brainer. Especially if she could find a spook or two to sprinkle through. If there was one thing sceptics loved, it was deniably reading about ghosts.

She opened her laptop back up, took a breath, and began typing:

THE DARK ROOTS OF BANYAN COURT

Too much? She could always revise the title if it turned out the history of the place was too mundane, but Cari was sure she could find something. When you had a man like Tobias Fell involved, you could be sure there was a skeleton buried somewhere.

A Whitechapel History. The title was as unassuming as the book, a worn paperback from sometime in the 1980s with a poorly cropped photograph of the distinctive arch of the Whitechapel Gallery over a navy-blue background. She had found a battered copy in the nearby library. It was thick, which was encouraging, and even more encouraging was the fact that the index didn't have a single entry for 'Ripper, Jack the'.

When Cari had decided to start researching her article, she hadn't reckoned on just how difficult it would be to escape his shadow. After all, not to be insensitive, but he was a single serial killer who didn't even hit double digits. A historical curiosity. Right? Surely he wouldn't be the focal point dominating every single work of local history about the area since? It wasn't that there weren't any books focusing on other aspects of Whitechapel's history, it was just that she had a hard time finding them under the deluge of breathlessly salacious books aimed at morbid tourists that saw the area as little more than a backdrop for ghoulish titillation. It was exhausting and unless it turned out Banyan Court was being haunted by the man himself, utterly useless.

Maybe *A Whitechapel History* wasn't the best book out there, but it was the one that she could find. Online research hadn't been much better. She didn't have her JSTOR login anymore, and without an angle to focus on yet the information she'd found had been even shallower than the pop-history books littering the library shelves. Plus, if the article was going to be grounded enough for mainstream publication it would need to be as much about the history of the building than about anything that might be haunting it. Unfortunately, the library copy was reference only and there wasn't an eBook edition, so she had to go home and order a second-hand copy from Amazon.

So, what to do until it arrived? She'd already scoured the non-paywalled side of the internet, filling her notepad with shallow details. She stood up, stretched and started to take stock of her kit, making sure that tapes were blank, batteries were charged, and everything was working properly. She could feel an anticipation building inside her, something she hadn't felt since she was a child. Soon she was going to have the history covered; maybe it was time to start sourcing her ghosts. It was for the article, after all.

The big question was where in the building Cari was most likely to find her ghosts. She'd mainly been trying the corridors around her own apartment until now and had determined that there were no spiritual emanations near the health suite, which wasn't entirely surprising.

Her online research had brought up plenty of articles on the 'back half' of Banyan Court. A few more affordable flats alongside the maintenance and storage areas, from what she understood. If it was less well kept or frequented than the main building, that was almost certainly the best place to start her hunt properly, not to mention the fact that, well, she didn't really like to think about it, but she reasoned that if the residents were poorer then there was more likely to be tragedy, trauma … all the stuff that made good ghosts. Her efforts to find a way back from the corridors around her flat yielded nothing, so she decided to try the long way. Cari headed down and past the creepy concierge, then began to make a circuit of the building, looking for an entrance.

She crept past the huge bins, relishing the feeling of trespass, of finding something hidden. The first thing she found was an old concrete basketball court, netless hoops rusting gently in the humid summer air. There it was: an unassuming door marked with a large 'B', the windows flanking it on either side protected by heavy bars painted a bright warning yellow. Cari was on CCTV, a sign warned her, an announcement that caught her unawares. As did the decidedly well-kept lock on the door. She paused for a moment, the question of how to get in suddenly a very pressing one.

It was, however, solved a few moments later when the door swung open and an exhausted-looking woman shuffled out, followed by an excitable little boy in bright green dungarees. She gave Cari a nod and wordlessly held the door open. Hesitating only a second, Cari mumbled a thank you and headed inside, jumping slightly as the heavy door slammed shut behind her.

This part of Banyan Court was something entirely new – or old, rather. Gone was the plush carpet and tasteful floor lighting of the main building, but this wasn't an afterthought: people clearly lived here. A lot of people. The bank of letterboxes set against the wall must have numbered almost eighty, and a rack of bikes in various states of repair sat off in a small side room. How could she not have known this was here? The estate agents certainly hadn't mentioned it. It didn't make sense. She'd searched so hard for doors that led back here from the front and found nothing. How could this many people be living here and there was no way to reach them directly? Cari pressed on, down the corridor, before stopping with a gasp.

Stretching up and away from her, right through the building, was an old wrought-iron lift. It was looped by a stairwell that gave access to the rest of the floors above her and had obviously been part of whatever Banyan Court had been before it was a residential tower block. The structure of it was tinged with rust but had stood the test of time far better than might have been expected. A thick yellow chain sealed the sliding grate shut, marking the thing as off-limits. No doubt it had stopped working decades ago.

Cari let the bag slip from her shoulders and knelt over it, rummaging for her remote cameras. She'd found what she was looking for, she was certain. If anywhere was going to be haunted, it was here. She allowed herself a smile of anticipation.

The next day was lost to googling her new discovery. The articles from Cari's initial research were just the tip of the iceberg. She wasn't the first to stumble onto the fact that there were people being rented sub-standard apartments. In fact, there were a good half-dozen thinkpieces on it from a few years ago when the building had first been completed, each holding up the back of Banyan Court as an example of everything wrong with current housing policies. Nothing had ever actually been done about it of course, but it did make Cari feel a little better that she wasn't alone in feeling uncomfortable about the whole situation.

And it did leave a bad taste in her mouth. She had started to take photos, framing them to emphasise the dingy atmosphere, but as the shutter clicked, she felt a curious sense of shame creep over her. This place wasn't some tourist destination for her to indulge her aesthetic tastes. She was safe from an existence like this, but at what cost? Her father's business dealings were not always the most ethical (from what her mother had cited in the divorce, neither was his personal life) and he'd never fully explained his relationship to the building's owner. Walking through the damp-smelling hallways of Banyan Court's back half she couldn't completely evade the sting of guilt.

It was still preying on Cari's mind now, as she tried her best to concentrate on the video footage she'd taken. She sighed and clicked back to a few minutes earlier, trying to keep her attention focused on the empty corridor. Don't get distracted. After all, if she didn't get this article picked up her father might cut her off, and then maybe she would be in danger of poverty herself. She was optimistic, though. She'd sent some article pitches off a couple of days ago and had already had a couple of interested emails from a few decently prestigious magazines. Admittedly, she hadn't explicitly mentioned ghosts in her approach, pitching it more as an insider's view of Tobias Fell's grand folly. Still, they'd seemed very keen on her intimations about 'dark secrets', so if she had something compelling enough she was certain they'd take it. No doubt they were expecting dirt and scandal, but she'd do them one better. She was sure of it.

She moved to the next video: footage of her finally finding a door between the two sides. She smiled slightly as her laptop speakers played back her own tinny squeak of triumph. Even once she'd discovered what was back there it had been a day's work to hunt down a door that linked the two halves. It had been so out of the way as to feel almost deliberately hidden, lurking down a thin, nondescript corridor and requiring her to go through a cleaning cupboard to access it. It even had a fierce-looking 'Keep Out' sign on it, though for what reason Cari couldn't understand. The more she learned about the layout of this place, the less sense it seemed to make. Perhaps that was another thing she could explore in her article? Turn it into a proper longread?

Regardless, it had made retrieving the footage from the

cameras she had set up relatively simple. She'd managed to tuck them into an out-of-the-way corner and on top of door jambs, and it didn't look like anyone had interfered with them. Forty-eight hours' worth of footage of the two spots with the most EMF activity; if this didn't do it, she might have to abandon the classic ghost hunting methods and try something new.

Now settled in with a blanket and a large glass of wine, she continued scrubbing through two days' worth of footage, looking for strange figures or rogue shadows. Unfortunately, the shadows all seemed pretty normal, and the figures that passed were solid enough, haunted only by their own difficult position in life or the harsh realities of living in a place like that. Again, she felt that twinge of shame at watching, comfortable and insulated, mining these people's situation for an article. She watched as a young woman left each night at dusk, clearly heading towards some awful night job, only returning after dawn could be seen through the hallway windows. Cari felt a swell of pity. It must be awful to work like that, slaving away in the dark. She was kind of cute, though.

Perhaps she was wrong. Perhaps Banyan Court was only haunted by the people who lived there. Still, she kept combing through the footage, going back and forth over individual frames, trying to judge if she was seeing anything significant and coming to the conclusion that no, she wasn't. Then she stopped, wrinkling her brow in confusion, rewinding and just letting the video play. A man was standing there, at the section of corridor she was monitoring. He was dressed in tatty jeans and a Simon & Garfunkel T-shirt, and what he was doing caught her eye. He wasn't going anywhere or waiting for someone from one of the flats. He was going from one wall to the other and gently placing his palm on each. She could see he had a camera of his own hung on a strap round his neck. Back and forth, back and forth, taking a few moments to consider each time. Then he took out a tape measure and stretched it between the two walls. He retracted it. Stretched it again between the same exact two points, checked it, then retracted it. He did this four more times, before pulling out a small notebook and jotting something down. Then he left, vanishing off camera.

Pulling the slider back, Cari watched him go through the motions again. A builder, maybe? Someone looking to do some DIY? So why did he look so furtive? She kept watching the screen. Somewhere under her confusion were the seeds of intrigue. The man's movements hadn't been erratic or compulsive in any way.

He was performing some sort of experiment. The more times she watched it, the clearer that became. He was, as far as she could tell, real; no strange shadows or video anomalies accompanied his appearance. So why did it feel to Cari like she might have finally found her ghost? What was he doing?

She pushed herself off the sofa, a little worse for wine, and headed over to a chest of drawers. Pulling out the lowest one, the one she thought of as her 'grown up' drawer, she began pawing through screwdrivers, possibly dead batteries, gaffer tape, warranties and light bulbs until she found what she was looking for. A tape measure of her own.

This was ridiculous. She should have been reading back through her books, making notes for the article. Instead she found herself pushing through the 'Keep Out' sign on a door in a cleaning cupboard and going to look for that corridor. It was late, but that didn't matter.

She stood there, trying to keep the tape level as she stretched it across the gap, as close as possible to where the man on the video had done so.

One hundred and ninety-eight centimetres.

Cari paused, letting the tape measure snap back, then walked over and pressed her hand against the small black cross she had drawn on the dingy wallpaper, closed her eyes and focused. Nothing. The wall was completely still. She walked to the other side and did the same thing again. Still nothing.

She took a deep swig from her water bottle and began to extend the tape measure again, making sure each end lined up perfectly with the cross she had drawn on its respective wall.

One hundred and ninety-five centimetres.

She stared at it for a long time, holding the tape measure in position for almost three minutes, watching for any change in the length, and movement in either wall. It was still one hundred and ninety-five. Three millimetres. That could easily have been her own error the first time.

She retracted it, waiting only a few moments before once again extending it to measure the width of the hallway.

Two hundred and one centimetres.

Cari's legs went slightly weak as she started to accept what she was seeing. All at once she was seven again, watching her mother pile up dancing shoes outside her wardrobe, shining a torch into all the corners to show her there was nothing there, but there had been something there. She'd known it then and she knew it now, no matter what her father and his 'professionals' might have said.

This wasn't the haunting she had been looking for, and she wasn't even sure how well it would work in the article, but she absolutely had to go deeper. If she needed to, she'd write an entirely new article. Heck, if it ended up in the *Fortean Times* after all her dad would just have to lump it. Right now, though, she needed to find the man from her camera, and she needed to get a look at the building plans. First the door, now this. What else was Banyan Court hiding in its strange, mutable spaces?

The on-hold music for the estate agent droned on from her phone's speakers. Half an hour now and counting, but Cari was patient. She had her phone on charge, thousands of unused minutes on her contract, and *A Whitechapel History* had finally arrived to occupy her while she waited. They could keep her hanging for as long as they liked: she wasn't going away. After all, they might be her last hope to get her hands on anything resembling building plans, having been firmly rebuffed by everywhere else that might have had them on file.

Part of her was still trying to justify this as 'article research', but she knew that wasn't it anymore. Something about this place had wormed its way into her and she needed to know more.

When she slept, she dreamed of her mother, telling her softly there's no such thing as ghosts.

The automated voice reassured her how important her call was, but Cari barely even heard. Her gaze was firmly focused on the book in her hand. She had finally found something she thought might relate directly to Banyan Court. From what she had seen in the back of the building it was clear that the place had parts that were far older than she had initially thought. She couldn't figure out the exact date it would have been built, but she was sure the original structure had been part of what was referred to by the book as the 'Collingwood inferno': a string of three fires in 1869, all affecting brick slum tenements in the area around Collingwood Road. Each caused tremendous loss of life within the cramped and unprepared confines of the over-crowded buildings. Arson was suspected, though no culprit was ever caught. Some even suggested that the police themselves might be responsible, as two officers had lost their lives to violence in one of those tenements the year before.

One of the tenements involved was a run-down building named Westerland House, after the Sir Henry Westerland who had originally commissioned its construction. The streets referenced seemed promising, and having a look over the historical map of Whitechapel ... The thrill of discovery rushed through Cari, as she realised that the foundations of the building in which she sat might be the very same that had once supported Westerland House. She looked up from her book with a start, suddenly worried she might have ignored the phone for too long.

'... call is important to us. Someone will be with you as soon as possible.'

Or maybe not.

Armed with a name, she attacked the internet, as well as cross-referencing with a few of the more respectable volumes she'd taken from the library. There wasn't a lot of information online, but she did find a photograph that claimed to be of Westerland House after the fire, on a website dedicated to (what else?) the crimes of Jack the Ripper. For all the ghoulish fonts and salacious copy, though, the thing that chilled Cari was the picture itself. The lower levels were blackened and scarred. Around the base were piles of rubble, and in the blurry silver of that nineteenth-century photo were a dozen indistinct shapes and lines, any one of which might have been the remains of a victim, as fire-twisted as the structure that loomed over them, still pleading to be saved. And above the third floor it was just gone, the brick below where it should have been warped and scarred by heat. Wait. She recognised those bricks. The fire-hollowed windows that would one day be covered with bright yellow bars. A shiver ran through her, though she wasn't sure exactly why, and all of a sudden, she felt very small indeed. Cari closed the laptop.

A Whitechapel History had a bit more detail on the specific fate of Westerland House. After the fire, the land was bought by Charles Fell, a man who made his fortune in gemstone mining. Cari smiled with vindication when she saw the name. He had it rebuilt and knocked down several nearby buildings to expand it into a dye factory in 1876. It had brought much-needed work to the area, but also its fair share of problems.

Blame was placed on the toxic fumes from the factory as the culprit for several infant deaths in the area over the next decade, with one newspaper dubbing Fell's factory 'The Poison Palace'. It certainly didn't help that, while most other factories had switched entirely over to William Henry Perkins's aniline dyeing methods, Fell insisted on continuing the use of arsenic in making their rich green dye, and many workers reputedly fell ill. This, combined with lax safety standards even for its time, led to a high turnover of employees. When a worker was forced to leave a job due to illness, injury or death it was joked that they had 'gone to the ballroom', due to a persistent rumour that Fell had constructed a hidden ballroom in the heart of the factory, gilded in gold and bedecked in Zambian emeralds and rubies extracted from Fell's brutal Burmese mining operations. A place of secret parties, exclusive invitations, and esteemed guests who never spoke of what occurred within those walls. How and why this idea began is impossible to say, and there seems to have been no concrete evidence for it, but the ease with which it took root in the imagination of his employees can maybe give us some inkling of the regard in which Charles Fell's workers held him.

Kirsten Dawes, *A Whitechapel History*, Chapter 14
'A Second Revolution'

Cari put the book down slowly. A ballroom. Something in those words resonated: an image of a grinning Victorian industrialist, sitting in the centre of his gilded and glittering sanctum of wealth, listening to the distant cries of suffering from the people below ... She had seen her mother dance once, a year or so before she left, and Cari found it hard not to picture that room, the shining marble and glowing chandeliers. It was better than a secret door, at least. But if she was going to find evidence of it, she needed a look at those building plans.

As if in reply, the hold music abruptly stopped.

'Hello? Hello? Dean Bishops Estate Agents, Laura speaking? Is anyone there?'

Cari almost leapt off the chair, fumbling for her phone. She'd gone almost completely deaf to the hold music that had been gently continuing through her research, and now she found herself almost unable to speak.

'Yes, uh, hi. Hello. Um, I'm ... I live, uh ...'

She could sense the woman on the other end about to hang up.

'Banyan Court?' Cari finished.

A pause.

'You rent one of our Banyan Court properties?' The voice of this 'Laura' was much warmer now, though Cari thought she could detect a hint of wariness in it.

'I do. Through my father.' Cari didn't need to have said that part. Why did she say it? She tried to calm down, get some control of the conversation back.

'What number is the property?' Laura asked, a little too eagerly, and then Cari understood. The estate agent needed to know which side of the building she was talking to.

'Four,' she said, suddenly aware of her position. 'I'm in flat four.'

'Ah, excellent!' The voice on the other end finished its journey into warmth. 'What can I do for you today? Many apologies for the wait, my colleagues are all out on viewings.'

'No problem,' Cari muttered, fidgeting in her seat. 'I had some questions about the floorplan?'

'Certainly. Send me your email address and I'll shoot over the one for your flat.'

'Actually, I was hoping I could get something a bit of a larger scale.'

'I'm ... not sure I understand.' Laura sounded genuinely confused.

'I'm looking for a floorplan for, uh, for the whole building. If I can.'

'I don't know if there's something—'

'Both sides.'

Laura was silent on the other end of the phone.

'I think you should probably check with Tower Hamlets' local authority. They might have something in the record—'

'They don't.' Cari knew she was pushing too hard, but it was like a dam had broken, begging her mother to check again. 'Nowhere does, but you rent out almost half the flats in this place. You've got to have something. And I need to see it.'

'Look, there's nothing like that here.' Laura's voice was oddly defensive. 'We just deal with the rent and maintenance.'

'So, you have plans of the wiring, the plumbing, stuff you can give the workmen.'

Now Laura's tone was cold. 'Just leave it alone.'

Cari didn't reply. The warning was so clear, so oddly forceful, she didn't have a response.

'Please,' Laura said.

'What have you seen?' Cari asked at last, her curiosity winning.

'Nothing.' Her voice was hollow and resigned. 'I haven't seen anything. Sorry we couldn't help you.'

Click.

Cari sat there a while longer, the phone still to her ear, staring out the window, lost in thought. The sun shone down on the same streets as it had for hundreds of years, and it wasn't going to set for hours yet.

Without a clear next step, Cari found herself wandering the halls, drifting through both sides of Banyan Court like the very ghosts she was hunting. She knew what she was looking for, but as for how to find it, she didn't know where to start. She took to drawing crude maps of each floor on graph paper, but without the skills to properly lay it out there was only so much she could do. She had no idea how large any of the other flats were, and there were so many locked doors, any one of which could have led to something that would have completely altered her amateurish schematic. They could be a cupboard. Or another corridor. Or a ballroom.

Why couldn't she shake this idea? She'd dreamed about it last night. Her father, dressed in a woollen suit and an old top hat, waltzing over the marble floor of an impossibly ornate room. No windows. No doors. Utterly hidden from the world. He held a woman in his arms, arrayed in jewels and fine fabrics. Her face was fixed in an empty smile and she did not move.

'Caroline never finished her lessons,' she had said.

'Such a disappointment,' her father had replied.

Cari didn't recognise the woman, but her father waltzed with her nonetheless, his feet not slipping once, though the dance-floor was slick with blood. Then she woke up.

Cari shook her head. The whole thing was absurd. Not even a difficult dream to decipher. She hadn't met her dad's new girlfriend, but the rest of the imagery was pretty basic. There was a certain degree of psychological baggage that came with coming from a successful, driven family and the pressures of it. Not to mention everything with her mother. Perhaps her dad was right: she'd stopped her counselling sessions too soon.

Or perhaps the ballroom was real. Whether you could call them ghosts or not, Cari did believe there was some sort of spiritual residue that could be left behind after death. The sort of thing that, if you were sensitive to it, might reach out and give you just a little bit of subtle guidance; planting an idea deep in your mind where you can't quite shake it. And she couldn't get the music from her dream out of her head. That gentle, rhythmic swell.

Cari paused at the thought. Did she really think that ghosts were trying to guide her to the hidden ballroom at the centre of the factory which had been hollowed out to make Banyan Court? Surely this was absurd. Even if it was true, it might not be something she could use in her article. Why was this the feeling that gripped her?

She broke into a smile. Why not? On the phone, the estate agent had clearly seen something unnatural in this place, and what about the guy measuring the corridor? Something was going on and if her instincts were drawing her to an impossible room, maybe it was best to follow them.

She returned to her flat and began to pore over her rough layout of the building. The old dye factory had stood about 94 feet tall, dwarfing many of the surrounding buildings, at least according to one website dedicated to the skyline and layout of (Cari sighed) Jack the Ripper's East End. That was about seven stories. After it was bombed during the blitz, it looked like the factory was abandoned and the building left to rot for over half a century.

A shiver went through her again. Tobias Fell, Charles's great grandson, had built Banyan Court on a ruin built on a ruin. Had they owned the building all this time? Why? It wasn't that strange, though, surely? Most of London is three ruins deep at least. Cari tried to focus. From the photos it looked like the V2 rocket had destroyed the top half of the building, anything that had survived would have to be below that. And the line from the book kept running through her head: 'the heart of the factory'. If the old ballroom was going to be anywhere, which it obviously wasn't, it would be on the fourth floor. She was sure of it.

What was she expecting to find? A rotten ruin the builders somehow overlooked? A pristine, sparkling artefact, preserved in secret by the current owner? A clustered huddle of ghostly figures, the ranks of dead miners and exploited workers, weeping over the pointless riches stolen from their broken hands? Of course, she told herself she expected to find nothing at all. It had only ever been a myth. But she was lying.

'Mr Erikson?'

The figure spun round at Cari's words, revealing himself to be exactly who she thought he was.

'Uh, yes. H-hello. Good to see you again.' It was clear the man had no idea who she was. He shuffled backwards slightly, like he'd been caught doing something he wasn't supposed to and was preparing to run.

Now that he wasn't interviewing her for a staff writer position all the power seemed to have left David Erikson and Cari found her respect for him fading away as well. He wasn't behind an imposing desk now; no framed front pages lining the wall. He was just ... some guy. His suit was clearly nearing the end of its life and his bag was held together on one strap by duct tape.

In many ways he seemed to match the shabby wallpaper of the building's rear and she felt a slightly petty joy seeing him like this. She didn't bother to refresh his memory on who she was.

'What are you doing here?'

She was pretty sure that it was something more sensible than hunting down a ghostly ballroom, but she couldn't resist asking. Last she'd heard he was still working as a contributing editor at the *Post*, and to find him skulking around the back corridors of Banyan Court was surprising to say the least.

'I can't say, sorry.' David threw his hands up in mock exasperation, his voice condescending. 'NDAs, you know?'

'OK.' Cari was feeling a little bit cruel. 'So, if I were to give Bill a ring? At the front desk? He'd know you were here. Right?'

She had no idea what any of the concierges' names actually were, but she was sure none of them were Bill.

'Sure,' David said. 'Call Bill if you want. It's all above board.'

Cari had to admit he was a decent liar. She almost believed him. He saw her grin and deflated.

' ... Or whatever the hell his name is. Fine, you caught me. Please don't get me thrown out.'

'What are you doing here?'

'Who even are you?'

'I'm—' Cari considered telling him the truth, but instead found herself surreptitiously dropping her tape measure back into her bag. 'I live here. And I know your work, so just wondering what brought you to my neck of the woods.'

She'd never used that idiom before in her life, the faux-casualness not really suiting her. The veteran journalist could clearly sense it too, and she could see him deciding whether to challenge her. His eyes moved from her expensive bag, to her high-end shoes, to the dingy, discoloured wall of the corridor.

'You live here?' It wasn't a challenge. It was an opportunity.

'I do,' she said, neglecting to mention which side. 'Now tell me what you're doing here.'

He sighed and shrugged. Clearly she was one mystery too far.

'Fine,' he said at last. 'But not here.'

Wetherspoons isn't exactly famous for their coffee, but the nearest available seats were at the Moon On the Water, a nearby pub with booths that were just private enough. At that time on a Tuesday morning there were only a few other souls there and none of them looked in a state to bother anyone.

David sat there, ignoring a steaming white mug that sat in front of him. Now Cari could get a decent look at him it was clear he'd recently been the recipient of a black eye. She waited patiently for him to start.

'So, a few weeks back a story broke about one of Tobias Fell's companies. They were involved in some slash-and-burn stuff in the Amazon, not unusual, but apparently this time it ended up killing enough people that there was a real outcry. Combined with all that additives story last year ... you hear about that?'

Cari shook her head.

'Nasty business. Couple of kids actually went blind. Anyway, we reckoned it was about time to do a proper article digging into Fell's connections with all these companies. Y'know, how much was he unlucky in the companies he chose to buy or invest in, how much was he complicit in all the shit they got up to. Obviously, I wanted to get a comment from the man himself, but as usual his office rebuffed me. Billionaire recluse doesn't want to talk to the press, go figure.'

David was talking faster now. It was clear he'd been holding this all in for a while. Cari sipped her burnt coffee and just listened.

'So I think no biggie, we can run the story without him, but I got curious. I'd never actually seen that place, Banyan Court, up close. I've been poking around, managed to get a comment from a few of the residents, but I don't know, something felt weird. Then they found this old woman last night. Edith Kinney, dead in her apartment. Cause of death says natural causes, but a police contact mentions there's this guy been seen hanging around. Heavy smoker, probably South American from the descriptions. Might be involved.'

David was staring at her, eyes gleaming.

'I reckon there's maybe a different story now, and I try to talk to the concierge, get some more details. He gave me this.'

He gingerly touched the bruise around his eye.

'Kind of an overreaction.'

'You think? I don't know. I've been doing this job a while now and I know when something's going on, but usually I can get a feeling for what it is. This, though? I feel like I'm just fumbling in the dark. No one from your side of the building's given me the time of day.'

Cari was taken aback at how easily he'd pinpointed which side she was from, but if David noticed her momentary discomfort, he didn't show it.

'Talked my way into a chat with some tech guy and he chucked me out before I could ask any real questions. Though I've talked to a few folk in the arse end of the building.'

'And ...?' Cari leaned forward, no longer bothering to hide her intrigue.

'More questions than anything else. Still no clue about this South American guy, or what's going on with Fell.'

'Never met either of them.' Cari shook her head. 'Sorry.'

'You feel it, right? All the little things that don't quite add up? I just need some answers.'

'Will you publish it?' An uncharitable thought about possible competition flitted across Cari's mind.

'What?' It was as though the question hadn't occurred to him for a while. 'Sure, I guess. If I'm not obsessing over nothing. But I trust my instinct, y'know? Can't get far in this business if you don't.'

David sighed, looking every one of his forty-three years. It seemed like he was done, and an uncomfortable silence settled over the conversation.

'So, what about you?' he finally continued. 'What's the daughter of Howard Fairley doing wandering around the slum side of Banyan Court with a notebook and a tape measure?'

Cari nearly choked on her coffee at the mention of her father's name.

'Took a while to recall exactly where I recognised you from,' David continued. 'But I'll never forget when he phoned up the office to shout at us for turning you down. Blaming me for wrecking your chance at getting "a real foothold in the industry", while not exactly helping your chances himself.'

'I'm really sorry he did that.' The white mug wasn't big enough to hide Cari's bright red face. 'I didn't ask him to.'

'It's history.' He waved his hand as though dismissing the thought. His voice finally lost the last faint traces of condescension 'So are you going to tell me what you're up to?'

Cari took a deep breath.

'Would you believe I'm hunting ghosts?'

David laughed. It wasn't a cruel laugh, but it was clear that no, he wouldn't believe it.

Then he nodded, surprising her. 'You picked the right place, I reckon.'

*

Cari wasn't sure she shared David's confidence, though, and pretty soon she was almost certain she'd made a mistake. Her 'map' of the third, fourth and fifth floors was as complete as she could make it, but still consisted mostly of question marks. Flats and locked doors barred every further avenue of exploration and though none of the measurements she'd done seemed to match up properly, she couldn't be sure if that was some supernatural property of the building or just mistakes in her own calculations.

She slumped against the wall next to the old stairwell. She wasn't going to cry. She refused to give her father the satisfaction.

'Hey, are you OK?'

The voice was soft and hesitant, and Cari didn't recognise it. But turning her head she found herself looking into a face she'd seen before. In person, weathered skin showed evidence of more hardship than matched his relative youth, and his eyes shone with a quiet intelligence. The T-shirt he wore was different to the one she'd seen on camera, but just as faded and tatty.

'It's you,' she said, before she could think about it.

Immediately the man's face changed. He backed off slightly, his posture turning defensive and his eyes instinctively scanning his surroundings as though for possible exits.

'You know me?' His tone was wary.

'Yeah. I've seen you around. I live in the building.' Cari thought it best not to mention exactly how. 'You were taking some measurements. In one of the corridors?'

'Oh. Right.' He was considering her words. 'That was you. With the hidden cameras?'

She flushed. 'You saw them?'

'Yeah.' He nodded. 'Not sure that's OK.'

'I know. Sorry.'

'Can't really criticise.' He opened his bag to flash her a camera of his own, then held out a hand. 'Damian.'

She shook it. 'Cari.'

'So, Cari,' he said. 'Why are you secretly recording here?'

She considered the question, running through the list of lies she could tell. She was sick of lying.

'I'm looking for the ballroom,' she told him. The words felt odd to say out loud.

Damian let out a low whistle.

'You sure that's a good idea?'

'You know it?' In an instant she was upright, electrified by curiosity. Her new friend grinned, clearly glad to find a kindred spirit.

'No. But I think I know what it means that you want to find it. Could probably tell you how. But I don't think you want to, not really.'

'You can't tell me what I want.' Cari bristled.

'You're right, I can't.' He eyed her, as though assessing. 'But I can tell you that so far, it doesn't look like this place has really noticed you. You keep pushing, though ... Maybe that changes. Trust me, you don't want that.'

Cari tried to digest his words, to understand what he was saying. Finally, she nodded.

'I accept that.' She considered her words carefully, sensing their importance. 'But I need to know.'

Damian sighed.

'OK.'

Follow the music. That's what he'd said when she'd told him everything she knew. The spaces in this place aren't only travelled by your feet. There are directions you cannot find on a compass. Listen in the dark and follow the music.

So Cari sat in the dark, ears straining. She'd lost track of time, but it had been night for a long time now. *A Whitechapel History* lay forgotten on the floor. Her laptop sat uncharged on her desk. The article wasn't important, not now. She could find another way to make her name. This was something else. A burning need to find the heart of this place, to push her way through a fog of history to the pure essence of greed and dispassionate cruelty; a world where people are allowed to suffer out of sight simply because it is *easier*. She'd seen glimpses of it since she was a child. Could she be better or was it her fate too? Perhaps tonight she would find out.

She sighed, opening her eyes, though the room was pitch black. Nothing. It had been almost a half-hour and she felt like an idiot. She stretched her aching legs and stood up, turning towards where the light switch should have been.

Wait. There. A note, so distant it might have drifted in from another building entirely. And there, another. The softest tone of a far-off cello. Cari stood, closed her eyes, and began to walk towards it. One step, then another. She knew she should have been standing in front of the wall, and when she took the third step she half expected to slam face first into plasterboard, but there was nothing there. Each motion felt longer than the last as she drifted effortlessly through the places hidden in the corners of Banyan Court, the unseen corridors and crumbled stairways, into the bare brick corridors of Westerland House.

She knew the door as soon as she opened her eyes, though she'd never seen it before. On the surface it looked unremarkable, no gold inlay or intricate designs, but there was an air of quality to it. The wood was solid oak, expertly aligned. The rivets and hinges were perfectly formed cast iron that had been well oiled and cared for. The lock was solid and intimidating. Whoever had installed this door had spent an awful lot of money making it secure.

But it was not locked. Not for her. Somehow, she wasn't surprised.

The music that had drawn Cari through the building swelled to a crescendo as it swung open. The strings sang in a swoon above the rumbling of the bass, laced with the delicate piping of woodwind, all flowing together in perfect three-four time. Warm light embraced her, as hundreds of gas lamps reflected off the gleaming golden walls.

She looked at her feet, now adorned in soft satin ballet shoes, like her mother used to wear. Like her father had picked out for her. For the first time in a long time, they felt right on her feet, urging her to twist into *en pointe*.

There was no orchestra, of course. No one had set foot in this place for over a hundred years. Maybe no one had ever set foot here at all. Cari was alone as the door closed gently behind her. It was so bright, and the polished marble of the floor echoed as she walked, despite the softness of her shoes, her footsteps mixing with the subtle harmonies of the waltz, falling naturally into perfect time.

Everything was covered with twinkling jewels. Diamonds, rubies and emeralds set into every light fitting, every wall panel, arranged in intricate lines across the dancefloor. And from each breath-taking gemstone leaked a steady stream of blood.

It flowed slowly down the walls. Across the floor. Filling up the lamps until one by one their lights were extinguished. Cari felt the slickness of it on her own hands, long before the gentle flood reached her expensive shoes, soaking into the satin, urging her to dance.

The music continued, faster now, as if in disdain of what was happening. It pulsed through Cari, pulling at every string within her, enticing her, demanding that she begin her routine, that she take her place in the blood-soaked choreography. Staying still took more effort than she had ever imagined possible, but she did it, taking in the suffering and pain that laced every penny of the riches that had built this place. A place that had never existed. A place she fit perfectly.

The music begged for her to dance, but Caroline Fairley shook her head and gently pushed herself backwards, allowing herself to collapse. She hit the rising tide without a sound and felt the weight of history wash over her, as she let herself drown.

Damian was waiting for Cari on her return. He didn't need to ask her what had happened. What she had found. Something had changed in his face, something had happened to him too. He didn't tell her what and she didn't ask, but he held his camera tighter than before, and wouldn't put it down.

'No need to cry,' he told her, offering his hand to steady her. Cari gently refused.

'Yes,' she said. 'There is.'

'Your invitation came,' he said wearily, handing her a thick piece of cardstock. 'While you were out.'

Cari knew she should have felt some surprise, should have been confused. But, somehow, she already knew exactly what it said. She was going to a party.

'Are you coming, Damian?'

'I am,' he replied, his eyes slightly nervous at the question. 'I still need to figure out a few things, though. It's going to be a big night. How are you feeling? Did it ... are you still you?'

Cari shrugged as she moved over to the sofa.

'Are any of us?'

Her legs were still weak from what she had seen. She would sit and wait and dream of her outfit for Tobias Fell's party.

Maybe she would let David know. He wasn't invited, but he should probably know. She smiled, dimly aware of Damian studying her. What should she wear? That was the question. The dress didn't matter, of course. What mattered was that she would wear jewels.

8th

Viewing Essential

Laura Lockwood
Formerly of 52 Henley Street

Laura couldn't stand the old man's flat. Even before he'd died it had been a never-ending headache for her. But now that it was unoccupied it felt like some tasteless joke being played on her from beyond the grave whenever she tried to rent it out.

'And in here we can see the bathroom. Fully fitted with a well-sized claw foot tub and an attractive tile finish.'

A bathtub still bearing the scars of the old man's assisted bathing chair and tiles still pock-marked with holes from the handrails he'd had installed. Laura had often suggested the landlords remodel, to exorcise these last lingering remnants of the previous tenant's existence, but they had always refused, leaving it to Laura and her agency to try and let the place in its current state.

'How's the water pressure?'

The potential tenants were a young professional couple, dressed in outfits that would almost seem shabby if you didn't know the designers who made them. When they'd first showed up Laura had made a silent guess that the man had a parent who owned the media company he worked for and the woman was climbing the ranks of a successful PR firm.

'It's just about perfect.' She smiled, picking up the shower head and turning the tap to send out a powerful cascade of water. 'Exactly what you need after a hard day at the office ...'

Whatever they did for a living (if they did anything), they weren't saying. Luckily, they also weren't saying anything about the various damage the old man's mobility aids had done to the flat. Objectively, it wasn't a lot. A hole here, a line of removed plaster there, the odd scrape mark on the bamboo wooden floors. The trouble was that this was 21 Banyan Court, and the sort of people who looked at a flat like this wanted perfection.

'Can we see the bedroom?' the young man asked, giving his partner a wink he clearly thought Laura wouldn't notice.

Laura did, of course, but she also had high hopes for these two. Not only hadn't they made a peep about any of the little imperfections that had scuppered her previous viewings, they hadn't had what she was starting to think of as the 'Number 21 freakout'. She might finally be able to shift this real estate albatross.

The bedroom at least was tastefully appointed, with wide floor-to-ceiling windows looking out towards the centre of London. She carefully avoided drawing attention to the view as she was well aware that on a day like this the grey miasma of fumes formed a clearly visible aura around the skyscrapers of the Square Mile. While she was perfectly used to the sight, she knew from experience it could easily turn the stomach of potential tenants imagining a view of London would be a little less guilt-inducing.

She need not have worried though, her prospective clients made a beeline straight for the queen-sized bed and lay down, testing the mattress.

'Yeah, I can see us in this.' The young man gave his partner another wink and she swatted his arm playfully.

Laura ignored the feeling of unease she always got in the bedroom. She'd all but begged the landlords to change out the bed after the old man died. But decent beds are expensive, and apparently the luxury mattress cost more than she made in a year. Not more than letting a flat like this go empty, of course. It was the sort of false economy that really got under Laura's skin.

The couple were lying quietly now, their eyes closed in mock-sleep. The room was still and Laura became slightly too aware of her own breathing.

Seconds turned into a minute.

'So,' she said, 'are we—'

The couple sat up simultaneously, as though they'd had some sort of electric shot. The man let out a noise that almost sounded like a sob, while the woman just stared, silently.

Laura didn't even bother to ask them what was going on. She knew exactly what was happening. She sighed as they grabbed their bags and all but ran to the door, slamming it behind them, leaving Laura alone in the silent flat.

The flat she was apparently cursed to show forever.

The keyboard seemed very loud as Laura typed up the notes from her viewing. The offices of Dean Bishops were always quiet at this time of year. It was still busy, of course, but the summer heat meant everyone tried to spend as much time as possible out at viewings, doing open houses, enjoying the weather. Admin was for the colder months. It didn't help that the air conditioner was in poor repair and several of the office windows didn't open. There was a joke to be made about the poor quality of the estate agents' building, but Laura had heard it too many times to laugh.

When she reached the end of her notes, she tried to decide

how best to phrase what had happened this time. Why these potential tenants had taken off so abruptly. She could have written 'Haunted by an old bastard', but she wasn't sure anyone else would appreciate the joke. She didn't believe in ghosts, naturally, the whole idea was ridiculous, though Laura had started to suspect that perhaps *she* was haunted. The mental and emotional baggage she had around that flat was leaking out somehow, in her words or mannerisms, and scaring people off. It was a reasonable explanation, though not one that had allowed her to offload the flat on to someone else.

She left the notes unfinished and headed over to the silent staff kitchen. Laura had never cared for the old man, even when he was alive. Before the difficulties, he'd always had that over-familiar tone, even when talking on the phone, and she'd quickly taken against him. Mr Robert Audley. A forgettable name for what should have been a forgettable tenant. The most notable thing about him had been his partner, Sir Arthur Charles, a former army general and legitimate knight of the realm. Exactly why he'd rented out an extremely expensive flat for Mr Audley without living there himself, well, that wasn't her business, but when the old man's health began to fail it was Sir Arthur who paid for the changes to make the apartment liveable for him. And then the treatments and machines and live-in carers that kept the old man alive. It was a special sort of tragedy that Sir Arthur died first.

Whatever the specific reasons, probably lack of legal recognition or a vindictive family, the old man saw exactly none of Sir Arthur's money after the stroke took him. And without any real income beyond a meagre pension, Mr Audley had no hope of keeping the flat. But neither could he really move out, as everything he needed to live was trapped in there with him and he had nowhere else to go. So, once the rent payments stopped it had become Laura's grim responsibility to have him evicted.

She still remembered the calls. The wheezing, laboured breaths; the desperation in his voice as he pleaded with her. Again and again he had called, endlessly, though neither of their situations ever changed. Laura had always prided herself on remaining detached in such situations, but that was too much. At first, she had pitied him, but by the end she'd despised him. This sad old man throwing himself on the mercy of someone with no power to grant it. To place the responsibility on her when she had no part in putting him in that position. It simply wasn't fair.

He'd died about a week before the bailiffs were called in. Natural causes, the inquest said, so at least there was that. At the time it had been a relief, but now here she was. Almost as trapped by 21 Banyan Court as he'd been by the end.

She returned to her desk with a green tea and resumed typing. She disliked that whole building, really. She considered each side with equanimity, disdaining both. The oblivious rich in the front half were never-ending in their demands and impossible to get hold of on anything other than their terms, while those on the poorer side were a constant stream of damages, deposit drama, defaults and evictions.

Laura wasn't sure which side wasted more of her time. But Dean Bishops dealt with so much of the property there that they all sometimes joked that Tobias Fell was her real boss. It wasn't even that much of a lie; he paid a lot of money to the firm to make sure that the properties in his building were dealt with quickly, professionally and discreetly.

She finished off – stating a difference in expectations – and started on her next task, opening a fresh email.

This notice is given under Section 21 (4) (a) of the Housing Act 1988.

She didn't like typing out the words, so copied them from a previous eviction notice. She sighed and checked the calendar. Five days until they had to send in the bailiffs. One of the few parts of her job she genuinely hated. Laura had never met a bailiff who hadn't been a thoroughly unpleasant person, which kind of made sense. Their profession was, to one degree or another, to destroy people's lives, and to be skilled at the job meant hardening themselves against the sight of the pain and misery they caused. If you didn't go into the job a nasty piece of work, it seemed perfectly crafted to make you one.

But they were a necessary evil, and Laura's distaste didn't change that she had to compose an email arranging for them to make a visit.

Her computer fan whirred below her desk in rhythmic bursts, like the rasping hiss of a respirator. Laura sipped her tea and thought about flat 21.

'Hello, Dean Bishops estate agents, Laura speaking,' the phrase rolled off her tongue lightly, disguising how irritated she was at having her work interrupted. She had just got used to the silence, and the bleating of the phone was deeply unwelcome.

'Hi,' the voice was quiet, but determined. 'I'm calling from Banyan Court.'

Just what she needed. What was it going to be? Plumbing issue? Wiring problems? Broken boiler? Place your bets. At this point she'd heard them all.

'And what can I do for you today, sir?' she said pleasantly.

'I'm after some blueprints.'

'I'm afraid we don't keep building blueprints in our files, sir. You might want to try Tower Hamlets' local authority.'

'Yeah, I just ... I need to see them.' He sounded exasperated.

'I'm sorry,' she lied.

'How about floorplans? For the flats?'

Laura paused. Something in the back of her mind told her she wasn't supposed to. Maybe something from Mr Fell? A request that building plans not be shared?

'If you're renting your flat through us, we can certainly send you your floorplan, sir. But I'm afraid we can't provide them for other properties.'

That sounded good. Convincing. It made sense, actually. Maybe it was already official policy and Laura had just forgotten.

'No. I know about my flat. I need to see what the measurements are supposed to be elsewhere.'

Just an oddball then. 'Well, I'm sorry I couldn't be more help.'

'It's just ... It's wrong, you know?'

'I'm sorry you feel that way.' Laura was keen to finish this conversation quickly. 'But I'm afraid it's official policy.'

'No, I mean, the building is wrong.'

Laura froze. There was something in his voice, a certainty, that made her hand clench around the phone. Because she understood what he meant. The small sensation she had spent almost two years dismissing as it wrapped around her spine, all condensed into a single sentence.

'W-what do you mean?' she asked, her crafted phone voice slipping just a fraction.

'I've been taking measurements. I've got notes here, they—'

'I'm sorry I couldn't be more help, sir,' Laura repeated, firm this time, as she willed the unease away.

'Well,' he said, taking her meaning. 'Thanks for your time,'

He hung up. Laura sat there quietly. Her mind wanted to dwell on the conversation, to pick it apart and dissect it for meaning. Instead, she pushed the impulse away and returned to typing up mortgage details.

Hsssk.

'Hello?' Laura's voice was clipped, trying to find a level between professional and impatient.

Hsssk.

The sound came down the phone line again. Hissing, mechanical.

'I think you've got a bad connection,' she said for the third time. It was the end of the day and she'd just about had enough of unsettling calls. 'Hang up and try again. Maybe somewhere with better reception.'

Hsssk.

'Right. I'm hanging up now.'

Hsssk.

Laura placed the phone down and turned to return to her work. She hadn't even got three words into her email before it rang again. She allowed herself a brief moment of anger before snatching it up.

'Hello, Dean Bishops,' she said tightly. 'How can I help you?'

'Yes.' The voice had a soft accent that Laura couldn't place. 'There is a problem with one of your properties. It is in Banyan Court.'

The doors to Banyan Court always seemed freshly cleaned, at least, the ones at the front. Laura was meticulously turned out as she strode through them, as she always was when the stress started to get to her. When people insisted on *wasting her time*. She went straight to the front desk and groaned inwardly as the smiling, round-faced man ambled out of the back office. His name tag read 'Jason'.

'Alright, Miss Estates?' He grinned, rolling out the same not-quite-a-joke he used every time she came by.

Why couldn't it have been Kirsty? If Laura had to rank the three concierges who worked at Banyan Court, Kirsty was easily the top. She was easy-going, witty and professional. Jason not so much. As if it wasn't enough that the old man's flat was refusing to rest quietly.

'I need the key to 21,' Laura said, trying to keep the conversation as short as possible.

'Oh yeah?' Jason stood up and went to retrieve it, glancing over his shoulder. 'Didn't you show people around like two days ago?'

'It's not a viewing.' And this wasn't a conversation.

He snapped his fingers like a cartoon character remembering a birthday. 'The banging.'

'Yes.' Laura was in no mood. First the dud viewing, then the weird phone calls, now this. She was adept at compartmentalising, putting it all out of her mind, but she couldn't deny it was starting to get to her. Still, she kept her face calm.

'I mean, we checked it.'

'And apparently that didn't stop it, so they phoned me. And given how loud it is, I have to make sure it isn't something that's causing any damage.'

'I wasn't the one who went,' Jason said, holding his hands up in defence. 'I sent Max, but he didn't see anything or anyone in there.'

'Just give me the keys.'

'Sure thing.' He tossed them over the front desk. 'You want me to come up with you? After all, it's number 21, right, where the old dude died? Preeetty spooky!'

Laura looked at him coldly. Obviously, it wasn't actually a ghost, but she really should get him to come up with her.

The owner of number 20 had been quite colourful when he'd described the sounds that were coming from the neighbouring apartment, and if someone had broken in then going up with someone – even Jason – wasn't a bad idea. But she wasn't going to be afraid of a dead man's flat. She couldn't be.

'No,' she said firmly. 'I'll be fine.'

'OK, well, if you don't phone down in five minutes, I'll come check on you.'

Laura didn't reply, walking past him over to the lifts. No doubt it was something that had broken because the landlords refused to do proper maintenance. Burst pipe, maybe, or something collapsing. Laura just wanted it sorted. So far that week she had barely managed to go a full day without thinking about 21 Banyan Court. Normally she got at least a month or so of peace between viewings, but apparently this week it had decided it needed all of her attention.

The lift opened on a clean, well-lit corridor. The aroma told of a recent visit by the cleaning staff, and she took quick stock of herself, making sure her dress and blazer hadn't been creased or dirtied by the tube ride over. These were the sort of people you needed to look your best for.

She walked quickly and purposefully towards number 21. As she approached, a short woman in a tailored dress emerged from the door opposite and scowled at her. Number 20's iron-grey hair was pulled back above a pale, angular face that looked like it knew how much you were worth by smell alone.

'You are here for the issue next door.' In person, the woman's accent sounded Scandinavian. Swedish, maybe?

'Yes. Laura Lockwood, from Dean Bishops.' She didn't offer her hand, not wanting to seem presumptive.

'The man on the front desk said no one was there. But he is

a fool. You want to check. It was very noisy. And I saw nobody leave.'

'Of course, thank you.'

'There was the sound of banging,' the woman continued. 'Something fell over, I think. Running water. At one point shouting. Or crying, perhaps. Hard to say.'

'Right, well, thank you very much. I really appreciate—'

'Tell that oaf at the desk to be more careful,' the old woman snapped. 'Not let anyone here that shouldn't be here. I think they're coming in from the back of the building. You should be more careful as well.'

'I ... I see. I will.'

The woman nodded and shut the door.

Laura pulled out the key to number 21.

The flat was silent, as it should be. The bright rays of sunlight beamed through the windows, out through the bedroom door, splitting the gloom of the entry hall in two. Laura paused, getting her bearings as her eyes tried to adjust to the contrast between light and darkness.

'Hello?' she called out, tentatively.

Her voice seemed to vanish almost as soon as it passed her lips. She waited, but there was no response. No sound of movement from deeper inside the flat. She was alone.

Confident she wasn't about to immediately get jumped, Laura moved into the hallway and started turning on the lights.

'Nothing out of place.' She found herself talking out loud as she moved through the flat.

'Tables as they were before.'

Who was she talking to?

'Sofa ... no sign of use.'

She didn't talk to herself. But it was better than the quiet.

'Bathtub dry. No sign of flooding or water damage.'

This was ridiculous. But being silent felt like inviting something else to break it.

'No new scuff marks or scratches. Windows securely locked.'

Laura breathed out, that last point was attested to by the prickly heat that filled the apartment. The air conditioning hadn't been turned on since her last viewing and the tall windows had turned the place into a tastefully laid-out oven.

She sat on the sofa, pulling a sports bottle from her bag and taking a swig of the lukewarm water. She considered refilling it, but the heat pressed into her, sapping her will to stand up again. A bead of sweat rolled down her hand as she took another sip. The droplet hung for a second at the base of her palm then fell with an almost inaudible *tch* onto a sheet of white paper.

It took her a second to refocus. Poking out from below the sofa was what looked like a headed letter. She picked it up. It was cold, which might have felt refreshing if it hadn't unsettled her so much. It looked like a page from some sort of legal agreement. Two columns of small, dense text. The names had been scratched out with a ballpoint pen, but it seemed to be a life insurance agreement. The company was listed as United Continental and at the bottom, stamped in red ink, was the word REJECTED.

Laura had been giving viewings of this flat for months now, showed it to dozens of potential renters. Cleaning crews had been in and out at least five times. She'd personally examined every inch of it. This piece of paper had not been here before. Her thumb brushed over the rejection stamp and came away red with fresh ink. She shoved the thing into her bag.

'No sign of damage or intrusion,' she resumed out loud, trying to reassure herself. 'No one's been here.'

A sound cut through the silent rooms and Laura spun around, panic stabbing through her. A raspy, mechanical noise that hissed out for a second, two seconds, then stopped. A pause, then it came again, the wheezing breath of a machine. She looked towards the closed door of the bedroom, from behind which the sound came again in rhythmic, steady bursts. Laura had never actually heard a ventilator in real life, but she'd always imagined it might sound exactly like this.

Her legs were numb as she stood and walked unsteadily towards the bedroom. She needed to leave. It was like the woman next door had said, someone had broken in. They were playing a horrible joke. The other explanation was literally impossible. Unless it was in her head. In many ways that was the scariest possibility, but at least she could accept it. There were treatments for that sort of thing. She had to know, but still she couldn't quite bring herself to reach out and take the handle of the bedroom door. She wanted to. She needed to. To know what was haunting her. A cruel tormentor, her own mind, or ...

She gripped the handle.

'You shouldn't be here,' she found herself saying. 'Mr Fell wouldn't like it.'

BANG.

It came from behind her. She whipped around in time to see the front door shaking on its hinges from the impact.

Bang bang.

A bolt of adrenaline and her instincts kicked in. She tried to run, but in her panic lost her footing on the waxed bamboo floor. Her legs went from under her as the front door opened, and she looked over to see a figure looming there.

'Everything alright, Miss Lockwood?' Jason's voice called out. And flat 21 was quiet again.

*

Laura's hands shook ever so slightly as she sipped her coffee. The office wasn't quite as silent as it had been before, but the gentle typing and distant phone-murmur of Kristen and Hadi didn't do much to reassure her. They were colleagues, but not really friends, and the idea of confiding her worries in them made Laura feel faintly sick. She'd been trying to put what she'd seen and heard behind her. It had been two days now, but the experience still pushed its way into her mind whenever she found herself alone with her thoughts. She didn't believe in ghosts. Never had. Never would. But she didn't want to be mad, either, and that was what madness meant to her: hearing things, seeing phantoms, the gradual erosion of your ability to trust your senses. But what was the third option? There'd been no one in that flat, they'd checked every corner.

It didn't help that her work seemed determined to keep it fresh in her mind. She'd already had another wannabe architect looking for blueprints and ranting about her own encounters, the Fairley kid this time, asking Laura *what she had seen*. Nothing! Laura had seen nothing. And that's how it was going to stay.

That and the fact that she'd finally had to pull the trigger on sending out those bailiffs. She desperately wanted to call in sick, just to take a few days off, but there was so much that needed doing. Not that she was actually getting anything done with her nerves shredded like this.

She jumped as the phone rang, a small spike of fear paralysing her, leaving her staring at it mutely. She heard Hadi pick it up on his line, answering in his gentle cockney lilt. Laura leaned back in her seat and took another sip of coffee. It was cold.

'Laura!' Hadi called from the other end of the office, his voice light and jovial. 'One of yours! Banyan Court, so don't upset the boss.'

She closed her eyes and swore silently to herself before giving

206

her extension number to him. At this point Laura couldn't care less what Tobias Fell thought. It wasn't like she'd ever met the man. A few seconds passed, then her phone was ringing again. Just for her. She set her jaw and picked it up.

'Hello, Laura speaking.' She sounded so pleasant and helpful it hardly felt like her.

'Yeah, yes. Hello.' The voice on the other end was deep, but strangely rushed, like they were expecting to be cut off at any moment. 'I'm calling from 15 Banyan Court. You're the one who looks after us, right?'

'More or less,' Laura said. 'We're hired by your landlord to look after your property and act as a go-between when necessary. What seems to be the problem?'

'There's a stain. On the wall of my study.'

So, either accidental damage or plumbing. Could be an easy fix, something to get her head back in gear. Or it could be a colossal headache.

'OK, what sort of stain?'

'Grey,' he replied. 'The stain is grey.'

Laura finished typing the address into the database and the tenant details popped up. Leon Copeland. Number 15. Age 38. Last credit check scored 821. Looked like a model tenant.

'Sorry, I mean what substance caused the stain? Or is it coming from within the wall?'

'That second one. It's in the wall.'

'It might be a plumbing problem, then. Does it seem like water?'

'No. No, it's not water.'

'Possibly a sewage pipe, then. I do apologise, Mr Copeland, I'll have—'

'It's not the plumbing. There's no pipes in there. We had

someone check. And it's not sewage. It's grey. And it won't go away.'

'I know it can be upsetting when this sort of thing happens.' She was losing control of the conversation. 'But it's probably best to wait for a qualified profession—'

'It won't go away!' There was panic in the man's voice now. 'I've cleaned it and cleaned it and it keeps coming back bigger. There's no pipe, there's nothing, it's just a wall and it won't be clean!'

'OK, Mr Copeland, I, uh ...' She was floundering, her whole body starting to shake. 'I'm going to—'

'What's on the other side?'

'The other side?'

'Of the wall! What's on the other side of the wall?'

'I, uh ...' She pulled up the floorplan. Which room was the study? 'I think that wall would be between you and another flat. Number 71. In the back of the building.'

'Is it their fault?'

'I don't ... What?'

The line went dead. Leon had apparently hung up.

Laura felt sick. She stood up, needing some fresh air, and feeling strangely grimy at just having to hear the desperation in the man's voice.

The phone rang again. She sat heavily back down and picked it up.

'Mr Copeland?' she asked.

'Is that Dean Bishops estate agents?'

It wasn't Leon. The tone was clipped and official, not used to having its time wasted.

'Uh, yes, Laura Lockwood speaking.'

'Do you have a tenant named Edith Kinney?'

The flat smelled horrendous. Laura had been so used to the smell of number 21, the antiseptic of professional cleaners and the balmy summer humidity, that she'd almost expected that when she came to check Edith's former home. But no, this place had seen a human life wither away in cramped isolation and that fact clung to every surface, in every fibre of the moth-eaten carpet.

Edith Kinney. Laura hadn't even known her name. She'd been quiet, always paid on time, never raised any problems. Hadn't been any bother at all. But now Laura did know of her she couldn't stop herself hating the woman. She had to choose to die here? She had to choose now? Laura didn't have the emotional reserves left to feel sadness for this lonely old woman, no capacity for grief. All that was left was the burning resentment that Edith had decided to go and die in one of the properties that Laura managed and give her another haunted fucking flat.

Laura stopped. She couldn't think like that. Number 21 was hard enough to deal with, she couldn't afford to be taking on new paranoias. She'd seen what she needed to see. She'd taken an inventory and made an assessment: There was no structural damage, a few cigarette burns on the carpet, but that was going to need replacing anyway. And it was going to require an extremely deep clean before it could go back on the market. What was the name of that cleaning service Hadi used for the Wicker Street murder house last year?

The police had been less considerate in their questioning than when the old man had died. They were keen to find out if Dean Bishops had details on other tenants who lived there, or whether Mrs Kinney might have been subletting to someone else. When the answers turned out to be no and no, they had got irritated and borderline aggressive. Laura had briefly wondered why, but she was too shaken to consider the mystery for long.

She stood in the living room, staring at the stained and discoloured armchair where Edith Kinney had died.

'I'm sorry it's not my job to care,' she said.

Nobody answered.

'See you tomorrow, Lockwood!' Hadi called, waving as he hoisted his bag and headed towards the exit.

Laura made a non-committal throat noise, barely registering his absence.

The office was silent again. It was late, far past the time anyone was expected to be working there. She knew she should go home. Get some sleep in her own house.

Soon the faint glow of the monitor illuminating her face was the only light in the room. The fluorescents in the ceiling were motion activated, but they'd turned off after about ten minutes. Laura wasn't even sure what meaningless paperwork she was supposed to be filling out at the moment, her fingers barely moving over the keyboard.

A small ping alerted her to a new email. Mechanically, she moved to click the notification. It was the bailiffs again, confirming a team had been sent out to handle the eviction. Laura could imagine them, rolling steadily towards their destination in their painted van, faces hard, dressed in black vests that invoked the authoritarian air of legally deployed violence. She felt sick, like it was her that they were coming for.

'It's my job,' she told the empty office.

Her eyes passed once again over the email. Who was it they were coming for this time? Which poor soul was being thrown out of their home tonight? She located the address and froze. She stared at it, tried to convince herself it was her eyes playing tricks, but the words stayed the same.

They were going to 21 Banyan Court.

Why hadn't she noticed that before? She scrolled through the previous messages. Sure enough, they had all been about the old man's flat. The one that had been empty for months. But it couldn't be – she'd overseen all the legal procedures herself, there weren't any outstanding issues that could possibly have got the bailiffs involved. So, what was going on?

It was a trap.

The thought just popped into her head. It was breathtakingly absurd, but she just couldn't shift it. A trap for who? The bailiffs? By what, an old man's vengeful spirit?

Or the building itself.

She was fully alert now, mind racing, and the lights overhead sputtered to life as she reached for the phone and dialled the service number at the bottom of the email. She waited as it rang. And rang. And rang. And went to voicemail.

'Thank you for calling Cooperston Commercial Services. Our office hours are—'

Laura slammed the phone down. She was worrying over nothing. She'd email them to say it was a mistake. At worst, they'd arrive, have a confused Kirsty let them into the flat, see that there was hardly anything there and leave. If they took the furniture, she could follow up with them tomorrow. It's not like anyone was about to move in. This was nothing to worry about. Worst case scenario she'd get a talking-to about giving them the wrong information.

But a deep sense of dread sat in her stomach like a rock. Nothing about this was normal. She had to warn them.

The streets seemed quiet as she walked from Whitechapel station. A few figures wandered slowly along the pavements, but they seemed lost in their own world, their faces never lit enough to see clearly. There was no traffic, and the steady background roar of London seemed a long way off.

When there'd been no response to her emails, she'd decided to try to head the bailiffs off. Their van was in the parking bay of Banyan Court, cutting across two spaces. Laura hurried towards it, tapping on the tinted glass of a passenger window. There was no response and pressing her face close she saw that it was empty. A night breeze picked up, whistling as it came around the side of the towering building, the sound not entirely unlike a scream. She braced herself against it and headed to the entrance.

'Hello?' she called as the front doors slid open. 'Kirsty? ... Jason?'

There was no answer. The front desk was empty. She stepped around the side, staring into the small room behind it. Nobody was there. The small chair lay on its side and the phone looked broken. Had there been a fight here?

She steadied her breathing and headed for the lift. It took almost a minute to arrive, and when the doors opened an awful smell rolled out of it. Two grey shoeprints stained the carpeted floor, the only possible source of the odour. Laura hit the button for the fifth floor, keeping her breaths as shallow as possible. The lift rumbled and began to rise.

The door to the old man's flat was open. Not wide, but just ajar enough for it to be a clear invitation. Laura looked down the corridor; no sign of anyone else. No bailiffs, no concierge, and no one to tell her if what she was seeing was real. It wasn't too late to run, she told herself, but the sound of the lift doors closing behind her rang with such finality that she knew it wasn't true.

Telling herself the bailiffs were just inside, that they were perfectly fine, she stepped over the threshold into the darkness of number 21.

'Is ... Is anybody there?' Her voice was so quiet. She didn't want to be heard.

The door swung closed behind her, the latch sliding into place with the softest of clicks, and Laura realised that it had been a trap, after all.

All the doors in the hallway of the flat were closed, and none of the city's nocturnal glow filtered through to break the thick darkness. She fumbled for the light switch, desperately flicking it back and forth, but if the bulbs were still there, they didn't respond. She stepped forward, feeling her way along the sideboard she knew so well, her fingers lingering over the gouges where grab bars once sat.

Almost on cue, she heard it. The sound Laura had been waiting for since she arrived. The slow and steady hiss of a respirator. From behind the bedroom door it came, pulsing with the relentless regularity of a pendulum. This time, she knew, nobody was going to be knocking on the door. No one was coming to get her.

'Just go,' she whispered. 'Turn around and leave.'

Maybe, if she tried, really tried, she could choose not to open that door. Not to see what was on the other side. To run, to escape, to flee back to her own front door, to her own house in ...

Laura stopped. Where did she live? She suddenly didn't feel sure. She slept alone, she knew that, ate alone, and if she tried, she could almost picture where. But could she? Was it her home she was remembering, or the thousands of real estate photographs she had taken, superimposed over her life? She must have somewhere to live, to exist. A flat of her own, or even a house. But it was gone. Taken from her. She stared at her keys, glinting faintly in the gloom, and recognised none of them.

Defeated, she grabbed the handle of the bedroom door and turned it.

The room beyond was brighter, though not by much. The curtains were open and the lights of the street below cast everything in the room in dim outline. In the bed lay a shape, completely covered by a sheet that smelled of antiseptic. The hissing continued, rhythmic, as the form beneath the covers rose and fell with each pump. Laura didn't need to see a face to know who was below that sheet.

'I—I'm sorry,' she said.

Hsssssk.

'I was just trying to do my job.'

Hsssssk.

'Did ... Did I kill you?'

Hsssssk.

'No. No, I guess ...'

Hsssssk.

'I guess we all did.'

Hsssssk.

Laura paused. The guilt rolled over her, breaking out from where she had hidden it.

Hsssssk.

'What do you want?' She tried to make her voice demanding, confident. She failed.

Hsssssk.

'What can I do?'

There was a shift. A stirring on the edge of the sheet. Then an arm appeared, falling limply over the edge of the bed. It was thin, wizened, with paper-thin skin stretched over blackened veins. In its hand it held something. A small rectangle of cream-coloured card.

Laura slowly walked over and gingerly pulled it from the

cold, stiff fingers. The sound of the ventilator stopped, and the flat was silent, as it always had been.

She looked at the message in her shaking hands. It was an invitation to a dinner, in her boss's home.

'OK,' she said, understanding. 'OK.'

Nobody answered.

9th

A Stubborn Stain

Leon Copeland
15 Banyan Court

'What are you talking about?'

'You don't see it?'

Leon Copeland ran his fingers over the magnolia wall of his study, trying to make out the edges of the shape Andrea was pointing at.

'Not really,' he said. 'Sorry.'

'From here, all the way round here. It's darker. Like there's some kind sort of grey underneath.'

'I ... guess?'

'Hm, weird.' She shrugged. 'It's really obvious from here.'

'Honestly, I don't really see it.'

'Maybe it's just me,' Andrea sighed. 'I guess spending so much time here on my own, it ... I guess you just start obsessing over things. Noticing imperfections.'

'I know, and I'm sorry.' Leon put a hand on her shoulder. She leaned into it. 'On the plus side I should be working from home for a while. We can spend some more time together.'

'That would be nice.'

'I've been thinking about repainting in here anyway. I could just go over the wall.'

'Are we actually allowed to paint the walls?'

Leon paused, as though unsure.

'You know,' Andrea teased him, 'if we'd bought that little place in Harrow we could have done whatever. Could've painted the light bulbs if we'd wanted to.'

'Andi, please don't start.' Leon's face shifted in discomfort. He dropped the hand, leaving her shoulder cold.

'Alright.' Andrea pulled a cigarette from the packet in her cardigan. 'It was just a joke.'

'I know, I know. It's just … you know how important appearances are to these people. You've got to *look* successful.'

Andrea felt a bit bad; she knew how stressed Leon was about the new position and revisiting old arguments wouldn't help any. She tried to hold her tongue and not start it again.

'And owning a house isn't success?' she said, failing.

'Come on, Andi. You think the board's going to respect a semi-detached at the end of the Metropolitan line?'

'Well, that's their problem.' Andrea wandered over to the wall, tracing the edges of the dark stain.

'Sure, but they're the reason we can afford to have the choice. And the reason you can afford to spend all your time making fancy soaps.'

'*Boutique toiletries*, thank you very much,' Andi shot back with the practised smile she used whenever talk turned to the finances of her business. 'And it would be easier if I had more space, expand a little.'

'I promise, a year or two here, then I'll be earning enough that we can buy somewhere actually nice. And who knows, maybe this is the year your soaps explode.' Leon grinned. 'Figuratively speaking.'

'OK, OK,' she conceded. 'I guess we're here now. And I don't think it's unreasonable to expect the study wall to not be all messed up.'

'It's just going to be me in here most of the time. And I can't really see it.'

There was a moment of quiet as they both stared at the patch of magnolia. Then Andrea turned and surprised her husband with a kiss. He laughed, then returned it, the tension broken. 'Fine.' She returned her focus to the unlit cigarette in her hand. 'I'll be on the balcony. Anyway, don't you have work to do?'

'Not much of it yet.'

'They still doing their "reorganisation"?'

'Yeah, once this round of restructuring's done and we've got the new acquisitions sorted then I'll be actually overseeing the operational integration ...' He glanced at her, and she hoped her eyes weren't too glazed.

'Go smoke,' he said, shaking his head with a smile. Andrea couldn't hide her relief.

'Thanks, love you!'

When she dipped her head back inside to ask him about dinner, she caught him standing by the wall, his fingertips brushing against it, as though feeling for the shape of the stain.

'There, that's looking a bit better.'

'If you say so.'

'The colour's pretty much an exact match. I think.'

'Yeah.' Andrea seemed unconvinced. 'Yeah, it's fine, I guess. It's gone.'

Leon stepped back as she touched the newly painted area again, testing its edges. His wife frowned, as though concentrating. She made a very odd picture, prodding a wall in sweaty gym clothes, and he found it hard not to chuckle. Still, he knew the move hadn't been easy on her. Covering up the 'stain' was the least he could do.

'Is there ...' she mused. 'I don't know, the texture is different?'

'Well, I'm not planning to spend my days stroking it, so I reckon that's OK.'

There was a long pause as Andrea considered this.

'Yeah,' she said, making a clear decision to be OK with it. 'You're right. Thank you for this. Anyway, I'm getting a shower. Oh, and I've got a call to some potential buyers later, so it'll be takeout for dinner.'

She gave Leon another kiss on the cheek and headed out of the room.

'Plus,' he mused, 'now I've found the paint I need we can sort it if it ever comes back.'

Andrea turned and gave him a smile. 'If you're happy, I'm happy.'

'Knock knock.'

Leon looked up from his desk to see Angela standing in the doorway, grinning.

'Hi.' He tried to smile back.

'You want some lunch?'

'Going out or staying in?'

'Well, I was thinking of going to that new vegan place, but it looks like you might be a bit preoccupied.'

'Yeah.' Leon looked over the various charts and reports that now littered his desk. 'Probably not going to be able to get away.'

'It's fine, I can bring something back for you. I hear their risotto is good.'

'Thanks.' Leon tried not to sound too dismissive as he stared at a print.

'At least they're keeping you busy.'

'Yeah, well, it's not exactly ...' He swallowed. Why was he so afraid to tell her? It's not like it was his fault. 'News story broke yesterday, apparently we've turned some river in India toxic. I've been trying to get ahead of it, but ... Well, it's not good.'

Andi took a moment to consider.

'I mean, we knew when you took the job. Petrochemicals is ... It can be a bit ...' She paused. 'Hang on, they can't blame *you*, right? You've only just got there.'

'They've got to blame someone. And it's not like Donovan can step down twice.'

'It's not your fault, though. It's not fair.'

Leon shifted uncomfortably. Andi breathed out slowly, trying to get her humour back.

'Hey.' She leaned forward with a smirk. 'Why not have a word with the man upstairs? I'm sure he could make it go away.'

'Or make *me* go away.' Leon shook his head. 'Besides, from what I hear, we might be in the same building, but we're kind of on different planets.'

He leaned back in his chair, stretching.

'It'll be OK.'

'Oh yeah, I know.' He nodded. 'It'll be a share price hit and a grovelling press release, but these things run their course.'

'Unlike that river,' Angela joked darkly.

'Andi!' In spite of himself, Leon laughed.

'I know, I know. It's very serious. I get it. I just hate to see you so down. It's—'

She stopped abruptly, her focus suddenly elsewhere.

'Andi? You good?

'Did Malia come yesterday?' she asked, her voice distant.

'You think I did all that vacuuming myself?'

'No, it's just the wall.'

Leon looked over and stopped. There it was, the stain. Clear as day. Almost a foot and half wide, a sort of greyish patch on the bright paint of the wall. How had he not noticed it before?

'Bloody hell.'

'Oh, so *now* you can see it. Unlike Malia, I guess.'

'I ... Well, it was freshly painted. Besides, does she even do the walls?' Leon was still rattled by its appearance.

'She wiped down the kitchen when you sprayed smoothie everywhere. I'd have thought she'd have at least given it a go.'

Now he'd noticed it as well, Leon was almost surprised at how composed his wife was about it. It was revolting.

'You want me to get her in again?'

'We might need a specialist.'

'I'll talk to her, at least. Worst case scenario I could always do it.' Leon ran his fingers over the wall, trying to find that difference in texture she had mentioned.

'Do you have the time?' Andrea was sceptical.

'I'll make time.'

She shrugged and headed for the kitchen. Leon was still focused on the stain that covered the wall. A sudden pain shot through his leg. He looked down to see his hand pushing against his leg, pressing the tip of his pen into his trousers. He pulled back just before he drew blood, forcing his clenched hand to place the pen back on his desk. He must be more stressed than he thought.

'You know, maybe we should go out,' he called.

'Where'd you get this paint?' Leon called over his shoulder.

There was no response for a few moments, then Andi appeared in the doorway, her stained work apron still damp and her hands smelling of patchouli.

'Sorry, what were you asking?'

'The paint, where did you get it?'

Her head tilted in confusion. 'I thought you got the paint.'

'I did' – he stood up, brush dropping to his side – 'but this isn't the same stuff.'

'Pretty sure it is.'

'No, the paint before was really thick emulsion, this ... I mean, it's so thin. Hardly covers anything at all.'

He pulled the brush across the stain, leaving a streak of magnolia behind, but he might as well have been spreading water for all the good it did.

'Well,' Andi sounded nonplussed. 'I certainly didn't buy more paint. So, unless there's someone breaking into fancy flats and leaving tins of ...'

Leon looked at her and the joke seemed to die on her lips.

'Is everything alright?' she asked, suddenly concerned.

Nausea crept through his stomach and he sat down heavily. Had it been the lunch? Or was the stress getting to him already? He always had digestion trouble if he was stressed. Before his interview for the new executive position he'd ended up trapped in the toilet for almost the whole hour.

'I just want it gone,' he said at last. 'I know how much it's been bothering you.'

His wife walked over, leaning so close to the dirty grey patch that Leon found himself recoiling on her behalf.

'I mean, I don't like it, Leon, obviously, but if you're not feeling well ...'

'I know, I know. I just want you to be comfortable here. In the flat.'

Andrea smiled.

'You're here, so I'm comfortable.' She paused. 'I'm never going to love it, Leon. Stain or no stain.'

'Well I choose no stain,' Leon declared, getting to his feet.

'Mr Copeland?'

'Speaking. What can I do for you?'

'It's, uh, it's Suzi.' The tinny voice blared from the speaker-phone. 'From Invidious. We do your PR?'

'Yeah, I know who you are, Suzi. What do you need?'

'We've been fielding a lot of press calls over the last week about the East Rapti River. We just wanted to make sure you'd got the pack we sent through with the guidance on your proposed response line.'

Leon stopped scrubbing, the foaming sponge still in his hand.

'Oh, yes. That came through.'

He glanced over at his computer, where the email sat un-opened.

'Right, right. Did you have any thoughts?'

'Yeah, sure,' Leon said absently. 'It all looks good?'

He walked over to his desk, trying to figure out a way to open the email without touching the laptop with his dirty hand. His gaze drifted to the small washing-up bucket he'd brought in, but by now the dirt had turned it murky and the thought of the sponge absorbing all of the filth back up made him a bit queasy. Leon stood there, unable to make a decision.

'Did you get that?'

'Uh, no,' Leon said, suddenly aware that he hadn't been listening. 'Could you repeat?'

'Of course,' Suzi said with the infinite patience of one ad-dressing a very important client. 'I was just saying that, given your role was not intended to be PR focused, we're happy to offer whatever guidance or direction we can.'

'Sure thing.'

Suzi said something else, but Leon was thinking about

whether to get a plumber. If it kept reappearing, that meant there must be something inside the wall, right?

'Brilliant. Thanks for your time, Mr Copeland.'

The click of the phone left Leon standing in silence, still contemplating his sponge. He looked from it, to the wall, and back again. The area where the stain had been was much darker now, but that was just because it was wet. Dish soap to begin with. A lot of how-to sites swore by it. He'd need to wait until it dried, of course, before he would know for sure if it was gone or not. And he wanted to go over it a few more times first. Just to be on the safe side.

Leon wiped his hand across his forehead, leaving a small mound of bubbles at his hairline. He looked over to his laptop. He could do it later. First, he had to get a handle on his space. Then he could get a handle on the wider situation.

He returned to his scrubbing.

'What is that smell?' Andrea wrinkled her nose.

'Hm?'

'It reeks in here.'

'Oh, sorry. I thought you liked vinegar?'

'Yeah, on chips. No sure I want my home stinking of it.'

'Sorry,' Leon repeated, shrugging. 'Plumber can't make it for a few days, so wanted to give it a try.'

'Is that ... Is that a thing?'

'You're the soap guru, you didn't know this?'

'I clean premium faces, this all seems a bit more, uh, abrasive than what I work with.'

She nudged a plastic crate with her foot. In it stood an array of brightly coloured spray bottles, each adorned with energetic promises. MAX POWER. MOULD KILLER. NO MORE DIRT.

'Well, to be honest I think the chemical ones just made it worse.'

There was a thick silence between them. For a moment Leon thought she was about to make some joke about the river, one of her attempts to break the tension, but she was quiet.

'You know,' Leon said, his voice thoughtful, 'when I was a kid, my mum had this friend Tori. I think she was technically a second cousin, but they'd known each other most of their lives. When I knew her, Tori had a lot of cats. Don't know much about why, but my mum always seemed angry about the cats somehow, like they shouldn't have been there. I liked them. I mean, of course I did, I was a kid. But there was always this smell in Tori's house. This horrible sharp cloying smell. Didn't know what it was at the time, but I was doing some reading about vinegar, and I reckon I've figured it out. You use vinegar to clean up cat urine. That's what the whole place stank of: cat piss and vinegar. Isn't that wild? Thirty-eight-years-old and still learning new stuff about your childhood?'

He turned to look at Andrea, but she was gone. Just as well. He wasn't sure he wanted to continue the thought anyway. To follow that half-remembered feeling of disgust, of contamination. That lingering oppressive scent and the knowledge that you had no control over your space. No escape from it.

Leon shook his head slightly and poured some more white vinegar onto his cloth. It was fine. Soon the plumber would be here and that would be the end of it. The spreading stain stared back, impassive and patient.

'Hello?'

Leon's greeting was terse, spat out through the gritted teeth of a jaw set in an expression of deep irritation. His eyes didn't waver from the wall.

'Mmhm. Hi, Suzi, what do you need?'

It was back, now almost black against the muted magnolia of the rest of the wall.

'Yeah, I know.'

He had been so certain it was gone, scoured from the wall, but not only had it returned, it seemed even worse than before.

'Sorry, when did we agree to that?'

Leon shifted uncomfortably, trying to cradle the phone against his shoulder while he considered the stain. It wasn't just darker, it seemed ... lumpy somehow.

'I mean, I'm not exactly, what's the word ...? Like photogenic, but for video?'

He looked down, imagining himself being filmed. His suit was stained and discoloured from his cleaning efforts, a lot more so than he'd thought.

'Yeah, exactly. I don't come across great. Hold on.'

He shifted again, laying the phone down on the table and jabbing the speaker button as he collapsed into his chair. Immediately Suzi's voice boomed out. He must have turned the volume up somehow.

'—just a quick interview. Like we said on our last call, you're the senior executive here, so we really need you to be the one to comment on it. We've put together a briefing for you. We strongly suggest taking the position that lax local safety standards were responsible for the accident.'

'Is that true?' Leon said. The thought of standing there, the camera focused on him, as he desperately tried to defend a mistake that wasn't his ... 'I thought the investigation wasn't finalised yet?'

'We're very confident it's the correct position.' Suzi's voice didn't betray a hint of doubt.

'Right.' Leon wasn't sure what else to say. 'I suppose I'll need a new suit.'

'Excuse me?'

'Nothing.' His eyes were already moving towards the bucket of cleaning products. 'Just let me know when it is, I suppose.'

'Will do! Thanks again.'

A click and she was gone. Leon sat heavily in his chair, the scent of bleach already clinging to him, engulfing him. He felt light-headed. He needed some fresh air.

He pulled himself up and started cleaning the wall.

'I don't understand.'

The plumber shrugged, his face impassive.

'It's what I said. No pipe.'

'How? I'm sorry, what did you say your name was? John?'

'Sure.' The plumber shrugged again, his accent grating on Leon.

'How can there be a leak if there isn't a pipe?'

'Right. There isn't.'

'Isn't what? A leak or a pipe?'

'Both. No pipe, no leak.'

'So what the hell is this?' Leon gestured desperately to the huge area of wall now a rotten bluish black.

The stain was spongy and clearly damp, with small bumps all over it which might have been lumps of decaying plaster or might have been mounds of growing mould. He itched all over to scrub them but swallowed the urge down. Leon had just been doing his best to keep it contained until the plumber arrived. Now the plumber was here. He had to fix it.

'Dirt?' the man said at last.

'How is this dirt?!' Leon exploded. 'Look! Look at it! Something is coming through that wall, I know it is. And I need to know where it's coming from. I need to stop it. Tell me what's doing this.'

'Well, not a pipe. We can be sure of that. The rest ... Not my department. Sorry.'

A creeping suspicion surfaced in Leon's mind.

'You can see it, right?'

'I see... Something. I think. Not as clear as you, though, I am sure.'

'Are you serious?' Leon felt like crying, but he set his face firm.

There was silence for some time as the handyman considered his words.

'It is this building, I think.'

'What are you talking about?' Leon asked. He put an edge in his voice, a clear warning. The plumber pursed his lips and changed the subject.

'The other side of the wall. What is it? Do you know? Another flat?'

Leon shook his head.

'Maybe find out. Might help with your stain. But it isn't a leak. No pipes.'

And with that the man picked up his toolkit and excused himself. Leon stood there a moment, thinking. The other side of the wall ... He shook his head.

As soon as the plumber was out of the front door Leon stormed back to the office, using a pencil to push the button on the phone for the front desk. He reached to pick up the handset, but his hand paused, suddenly alarmed it might have been contaminated by the dripping filth on the wall. He pushed the speaker button instead.

'Front desk.' The tone was bored, businesslike.

'Yes, hello, it's—'

'Mr Copeland, good to hear from you. How's Janek doing? Did he get it all sorted for you?'

'No. In fact he was absolutely useless. I need to talk to another plumber.'

'Another ...?' The concierge's voice tried to hide his confusion. 'Mr Copeland, Janek knows the plumbing of this building better than anyone, 'cept maybe the people who built it. What was the problem?'

'He said there wasn't a pipe.'

'Uh, say again?'

'He said there was no pipe, so I need another plumber.'

'Mr Copeland,' the concierge spoke slowly, like his tongue was navigating a minefield, 'if Janek says there isn't a pipe, then I'm not sure any other plumber is going to have better lu—'

Leon swept the phone off the desk, cutting the man's words short. He collapsed into the chair, his heart beating far faster than the conversation should have justified. He sat there in silence, staring at the wall. The whole room smelled, but it was no longer the scouring tang of cleaning products. The thick, earthy stench of rotten damp pervaded the place. He'd showered twice already today, but still it enveloped him. He stared at his hands, chapped and reddened by recent weeks, and strained his eyes, trying to see if any stain had transferred to him. He saw it, sometimes, in the mirror or in darkened windows: his reflection, discoloured and caked in mould, the creeping damp burrowing its tendrils into him and leaving nothing but a hollow shell filled to the eyes with rancid water.

The moment passed and Leon was left with nothing but the lingering disquiet.

'What's this?'

'What does it look like, Leon?' Andrea's voice was exhausted.

'It looks like you're trying to hide it, is what it looks like.'

'I just thought that it wasn't doing either of us any good, staring at it.'

'Putting a bookshelf in front of it when I'm not in the room isn't going to sort out the problem.'

'It's just a stain,' she said. 'I know it bothers you—'

'You were the one that spotted it.'

'I know, and it bothers me too, I just … How long are we here for, really? A year isn't that long, Leon. It's better if we just ignore it. This isn't good for you.'

There was a long silence before Andrea tried to change the subject.

'I saw you on TV the other night.'

'Oh yeah?'

'What, my husband goes on the evening news and I just miss it?'

'Your husband goes on to try and minimise the fallout from his company poisoning a bunch of rural communities … Yeah, maybe you miss it.'

'You know it's not your fault.'

'Mm. Was I OK?'

' … Yeah.'

'Yeah, what?'

'I mean, you did look a little, I don't know, squirrelly?'

'Squirrelly?'

'You know. You were talking kind of fast and some of the things you said about the water, I'm not sure how much sense they made. Like, you kept talking about a dam breaking, but they said it wasn't anywhere near a dam.'

'Oh, I … Must have been thinking of something else.'

Andrea looked worried.

'How's it going?'

'Fine.' Leon was dismissive. 'It's blowing over, like they always do. I sweated on TV and that's all they want really.'

'So, you're just a fall guy?'

'It's the job. You sit there and make money until someone goes too far, then you fall. If you fall softly it goes away; if you fall hard you get shuffled away like Donovan.'

'Hm.' For a moment Andrea looked intensely sad. Then it passed. 'What do the others think?'

'Oh, they think it's hilarious. Albertson keeps calling it my "baptism" and won't stop telling me the story of *his* first major scandal. Blood diamonds, apparently, though he insists it was a misunderstanding.'

'Seriously?'

'Yeah, they said they might even be considering me for another position in a few months.'

'A promotion?'

'I don't know. Probably just a lateral move, but maybe.'

'And none of this bothers you?'

'It's a bit late for that. Anyway, you're the one always making those stupid jokes about this stuff.'

'That's not the point.'

'So, what is? Because apparently someone has to get their hands dirty so you can throw money away making ethical soaps.'

The air between them was icy.

'Well,' she spat. 'I'm glad you've made peace with it. Guess you can get back to cleaning. At worst it'll be a bit of a stain on my record.'

Leon's mouth twitched slightly, and she immediately regretted saying it. It hung in the air between them.

'I can get it clean,' Leon said, his voice suddenly small. 'I know I can.'

Andrea took a long second to steel herself, then shook her head.

'I've been looking into some counsellors. Clinics that special-ise in OCD.'

'I'm not …'

'It's not anything to be ashamed off. You remember Krista? Her girlfriend has it, and she's been doing—'

'Andi, I know you don't want to be here, to live like this. I just—'

'Leon.' Her voice was quiet and insistent. 'This isn't about me. You know it isn't.'

'I'm moving the bookcase away. It's not something we should just ignore.'

'Fine, OK. Just please …' Andrea held out a sheet of printer paper. 'I've put together a list. Please have a look and give one of them a call.'

'It's not in my head. I know it isn't. You can see it too.'

There was a long pause.

'I don't know anymore, Leon. I really don't. But if you're going to keep cleaning, I can't stay here. All these fumes, it's giving me a migraine. I can't sleep for the smell.'

Leon didn't respond. His gaze focused on her arm. He felt his legs go slightly weak. There, just below her elbow, there was a tell-tale patch of light grey. Bile rose in his throat. It was spreading.

'OK,' he said at last. 'I'll get it sorted.'

Number 71. It had taken a lot of effort to find out which flat was the other side of that wall, and even more to find a way into the horrible back area of the building. No one wanted to talk about how this place was laid out, but that didn't matter now. He was here. He'd made it. This is where the plumber had said it was coming from. This was it. He was going to get it sorted. Just like he said.

Leon stood in front of the quiet, unassuming door and took a deep breath. Could he smell it? That faint stench? Was it coming from in there? Hard to say. But he knew it was here, it had to be. This awful, squalid place had to be it. Whatever was pushing that awful diseased mark into his home was inside. He could see it, there in his mind, all the awful festering horror that was lurking beyond this door. The rancid squalor that must have given birth to this filth reaching through his walls.

He prepared himself, raised his fist, and knocked.

'Where were you last night?' Andrea's face split the difference between anger and concern.

'What do you mean?'

'Before that. You were out when I got home. You didn't get in until midnight.'

'Sorry. Thought you'd be sleeping.'

'That's not an answer.'

Her husband didn't turn around, eyes still resting on the wall. He dragged his finger down it, making a face as though touching something slick and oily. The smell of bleach rolled off him like a wave.

'Number 71.'

'In this building?' she said, her anger giving way to confusion. 'Do we know them?'

'There's no one to know. It's empty. Completely empty.'

'Please, Leon. Just tell me what's going on. What's—'

'The other side of the wall.'

He turned to look at her.

'This is about the stain,' she said, resignation on her face.

'Have you ever been to the back of the building?' Leon continued, his voice distant. 'It's quite something. How the other half live, you know? Except it's a lot more than half, isn't it? But I was so sure. So certain that it was there.'

'Leon ...' She pleaded. Her bag was packed, she could leave at any time, but she couldn't leave him like this. God knows what he'd do.

'I knocked for so long. Hours.' He held up his bruised, swollen hands and she gasped. 'But there was no answer. So, I waited, and then I decided to see for myself.'

She reached for his bruised hands, but he pulled back. Her shoulders sagged. 'Please don't tell me you broke in, Leon.'

'Do you know what I found?'

'Well, you said no one lives there, so I'm guessing nothing.'

Leon paused, momentarily thrown. 'Well, yes. But not just nothing. I found the wall, Andi. The other side of this one. And there was nothing there. At all. It was clean.' He moved towards her now, as if to hold her, before he stopped short, as if he couldn't bear to touch her. 'You know what this means?'

Andrea said nothing.

'It means it can't be what this wall connects too. There's something else. Something between us and flat 71. Something *inside* the walls that's bleeding through!'

There was a look of triumph on his face, like he'd solved all their problems.

'I'm going to go now,' Andrea said.

Leon's expression crumpled. 'What?'

'I'm going to go and stay with Krista for a while. Please call me when you've had a chance to get some sleep. And made an appointment with a counsellor.'

Leon's tone became desperate as he gestured wildly at the wall. He couldn't look her in the eye.

'I'm sorry, I know it's hard to live with, but I've solved it now! I can sort out the stain, I can get rid of it!'

'I don't care about the stain, Leon! I can barely see it anymore. It's you. You're not well.'

'No, it's because it's awful, and the smell—'

'The only thing bothering me is *you*, Leon. All your chemicals and your scrubbing and ...' She was crying now, as her voice started to break.

'I can fix it.'

'No,' Andrea said as she turned to leave. 'You can't.'

Leon looked up. He forced himself to look at it now, the grey, stretching up her neck, over her face. In her mouth. Was that it? Was it making her say these things? He tried to reach out, to grab her as she walked out the door and explain that she wasn't herself.

But as he did so he saw his own hand clearly, as if for the first time. It was discoloured and stained a ghoulish grey.

'Are you in my head?'

The stain simply oozed in reply. Leon swallowed, throat dry. His legs shook, both from fear and from hunger. He couldn't eat anything from the kitchen. He'd already checked. It was all contaminated.

'What do you want? You must want something. Or maybe Andi's right. You're not real, and there's something in my head that's making me see you and that means there's something I can do to fix it. Medication. Or one of those therapists Andi was— Oh God, Andi...' He slumped back in his chair. The office was silent.

'But if ... If you are real. And no one else can see you – not even Andi anymore – that means you've chosen me. You're revealing yourself to me. Why?'

He knew the answer. His eyes travelled over the desk. The testimonials, reports, inquest files. There were so many. He hadn't talked to anyone, hadn't answered the phone or his emails in days. Would he be fired? He almost laughed. It was too late for that. He wasn't someone who got fired, not anymore.

'That's bullshit. I'm working to fix it. We're cleaning up the river, we're putting things in place to stop it happening again. I didn't even have this job when it happened! It's not my *fault*.'

A thick rivulet of pus dribbled its way down from a patch of mouldy grey plaster.

'This isn't fair. I don't deserve this.'

He tightened his grip on the claw hammer. It had still been attached to his high-end toolbox with a cable tie. Apparently, this was the first time he'd ever had to use it.

'Go away. Let me clean you or I will make sure there isn't any wall left for you to fester.'

Leon had no idea if he could actually destroy an entire wall with a claw hammer, but he was willing to give it a shot. If it was coming from inside, this was how to get it out.

'This is my home. Get *out*.'

The stain disagreed.

Leon screamed, a guttural cry of anger and panic, and ran towards it, slamming the hammer into the centre. The wall dissolving beneath it like wet tissue paper, collapsing in on itself with a sick pop. There was a beat, then the putrescent grey rot flowed out from the dark hole in a wave, hitting Leon with all its force. It pinned him, gagging, to the floor as he struggled to pull himself to his feet, slipping amid the slickness of the filth-covered floor, unable to get a grip on the desk to pull himself up. The smell was like nothing he'd ever experienced. It was the smell of death, of decay, of a thousand mouldering poisons cast thoughtlessly into the world. It clawed at his mouth, pushing itself through his clamped teeth, gushing in through his nose and down his throat, filling him, killing him, hollowing him with its awfulness.

Then, just as quickly, it released him, vomiting itself up and out of his throat in a rancid geyser, until he lay on his side, sputtering weakly. There was something in his mouth, something solid the foulness had left behind. With wet, filthy fingers, he pulled it from his mouth, unfolding a piece of pristine white card.

Reading it, he knew what he had to do to be clean.

'Of course, Tobias,' Leon said, sitting in his empty, grime encrusted office. 'Of course I'll come to your party. The invitation is appreciated. We'll see you shortly.'

A thick droplet of grey sludge fell from Leon's nose, impacting the thick cardstock where the invitation was printed. It left a familiar stain.

10th

Round The Clock

Jason Brown
6 Chigwell Lane, Debden

Max's bootsteps were always loud. Whenever he was walking the halls or doing rounds, even over the soft carpet of the residential areas, Jason could always hear him coming. They were thick black leather, well cared for though the shine had clearly worn away from hard use, and their dark red laces looked almost black from a distance. They added another half inch to Max's already towering figure and were the only part of his dress that was always meticulous. Jason had once asked him where he could get a pair of boots like that, but Max had just laughed and shaken his head.

'Oh, you could buy boots look just like 'em, sure,' he'd said. 'But it's not the same. You gotta earn boots like this.'

He'd never explained exactly how they had been 'earned', and simply went back to brushing them.

None of this was to say, of course, that the rest of Max's appearance was slovenly. His hair was neatly cropped close to his pale scalp, and he kept his concierge uniform in good condition. But his shirt testified to a lack of skill with an iron, a slight beer belly strained gently against the buttons of his jacket, and he never seemed quite able to shift that last millimetre or two of stubble.

To Jason, though, these were points in his favour. Kirsty and Ryan, the other two who worked the front desk at Banyan Court, were always absolutely fastidious in their appearance, and it often made him feel self-conscious. The long tube rides of his commute from Debden meant that keeping his own uniform pristine was a constant challenge. He'd tried getting changed at work, but if he packed it in his backpack the uniform arrived a crumpled mess and a full suit bag was too bulky to be constantly carrying to and from work. Jason had even tried leaving the uniform at work but had got a firm talking-to from Toby about it. Toby was their manager at the personnel company that hired them out and was very keen that their appearance and conduct be in keeping with the 'luxury lifestyle brand' of the building they worked in from the moment they arrived. Toby stayed in the central office and didn't have to wear a uniform.

All in all, Jason found Max a very reassuring presence, and was pleased with how often their shifts overlapped.

'Hey, Jace, you dreamin'?' Max called, deep voice punctuated by the thumping tread of his footsteps.

'Hm?' Jason looked up from the pad where he'd been doodling. 'What's up?'

'Dickhead alert, twelve o'clock,' Max said, not quietly enough for Jason's comfort, and ducked into the small room behind the front desk.

Jason looked up to see a figure striding through the doors. The metal tip of a cane rapping gently on the marbled floor. He recognised the sky-blue suit with aquamarine tie and pocket square before the face of the figure had cleared the glass front of the building.

'Good morning, Mr Candido,' Jason said.

Jésus Candido regarded the concierge with a face like he was checking a vegetable for mould.

'No,' he said at last. 'It is not.'

'Hey,' Max stage-whispered from the back room. 'Ask him if he's lookin' to buy a bold new piece for his gallery.'

Jason said nothing, smiling blankly at Mr Candido, hoping he hadn't heard.

''Cause I dropped a huge piece of modern art in the loos this morning, and I think he might be interested.'

Jason tried to stop himself, but a grin split his face and a few snorting laughs escaped. Mr Candido stared at him, his disgust now laced with confusion, but the immaculate man said nothing. After a moment, he simply turned and walked towards the elevators.

'Jesus! You're going to get me fired.' Jason spun to face his friend, trying his best to sound as angry as he knew he should be.

'Firstly, Jésus just got in the lift.' Max grinned at him. 'And, second, if I did get you fired from this dump, it'd be the biggest favour I ever did you.'

'Well, I'm not sure my folks would agree.'

'Well, that's cause you're a pushover, ain't it?'

Jason turned away as the jibe landed, but not before catching Max's face darkening.

'This place's rotten, Jace, all of it. Soft poshos one side and whining grot the other. Only difference is this half of the rot pays us. That's all there is to it. Remember that.' Max smiled and stretched his neck, the crack of the bones ringing out through the foyer like a gunshot.

The cot bed creaked under Jason's weight. It wasn't remotely comfortable, but when a shift ended the wrong side of the last

Central line tube, there wasn't much in the way of options. It wasn't like he was making the sort of money he'd need for regular hotel stays, nor did he have the kind of friends that might have sofa space in central London. The cramped cot that could just about squeeze into the back room was management's only concession to the '24-hour' part of 24-hour concierge, and even then it had only been agreed after the team had comprehensively proved that it couldn't be seen from the foyer when the door was open.

The metal frame was slightly too small for Jason, and the hard metal always ended up digging into some part of his back, but the thing that really kept him from sleeping were the monitors. There was a bank of about a dozen screens, each cycling between the different security cameras that watched the corridors and lifts of Banyan Court. The front of it, at least. Jason didn't think much about the back. It wasn't his problem.

The cameras meant that even with the ceiling lights turned off, he found himself bathed in the monochrome glow of the screens, an eerie night light that made drifting off difficult, and he would find himself staring for hours at the silent corridors. Occasionally, he'd see one of the residents coming or going, but not often. He was pretty sure some of the upper floors had never been lived in: valuable properties bought as investments by overseas oligarchs and billionaires. This was London, after all; if you were actually *living* in the property you bought, you clearly weren't rich enough to properly afford it.

From the front desk he could make out the sober tones of the Shipping Forecast, just before Radio 4 turned over to the World Service. Ryan liked to have it on when he did overnight desk duty. Jason knew his smartly dressed colleague actually spent the dead hours of the night working on his screenplay, but he claimed the quiet muttering of the radio helped him concentrate.

Jason's gaze drifted over the monitors. Max was doing some rounds on the fifth floor, his tread firm and steady. Jason wasn't sure why there needed to be two concierges on duty this late, but Toby had put together the rosters and he wasn't going to make waves about it. Besides, he liked having Max with him. Jason always found doing the rounds a little bit unsettling. The hallways of Banyan Court always seemed too quiet, too long. He kept thinking he could hear muffled voices behind the closed doors – even an empty cleaning closet, one time – and the way the thick carpet muffled his footfalls set his teeth on edge. Max had no such qualms.

He watched as his friend wandered the hallways, swinging his baton slowly back and forth. It was an antique, he'd once said, a genuine Victorian policeman's nightstick that had belonged to his 'ancestors' (which Jason took to mean a great-great-grandfather or uncle). It was made of a heavy, polished wood, and always seemed slightly cool to the touch regardless of the heat. It wasn't technically legal for Max to have it in public, but no one had mentioned it, and it wasn't exactly as if he'd had cause to use it. But it was a symbol for him, a talisman of sorts. Jason thought the residents must quite like it, the firm reassurance that someone was willing to fight for their safety. At the very least, no one had complained.

'You gotta find how you want to change the world,' Max had told Jason when he first brought it in. 'An' when you find it, keep it close. I wanna change the world by bustin' any heads tryin' to ruin it.'

Max said a lot of stuff like that, and certainly had plenty of opinions on who was trying to 'ruin' the world, but Jason couldn't deny that even he felt a certain security watching that heavy stick swinging back and forth through the building. He lay back and drifted into sleep.

*

Jason opened his eyes resentfully. There had been a time when he would have had a moment of panic and confusion as his mind tried to process waking up somewhere it wasn't used to. But by now the cramped cot bed and the tiny room had imprinted themselves deep enough on his psyche that waking there felt mundane and familiar. More familiar than Jason would have liked, really.

He fumbled for his phone to check its clock. The small room had no windows, so with the lights off and the door closed it could have been any time at all. The screen showed 05:12. Jason groaned to himself and started the process of getting up. There was another hour or so until the first tube, but he should be home in time to get a shower and some breakfast ... before coming back for his next shift. He let out a slightly bitter sigh and turned to look for his shoes.

'Sleep well?'

Jason jumped at the sound of Max's voice. Looking over, he saw his friend sitting in the chair that looked over the security monitors, though he was turned towards him. The glow of the screens covered that hard face in shadows, save for Max's eyes, which glinted out.

'I ... guess. Sure. Were you watching me sleep?' The question was intended as a joke, but the laugh that tried to follow came out as a nervous chuckle.

'Keepin' an eye out.' Max's thumb gestured at the bank of displays.

'Right ...'

'Somethin's comin'. I can feel it.'

Jason tried to rub the sleep from his eyes. He wasn't awake enough for this.

'What ... I mean, did you see something, or ...?'

'Somethin's brewing. I can feel it, like I said.' Max's hand unconsciously drifted towards the nightstick on his hip. 'I can smell it on the grot.'

'They're not—' Jason caught the warning look in Max's eyes and stopped himself.

'Don't start with your pushover bleedin' heart bullshit. They don't pay your fuckin' wages so you don't have to pretend you like or respect 'em. Those over there, they're grot, Jace. They build up in cracks when you're not paying attention and if I had my way I'd clean 'em all out.'

'They live here too, Max,' he muttered quietly. Given his own financial situation, Jason sometimes wondered how close he was to becoming like them in his friend's eyes.

'Same building. Different world. They're penniless whinin' deadweight, Jace. Grot. Sooner you realise that, the better.'

'You're in a cheerful mood.'

This was not the first time he'd heard Max go off on a rant about the residents of Banyan Court's back half, but usually he at least had the chance to get a coffee first. He wondered what had triggered this one. Max had strong opinions on pretty much everyone who wasn't paying him, with particular ire reserved for 'hippies, lefties, chavs, tramps, weirdos, whiners and the fuckin' unions', all of which he could go on about for hours, nightstick waving like a conductor's baton. Jason would nod along, privately wondering what made Max, who would proudly proclaim himself working class, see himself as so far above those he decried.

Still, Jason didn't actually object to these tirades. He didn't agree with them either, of course, personally, but Max was older than him by a couple of decades at least, and at times reminded him of his grandad, a fiery red-faced contrarian, in the years before he died. Besides, Jason couldn't help but get a slight kick out of the fact that this man who hated everybody had chosen him for a friend.

'Somethin's comin',' Max repeated, scowling as he turned away. 'I can feel it. So can they, they're just too thick to notice.'

He sat there, glowering at the screens as they flicked through the corridors of the building. The room had got uncomfortably humid with both of them in there and had started to fill with the scents that Jason associated with Max's presence: machine oil and boot leather. He needed to get some fresh air.

'Whatever, man.' Jason shrugged. 'I got a train to catch.'

Technically, the journey from Whitechapel to Debden wasn't a difficult one but depending on how the transport systems lined up on any given day it could be up to an hour and a half's journey.

It wasn't the time that wore on Jason, though. There was something about the long stretch of train ride rattling out towards the suburbs and countryside that he found strangely oppressive. The same landmarks passing him by every day, again and again, marking the passage of time between a deeply unfulfilling job and a house his parents were clearly sick of sharing with him. A huge pendulum, back and forth, each swing another tally on a wasted life he'd never get back.

The heat didn't help, of course. He'd read somewhere that it would have been illegal to transport cattle on the Central line during summer, because there were laws about how hot a container carrying cows could be. Not people, though. No laws about that. Jason supposed this was because people could choose to not get into a carriage they thought was too hot, but as the beads of sweat started to soak through his uniform shirt, it didn't feel like much of a choice to him.

He watched, bleary-eyed and uncomfortable, as the

pseudo-countryside of London's suburbia rolled by. It looked like it should be refreshing, full of invigorating breezes and the sunshine of a new day. But Jason knew the air was still laced with motorway fumes and sticky with the heat of summer.

His parents' small house was just big enough for a retired couple, as had indeed been the intention when they had sold Jason and his brothers' childhood home in Muswell Hill and moved out here. He unlocked the side door and slipped in as quietly as he could. There was always a slight flush of guilt when he got out the key, noting the tag still read 'SPARE' in thin black letters, despite it having been on his keyring for almost half a year now. Another failure.

His parents weren't up yet, so no need to small talk about his day. He moved quietly up the carpeted stairs, avoiding the creakier steps, and into what his father still insisted on calling the 'spare room'. This was one door he couldn't open quietly, given how many boxes were piled up behind it, but it didn't sound like he'd woken anybody up. After picking his way through the maze of brown cardboard that still held the majority of his worldly possessions, he stretched himself out over the unmade bed.

Exhaustion washed over him. It wasn't his childhood room, far from it, but he'd done his best to cover the walls with any-thing that felt like his. Posters for power metal bands he hadn't listened to since he was fifteen; framed stills from his university cinephile phase; a piece of abstract art he'd picked out with Tammy when they'd first moved in together. His gaze lingered on the last one. He shouldn't really have taken it. Technically it had been a gift to her, but he'd half-hoped if he packed it up with the rest then she might have had a reason to call. But she never did. It was stupid, might as well frame the divorce papers if he wanted something on his wall that was going to upset him whenever he looked at it. He should just take it down. Later.

He reached into a box that had been marked 'Kitchen' in Tammy's handwriting four years ago. Then changed to 'Kitchen – Pans' two years ago when they'd moved into their 'forever home'. And, finally, 'Books' six months ago, in his handwriting. He pulled out a weathered old paperback, a Matthew Reilly thriller he'd read a dozen times, and lost himself in a world of grizzled marines with nothing left to lose until he drifted off into a fitful nap.

A package sat on the front desk when he got in for his next shift. It was large and square, unremarkable except for the fact that it was addressed to Tobias Fell. Max sat behind the desk, eyes sparkling with dark amusement.

'Is it ... You haven't sent it up?' Jason felt suddenly on edge, though he wasn't sure why.

'Was waitin' for you. I know you like to handle things for his highness up there.'

Jason felt himself blush, ever so slightly. It was true; he did get a small thrill from sending things up the small private dumbwaiter that travelled all the way to the penthouse. He didn't really know much about Mr Fell, except that he was important and very powerful.

'Sure thing,' he said, trying not to betray his excitement as he picked up the surprisingly heavy box and carried it around the corner where the small lift was concealed.

Jason adjusted himself as he walked, bearing the weight against his chest as he tried to get a better handle on the unwieldy corners. A sharp stabbing pain pierced his shoulder. He cried out at the unexpected sensation, releasing the box. As it tumbled to the floor, as though in slow motion, his hand instinctively felt for a wound. He just had time to register the feeling of slick, wet blood before the box hit the ground and split, sending sharp metal spilling out in all directions.

Heavy chefs' knives. Meat cleavers. Stainless steel hooks. A thick apron and what appeared to be some sort of electric bone saw. Butcher's gear – some of which had apparently been improperly packed enough that it had stabbed him through the box.

Jason examined the cut. It was shallow but bleeding freely, and he couldn't help but be shaken by what was splayed out before him, even as he felt blood trickle down his chest.

'Told you.' Max's voice came from behind him as Jason tried to carefully repack the box. There was a note of smug triumph in it.

'Are you going to help me with this, or ...?'

Max nodded at the implements flashing under the tasteful lighting. 'I reckon it's just startin'.'

His friend grinned darkly as he turned away.

'Of course, sir, I'll arrange a cleaner,' Jason said for what felt like the sixtieth time.

'You're not listening,' continued Mr Copeland of number 15, clearly trying very hard to keep his voice level. 'I've got a cleaner, but it hasn't helped. My wife—'

Jason glanced over at Max, who made a violent 'wanker' motion with his hand. It wasn't clear if it was aimed at him or the phone, but Jason appreciated the support.

'Look, Mr Copeland, I don't know what to tell you. I can arrange for a cleaner to come in, though ...' He paused. 'I've got a plumber in later, actually. Working on one of the upper floors. I could ask him to stop by? Have a look?'

'Fine, fine, let me know when he'll be up.'

'Will do, glad I could h—' The phone went dead. '—elp. Brilliant.'

Jason gave Max a half-hearted smile.

'Successfully made it someone else's problem?' his friend said, huge head splitting into a grin.

'Guess so.'

'I told you.' His friend shrugged. 'Something's goin' on.'

Jason was about to wave away the sinister implication when his friend's eyes flashed up to the front door and he nodded a warning. Following his gaze, Jason tensed up as he saw the figure approaching.

'Mr Erikson,' he started to say. 'Please, we've been over this. You can't go—'

His view of the journalist was interrupted by Max's massive frame as he stepped in front.

'Not gonna warn you again.' One hand rested on the solid wood of the nightstick.

'Look, I understand you may not like the press.' David Erikson's voice was calm. 'And I'm sorry for all the bother earlier, I really am. I'm not interested in sneaking around. I just wanted to check something with you.'

The newspaper man was clearly practised in de-escalating exactly this sort of situation. But he hadn't met Max before, and Jason could see in the set of his partner's jaw, the tense of his muscles, that he was just as determined to keep escalating it. He began to walk slowly towards David, like a stalking cat.

'Mr Erikson.' Jason's voice was quiet. Why was he so scared all of a sudden? 'Please leave before we're forced to remove you again.'

'OK, OK, I'm going.' Jason made himself relax when the journalist turned and began heading towards the door. At least he knew how to take a hint.

Then he stopped. Paused. Jason's stomach dropped as the man turned back.

'I just wa—'

Whump.

The sound of the nightstick impacting his face was oddly understated; a muffled wet noise like a joint of beef being dropped onto the floor. It hit David just above the cheekbone, next to his left eye, and he fell to the ground without a peep, too stunned to speak.

'Get outta here,' Max's voice rumbled. 'Now. Or next time I'm not holding back.'

And much as Jason hated to admit it, Max had been holding back. As David struggled upright, he could see that, while he'd have a nasty bruise, the baton hadn't broken the skin. There was a moment as the injured man looked from the huge figure before him over to Jason, silently pleading for him to intervene.

'Go,' Jason said.

David scrambled to his feet and ran out of the front door.

Max cracked his neck and let out a sigh of satisfaction, a huge grin plastered over his face.

'Can't stand journalists, you know?' he said to Jason as he returned to his lurking spot behind the desk.

Jason did know. Max had always been plenty vocal about it, but the violence … The violence was new. He tried not to catch his friend's glowering eyes and swallowed down his growing unease.

Jason slammed the phone down.

'Christ.'

'Copeland again?' Max called from the back room.

'Mm-hm.'

'I told you, man. All the crazies are comin' out.'

Jason exhaled. He wasn't entirely wrong. In the last few days he'd had a bunch of calls from upstairs. Not just from number 15, either. That tech guru guy kept sending down weird requests,

Jésus whatshisface was demanding taxis at all times of the day and night, and the plumber, Janek, had been in and out more times this week than in the last year, looking more and more unsettled. That was without the old lady they'd found dead in one of the back flats (not technically their responsibility, but still pretty unsettling) or the thing with the reporter. Things were ... Well, they were getting strange.

It didn't help that Max seemed to be taking all this as some kind of vindication, giving that same shit-eating grin every time something weird happened. There was something else in his eyes, though, a sort of anticipation, like he was waiting for just the right time to deliver a punchline.

After what happened last week, when he saw Max on the monitors now, he couldn't help but notice the way he moved. It was slow, but purposeful, nightstick no longer swinging, but still and ready, his head scanning from side to side. Jason had almost begun to fear what might happen if a resident bumped into him when he was making the rounds. Truth be told, a lot of the things that used to amuse him about Max had started to scare him a little bit.

'Hey,' the deep voice rumbled from the back room. 'You with me?'

Jason jumped slightly at the question, his thoughts broken.

'Yeah, Max. Yeah. Sorry.'

'No worries, man,' Max said lightly. 'So, what d'you think? About all of it? What's goin' on.'

'I don't know,' Jason replied, trying to match the tone. 'Above our pay grade, I reckon. It's a story, I guess, isn't it?'

Max was quiet, as though considering his words. Jason's gaze moved down to the heavy baton cradled gently in the crook of his arm, and he was all at once very, very worried that his friend might not like his answer.

'What ... What do you think?'

'Me?' Max's smile and carefree tone was gone. 'I think some grots are trying their luck. Messin' with us. Hasslin' the folks we look after 'cause they're jealous. 'Cause boo hoo their lives were so hard. I think we need to find who they are and teach a lesson. Bust some heads. After that everything'll just fall into place. You wait and see.'

The blunt confidence and cool tough-guy act no longer seemed impressive or reassuring. The take no shit attitude had congealed into the hanging threat of violence and Jason briefly wondered if the other concierges had noticed. They seemed to avoid Max anyway. Maybe this was how they'd always seen him. Or maybe he was overreacting? It was just talk, and Max had always talked like this. Well, maybe not *all* talk. He had smacked that journalist around. But if he was dangerous, what could Jason do about it?

The foyer doors opening caught his eye and he looked over to see a new face walk in. The guy was young and still had that teen lankiness to him. His step was slow and self-consciously casual. He wore a dark hoodie with some videogame logo on it and a blue baseball cap. He sauntered up to the desk and leaned against it heavily, his elbow pushing the visitor book out of alignment.

'Evenin'. What can we do for you?' Jason asked, trying to keep his voice professional and helpful.

The kid ignored him.

'Hey.' Max wasn't quite as friendly. 'Do you need something?'

The blue cap shifted as the young man looked between the two. His eyes were bloodshot and rimmed with red, an effect that, combined with the hazy smile, made it quite clear what the kid had been doing with his day.

'Yeah. Yeah, sure.' His voice was gentle, with none of the focus sobriety might have given it. 'I got, uh, got a phone.'

'We've all got phones.' Max's voice gained an edge. 'Can you be a bit more specific?'

'Violet. It's Violet's phone. Says on it. "Vi-o-let". She lost it.'

He reached into his hoodie and pulled out the mobile, placing it on the desk in front of him. It was square and functional, with a fresh crack snaking up from the corner of the screen.

'Oh.' Jason nodded, suddenly understanding. 'Lost property?'

The blue cap nodded twice in affirmation. Jason turned to his terminal and started tapping quickly.

'Violet Ng? Number 114?'

'Sure.' The kid shrugged. 'I guess.'

'Well, she lives the other side of the building.' Jason glanced at Max, but if he had a reaction to this news, he was hiding it well. 'I guess we could look after it and let her know.'

Jason called up the lost property page and stifled a groan. He always forgot how much of a chore this was on the building's management system.

'Sorry, got to fill this in.' The kid simply shrugged again. 'Name?'

'Violet.'

'No, your name.'

'Andre.' A pause. 'James.'

'Sorry, which one?'

'James.'

'Sorry, wait, so ... James Andre?'

'Yo.'

Jason sighed. It was going to be a long evening. He steeled himself to ask the next question, when he felt Max's huge hand settle on his shoulder.

'It's alright,' the deep voice rumbled in his ear. 'I got this.'

'You sure?' Jason said, trying not to sound too worried about leaving Max alone with someone.

'Course.' His friend's voice was relaxed. Was he just being paranoid after the journalist thing? 'Anyway, you're late for rounds. I'll take care of all this.'

Jason nodded, getting to his feet and stretching. If there was any tension, James didn't seem to register any of it, lost in his own mellow world. Max settled into the seat that always seemed a little too small for him and stared at the computer.

'What's the address?' he asked.

Jason gratefully hurried towards the lift. He glanced back for a moment, trying to ignore how much of the relief came from the fact he was leaving Max behind as well.

Doing 'the rounds' had always felt to Jason like a deeply point-less exercise. It wasn't as though they worked in a warehouse where they could check every room or compare things to an inventory. Anyone who broke in would be looking for a posh flat payday, and the flats were exactly the places the concierges couldn't check. Still, tonight it was a relief to have a little bit of quiet, a bit of space to himself. He walked the same repetitive stretch of corridor on each floor confirming that, yes, no one had stolen the hallway carpet yet. Jason was pretty sure the other concierges skipped the rounds entirely, but Max had been very adamant when training him about how important it was.

He also wasn't keen on having so much time alone with his thoughts. Traditionally they eventually circled round to Tammy and his parents and his many, many failures. Tonight, though, they were dwelling on Max. Should he have stood up to his friend more? A flush of shame and anger spread over Jason as he thought about how much of a pushover he'd always been. He knew it, no matter what anyone else said, and even privately blamed it for the divorce. Tammy had never said anything, in fact she always used to say that she liked how 'gentle' he was.

But they said that, didn't they? Women. Jason knew, deep down, that he just hadn't been strong enough to keep her. He choked down the rising feelings of inadequacy and pushed on. Yeah, next time Max was being a dickhead, Jason was going to say something.

He finished off the twelfth floor, entered the lift and hit the button marked 'G'. Nobody went up to the penthouse, naturally. He'd been told once that Tobias Fell had a secret, private lift, but Jason had never seen it for himself, despite looking on a particularly long night shift. Twice since he'd been working there a swarm of shiny black cars and armoured jeeps had descended on the building, blocking traffic and filling the foyer with generic-looking men in dark suits and earpieces. He'd later been told Mr Fell had been going out, but Jason hadn't seen him, nor did he know where he'd entered or left the building. There was a specific room on the ground floor, just opposite the lifts, with a dumbwaiter where they left packages for the penthouse, and they were always gone within a few hours.

Jason absentmindedly rubbed his aching hands as the lift descended. He was restless, though he couldn't be sure exactly why.

He found Max sitting behind the desk. There was no sign of James Andre, but his partner was talking quietly to a group of men in official-looking black vests. There were four of them, each with close-cropped hair and the sort of broad, dumpy build that came from a physical job and unhealthy lifestyle. As he got closer, Jason could read the worlds stitched in white on their pseudo stab vests: BAILIFF.

Jason couldn't hide his surprise at seeing them on this side of the building. Normally they were asking to be let in the back.

'We need the key to number 21,' the oldest one was saying.

He was a middle-aged man with a red face surrounding a moustache that he clearly thought was intimidating.

'I'm checkin'', Max growled, reading over some forms that had clearly just been handed to him.

'Then check faster,' the ruddy bailiff said, his finger tapping on the counter. 'We've got a job to do and it's late.'

Max stood up. Without the chair he was easily a foot taller than the leader of the group, and the bailiffs instinctively took a step back. Max smiled and put down the documents. He glanced over at Jason. His face was slightly flushed, as though he'd just been jogging.

'Here's my colleague now.' He picked a key up from behind the desk. 'Everythin' looks in order. I'll take you up.'

'It's about time,' the moustachioed man grumbled, following behind Max as he led them towards the lifts.

'Watch the desk, Jace.' Max winked at him as they passed.

'R-right.' Jason nodded as an uneasy feeling passed through him. He felt oddly weightless all of a sudden, as though detached from the scene he was watching, but as requested he walked slowly over to the front desk and sat down.

The foyer was peaceful, the quiet only broken by the occasional taxi rolling down the streets outside. He glanced at the computer screen, then back outside, then back to the computer screen in slight confusion. The lost property form was still up on the screen. It hadn't actually been filled in past the address line. Well, that wasn't particularly surprising, on reflection. James Andre had not seemed the most reliable sort and had probably given up and wandered off. Or maybe Max had snapped and said something that sent the kid running.

Either scenario was a bit of a relief for Jason. He sat down and went to close the program. The mouse felt weird. Sticky. He pulled his hand back to find it was red.

'The fuck?' Jason said, though deep down he knew exactly what was happening. He knew it even before he became aware of the low, pained breaths coming from the back room.

James Andre was in bad shape. His eyes were almost entirely swollen shut and blood still flowed slowly from his nose and mouth. He held his hand at his side, the arm above it bent at a painful-looking angle. Somehow his blue cap was still on his head, though now streaked with blood. Jason stood in the doorway, his mind racing, frozen in indecision. He still had time to leave, a few seconds in which he could decide to not have seen this.

Then James tried to speak. The croaking noise was barely recognisable as language, but within it, Jason could still clearly make out the word 'Help.' He turned and hurried back to the desk, fear making his hands shake as he fumbled for the phone. His finger was poised over the number pad, when a shadow fell across him.

'Really hope you're not doin' what I think you're doin', Jace.' Max's voice sounded different, heavier.

'What the hell have you done?' Jason wanted to scream at the figure towering over him, but when those dark eyes fell on him, he felt his conviction start to evaporate.

'Taught a piece of shit some respect.' Max smirked. 'You gotta keep 'em in line, Jace. It's like I always told you.'

'No, that was— You didn't mean it.'

'Not my fault if you weren't listening, mate.' Max sounded saddened, but unsurprised. His eyes glinted in the darkness. 'Now step back from the phone.'

'Max, listen to me—'

There wasn't a second warning. The nightstick came down with a crash, landing firmly on the plastic housing and shattering it into a hundred black fragments. Jason cried out and leapt back, dropping the now useless handset.

'Let's talk about what's gonna happen here. 'Cause I don't *want* to hurt you, Jace, but y'know, you put me in a real tough spot.'

Max was walking around the desk, now, eyes locked on his new prey, heavy wooden baton held firmly in his huge fist.

'You really shoulda minded your own business. Left me to the job of keepin' order in this place. Sometimes you just gotta squash disrespect. Always thought you might understand. But seems—'

James Andre lunged from the doorway straight for Max, his shout of anger and pain distorted by the damage to his face. The attack was weak and uncoordinated, almost missing his target entirely, but Max spun to face him anyway, giving Jason an opening. He leapt from his chair and kicked wildly with all his force, landing a heel squarely in the larger man's groin. Max let out a yelp of agony and toppled over. Jason noticed the solid corner of the marble-topped desk moments before his former friend's head hit it full force. Though even if he'd had the time to try and stop the impact, he wasn't sure he would have.

The crack of Max's skull was a sound unlike anything Jason had ever heard. It was nothing like the clean sounds of violence that he expected from when the bad guy goes down. It was a wet, gravelly crunch that seemed to reverberate through his own head and left him feeling weak and queasy. Max rolled off the desk and onto the floor, leaving fragments of himself on the corner. Everything was quiet, save for James's ragged breathing.

Jason offered the injured young man his arm, and led him out from behind the desk, over to the plush bench that ran along the edge of the foyer next to the lifts. His leg was clearly in bad shape, and he limped painfully, placing almost his full weight on Jason. The boy sat heavily and tried to offer up a smile, though his eyes were groggy and unfocused, and he seemed to be slipping closer to unconsciousness.

'Wait here,' Jason said. 'I'm just going to grab my phone and we—'

More than anything else it was the odour that tipped him off. It was something he'd briefly smelled when taking the police up to look over the old lady's apartment. Which shouldn't have even been his job, but who else was going to do it. He remembered the stench as he unlocked the door, but even then it hadn't been this strong or this close. It was the smell of death, but more than that, like something that had been dead for a *long* time. Jason turned.

Max stood between them and the front doors. He moved slowly, but there was no way Jason could get past him while carrying the injured youth. He stared at his tormentor. The skin on Max's face had somehow been torn clean away by hitting the counter and lay on the floor behind him like a mask. What stared at them now was nothing but a gore-drenched skull, a bloody death's head that stood atop a concierge's uniform that had now darkened to a dull, utilitarian black. Blood dripped onto his boots. What the hell was that thing? Was that Max? Had it *always* been Max?

Jason gritted his teeth, grabbed James, and started to pull him towards the elevator.

'Always knew you might be trouble, Jace.' Max's voice was untroubled by his lack of lips. He watched as the lift doors closed, his teeth on show in a macabre grin. 'And I hate trouble-makers.'

The lift opened onto the twelfth floor. Jason hit the stop button and jammed his key into the slot to override the control panel.

He wasn't sure if doing so would affect all the lifts, but he had to hope.

He stared at the other lifts, waiting to see if the numbers changed. If any of them were climbing inexorably up towards them. They were still. For now.

What was going on? That thing chasing them was dead. It had to be. It smelled dead, it looked dead, it *felt* dead. But that didn't make any sort of sense. Max had been ... I mean, Jason had never taken his pulse or anything, but he sure as hell hadn't been a corpse! That didn't change the fact that this was Max, the truth of Max, and he couldn't shake the feeling that it always had been.

'Stupid, stupid!' Jason cursed at himself as he dragged the nearly unconscious James out into the corridor. What was he doing? Max was stronger than he was, faster. He knew the building better and wasn't carrying another human being with him. Even without whatever freaky shit was going on with him basically being a corpse, Jason knew he was outmatched. Was he doing it again? Delaying the inevitable, trying to deny his own weakness and failure until push came to shove and he turned tail like always? No. Not this time.

He lowered his injured cargo down onto the carpet and started to pace back and forth, thinking through his options as fast as possible. First priority was to get access to a phone and call the police. Getting out of the building was tempting, but with James slowing him down there was no way they'd be able to outrun Max. Could he leave James behind? At the mercy of someone, something, that was clearly eager to kill them both? It didn't matter, not really. If Max was still downstairs, which he might be, he had access to the automatic security systems and could make leaving the building very difficult either way. Or maybe he was in one of the other lifts, or moving up the stairs.

It didn't matter: getting a call out was the best move, but his phone was still charging on the desk and a quick pat of James's pockets came up empty.

The situation wasn't entirely desperate. Max would be able to keep a close eye on them as long as he stayed in the security room, but as soon as he left, he was just one man and there was a lot of building to cover. Especially if the two of them could get into one of the apartments. That was probably the best move.

He dragged James back into the stopped elevator.

'Stay here,' he said, as though the bleeding teenager had a choice. 'I'll be back.'

The injured boy tried to say something, but his swollen jaw rendered it nothing but a groan. He tried to grip Jason's shirt, but his hand fell away. He was in real bad shape.

'I'm sorry,' Jason told him. He started to run. Down the hallways, hammering on doors, trying to remember which ones were actually occupied and which were just empty property investments. There on the twelfth floor, it was mainly the latter. This was a bad choice. Another failure. Jason could almost feel his parents' sneers, Tammy's disappointment.

No, they were going to make it. They had to. He rounded the corner.

'Hello? Hello! We need help!' Jason's fist pounded on the door of number 3. He was acutely aware of how solid it was, how much protection it would give him if he could just get the other side of it. But right now, it was only protection for those who didn't want to come to his aid.

At the other end of corridor, he heard the door to the stair-well opening.

Thump. Thump. Thump.

Max's boots fell heavier than seemed possible, reverberating through the floor as he approached.

'I hope you're not botherin' the residents,' his old friend's voice echoed down the corridor. 'They don't need to see this.'

Jason's stomach dropped when he saw the window. Beyond number 3 was a dead end. His only way out was past Max. He crouched, trying to quiet his breathing.

'You're just drawin' this out, Jace,' his pursuer called. 'It's no use. I've dealt with thousands of troublemakers before and you and that punk are no different. You don't matter. *We* don't matter. Important people need their world orderly. And you're disrupting that. Raisin' a fuss.'

Jason pushed back against the wall, willing himself to be smaller, to be hidden, for his pursuer to not come around the corner.

Max walked into view, the bloody grin on his face seeming to get wider still as his lidless eyes settled on the cowering Jason.

'And no one likes a fuss.'

His bootsteps were deliberate and slow, but he seemed to move the length of the hallway in only a few strides. He loomed over Jason, who tried desperately to say something, but found his breath caught in his throat.

'Where's the kid?'

Jason started to smile, his lips ready to curl into a sneer of defiance, to swear he'd never tell, that the kid was under his protection. That he wasn't going to be a pushover anymore. But Max didn't even give him time for a response before the baton came down hard and Jason's world exploded into white light and pain.

He tried to focus his thoughts, but something, maybe a boot, maybe the club, struck him hard in the chest and he felt something crack. He collapsed, the wind going out of him all at once, and the nightstick hit his back once, twice, three times, each impact a spike of agony travelling through his body. He'd been in fights before, but he'd never been beaten, properly, savagely beaten, and he felt his resolve leaking out of him with his tears.

Then he heard something. A door opening, ever so slowly. Jason looked up to see the entrance to flat 3 ajar. A middle-aged man stood there in a tailored dressing gown, looking concerned. Jason started to reach for him, to say something.

'Don't worry, sir.' He heard Max's voice from above him. 'Just a couple of troublemakers. I'm taking care of it. Sorry to disturb you.'

There was a long moment as this stranger looked over the situation before him. Jason tried to cry for help, but the words wouldn't come.

Then the man from number 3 nodded and closed the door.

'Now where's—?'

'The lift!' Jason felt the words come out in a terrified spurt before he'd had a chance to think about it. 'I left him in the lift!'

He waited for the next blow, but none came. Max let out a soft laugh.

'Good lad, Jace.'

The bootsteps began to recede, leaving Jason to catch his breath. He tried not to think about what he'd done, climbing painfully to his feet and limping towards the stairs, painstakingly following in Max's footsteps. He hadn't had any choice. Had he?

He managed to make it down to the seventh floor before he heard the shattering glass from high above, and saw the momentary blur of a body falling past the windows to the ground far below.

'So, Mr Brown. Thanks for coming back in.' The policeman's tone had changed. When they'd first taken his statement, they'd been polite, sympathetic. They'd nodded understandingly before sending him off in the ambulance. Now the pair that sat opposite him in the interview room were cold, their mouths set in hard lines.

'No, uh, no problem.' Jason sat on the uncomfortable metal chair, wincing slightly. 'Any luck finding Max?'

'Right.' A look passed between the officers. 'That's rather what we wanted to talk to you about.'

'Sure, if you need more information—'

'No, thank you. Your description of him was plenty colourful.'

There was a pause, then the other policeman spoke.

'What would *really* help us is a second name. Or an address. Or really anything to prove he exists.'

'I told you, I don't know his surname, he never said.' Jason could feel something was wrong. 'Prove he exists? What are you implying?'

'Not much of an implication,' the first cop said. 'There's no employment record for any Max at your company. No Max, Maxwell, Maximillian, Maximus, nothing. He doesn't work for them.'

'But—' Jason's head was pounding. 'The others. Kirsty and—'

'Your colleagues have no knowledge of anyone matching your description working alongside the three hired concierges.'

'Though they do recall you mentioning a Max on a few occasions,' the second one piped up with a sneer. 'So, you've got the groundwork if you want to try pleading insanity.'

'That's not ...' Jason felt faint, like he was drowning. 'That doesn't make sense. They've worked with us for years. They talked to him, I remember, I'm sure of it, they—'

'OK, I'm going to cut this short.' The first policeman leaned forward. 'What we have is a half-dozen bailiffs who claim that, shortly before the murder, you led them to a storage room on the ground floor and locked them inside. We've got hospital records that show a bit of light bruising, mainly on your knuckles, but none of the quite graphic injuries you describe receiving. We've got a day's worth of security footage conveniently wiped. And we have a lot of blood on your clothes, all of which seems to belong to your victim. Sorry, *the* victim.'

'But, the—' Jason's eyes lit up. 'The man in flat 3! He saw! He—'

'He didn't have any interest in making a statement,' the second cop said casually.

Jason reeled like he'd been punched The tears started to come, burning as they rolled down his cheeks. He looked up, and there, standing in the corner behind his tormentors, was Max. His face was still missing, and the bloody skull leered at him as it brought a black-gloved finger to its teeth.

Shh.

Right. That was it, then. Jason felt his shoulders sag in defeat. A deep numbness rolled over him as he tried to come to terms with what he was seeing.

'So, am I under arrest?'

There was a moment of awkward silence. He looked up to see the two police officers shifting uncomfortably on their chairs.

'No,' the first one said at last.

'You're free to go,' the second spat, like the words themselves were rotten.

'What? I ... I don't—'

'Get out of here.'

'But ... But James...' Jason couldn't believe what was being said.

'Was a punk who apparently no one will miss.'

The judgement hung in the air as the second policeman chose his next words.

'You, on the other hand, apparently have some very important friends.'

Max was waiting for him. Not behind the front desk in reception, or in the corridors of Banyan Court, but in his bedroom in Debden. He sat on the small single bed, almost buckling it under his weight, smiling at Jason. At least he'd had the decency to put his face back on, even though it was now half-rotten. He silently handed Jason a thick piece of cardstock.

TOBIAS FELL cordially invites JASON 'MAX' BROWN
to attend a dinner party at 1 Banyan Court
on the evening of 16th August 2014
Penthouse access will be available through the freight elevator

'Mr Fell wants some security at his function,' Max said, grinning.

'Then I guess we're goin',' Jason replied sadly.

11th

Old Plumbing

Janek Kowalczyk
41 Underwood Road

No one ever thinks about the pipes. Not really. You could corner almost anyone, point to the pipes on the outside of their house and ask them what they connect to, where they go, what they're full of, chances are they won't be able to tell you. Maybe, if they own the place, they had to get a plumber in once who talked them through it all, and they have vague memories of words like 'drainage' or 'inlet'. For most people, though, it might as well be magic. You flush the toilet and the waste simply vanishes. The kitchen sink flows out to somewhere that isn't your problem. The washing machine is fed from a hidden realm referred to simply as 'the mains'. It's even worse in a block of flats, where the intricate network of pipes and feeds and stop-valves is almost entirely hidden from view.

All this was just fine by Janek Kowalczyk, who was secretly of the opinion that it was exactly this ignorance and mystique that kept him in work. He'd always found plumbing to be a rather simple discipline, one that made a sort of intuitive sense to him. To his mind, all it really took was common sense, the right equipment and enough patience to see a job through safely. His colleagues disagreed, of course, said he simply had a knack for the trade, which was great for his ego, but he could never really shake the feeling they were just covering themselves. Certainly, there was plenty of competition in the industry, any number of cowboys looking for an opportunity to undercut a skilled tradesman and flood your home for half the price. Still, Janek had always had a way of looking at a place and seeing how it all connected. A building was not entirely unlike a human body, with its veins and membranes and intestines, and he often had a sense of how a structure lived.

Of course, the trouble with coming over from Poland as he had was that English landlords assumed Janek was just another cowboy, cheap and slapdash. They were patronisingly delighted when it turned out he knew what he was doing, and significantly less happy when he quoted them properly for it. It was one of the reasons he was so happy to be spending as much time as he was in Banyan Court.

He'd apparently become a favoured supplier for one of the companies that dealt with a whole bunch of the cheaper flats there, and they'd clearly been talking enough with the other letting agents that he'd even got some jobs in the high-end apartments. He still wasn't paid what he was really worth, of course, but Janek had long since come to terms with that, and the steady stream of work was very welcome. Even if the pipes there did, on occasion, utterly baffle him. They sprawled out in odd ways, connected in places that didn't make sense, and seemed to be all different ages and makes. If Banyan Court was a body, it was very sick indeed.

'Morning, Janek.'

Janek grunted at the concierge, whose name he suddenly realised he did not know. This was all a bit new to him, having clients regular enough that they learned his name, and he felt a brief, irrational anger that the man behind the desk had cheerfully put him at such a disadvantage. Realising his grunt might have seemed rude, he tried to smile, awkwardly raising his hand in an almost-salute.

'Which is the number?' he asked, maybe a little bit too quickly, but he was keen to avoid small talk.

'Uh, looks like number 17. Floor...' The concierge gave no indication he'd noticed Janek's impatience as he slowly checked his sheets. 'Floor eight. Problem with the shower. Mr Fowler's out at the moment, but he gave instructions to let you in. Said he'd be back about six which, between you and me, means he wants you out by then.'

Janek shrugged.

'It takes how long it takes.'

'That's what I said to him. Told him you did good work.'

Janek nodded his thanks and hoisted his toolkit, heading towards the lift. The concierge grabbed a set of keys and followed him. Of course. He needed to be let in. Even the lift needed a key. The people here trusted Janek to fix their shower, but it wouldn't do for him to forget his place. He stepped into the mirrored lift, shining and immaculate as always, and pressed '8'. The concierge joined him just before the doors began to close.

'Gotta say, I'm surprised how often you're round at the moment. I mean, like I say, you do good work, but still, new build like this ... just seems odd.'

Janek shrugged again.

'Old pipes,' he said.

The concierge nodded, though it was clear that he didn't understand.

*

Mr Fowler's bathroom was the sort of immaculate that you only ever got from a successful middle-aged businessman who lived alone. Three different reed diffusers sat on the windowsill, probably a hundred quid a piece, but it was obvious no thought had gone into how the scents would actually work together. They lent the room a confused odour that was by turns floral and citrus, with the occasional strong waft of patchouli. They weren't enough to mask the other scent, though, a slightly coppery undernote that made Janek grit his teeth and sigh deeply.

He had been told the shower was having problems with the pressure and had started producing 'bad water'. As far as complaints went it wasn't particularly useful, but Janek had dealt with far worse and, honestly, all he needed to know was that it was the shower. There were only so many problems that could affect a shower without touching the rest of the plumbing.

First task, of course, was to check the top-of-the-range electric shower system the guy had had installed. One advantage of getting callouts to flats like this was that, no matter how rich their occupants were, they rarely had space for the sort of fancy at-home spa systems that were a proper nightmare to navigate. Janek still allowed himself a small moment of snobbery, looking at the unnecessary and overpriced features some lucky fitter had managed to sell to Mr Fowler. Janek shook his head, imagining how much the man must have paid for it. He considered himself a good man, and always did his best to avoid passing judgement on others, but deep down he had an unshakeable conviction that all rich people were deeply, deeply stupid. Well, maybe not stupid exactly, but foolish, certainly. He'd seen it over and over again: there was simply no way to have that much money without it warping your relationship to the world in ways that made you laughably ignorant.

The shower itself looked fine, at least, save for a tell-tale residue that Janek was careful to wash off properly. Reassembling the thing took much longer than actually checking its function, as any indication it had been interfered with was a sure-fire way to get a complaint and lose Banyan Court as a client. And he was only getting started.

Next, he checked the hose and the shower head. Both had those same crusty remains dried along the inside of them, but it was nothing that couldn't be cleaned out with some descaler, followed by a little bleach. Rinsing it through, watching the rusty-looking water drain away down the plug hole, Janek laughed softly, just to himself. Wash the dirt out of one pipe to flush it down into another. Such was the cycle of that invisible, unremarked network that kept the place alive.

The shower itself was fine, it seemed, so it must be the pipes themselves. Standing up, he took a moment to stretch out after so long hunched over, pins and needles tingling in his legs as circulation returned, and walked out to the kitchen sink. Turning on the tap, he watched carefully as the stream of water flowed out of it, strong and clear. He stood for a minute, before taking a guess at which of Mr Fowler's cupboards contained drinking glasses. He got it right on his second try, grabbing a highball glass and filling it to the top before turning off the running water. The silence that followed seemed ever so slightly thicker than it had been before. Janek nodded to himself, before holding up the glass to his face, carefully studying the liquid inside. It looked clean and clear, and a thin layer of condensation was starting to form on the outside. He sniffed it once, twice, nodded again, then proceeded to drink it, draining the glass in a few seconds. No taste except the slight chalkiness of that hard London water. Healthy.

Janek was stalling and he knew it. He sighed, placed the glass in a dishwasher that probably cost more than his van, and returned to the bathroom. He worked quickly, bypassing the shower so he could have a look at exactly what was coming out of the pipe that fed the bath tap. He checked his watch and opened the valve. It took a few seconds, but soon enough it was flowing just as he had expected, slowly and thickly onto the pristine porcelain of the tub. Janek's mouth twisted into an expression of grim vindication.

The blood that spurted and sputtered from the pipe was a rusty red colour, a long way from the bright scarlet of a fresh wound. It was still liquid, however, though didn't seem to be in any way diluted by the water in the system. The smell that came off it was putrid and sick, but Janek had already taken the step of opening all the windows in the flat. He kept watching, his face set in a hard expression. Glancing at his watch he saw it was half past two. Time enough for the smell to dissipate, he thought as he leaned out of the window and lit a cigarette.

He smoked slowly, deep in thought, keeping one eye on the sporadic rivulet of gore spurting from the pipe out into the bathtub. The smell of the cigarette laced together with the reek of old blood and essential oils, and for a moment he was glad he'd decided to wait until after the job for lunch. He took another drag, feeling the thick smoke fill his lungs. Everyone finds ways to poison themselves, he thought briefly, before tossing the tar-blackened filter out of the window, watching it arc away into open air, down onto the roofs below. Then he turned his attention back to the pipe.

By now the blood had started to thin, just as it had in the other flats, and what flowed from the pipe now was mostly water. That was something to be thankful for, at least. Janek remembered all to vividly how panicked he had been the first time it had happened, over in number 27.

He considered for a moment lighting another cigarette,

but by the time he'd decided against it the water was almost entirely clear. He checked his watch again: seven minutes and ten seconds, plus however long Mr Fowler had watched it in horror, before turning it off and convincing himself it was some sort of rust in the pipes. So far the longest it had taken was ten minutes, which was something of a relief, given everything he had to do afterwards. Maybe he'd measure the volume in whichever flat this happened next. He grimaced as he realised just how sure he was that there *would* be a next time. So far it had been all over this side of Banyan Court, and Janek was damned if he had any idea what he could do except run the blood out and scrub thoroughly afterwards. If nothing else, it was a blow to his professional pride.

As he finished cleaning the pipes and washing up any remaining mess, he listened closely, straining his ears for any new sound. Nothing. Unsatisfied, he began to pack up his tools. So far, the tapping in the pipes had only happened once, in flat 6 a few floors up, but Janek was somehow certain that it was the key to whatever was poisoning Banyan Court. He checked his watch again once he was all done. Four o'clock. It looked like Mr Fowler would be able to get a shower as soon as he got home from whatever high-flying financial career he had dedicated his life to, and wash off that lingering scent of blood.

There was only one armchair in the Kowalczyk house, and that was Janek's. The kids crammed onto the big sofa, and Lena preferred the small two-seater (although the second seat was always covered in her paperwork), so over the years the chair had gradually moulded around him, until the cushions seemed to instinctively conform to his shape. But as he sat there late that night he found, for the first time in recent memory, that he was uncomfortable. The image of those pipes stuck with him, and he just couldn't seem to find the right position to relax and consider them properly. The question that plagued him hadn't changed from any other night over the last month: what the hell was he going to do about Banyan Court?

When it had first happened, he had thought perhaps there was a body in the pipes somewhere. Maybe someone was trying to dispose of a murder victim, gradually draining and dismembering them. It wasn't as if the posh side of Banyan Court had any shortage of ruthless bastards. Hell, given some of the stories he'd heard about Tobias Fell himself ... But, no, that didn't make any sense. Everything he'd seen had been feeding through *into* the flats, a system that was obviously kept very separate from the outflow pipes, even with the building's twisted plumbing. Then he had considered the possibility of a worker accidentally trapped somewhere, hidden out of view when they were being installed. But that was ridiculous. Insegur Group, the conglomerate Fell had hired to build the place, had a pretty dreadful reputation for worker safety, sure, and Janek would know – he'd once worked for the international arm. But that still seemed a hell of an oversight. Besides, this had only started happening in the last month or so, and it had been several years since the new part of the building was erected. None of the obvious explanations made sense. Except, of course, for the one that didn't need to make traditional sense: the building was sick.

He couldn't vocalise exactly where the thought came from, or how it could possibly be true, but deep down it felt right. He had always been able to see a building as a whole, the veins of pipe and plumbing, and all his instincts screamed at him that this was a disease. Banyan Court was rotting. And more than that, it was getting worse. The blood was flowing for slightly longer each time, smelling slightly worse. He had to do something.

Janek told himself to go to the police. He wanted to, really he did. He wanted this to just be someone else's problem, to be able to lie in bed with his wife knowing that someone with the right skills was taking care of it. But it was never that simple, was it? Janek had had enough dealings with authority to know how poorly they reacted to things that didn't seem to make sense. In the best-case scenario, they believed him, tore the building's plumbing apart and found ... something rational. A body, maybe, or a serial killer's disposal method, or something equally awful. Janek would be a hero, sure, but a hero that had still alienated all of his best paying clients. And the worst-case scenario was he alienated them for nothing. That the sum total of his reward was another patronising talking-to from some piece of shit cop who had nothing better to do than make unsubtle implications about deportation. No, it would have to be a lot worse before he could bring himself to take that risk.

He'd promised himself weeks ago that he'd make a report if people started to get ill. If there was a body, human or other-wise, rotting in those pipes then it wouldn't be long before it started to affect the health of the people who lived there. If the blood was properly real and it got into the drinking water, it wouldn't be long before people started to get sick. He'd been keeping an eye on the news, even got little Julia to show him how to set up a Google alert for outbreaks of illness in the area – or more occurrences outside of Banyan Court – though she'd had no idea why. So far there was nothing. The only evidence of anything wrong were the calls he'd been getting more and more regularly.

So, there was only one conclusion. At least to Janek's mind. He'd never dare mention it to Lena, though. She was a doctor, after all, and not prone to superstition. Though he wouldn't dream of saying it to her face, Janek sometimes thought she could be a little bit close-minded. To her, disease was something physical that only affected people. He probably couldn't mention his theories to any of the people working at Banyan Court either. Perhaps they might not dismiss him outright, but they hadn't seen what he had seen, and he had no idea how they would react if they did. No, if he was going to investigate this properly, he'd need to come up with another angle. He sighed, picked up his laptop, and started to draft an email.

'So, how long do you reckon it'll take?'

Janek shrugged. 'Depends on what the problem exactly is. Could be weeks.'

The concierge, who today was helpfully wearing a name badge reading 'Jason', cocked his head with an apparently genuine smile.

'I suppose we'll be seeing a lot of you, then. Is this going to interfere with the residents at all? Folks this side can get a bit touchy.'

'Corridors and service rooms only,' Janek assured him. 'But I might need to go to the back.'

Jason stopped for a second, an expression of confusion briefly passing over his face, as though the idea of going from the front of Banyan Court to the back was entirely alien to him.

'Most, uh ...' He fumbled for the words. 'Most people just go round the outside, I think.'

'There must be a door.' Janek had no intention of going all the way round every time he needed to follow a pipe.

'I guess. Probably locked though.'

'Then you will have a key.' Something about the whole interaction was putting Janek's teeth on edge. Jason kept pausing, losing his focus. He turned towards the empty room behind his desk, as though looking for permission.

'Sure,' he said finally. 'I'll get you the service set.'

He pulled out a small ring full of keys and electronic fobs, and blew the dust off a sign-out book which Janek dutifully scribbled in. He couldn't help noticing that it had been almost two years since they'd last been signed out.

'Not many people get these keys?' Janek asked, and Jason paused a second before bursting into laughter, something that caught Janek off-guard as he most definitely had not made a joke.

'We normally head up with service guys like you, give them access to whatever they need,' Jason replied, looking back towards that small room again and shaking his head with a smile. 'But I'm told you've got a lot of work ahead of you, so I guess it's just, uh, easier this way.'

'Right. Well, see you.'

Janek turned as fast as he considered polite and started to walk towards the lift. To his relief, Jason made no move to follow him this time, and he was happy to be rid of the inquisitive concierge. He had plenty of lies prepared as to exactly what he was doing. His reports so far had talked about dirty water and leaks, a web of lies sufficient to get the building manager to sign off on his attempts to 'locate the source of the recent plumbing issues'. Even so, he really didn't want an audience for when he started pulling up expensive carpet, or knocking through walls to get a proper look at the pipes. And if he was right about the state they were in, he definitely didn't want anyone to see what he found.

On reflection, it shouldn't have surprised Janek just how confusing the pipes in Banyan Court really were. What else had he been expecting? Though he had to take a moment to stare in stunned silence when he got through a piece of wall only to be confronted by a huge cast-iron drainage pipe. The thing must have been at least a hundred and fifty years old and put Janek in mind of a massive varicose vein, swollen with age and neglect. Its existence might have made sense given the age of the original building, except for the fact that this was on the eleventh floor, storeys above where the old factory had stopped. If they'd used the old piping up here, they'd have had to specifically remove it and reinstall it several floors up, which would have been a pointlessly bad idea. Not that the old cast-iron pipes wouldn't still work with proper upkeep, but modern plumbing was a hell of a lot more reliable and generally much easier to install.

This was the most extreme example, certainly, but he'd been finding similar instances all day. There was modern pipework there as well, since there's no way the original building had enough to service all of Banyan Court, but the old iron tubes seemed to be the backbone of the system, the arteries and intestines into which it all connected. If he had to guess, Janek would even go so far as to say that there was more new pipework in the cramped and unpleasant rear of the building, with most of the older parts in the tasteful front section. It had been a long time since he had worked construction, but he could think of no conceivable reason to do this. Someone, somewhere, had specifically demanded it be done like this and, whoever they were, they must have been too rich or too important for anyone to tell them no.

He had to go deeper. If he was going to make a diagnosis, he needed to see the worst of the symptoms, and these pipes were the key, he was sure of it. So Janek spent a few hours finding the largest concentration of them and went to work.

It didn't take much work to unearth a short access pipe. Placing down the section of plaster he had cut away, he began to remove its covering. It started smoothly, but after a few turns the cap stopped abruptly, apparently stuck fast. Janek paused, running through all the possibilities of exactly what might be keeping it from opening. It was old, certainly, but it didn't look like it was rusted shut. He turned away for a moment, rifling through his toolkit for something to force it open, when a small noise froze him in place. He knew the sound, of course, of the access cover slowly rotating, unscrewing behind him. He was alone with the pipes, hadn't seen another living soul for over an hour, and if it was being opened, then it was being opened from the inside.

Janek had to turn around, he had to. What was the point of all this if he couldn't bring himself to actually look at what he had found? But in that moment, there was nothing on earth he wanted to do less than to see what was going to come out of that pipe. The noise stopped, and for a moment Janek almost felt relief, before there was the *tap tap tapping* of something small and hard on the inside of the cast iron.

It was calling to him. It wanted him to look.

He turned around to face the pipes just as the cap came off completely, falling to the floor with a clatter. There was a moment of quiet, as though pausing for effect, and then the stillness was broken by a gush of foul-smelling liquid spurting out of the pipe at him. Janek took an involuntary step back, his eyes still focused on the dark opening. There it was, white and slimy against the dark metal. A finger. The bone shone through where the flesh had rotted away, pale and cold, while what was left had swollen into bloated and waxy lumps.

Janek waited. Whatever this was, it wasn't finished. He was sure of that. The finger stretched out of the hole, which was far too narrow to permit anything wider than the decaying hand that followed it. It tapped again, this time on the outside of the pipe, the sound of wet bone on rusted iron, clearly calling for his attention. He almost laughed at the thought that he might be doing anything other than staring at the rhythmic movements of this insistent corpse's hand. It stretched towards him, and then slowly, purposefully, crooked its thin finger, gesturing him closer.

One step at a time, Janek approached, disgusted and intrigued by this strange invitation. He wanted to keep his distance, his mind fixating on the thought of an arm suddenly shooting out of the pipe and grabbing him by the throat; clammy, rotten fingers sinking into his windpipe. But he continued his approach, until at last he was in front of it. He took a moment, readying himself before bending down, his eyes now level with the hole, staring directly into the darkness of the pipe, visible around the thin wrist. He mechanically reached for his torch. The hand withdrew just as he clicked the button, sending the powerful beam of the Maglite directly into the opening.

What he saw inside took a few moments to fully register. His eyes kept fixing on tiny details, like they were trying their best not to comprehend the complete image. More white bones and bloated flesh, almost enough to make a full body, but so crushed and pressed together that it was impossible to be sure. The pipe was less than eight inches across and with only a twisted cross section visible; he couldn't make any anatomical sense of the compacted mess. He could see something there that might have been a foot. Squashed next to it was what could have once been part of a ribcage. All covered with a torn and stained grey jumpsuit, one Janek almost thought he recognised. At the centre of the mass, his torchlight fell upon a single blue eye. It blinked once, not cloudy and dead but shining, alert and focused. It fixed on him and a few things next to it that might have been teeth shifted their position. Was it trying to smile?

The whole thing shifted, bone and skin and fabric rippling around as the crushed corpse moved, revealing more of itself to Janek's torchlight. A second later and he could just about assemble the image into almost a face, all topped with the remains of a broken, off-white hard hat. Between that and the jumpsuit, Janek had a sudden, horrible impression of what he was looking at, and it was only the knowledge that his own eyes were a deep brown that managed to shake off the thought that he was somehow staring at his own mangled corpse. As it continued to move, he saw that knotted and twisted all around it was a broken safety harness, with torn polyester straps and shattered metal links all caught in each other, giving an impression halfway between an ensnared prisoner and a grotesque piece of gift wrapping.

Then all at once it started to slide backwards, disappearing silently back down the pipe like it was being sucked through a pneumatic tube. It took no more than a couple of seconds for it to be out of reach of Janek's light, leaving only a faint bloody residue on the iron interior. He was alone once again. He went to the opposite wall and leaned heavily against it, his body overtaken by a sudden feeling of intense cold. He slid down until he was sitting on the floor next to his toolkit, and he didn't even bother to check the ceiling for smoke alarms before he raised a cigarette to his lips with shaking hands. He wanted to think, to consider what he had just seen, but his mind was entirely blank.

Grey jumpsuit, white hard hat. A uniform so generic as to be almost completely unremarkable to anyone who wasn't Janek. Anyone who hadn't been wearing it the day they almost drowned.

It was years ago now, decades, before he came to England, before he worked for himself, back when he was still doing jobs with major construction firms. He was new in the position, young and brash, comfortable ignoring the comments from his older, more experienced colleagues when they warned that the company – one of the international affiliated of the Insegur Group – had dubious safety standards, about how he needed to be careful when using their equipment, and how it often wasn't properly maintained. But even if he had paid attention, he didn't know how much it would have helped.

They'd been doing some work on a reservoir, not even a very big one. A simple repair job on the tiny control station that sat near its centre, at the end of a long metal bridge that jutted out from the concrete edge of the still, dark water. There were plenty of signs warning of the dangers of swimming in there, promising hidden currents that would drag anyone foolish enough to try down into a watery grave. Young Janek hadn't really bothered to pay them any mind, not even as he'd clipped on his harness and had his bored, distracted co-worker lower him down next to the damaged pipe, eager to get a better position on the problem. The memory of those stark letters promising a messy end only came back to him when he heard the sound of tearing and saw the old, rotten straps suspending him begin to break.

Trying to describe the cold of that water had never been something he was properly able to do. It can't have been as cold as it was in his memory, it simply wasn't possible. In the years since then he'd gone swimming in literal frozen rivers, but even they had never seemed as appallingly, endlessly cold as the waters of that reservoir when he plunged into them. All sensation seemed to leave his body at once. He was a strong swimmer, even then, and it was less than fifty metres to the edge, but it was as though someone had simply turned off all his muscles. He'd flailed weakly, the harness that was supposed to have protected him now binding him and weighing him down. The endlessly icy water of the reservoir rushed down his throat and into his lungs, and he'd known with absolute clarity that he was going to die.

Young Janek, however, had clearly been possessed of a luck that had largely deserted him in his later years. The exact details of his rescue had never been clear to him, but the rest of his crew had apparently managed to pull him out before drowning or hypothermia was able to fully take him. He was alive, though the next few weeks were, as he recalled, deeply unpleasant. Not only was he unable to work, causing some financial problems for the rest of his family, but he had received a visit from some sharply dressed management types who made it abundantly clear what a bad idea it would be for him to raise any sort of legal issue around the company or their safety provision. The worst part was that he didn't even have the option of quitting, not without leaving his family in a truly dire position. It would be another year before he was able to go and work for himself. Another year of staring at that grey jumpsuit and not-quite-white hard hat, remembering the waterlogged death that was almost his.

'You alright?'

The soft question shattered Janek's reflection like a gunshot and he stood up quickly from the floor, shaking his head and muttering to himself, scattering cigarette butts all round him.

'Hey, hey … it's alright. Sorry. Lot of people smoking in doors at the moment. I won't tell.'

The speaker was a young man in a worn Budweiser T-shirt a few sizes too big for him. His features were soft, but his face had the look of someone who'd had more adversity than his years deserved. His skin had clearly seen the elements, and his eyes hardship. But his concern seemed genuine, and Janek didn't hear any of the condescension he so often encountered on the more expensive side of Banyan Court.

'I ... yes.' Janek tried to regain his composure. 'I'm fine. Had a ... bit of a fall. Trying to get my head correct.'

'Yeah, I'll bet.' The youth looked at him like they were sharing a secret. 'This place'll do that to you.'

A slight shiver passed down Janek's spine. Was this someone who had seen what he'd seen? Someone who might believe him? Was that too much to hope for? The young man stared at him, his face unreadable, until at last he offered his hand.

'Damian,' he said.

'Janek.' He took the handshake warily.

'Well, Yanik.' Damian grinned, and the older man bristled at his pronunciation. 'What do you think of our humble home. I'm guessing you don't like it here?'

Janek shook his head.

'I mean, I guess technically neither do I.' The young man gestured to his outfit. 'Not sure I'd fit in with the hobnobs over here. I'm the other side, you know?'

He gestured down the corridor, towards one of the well-hidden doors that connected the two halves of Banyan Court. Janek considered his response, but Damian didn't wait.

'Thing is,' he continued. 'They want us to think like that, y'know? They want us to be so very sure that it's all separate, us and them, my side your side. We're not the same kind of people if we don't live in the same places. But it's all a lie. You've got to look at the spaces, the ways they don't add up. They're trying to keep us apart, but it doesn't really work unless we're together. Makes sense, I suppose. If you keep everyone looking down on each other, they don't ever bother looking up. You get it?'

Janek most definitely did not get it, but the soft, intense voice of his new friend was making him feel dizzy.

'Sorry.' Damian smiled, embarrassed. 'Just getting used to monologuing, I guess.'

'I'm just here for the pipes,' Janek said, starting to gather his tools. He picked up the cap lying on the floor and moved automatically to reinstall it. His gaze fell on the opening into the pipe and his hand stopped in mid-air, the thing that had been inside returning to his consciousness all at once.

'Pipes aren't nothing, Yanik. Pipes are the guts of the place, they're what makes it work.'

'Yes.' Janek turned, surprised to hear someone else who understood. He pointed to the open pipe. 'It is the body, but sick, rotten. There was something there, something collecting the sickness together.'

'Like a tumour.'

'Maybe, or like a clot. But not the cause I think. I do not know what makes it sick.'

'Hm.' Damian considered for a second. 'This place is a cannibal, built from its own ruins. That sort of thing breeds illness, I guess. What did you see?'

His voice so serious, so earnest that Janek felt the lie he was about to tell die on his lips.

'Skeleton,' the plumber said, surprised at how readily he trusted this strange man. Then his face flushed red as he realised how daft it sounded to say out loud. 'I saw a skeleton. In the pipes.'

Damian nodded, either ignoring or oblivious to the ridiculousness of the thing.

'You know whose skeleton?'

Janek shook his head. 'Workman, I think. He had a jumpsuit, hard hat. Like me.'

There was a pause. The young man seemed to be considering his words. He clearly knew about this place, so Janek pressed on.

'What's happening here?'

'Banyan Court?' Damian said. 'Been looking into it. Not the pipes, though. Didn't think of that.'

'Did anyone die when this place was built? Plumber, perhaps, made to do unsafe work?'

'Don't think so.' A pause. 'But the folks around here, they all grew rich off screwing people over, never been any other way to do it. I wouldn't be surprised if some of them skirted a few regulations. Got some blood on their hands. Especially upstairs.'

His gaze flicked up to the ceiling, then back down to Janek.

'I reckon you'd better follow that skeleton, if you want to properly diagnose the place.' Damian's eyes twinkled with an intensity that made Janek uncomfortable. 'Just be sure you really want to know, because I don't know what the building wants to show you.'

Janek found himself nodding.

'And come find me afterwards. I've got a— I don't know. I'm working on a theory.'

The young man's words stayed with Janek, twisting around his head as he tried to continue his work. At first, he attempted to stay away from Banyan Court. For days he sat at home, ignoring the curiosity that tried to pull him back. But every time he tried to compose an email to the building manager to claim the job was done, his hand would hover over the 'send' button until he deleted the draft. In his darker moments, Janek imagined the thing he had seen was some strange echo of his own future, dead and hidden in the twisting pipework of Banyan Court. He lay awake at night, Lena snoring gently beside him, wondering if he was chasing his own death through the cast-iron labyrinth.

Lena tried to talk to him about it. He knew he had a tendency to be quiet, taciturn, but she saw the exhaustion in his eyes. What could he say, though? How could he explain what he had found himself involved in? He had reassured her that it was just a difficult job getting under his skin and then kissed his children good night.

But whether he would have chosen to go back or not, Janek couldn't escape his job. More calls came in, more 'bad water' that needed draining. And as much as part of him wanted to forget what he had seen and walk away, they could not survive on Lena's income alone. Turning the work down simply wasn't an option. So, he continued to find himself walking through the shining glass doors of Banyan Court. And as the blood drained from the baths of the rich, the tapping would return, gently imploring him to follow. And eventually he did.

Janek began to spend time in the corridors and service rooms of the towering building, listening for the tapping, senses sharpening to that faint coppery scent of old blood. Three more times he saw the 'clot', the thing that pushed itself through the old pipes, and he followed it as best he could, the tapping calling him, urging him further, more and more plaster falling away to reveal antique iron. Sometimes it seemed to stay within the main waste outflow pipes, other times squeezing itself through water feeds so thin that Janek had no idea how anything with bones could fit through them at all. He had come to the conclusion that the bones, the flesh, they weren't real, exactly, they were something else, something spectral, but it all looked so completely physical, smelled so real. The valves made no difference, it came and went as it pleased through the bowels of the building and he pursued it single-mindedly.

He always lost it when moving between the front and back of Banyan House, as though the divide was a barrier it couldn't cross. If Janek first heard it near the health suite, he'd have lost it long before he reached the rickety old lift and vice versa. A frustration began to build inside him, starting to drown out his fear. Wasn't he doing what it wanted? Chasing it all over the damn building? So why did it always decide to vanish there? Unless that was where it wanted him. Somewhere in between. The plumber's breath caught in his throat.

Jason had made no mention of retrieving the keys from him, and indeed hadn't even been at the desk the last couple of times he had passed. So Janek began to look closer at the doors between the two sides, the short corridors that led to them, so easily missed they almost seemed deliberately hidden. Those doors were heavy and refused to stay open, but something about what Damian had said still stuck around his mind. Something about the spaces not being right.

He began to take a few measurements, testing a theory. It was hard to be sure without knowing the exact dimensions of the flats, another frustration choked down, but Janek soon became convinced that there was a hollow space between the two halves of the building. A gap of about ten feet between the front and back where the pipes didn't continue. Where they disappeared. A hidden cavity at the heart of Banyan Court.

There was no way to access that space. Janek hunted for it, checking for doors or service hatches, but there was nothing. No, he would not accept this. After everything, after being dragged through this bloody horror story for weeks, a simple wall wasn't going to stop him. He had to walk all the way back down to his van from the eighth floor to fetch a hammer and crowbar. Not common plumbing tools, perhaps, but very much what was called for in this situation. He spent a half-hour finding the exact right point in the passage between the two sides. Janek took a deep breath. It was time for some exploratory surgery.

He grunted as the hammer sank into the wall, the anger flowing out of him as a burst of plaster erupted into his face.

He pulled it back and swung it again. And again. Each impact a crunch of violence as the ragged hole he made grew wider, beckoning Janek in.

The darkness stretched down below him, a pitch-black core in the centre of the building. All the way down to the foundations and up to the penthouse far above, a gaping wound between the two sides, held together by ragged pipework stitching. There were no lights along the walls his hammer had exposed, and though his torch picked out the bare brickwork, if Janek shone it up or down, the beam quickly disappeared into darkness, like it was being swallowed. From the walls that marked the back of each side of Banyan House those thick cast-iron pipes sprouted, their shapes irregular, turning and creeping down and out of sight in odd patterns like stiches, barely holding the two edges together. Were they moving? No, it was just a trick of the torchlight beam, surely. But leaning further through the gap he'd made, he saw the pipes were ever so slightly pulsing, like the iron was trying to mock the fleshy pipes of the living. And they all led down into the hole.

Janek stood back, trying to understand exactly what he was looking at, when he heard that familiar *tap tap tapping*. With a start, he realised that it wasn't just one clot. It had never been just one twisted thing he had been chasing. One unfortunate worker. Every pipe was filled with the sound of wet, cramped bodies shifting and crawling inside them. And it was more than just the pipes. The air was filled with the sound of dozens, hundreds of the forgotten dead moving the walls, the floors, the wires... All through the guts of this building they spread like a poison, shifting and clamouring for his attention, begging for him to notice their unnecessary and unmourned passing. Had any of them died here? Did it matter? This was where they had dragged themselves, shifting their pained and broken remains from wherever they were cast by a broken railing, an unmoored machine or a falling chunk of masonry. A broken harness that plunged them into an icy reservoir. This was where they made their accusation and called out to any who might be listening.

And it had been built this way. These things, these spirits, were not accidental clots or unseen tumours, they were part of the substance of the building. This place had not become sick, it had been built diseased. But why? And what did they want from him, these souls that had been used to infect it?

Janek's torch beam finally fell upon a set of metal rungs, passing alongside the hole he had made in the wall and stretching up and down and out of sight. They wanted him to climb, he knew that, and looking closer he saw why. The screws that held the crude ladder to the wall were far too short and rusted through. There was no way it would take his weight for more than a few seconds before breaking. He would fall into the darkness, where they waited for him, where they wanted him to join them. They had something they were desperately keen to share.

Janek stood there listening for a very long time before he finally made his decision.

Lena Kowalczyk had been worried about her husband for weeks now. He'd been sleeping badly, up at odd hours and always staring at drainage layouts for a job he refused to talk to her about. She gave him his space, though, and didn't press him about it. Not even the night the invitation came, after he had returned past midnight, completely soaked from head to toe despite the absence of rain. He mumbled something about an accident at work and faulty plumbing, then immediately went to take a shower. Lena had no idea what to do, so she just left the strange letter that had arrived on the kitchen table and went to bed. After all, it was addressed to Janek.

TOBIAS FELL cordially invites JANEK KOWALCZYK
to attend a dinner party at 1 Banyan Court
on the evening of 16th August 2014
Penthouse access will be available through the freight elevator

They could talk about it later. For now, she was just happy he was safe.

12th

Point of View

Damian Simpson
94 Banyan Court

Hey Cari,
Found this old tape in my files when putting together
background for the retrospective. Not sure when he sent it to
me, but I clearly missed it. I reckoned it was worth putting
together a proper transcript, since it's kind of degraded, and
thought it might be worth you having a copy. If only to have
something concrete if you ever start to question yourself. I
know we've been over this a bunch of times, but given what
happened, I think it might help to see where Damian was
coming from. Let me know if it jogs anything loose, memory-
wise. Still keen to get that proper interview someday.
  Best,
  David

[Timecode 03:11 02-08-2014]

[00:00] A man's face fills the foreground. He is white and clean-shaven with medium-length brown hair, greying slightly in patches. His features are those of a younger man, but his skin shows the signs of hardship, roughened and worn with the creases of someone much older forming around the eyes. He's wearing a T-shirt for the band Deep Purple. Behind him is the wall of an unremarkable living room. A calendar scroll of the sort received from a Chinese takeaway is hung next to a small framed photograph, the subject of which is mostly obscured by the man's head. Over his other shoulder is a window. It is dark, but the distance and quantity of lights suggest the room is several floors above ground level, overlooking the city of London.

The man stares into the camera, as if trying to decide what to say. His words are low and mumbled.

Damian: It's, uh … I don't know. Just [inaudible] I guess.

[00:11] He rubs his face, the camera shifting briefly, allowing a table to be glanced at the edge of the frame. It is covered with graph paper and what look to be hand-drawn maps.

Damian: Nah. Forget it.

[Cut]

[Timecode 14:39 09-08-2014]

[00:29] Damian is sitting in a chair facing the camera. The framing is more deliberate and the camera is stable, most likely mounted on a tripod or similar. He has clearly made an attempt to look more respectable than earlier, with his hair roughly combed and a rumpled button-up shirt. His face is slightly shiny from sweat. The window behind him now shows summer daylight, with the London skyline just discernible in the distance. More maps and diagrams can be seen on the small section of table viewable at the bottom of the frame. Damian takes a drink from a glass of water. He appears nervous.

Damian: The, uh, the spaces within a building are always strange. They never work quite how you expect them to. You look at a space, I mean, we're visual creatures, humans are very visual. You look and you feel like you understand it. Its dimensions. You know it. But eyes aren't actually good for this. Not really. I mean, of all your senses, sight is one of the worst for it. Smell and taste also.

[01:02] He smiles weakly.

Damian: But yeah, sight. It's not great. We think what we see is objective, a realistic version of what's in front of us, but it's all relational. Your mind, your eye, fixes on certain focal points, lynchpins for whatever you're seeing, and everything else kind of warps around them. Have you ever had that feeling, I think in French it's *jamais vu*, 'never seen', like *deja vu* is 'already seen'? It's when you look at something so familiar, your mother's face or a train station you travel

from every day, and it looks ... completely different. Alien.
Everything you remember being there is there, but it all seems
slightly off, like it's been rearranged. That's because your eyes
have accidentally settled on different focal points from the
ones they're used to, and so everything else is subtly changed
to reflect that. It all seems different. You can't trust what your
eyes tell you about spaces. Half of it's illusion and the other
half assumption.

[01:47] He takes another sip of water. The movement causes
the camera to defocus for a second. When it refocuses,
Damian is absently scratching his chin. A small, thin scar can
be seen across the jawline.

Damian: When you're homeless, you start to see spaces
differently. I've been on the street, I mean, I don't know,
maybe six years total, on and off. Kicked out of a bad home,
the old story, you know. Not for the last few years now; I've
got a job and everything, I'm ... [three-second pause]. That
stuff doesn't leave you. The lessons you learn. And I'm not
talking about what it teaches you about people [bitter laugh]
though that's some of it. No, I'm talking about what it teaches
you about spaces. Because you're always looking for a place
to sleep, and a back-up for if your first choice is dangerous or
you get moved on. All cops, yadda yadda. You have to learn
to consider sightlines, because places you reckon are nice and
secluded might actually be clearly visible from a main road,
and places that feel very public might have a quirk that makes
them almost entirely hidden. And that's fine. Those things you
learn quick.

[02:28] He gets up and moves to the window, causing the camera to defocus again.

[02:34] He turns the handle on the window and slides it open. There is a small change in the audio quality as the air pressure rebalances and a gentle breeze can be heard. Damian takes a deep breath but snorts it out in disappointment. Clearly it is not as refreshing as he hoped. He continues to talk from the window.

Damian: What takes longer to learn is airflow and temperature. If you end up on the streets in spring, summer, like me, you don't even think about it until autumn hits, but then you've got to very quickly learn about this stuff. If you can't get an actual roof somehow, you need to figure out how warm a sleeping spot is going to be, how windproof. And let me tell you, for that stuff, your eyes are lying to you. The shape of a space changes so much about how much it keeps the heat in, how it channels or avoids the wind. You get a sense for the movement of air currents, how draughts can tell you a lot about how somewhere is constructed, how deep it is. How much protection it gives you. It's a sense you get mainly from feeling, but the sound, really opening your ears and listening, that's also— [Laughter] I mean, bats have really got the right idea. They've got it made. [Pause] They wouldn't have a good time here. That's one of the ... I mean, that's kind of why I ... I want a record. I want some proof.

[03:30] He reaches out a hand and places it on the wall beside the window. He presses against it. Nothing happens.

Damian: And I know, right? I know what this is, what my

counsellor would say. It's another obsession, because life has got stable and stable means boring. I've got a place to live. I've got a good job. [Pause] Well, I've got a job. So, my mind starts looking for things to shake it up, to make being sober more interesting. I know where this ends if I can't leave it alone, but ... I don't think I'm wrong here. And I want a record. I want some proof.

[3:50] He gestures towards the camera.

Damian: Because the spaces here, in Banyan Court, they're wrong.

[Cut]

[Timecode 01:02 10-08-2014]

[03:59] Damian is in a different room. The frame is at a slight angle, as if the camera has been placed down haphazardly, without consideration for stability. An unmade bed can be seen, alongside a radiator with several socks draped over it. The wall above the bed has a poster for the Hawkwind album *In Search of Space*. Damian is walking slowly back and forth, holding a tape measure. His hair has returned to its relatively unkempt state, and his shirt is now partially unbuttoned. Beneath it can be seen a chest binder and what appears to be a battered St Christopher medal on a thin metal chain.

[04:18] He walks out of the frame, then back past the camera, trailing a tape measure behind him. He then returns to in front of the camera and holds up a section of the tape measure, pointing at the measurement: 192cm.

Damian: This is not about my living space. Though, yeah, it's a shoebox. London, I guess. Hm. Weird how quickly you get used to something. Anyway, hold on.

[04:26] He gathers the tape measure back up and walks off frame, repeating the same process of stretching it across the width of the room. There is a pause.

Damian: Ah, hold on, [inaudible] wait for it to do its thing. It's not always predictable.

[04:39] He sits on the bed and waits.

[04:45] Damian continues to wait, impatience crossing his face. He takes his phone out of his jeans pocket but glances up at the camera and puts it back, instead waiting in silence.

Damian: Right. Let's try [inaudible].

[05:03] He stands up, takes the tape measure, and repeats the process a third time.

Damian: Ha!

[05:26] He returns to in front of the camera, a smile of vindication on his face. He holds the tape measure up to the lens. It takes a moment to focus, but his finger is positioned a few millimetres before the mark for 195cm.

Damian: These are between the same two points.

[05:30] He picks up the camera and angles it towards another wall, where an X has been clearly marked in red electrical tape. Damian turns the camera towards the other wall, where a similar X has been marked over a bedside table.

Damian: I've been living here about three months now. My first real place since the halfway house, so I really thought it was just in my head. Been living close to a lot of other folk for so long I thought it was just because I was on my own again that the space seemed wrong. But the feeling stayed there, bothering me. The airflow doesn't work right. So, I started doing some ... Well ...

[05:41] Damian walks over to the desk and picks up a notebook. He returns to in front of the camera and holds it up. The lens refocuses to show pages covered with measurements, all of which are almost, but not quite, identical.

Damian: I don't know what it means. But it can't be— Jesus, I [inaudible]. I mean, it's not like I don't know there's weird stuff out there.

[05:59] He puts the notebook down out of frame and sits on the bed, facing the camera.

Damian: I mean, you hear stuff, you know. When you're on the edges, most people don't really see you and you kind of, I don't know, you sort of start to see the other things the rest of the world doesn't notice. Also, you've got the, uh, well you get to hear a lot of really out-there beliefs. Blaming society, government, addiction for where you're at – it's easy to fall into. You get a lot of conspiracy theories, a lot of weird ideas. You've got to be careful. I had a friend once, Opal, said she couldn't listen to what folks talked about like that. Said if you opened your mind the brain worms got in. Not literally, you know, but those ideas that warp your perspective, change how you see the world so you can't see anything else. I guess I see her point. But I always listened. Didn't believe, not much, but I listened. [Pause] Something in this building isn't right. Cold corners. Draughts that shouldn't be there. Doesn't measure right. I don't know. [Pause] I don't know.

[Cut]

[Timecode 11:55 10-08-2014]

[06:51] The image is dark and out of focus. A small amount of light can be seen from above, coming through what seems to be the opening of a bag. There is a voice speaking. It is muffled by whatever the camera is being carried in, but it is deep, with a gentle accent.

Speaker 2: —be dangerous.

Damian: Sorry, could [inaudible], could you say that again?

Speaker 2: It's not a joke. I'm not trying to scare you.

Damian: You just said I should be worried.

Speaker 2: Not of me.

Damian: Of who, then? Of what?

Speaker 2: Tobias Fell. He [inaudible]

Damian: He built this place, didn't he? It—

[07:19] The bag with the camera is shifted, drowning out the audio for the next few seconds.

Speaker 2: —just watch out.

Damian: What's wrong with this place?

Speaker 2: What do you mean?

Damian: It's not right. Is it? It's, what, haunted?

[07:24] There is a long pause.

Speaker 2: I don't believe in any of that shit.

Damian: So, what are you afraid of?

Speaker 2: People. Real people. People with power.

Damian: Yeah. I guess [inaudible] worse than ghosts.

Speaker 2: [Pause] But you can't let them go unchecked. You just can't.

Damian: Gonna be honest. A rich man suffering consequences sounds a lot less plausible to me than ghosts.

Speaker 2: We'll see. You should go home, don't look too close. Whatever's going on here, you don't want to be part of it. [Inaudible] meet you, Damian.

Damian: You too, uh ...?

Speaker 2: Diego. Good luck. And please be careful. There are strange and dangerous people here.

Damian: Sure.

[07:51] There is a blur of movement and light as the camera is pulled out. It is turned to point at the corner at the end of a dingy corridor. A dark-skinned figure in an old suit is briefly glimpsed disappearing around it. The camera turns back towards Damian's face. Behind him we can see a cross of red electrical tape on one of the walls.

Damian: Weird guy. [Laughter] I like him.

[Cut]

[Timecode 02:25 11-08-2014]

[08:01] Damian is in the same chair from the first few shots. Behind him, the takeaway calendar can be seen more clearly than before. It is a stylised blue and white 'evil eye' design in watercolours. The lights in the window are dimmer than earlier, and almost entirely out of focus. Damian has his hands clasped together, fingers nervously drumming against each other.

Damian: I've been thinking. I've only been able to check the corridors on this side of the building. Been wondering about the front, if all those rich jackasses ...

[08:10] He trails off. His hands start to shake slightly. He sniffs as though he has been crying.

Damian: Christ. Don't know if [inaudible] this. Just a distraction, really, I guess. I mean who the hell cares? Like, really cares, if the rooms, corridors and all that aren't the right size all the time? Me, I guess, maybe. [Sighs] It's as good a distraction as any. I just wish I could get to sleep properly, you know? Wouldn't be as bad if I could just sleep a bit, but Christ here we are. As if getting deadnamed in Dad's obituary wasn't enough, I got a haunted fucking floorplan messing with my bedroom. Least work gave me a couple of weeks for 'bereavement'. It's [inaudible]. They don't need to know it's a 'glad the piece of shit is dead' kind of deal. Man throws out his kid, still gets a rosy write-up when he kicks it. Really want to talk to Ruth about it, but it's not like the AKT doesn't have enough to deal with without me bothering them more. I'm a success story, after all. [Joyless laugh] Still, time off gives me space to measure hallways, I guess. [Pause] God, I want a drink.

[08:50] There is a pause. Damian looks directly into the camera.

Damian: Delete this bit, OK? When you're— No one needs to see you like this.

[Cut]

[Timecode 07:42 11-08-2014]

[08:59] A corridor, similar to the one from the Diego recording. The camera is pointed at a corner above a doorway. There is a small black shape just visible. The shot zooms in on it, refocusing until it is clear that it is looking at another camera, small and tucked almost completely out of sight. The smaller camera is angled to be covering most of the corridor.

[09:10] The two cameras stare at each other for several seconds.

Damian: Looks like we might have a friend.

[Cut]

[Timecode 14:01 11-08-2014]

[09:19] A blonde woman in a navy-blue concierge's uniform is standing behind the front desk, a wall of marble tiles at her back. Daylight floods in from the floor-to-ceiling windows at the edge of the frame.

Concierge: Please put that away, sir.

[09:22] Damian's voice comes from behind the camera.

Damian: I just want to document what happens when I try to get into the building where I live.

Concierge: You don't live here, sir.

Damian: No, I guess I live in the paupers' ghetto that just happens to share walls, right?

[09:32] The concierge shrugs, clearly uncomfortable.

Damian: Look, I'm not going to hassle anyone. I just [pause]. I want to use the gym.

Concierge: I'm sorry. The health suite's only for people in the premium apartments.

Damian: Sure, figures. Only the rich get stuff for free, eh?

[09:41] The concierge chuckles once before catching herself.

Concierge: Look, I'm sorry, but I really can't let you up. It's policy. Check your tenancy agreement or whatever, they always slip it in there. I can't let you in. I'm sorry.

Damian: Of course. Just doing your job. Better than your colleague.

Concierge: What? Was one of my colleagues rude to you?

Damian: Basically threatened to have his friend beat me up if I didn't leave.

[10:01] The concierge's face darkens.

Concierge: That'd be Jason. Let me guess, he warned you about 'Max' and his 'temper'?

Damian: Yeah.

Concierge: [Sigh] Thanks for letting me know. I'll have a word with him. Again.

Damian: I mean, yeah. That's kind of why I brought …

[10:13] The frame shakes as Damian gestures with the camera.

Damian: In case anything happened.

[10:15] The concierge leans slowly forward, over the desk.

Concierge: [Whispered] Look, I don't [inaudible] you this, but there are some doors between your [inaudible] and this side. I don't know where they are, but I don't think they're all kept locked. Obviously [inaudible] best I can do.

Damian: Thank you. That's … Thank you.

Concierge: Yeah, sure. I'd appreciate if you don't put this footage anywhere my bosses would see it.

Damian: Sure thing.

[Cut]

[Timecode 14:19 12-08-2014]

[10:54] The camera lingers on a door, number 80. The walls surrounding it indicate it to be on the poorer side of Banyan

Court. There is a faint rustling sound that at first seems like an issue with the microphone, but as the camera gets closer to the door it becomes clear this is the sound of papers being moved, crumpled and shuffled from inside the apartment. It is replaced by the rhythmic scratching of a pencil writing at great speed. It's loud. Louder than you might expect.

Damian: No sign of those connecting doors. But I did stumble across ... well.

[11:12] The camera pans down to the ground and the edges of several sheets of legal paper are protruding from beneath the door. The camera defocuses as Damian kneels down to retrieve one of them.

[11:19] The paper comes into sharp relief. The header 'Akman Blane' can be seen.

Damian: Tried knocking, but no answer. Quick google says this is a bunch've corporate lawyers. Biggest client? Tobias Fell, owner of the building. Maybe a coincidence. Maybe.

[Cut]

[Timecode 23:40 12-08-2014]

[11:31] Damian is in his bedroom, sitting on the edge of his bed. He wears flannel pyjamas and a glass of water can be seen on his bedside table. He is holding three sheets of paper. His face is troubled.

Damian: 'They're not real.' That's what I said to her. She was scared and I wanted to reassure her, but ... [Pause] Hm.

[11:37] He looks down at the sheets of paper and picks one out, putting the others down on the bed.

Damian: I went back. To the door with the paper. Thought I'd do some measuring. I met the woman who lives there. Scared her half to death. I thought others might have noticed whatever's going on here, but this isn't just shifting walls, She seemed ... I don't want to use the word 'haunted', but ... [pause]. In a way it's almost reassuring, it's not just my brain seeing connections that aren't there, poking walls for no reason. But in another way, it's terrifying. It means it's real. And it means it's not just the layout, it's not just the place. It's doing something to the people here. Maybe even targeting them. I don't know how many, it might just be the two of us, but I don't think so. I've seen a couple of others around who ... I don't know, it's like you can see it in their faces. [Pause] 'They're not real.' Why did I say that to her? Diego said don't look too close, to leave it alone ... Maybe it's one of those things, you know, if you don't believe in it, it can't hurt you. You stare so long this place drags you in. Maybe I was trying to protect her. Maybe I just thought she needed to hear it. What even is 'real' when we're talking about something like this?

[12:22] He holds up the piece of paper to the camera, which tries unsuccessfully to focus on the text. Damian shifts the positioning and a dark smudge can be seen on the side of the sheet. The image clears. It's a thumbprint in what appears to be dried blood.

Damian: 'Not real' doesn't mean harmless. Never has. Some of the most harmful things in the world aren't real. The woman at number 80, she isn't safe. Don't think anyone here is. I don't know what to do, to be honest. I can find somewhere else to live, but it'll take time. I'm not going back to the streets. And if there are other people this place is affecting, can I leave them? They're not my responsibility, I know that. But who else's going to look out for them? Folks this side, folks in need, nobody [inaudible]. Maybe I'm just curious.

[12:44] Damian lets the paper go and it falls gently out of frame. He reaches for the camera.

[Cut]

[Timecode 02:44 13-08-2014]

[12:49] It is dark. There is the sound of agitated movement and the camera is clearly moving violently. Something is scraping, like brick or stone being dragged. Damian can be heard breathing heavily.

Damian: What the fuck what the fuck what—

[12:58] A switch can be heard being flicked and the room illuminates, causing the camera feed to briefly overcompensate, saturating a shot of Damian's bed. For a split second it appears as though the walls next to it are shifting, but when the camera finishes compensating for the new lighting, they are still.

Damian: That's ... What?

[13:07] He brings the camera closer to the corner of the room where his bed is situated. He runs his hand slowly across the wall next to it, then the one behind it. There is no reaction from the wall. Damian curls his hand into a fist and hits it against the section above his pillow. Nothing happens.

Damian: They were moving. I swear. Woke up and I could feel it, the space around me changing. God that felt ... Did not like that.

[13:20] The camera continues focusing on the walls. They remain static.

Damian: Why, though? Were they trying to crush me maybe? Don't know. Feels more aggressive than what I've seen elsewhere. Still, guess it's noticed me. Is that good news? Hm. Probably not.

[13:32] The camera moves close to the walls, causing it to defocus as it gets close to the texture of the plaster.

Damian: What's wrong? Don't want to perform for an audience? Interesting.

[13:36] He pulls the camera back.

Damian: If they don't like the camera, it's worth keeping it closer from now on. All the time, not just when I'm hunting. Big if, though.

[13:43] The camera is placed on the bedside table. Damian can be heard sighing.

Damian: Probably move to sleeping on the couch.

[Cut]

[Timecode 13:49 13-08-2014]

[13:47] A woman's face fills the frame. Caroline Fairley. She is young, with light hair kept short and stylish and a pair of expensive-looking earrings.

Damian: You sure this is OK?

Caroline: Yeah, it's fine. More evidence, y'know?

Damian: That's the idea. And I guess I kind of always wanted to be a director.

Caroline: [Laughing] Oh yeah?

Damian: Seriously! I mean, [inaudible] not seriously, seriously, but I always loved the idea. When I got my job, actually had a bit of money, this camera was the first thing I bought.

[14:01] The camera shakes as Damian indicates it.

Caroline: And did you use it before all this?

Damian: Hm. Not really. I guess it was more of a dream than

a plan. But then I started getting paranoid about this place and ... Just feels safer to keep it around. [Pause] So you ready?

Caroline: Sure. How did you want to do it?

Damian: Just say your piece, I guess.

[14:13] A look of resolve passes over Caroline's face. She stares directly into the camera, addressing the viewer.

Caroline: My name is Caroline Fairley. I live in number 4 Banyan Court. I have, over the last few weeks, become convinced that the building I live in is haunted. I intend to find proof of this in the form of a room that I believe does not exist in the physical world. I'm being helped in this by Damian, uh—

Damian: Simpson.

Caroline: Damian Simpson, who had also been investigating this place. He has offered help and guidance in my search.

Damian: Best I can do, at least.

[14:47] The camera pans wildly as it is passed between them. It settles on Damian's face.

Caroline: So, what's the deal? How do I get to the ballroom? You said you had a theory.

Damian: Yeah, sort of. I'm still trying to figure the why of it all, but I've been putting the pieces together, doing some research of my own and, well, this building isn't normal. It's like, you know the standard ghost spiel, right? The things a place has seen, the terrible crimes and awful suffering gets baked into the wall, caught in the fabric of a place. Like Janek said, an infection entering the body.

Caroline: Sure.

Damian: Not this place. It's ... I can't find evidence of anything happening here that might explain what's going on. But these ... echoes? They're still here, somehow. Like they were made part of the foundations, the actual walls. Like Banyan Court is a Frankenstein of second-hand shadows.

Caroline: Poetic. But Frankenstein was the doctor.

Damian: It's bleeding into people, especially those that look too closely, whose attention is too focused on the walls, the structure, the homes here. Or those that feel trapped. It's starting to reach out to them. What I don't know yet is why. Or what it wants.

Caroline: You think it has enough of a mind to want something?

Damian: Maybe, maybe not. If not the building itself, then maybe the spirits, the ... echoes, or whatever, that have been made a part of it. So far, the only connection seems to be with Tobias Fell. Which isn't much of a connection, from what I've seen.

Caroline: I mean, he was the one who had the place built. You think it might be deliberate?

[15:54] Damian says nothing. He looks thoughtful, then troubled.

Damian: I don't know. I don't know how you'd do this deliberately. Or why.

Caroline: So, who's it touched?

Damian: What do you mean?

Caroline: You said it was bleeding into people. Have you met many?

Damian: A few. [Pause] There was a plumber found dead workers in the pipes, he actually gave me the whole 'disease' metaphor. Um, there's a young woman trapped by a mountain of paper cover-ups and conspiracies. A few others I think might have been ... There was one man, said he was from Ecuador, he refused, I think. Said he didn't believe in any of it, that I shouldn't look too closely. It seemed to leave him alone.

Caroline: You think not believing protects you?

Damian: I don't know. Maybe. I've been hoping this helps.

[16:30] He gestures to the camera.

Damian: Maybe protection's not an option for us.

Caroline: Guess not. Who knows? Maybe I'll find some answers in the ballroom.

[16:34] Damian tries to smile, but it doesn't seem to sit well with him.

Damian: Maybe. Just be careful. You're really sure that you want to do this?

Caroline: I've got to know. And you said it can't hurt us.

[16:50] There's a long pause as Damian considers this.

Damian: Physically … No, I don't think it can. But there's a lot of other types of harm.

Caroline: I'm not afraid.

Damian: Maybe you should be. Maybe we both should.

Caroline: You said you'd help me.

Damian: Yeah, I know, I did. I will.

Caroline: So?

Damian: I think maybe the key is not to think about it as a space in the world. I've been thinking about this a lot. So much of the world, of the spaces in it, exist only in your mind. Maybe that's what you need to focus on – Banyan Court as it seems to you. Opening yourself up to it. To what it wants to say.

Caroline: There was one point [inaudible] I think I heard music.

Damian: Then maybe it's already calling you, and you just need to follow where it wants you to go. You said it was, what, a ballroom? Like dancing?

Caroline: Yeah.

Damian: Then follow the music. Ignore where the corridors should lead you. Go where it wants you to be. Listen in the dark and follow.

Caroline: Right. [Pause] Will I be safe?

Damian: I don't know. Maybe. This place ... I mean, I don't think it's killed anyone yet.

[Cut]

[Timecode 22:40 13-08-2014]

[17:59] The camera is focused on a section of corridor wall. The carpeting is plush, and the thick wallpaper is lit with tasteful up-lighting. He is clearly in one of the upper floors of the front part of the building. The frame is focused on a long section of blank wall slightly beyond the door to flat 7. It lingers there for a while, then swings around, pointing to the door to flat 8, opposite. When the camera is angled back to the original wall, nothing has changed. It remains a blank space.

Damian: Right. Cari's gone, off on her ... Journey. And it got me thinking. Maybe I've been hiding, pretending like I'm looking for something, but always taking shelter behind the lens. I told Cari what to look for, but I've been too afraid to open up myself. So, let's do this.

[18:35] The camera is shakily placed down onto the carpeted floor, and the frame is taken up by carpet fibres and a pair of brown Doc Martens boots.

[Cut]

[Timecode 22:44 13-08-2014]

[18:38] The camera turns on, pointed at the space next to flat 7. A new hallway now branches off from it, replacing what was previously blank wall. The sides of this new hallway, though covered in the same wallpaper, seem slightly darker than those we have already seem, as though the wall underneath is a different colour. The camera lingers on the new space. When Damian speaks again, his voice is less confident.

Damian: I was right. I was right. Let me show you.

[18:42] He tries to steady his hand as the camera struggles to focus.

Damian: Just watch.

[19:27] He begins to make his way down the new corridor. It seems to stretch off some way into the distance, but only has two doors – opposite each other on either side. They appear to be the same make and style of door as to the other flats on this floor, but there are no numbers on them. Around the edges, the heavy wood appears scorched.

[19:40] Damian reaches out to grip one of the handles, but his hand pauses just before making contact, and pulls back.

Damian: Too hot to touch, it's—

[19:43] The camera focuses on a point on the wall next to the door, there is a slight difference in the texture of the wallpaper.

Damian: Let's try something else.

[19:48] His hand reappears in the frame, this time holding a small pocketknife with the blade extended. He pauses, clearly trying to decide where to cut, before choosing an apparently arbitrary section of wall and begins to push it in. It goes through far easier than would be expected, and as Damian begins to pull downwards a small shower of black ash begins to fall from where he is cutting.

[19:56] He puts away the pocketknife and takes hold of the edges of the wallpaper where he's cut it. Tearing it away reveals the wall beneath is blackened and burned.

Damian: What is this it's—

[20:17] He starts scraping at the blackened wall with his hand, now grimy with soot. Something lighter can be seen just underneath the ashes, embedded in the wall.

Damian: No. No way.

[20:40] He grips the small white object in the wall and twists it out, holding it in front of the lens. The camera takes a moment to refocus. It is a human tooth, slightly warped and deformed as if from intense heat. Damian takes a breath in disgust but composes himself quickly.

Damian: You think about all those people in Fell's properties, his companies. If they burn, is it his fault? How much is he responsible for, what did he encourage, where did he turn a blind eye? However you try to cut it, somewhere down the line he had a hand in a lot of people burning alive.

[21:03] He turns the camera back to the hole he has made in the wall. Pale shapes can be seen among the ashes, possibly other bones.

Damian: And now it looks like they're here. Echoes. In the pipes, the walls ... God, what if—

[21:13] He is interrupted by the sound of someone screaming. It seems to be coming from the floor above him.

[Cut]

[Timecode 22:49 13-08-2014]

[21:16] There is the sound of muffled screaming. Damian is running up a staircase and the camera bounces around, unable to focus as the stairs fly past. The lighting and chrome of the handrail indicates he is in the front of Banyan Court. The screams seem to be coming from somewhere further above.

Damian: Shit shit [inaudible] shit.

[21:26] He reaches a door at the very top of the stairway. The distressed cries are clearer now and seem to be coming from the other side, along with the sounds of a physical struggle. Damian reaches for the handle, then pauses for a second. He takes a deep breath, then opens the door slowly. His hands are shaking, causing the frame to shake in turn.

[21:45] The camera is lowered to ground level and looks round into the corridor, though it is unclear whether Damian himself has actually gone through the door or is simply holding the camera out to get a better look. The hallway is identical to the previous ones seen on this side of the building, except that this one terminates in a large glass window, through which the night skyline of London can just about be seen. Near to it, two figures appear to be struggling.

[21:49] The camera zooms in on the pair and it becomes clear that the struggle is very one-sided, as the larger of the two men, a hulking figure in a black uniform, is easily restraining his victim, a scrawny teenager in a dark jacket and blue baseball cap. The man is striking his victim repeatedly with a heavy-looking wooden baton. There is a pause as he surveys the damage his weapon has done, then he hoists the bloody youth up higher.

Assailant: [Inaudible] you, right, punk?

[22:00] The uniformed attacker hurls his victim against the window, shattering it completely. The boy disappears into the night sky. After a second there's a thump that might be a microphone issue or could be the sound of a body hitting the street outside.

Damian: [Breathing hard] Shit.

[22:03] The assailant turns around, though it is unclear whether or not they have heard Damian. In full view, it is clear there is something very wrong with the killer's body. It is distorted, as though the skin of a much smaller man were stretched out over the frame of this larger one. The face is distended, and the fingernails stop partway up the enormous hands, though there appears to be no discomfort in the man's movements. When he takes a step, it's as though the camera had taken a double-exposure, with two human figures, both uniformed, superimposed over each other. The figure takes another step towards the camera, and a name badge comes into focus for just a second. Freezing the frame allows it to be read as 'JASON'.

[22:10] The camera is withdrawn rapidly and there's a blur of motion as Damian flees down the stairs.

[Cut]

[Timecode 23:54 13-08-2014]

[22:15] Damian is sitting in his kitchen. His face is pale and his hands tremble as he drinks a glass of water. Each time the liquid touches his lips, his eyes flick down to it, as if in disappointment. He sighs shakily and places the glass down out of frame. He stares blankly into the camera.

Damian: I don't, uh—

[22:27] He looks up sharply as though he has heard something. He stands up and walks out of the frame. There is the sound of a door being unlocked and then relocked.

[23:11] Damian returns and sits back down. He is visibly pale.

Damian: He didn't see me. It didn't see me. And if it did, there's no way it knows who I am, or where I— Unless the building tells it. This place knows.

[23:23] He looks up at the walls surrounding him, suddenly aware of their presence.

Damian: I was wrong about what's here. These echoes, they're so much more dangerous than I thought. God, what have I done I've sent Cari to— No, that's not— She would have gone there without me. And she might still be OK. She might [pause]. Shit.

[23:44] He continues to stare into the camera.

Damian: I should go to the police. They're already here. I think. I heard sirens. I don't know what I'd— I looked over the footage. It's, I mean, you can see the poor bastard go through the window, but the guy who did it, there's no way you could identify him from what I've got. They'd say I messed with the video. Best case scenario they think I'm wasting their time, tell me to get lost and guy— the thing that did this doesn't notice me. And given my history, if I get involved with the police, even as a witness I'm— I know what it's like to lose everything. And I can't do that again.

[Cut]

[Timecode 09:17 15-08-2014]

[24:19] There is a knocking coming from somewhere further down the corridor. Damian moves the camera slowly, cautiously. The state of the corridor indicates he is in the front of the building. He is breathing slowly, nervously, as he approaches the noise. It sounds like someone is knocking on the front door of one of the flats, but it is rhythmic and constant, not pausing or waiting for any response.

[24:36] The camera is held round a corner to reveal a man standing in front of the door to number 30 Banyan Court. He is dressed in what was once clearly an extremely fine tailored suit in an ocean blue, but what remains is torn, dirty, dishevelled. His features are Hispanic, and his face is blank as he knocks again and again on the door to number 30.

Damian: Hello?

[25:00] The figure does not respond. Damian begins cautiously approaching.

Damian: I don't think anyone's home. Do, do you need help?

[25:21] As he gets closer it becomes clear that the man is holding something in his hand. It appears to be a piece of cream-coloured cardstock. He does not respond to the camera's approach.

Damian: Hey, man, look, you seem in really rough shape. Can I call someone for you? Where do you live?

[25:32] The stranger's response is so quiet the microphone barely picks it up.

Knocker: Here I [inaudible] mine. Stolen. Stolen [inaudible] me.

[25:38] Damian doesn't immediately respond. The camera lingers on the man as he knocks again and again on his front door, waiting for a response.

[25:47] Damian tries the handle, but the door is locked. He sighs. The knocking man does not respond to the attempt.

Damian: This place really did a number on you, huh?

[25:53] He reaches down and gently prises the cardboard from the man's fingers. He holds it up in front of the camera, which takes a moment to focus on the words. It reads: *TOBIAS FELL cordially invites JÈSUS CANDIDO to attend a dinner party at 1 Banyan Court on the evening of 16th August 2014. Penthouse access will be available through the freight elevator.*

Damian: That— Is that what I ...? I guess that changes things. [Pause] I need to check something.

[26:05] He reaches out and tucks the invitation inside the jacket of the unresisting Jésus, then turns around to leave.

[Cut]

[Timecode 11:32 15-08-2014]

[26:11] Damian is back in his kitchen. There is an odd smile on his face. In his hands he holds two pieces of card. His fingers are grey with ash.

Damian: I was right. I made my choice. I went back to the corridor, the one with the ... The burned one. Did a bit of digging in the walls and there it was. If I wasn't haunted before, I sure am now. Cari got one as well, found it slipped half-under her door. She's OK. Or at least alive. Maybe that's the best we can hope for right now. I don't know exactly what this means, but I have my suspicions.

[26:28] He pauses, deep in thought.

Damian: Trapped in the walls. Trapped in the pipes ... Trapped.

[26:31] Another pause.

Damian: I was hoping I'd have a chance to see Janek again before all this, confirm a few things ... Well, too late now.

[26:37] He shakes his head.

Damian: None of this is an accident. Maybe Fell organised it all himself, maybe he's been put at the centre of it all by someone else, something else. These invitations were sent by the building, though, no way did a human being go round putting these in the hands of the haunted. Which is me too now, I guess. No getting off this ride now. Just got to hope I know what I'm doing.

[26:50] He holds up the cards. His and Caroline's names can be briefly seen, but otherwise the text is an exact match for Jésus' invitation.

Damian: I don't want to go. I'm— I mean, I'm terrified. But I'm more scared of not going. Of what happens without me there. I don't know if I'd even be able to *not* go. I do have theories. Some ideas about ... Well, I'm not going to say on this thing. Maybe it's just paranoia, but I'm starting to think the only safe place to keep my plans is in my head. Still, there's time yet before the party. Hopefully I—

[27:09] There is a knock at the door. Damian looks up, apprehensive. He starts to rise, but stops as the camera's microphone picks up, just for a moment, the faint strains of an orchestra. He smiles sadly and his eyes return to the camera.

Damian: There she is. I guess wish us luck. Whatever happens, I think it's going to be messy. Cari gave me the address of some journalist she was talking to, so, uh, if you're watching this, then ... Hi. [Pause] Really hope I made it back.

[27:25 – End]

13th

The Builder

Tobias Fell
1 Banyan Court

Tobias

The penthouse was prepared. In many ways it always had been. The wide, open central room had been kept largely empty, devoid of furniture and simply adorned with tasteful mood pieces around the edges – ready to receive tonight's guests. Was that dreadful little art dealer coming tonight? He'd actually provided Tobias with a few of them. Not directly, of course, Tobias had people for that. Still, the penthouse had always been ready to receive these visitors. It had, after all, been built for them.

Tobias wandered down into the grand dining room, limping slightly on the still-new prosthetic that had replaced the lower part of his right leg. He brushed his fingers lightly along the fine polished oak of the immense table. They'd had to bring it up in parts through his private elevator, the location of which he was uncomfortable at having revealed, and then build it up here. But it had been worth it. He counted the place settings. Twelve. He wasn't entirely certain of the number of guests that were expected, but he had been told this sort of thing tended to work in certain numbers. Twelve just seemed right. If there were more guests than that, then he would figure something out.

Tobias hadn't been there when the table had been put in place, of course. He liked to imagine it, though, the sort of people who did the work. Who would have been hired to set this sort of thing up? He'd given his assistant, Jeremy, very specific instructions, and they had certainly been carried out, but who would the man have got to do it? A local firm, all rough features and gruff shouting? Or a team of elegant professionals, skilled and expensive, with cotton gloves and hushed tones? What human experience had brushed against this, the culmination of his strangest project?

He sighed, clearly it would have been the latter. Jeremy would never have trusted local workmen to have the discretion a task like this required. In many ways he was far more prejudiced about that sort of thing than Tobias. He'd been against building Banyan Court in Tower Hamlets at all. Of course, he couldn't be told exactly why it had to be built there, that powerful psychic frisson that seemed so very important: the history of poverty, tragedy and exploitation these bricks had born witness to at the hands of Tobias's own ancestors. Still, the billionaire fundamentally had nothing against the people who lived here, in the paupers' tenement he had designed. Their poverty, their lack of education and class, it wasn't their fault. It was simply the by-product of a system. And Tobias had no respect for those who benefited from a system but could not stomach looking at the waste produced by it. This world was designed to generate winners and losers, and it showed a lack of character to wish yourselves a winner without accepting what it does to those who lose.

Someone had once, years ago, asked him in an interview whether he considered himself a good man, and he still laughed to think about it. About the crude concept of goodness and how the ignorant still clung to it in defiance of the world they helped to create. He was simply a man who had learned early how the system worked and used it as it was designed. Anything else was pretention and self-delusion.

The sun was beginning to set, the city beyond the glass walls of the penthouse illuminated in deep oranges and crimsons. Tonight, for the first time in years, he had drawn the curtains back, allowing the light to enter. If any nosy paparazzo had had the patience to be watching for him all this time, then perhaps they should be rewarded. The dining area was, of course, curtained and hidden. Some things tonight must still remain private.

The light played across his skin. It was so pale now that he had to use colour correction during video conference meetings. The one time he had forgotten to do so one of his directors had tried to insist he see a doctor. They didn't understand, of course, but that wasn't their fault. They hadn't seen what he had seen. Soon he could leave, see the sun again. See people again. If he wanted to. He'd found isolation more agreeable than he'd originally thought possible. Perhaps he would remain a recluse – but it would be his choice this time. Tobias smiled. Maybe tonight would be an opportunity to see how the presence of real people affected him after all this time. Not *normal* people, of course, but it was a start. But there was work to do first.

The sound of grinding metal echoed from the other side of the penthouse. Somewhere, deep below, the old iron freight elevator was gradually groaning its way up the building for the first time in almost a century. He listened, the grinding of gears a stark contrast to the secretive silence of his own private lift.

Tobias took a moment. Was he nervous? Guilty? No matter. The first of his guests was about to arrive.

Jason

The old iron cage wasn't small, but next to Max's bulk Jason felt as if he was being pressed into the latticed bars like sausage meat through a mincer. Every ragged breath Max took, it was like the floor was going to buckle, but still the tiny platform crawled its way upwards. The smell of his old friend's rotten flesh seemed palpable, and Jason couldn't imagine what sort of dinner party a billionaire could possibly be throwing where it wasn't going to be an issue. Something in the back of his mind told him that that wasn't the weirdest part of the situation, but when he tried to focus on it his head began to swim.

'Don't worry about it,' Max growled through what remained of his lips. 'Just do your job.'

He rested one hand on the large wooden box that took up the rest of the elevator's limited space. It looked heavy and, notably, easily big enough to hold a person. Jason's eyes lingered on it for a second. Did he know what was inside? There was a memory there, but it didn't feel like his.

Far above, the ceiling began to approach, and the lift started to slow. Jason reached down for his nightstick, before remembering it was Max that had one, not him.

'I got you, Jace,' Max said. 'Any of them give you trouble, you just let me know.'

Then there was a juddering, clattering stop as they reached the top. Max reached over his head and grabbed the sliding grate, pulling it open. The lift now sat in what seemed to be a dilapidated engine room up in the roof. In front of them was a simple metal door, shiny and new among the old and neglected material.

'After you,' Max said.

The door opened outwards and Jason's breath caught ever so slightly in his throat. The room was huge, with the faintest hint of some fragrance in the air that was quickly overpowered by the decaying stench of his partner squeezing through the door behind him, dragging the wooden box.

'There's nobody here.' Jason looked around, confused. 'Are we early?'

'We're security. 'Course we're here early.'

'So, what do we do?'

'We keep an eye on things. When people arrive we make sure they're taken care of. One way or another.'

Tobias

The office from which Tobias conducted his business was surprisingly plain. He held no meetings there and, aside from a few construction workers, no one else had ever seen it in person. All he required was a comfortable chair, a phone and a computer, all of which were of the highest quality that money could buy. In some cases higher. But anything that would have required binders of documents or detailed filing was taken care of by people lower down the ladder and at this point even the things he did need to reference were almost entirely digital. He had a single bookshelf full of weighty-looking titles he hadn't read that was set up in the spot facing his webcam, but aside from that the room was spartan.

He sat at his desk, watching the video feeds from the main room. The man who stood there was not a particularly impressive specimen, but he was clearly talking to someone else. As he came more into focus Tobias could clearly make out a uniform, one he recognised from the security camera feeds he had made sure he always had access too. The concierge, then. He tapped on his keyboard and the images from the rest of the building disappeared, every screen now displaying this one sorry-looking figure. Then Tobias took a moment, closed his eyes, and focused.

When he opened them again the second figure was now visible on his screen. Thin lips split into a wide grin as he took in the rotting goliath. The little concierge's imagination had worked a grotesque wonder when choosing a form for his haunting. And they had brought the main course for dinner, as instructed. That was certainly a relief. It was one thing to watch the suffering of the poor souls below, but now it came time for them to play their parts he had been somewhat wary. But no, it all seemed to be going quite to plan. This was going to be delightful.

Violet

Several of the guests arrived together. Violet had no idea who any of them were, nor did she really care. They certainly hadn't arranged a time to go up as a group, but still they congregated at the bottom of that ancient iron spine, waiting silently for the lift. One of them, a middle-aged black woman who looked like she hadn't slept in weeks, tried to make small talk, but Violet ignored her. Then the rattle began as the elevator crawled its way back down towards them, settling finally at the bottom with a crunch.

'Is it safe?' asked a young woman in a long pastel-blue party dress. She wore a full face of make-up and a tasteful pair of earrings, and when her eyes passed over Violet's durable work clothes, stained with the remnants of a hard day's labour, there was a flash of confusion in them.

Violet didn't answer as she stepped into the lift. The young woman's hands were soft and clean; the two of them had nothing to talk about. The other guests followed, seven in all. Two little girls with a nervous-looking mother, the tired woman, the one in the blue dress, a young man in a suit several sizes too large, and a flamboyant gentleman in a maroon blazer who was leaning on his cane, trying desperately to keep his legs from shaking. They barely all fit, and Violet could feel herself pushed into the cold iron walls by the press of bodies. She smiled and placed her calloused, blistered hand on the lever. It felt so very familiar.

Gillian

Gillian arrived with the second group, knowing with crystal certainty she was going to be murdered. Obviously. That was the only real explanation for what was happening. As the giddy thrill of her discovery had begun to fade and the apparent reality of the situation started to assert itself, a deep terror had begun to grip her. She'd got too close, and now Tobias Fell was inviting her to her own assassination.

What could she do but go? She was tired of running. Besides, a man with such resources, such an intricately woven net, there was nowhere she could escape his reach. If he was able to go to such lengths simply to invite her to this event, then trying to avoid it would no doubt just make whatever end he had in mind for her more painful. Better to attend in the hope that it would be quick and maybe, just maybe, she could get some answers before she died. Even now, Gillian couldn't help but feel that if she got some real answers it might just be worth it. The others being here worried her, though. Did they know how much danger they were in? Were they a part of it?

The iron box continued its tortuous ascent and Gillian tried to ignore the stink rolling off one of her fellow passengers, a white guy in a stained grey suit who looked like he'd taken a bath in mould. The only other person riding with them, a middle-aged man who wore a newly ironed polyester suit and a shy smile, was also clearly trying to ignore the smell. She wondered what grim discoveries of their own must have led them here.

She looked up, trying to focus on the progress of the elevator to distract her from both the odour and the dread of her own imminent demise, and a thought struck her.

'Hey,' she said to no one in particular. 'If the old freight elevator was part of the original Victorian building, and that was only about five or six storeys, then how come it goes all the way up to the penthouse? The metal all seems about the same age.'

The man in the cheap suit smiled and shrugged, before replying in what Gillian guessed was a Polish accent.

'Ghosts?'

Gillian didn't laugh.

Carter

'Hey, hold the lift!' A voice rang out as the third and final group were about to ascend.

Carter looked up to see someone sprinting full speed towards them. He opened the door again instinctively, before he'd fully grasped who it was. That horrible journalist, David something-or-other, who'd had him do that dreadful interview. He climbed inside before Carter had a chance to reconsider and pulled the door closed behind him.

'David?'

This voice belonged to the other occupant of the elevator, a young woman who'd introduced herself as Cari, dressed in silver velvet and bedecked in an astonishing quantity of jewellery.

'Caroline?' David said, his mouth hanging slightly open. 'You look ... Uh, thank you. Mr Dwight. For the door. And sorry about—'

'Forget it,' he replied, trying to hide his anger. The old Carter wouldn't have hesitated to give the little troll a piece of his mind. Maybe he was a better person, after all.

'I didn't realise you'd got an invite,' Cari's voice was light, but there was a hint of something underneath it that sounded worried.

'Oh, I wouldn't miss this,' David said with a wink. She didn't seem reassured, but he was clearly too distracted to notice.

'Well, then,' Carter said curtly. 'Let's not keep our host waiting.'

He had always expected to at some point be travelling to the penthouse in Tobias Fell's private elevator, the one he'd heard talked about over long business lunches. This angular iron cage was a long way from that dream, but as Carter pulled the lever of the reassuringly primitive mechanism, he was glad this was how he got there.

And the last of the party guests began to ascend.

Leon

Tobias Fell's flat was immaculate. That was the first thing that struck him upon entering. The floors were polished to a mirror shine and what furniture there was seemed to somehow manage an appearance of being both antique and brand new at the same time. The walls had been painted in light, airy colours unblemished by any sort of mark and Leon had the strangest urge to press himself against them, as though their cleanliness might somehow become his.

He was under no illusions about his appearance. He had spent most of the day showering, buying new suits, watching shop assistants recoil in disgust at his appearance. It did no good, though, and perhaps that was right. He'd been embraced by Banyan Court, so perhaps it was only fair that he bear its mark proudly. He wondered briefly if it should have been Andrea there instead. Had he somehow stolen her invite? No, she had seen the stain first, perhaps, but deep down he knew it was his. And if there were any others who could understand what that meant, they would be here. Looking around the party he could smell the place on them as clearly as he could on himself. They were all stained, even if only he could see it. He saw the peacocking art dealer strutting by, what was his name? It didn't matter. He could preen all he wanted, but he reeked of it just as surely as Leon did.

'Arsehole,' he muttered under his breath. Then paused, smiled. 'Arthole.'

He laughed at his own joke, a small chuckle that came out far louder than he intended. A few of the other guests looked over at him with a pity in their eyes that made him wince. The two security guys also gave him a stare. Did he know that one from the front desk? Poor man looked almost as out of place here as Leon. His colleague, however, was a different story. Six foot four hunched over, with a face like the underside of a truck, his eyes scanning the assembled crowd with purpose. Even the front desk guy looked scared of him. What was going on here?

Turning his own gaze to the dozen or so other guests around him, Leon tried to spot any other familiar faces. Was that Carter Dwight? That made sense, he seemed like the sort of person to be invited to a billionaire's party. They'd met at a tech conference last year and he remembered the conversation coming easily.

'Hey!' Leon called. 'Hey, Carter, how'd the new Dodj rollout go?'

Carter pretended not to have heard. Well, that was fine. None of them were better than Leon, whatever they thought. They were all contaminated just the same.

Damian

Surveying the room was a fascinating experience. Every one of them walking, talking in a way they so clearly felt was normal. Even the knocking man was smiling and doing his best to socialise as if nothing was wrong. But none of them were quite managing it. It felt so much like he was watching them from a distance, from behind glass, and Damian wished, not for the first time, that he'd been brave enough to bring his camera.

To call them mad wouldn't have been right. Haunted didn't sit entirely well either, especially for those of them whose experiences had given them a certain manic quality, but all of them had been in some way touched by the building, taken by it. Damian wondered how each of them perceived the others, what they saw.

Even Cari had not escaped. She was perhaps more aware than the rest of them, or had seemed so when they talked about it earlier, but as Damian watched her move ably through the crowd, he couldn't ignore the fact that the glittering jewellery, which she had not owned until she walked into that ballroom, was gently weeping blood onto her skin. Did the others see it? Did she? He hadn't asked, afraid to confront the possibility that she was as adrift from reality as the rest of them.

Damian tried to take stock of his own mind, but how can you evaluate your own perceptions? He felt clear-headed, keenly aware of the space around him, the angles of the penthouse, the danger that they all found themselves in. Rational. But he was also aware that he was currently all but crouched in a corner, trying his best to make sense of how the room felt. It seemed at once like it was closing around them, pushing the group together, but at the same time infinitely too large, as though it had no walls at all and was open to the empty night air. Was he as compromised as all the others? Had he walked right into the jaws of the lion, ignorantly believing himself to be a Daniel?

At least he'd had a chance to talk with Janek about what the plumber had found in the heart of the building, but as much as it confirmed some of Damian's suspicious, it hadn't given him anything immediately useful. He was starting to feel very much out of his depth.

He almost retreated backwards, further into the corner, but caught himself just in time. He didn't want to touch the walls in the penthouse. The walls had always been where the pain, the imported suffering of this place, seemed most concentrated and he could feel it more strongly here than elsewhere in the building. Damian tried to decide if there was something he should be doing yet. No. Even if his idea was going to work, he had to wait for the right moment.

And he had to trust that he'd know when that was. For now he'd bide his time. Eventually their host would arrive. And then Damian would learn exactly how stupid he had been in coming here.

Jésus

Jésus was having a dreadful time. He felt like his whole body had been wrung dry and his right hand was swollen and bruised. His memory of the last week was patchy and confused, but he knew one thing with absolute certainty: his home had been taken from him and he could not return. Nonetheless, he was still Jésus Candido, and he would not be defeated so easily.

When he had returned to himself after ... whatever had happened, the invitation tucked into his jacket had been the only clue about his missing days. Of course, even without hoping to have some answers he would never have been fool enough to refuse an invitation from Tobias Fell. He had retrieved an outfit from storage (out of season, but it would have to do) and had booked a nearby hotel room to prepare. And now he was here, trying his best to admire the various art pieces (some of which he flattered himself to recognise) and wait for whatever was going to happen. For someone to explain the picture and the lost time and all the strange dreams that had been tormenting him. And, ideally, for someone to apologise.

He avoided the other guests as best he could, casting the occasional withering glance at how they were dressed. The rancid man in the filthy suit didn't really bother him, if he had had an option to turn up any other way no doubt he would have taken it, but Jésus could not forgive the cheap polyester effort of the rough-handed workman gawping at the Csaky sculpture near the door to the dining room. To make matters worse, that lazy fool from the front desk was here, working security of all things, though luckily neither he nor his grotesque companion seemed to be paying Jésus any notice. And there were children here.

WITHDRAWN

Then there was the man in the corner. Young, a face lined with hardships, and a cheap, but tastefully chosen, suit. There was something in that face Jésus recognised.

'Excuse me, do I ... know you? We have met before?'

'Maybe around the building,' the young man said, dodging the question. 'We both live here, after all.'

'No, but I have seen you,' Jésus insisted. 'Were you the one who gave me my invitation?'

The young man shook his head, backing away slightly, as though nervous. Which was ridiculous, as Jésus was just trying to have a *normal* conversation.

'What is going on here?' Jésus was losing patience.

'I don't know for sure. I'm trying to find out, but ... you can help me. If you want.'

It was that infuriating tone used to mollify the delusional. Jésus did not need to be humoured.

'Tell me what you know.' He advanced on the wary looking young man. 'What do you know about the painting that stole my home?'

'Nothing. But I'd guess it had history. And it wasn't acquired innocently.'

A pause.

'Who died so you could own it?'

Jésus' whole body went cold. His hand knocked twice against his leg.

'I-I have to go,' he stammered.

The young man couldn't hide his look of relief, but shook his head.

'Don't think we can. Not until the party's over.'

Janek

The tie felt tight around Janek's neck, and he tried not to look desperate as he glanced around to see if there was anyone serving drinks. He had never felt so drastically out of place. He recognised a few of the other guests as living in the building, but he was neither wealthy nor a resident. So what was he doing here? He wanted to move on, forget what he had seen and felt at the sick heart of Banyan Court, but instead he had come here, to the building's head. What culture was it that believed your soul lived in your head? Was it the Egyptians? Where had he read that? He looked around again, but still there were no drinks.

At least he wasn't the worst dressed here. The poor bastard from number 15 looked to be in a dreadful state. Janek could only assume that 'stain' of his had spread. He was still certain there hadn't been any pipes in there, but there were worse things lurking in the walls of this place. His mind flashed to the cold black water, the pleading, gripping hands. A deep breath. The memory faded.

He considered saying hello to Jason, one of the only friendly faces he could see around here. But that face was currently pale and casting terrified glances over to another man Janek had never seen before, who wore a black version of the same uniform. Could that be 'Max'? Jason had apparently undersold how deeply intimidating his friend was. Why would a dinner party need security like that? He knew Fell was a recluse, maybe paranoid, but it still seemed excessive. Maybe he was best leaving them to their duty.

Damian had been keen to talk when he arrived, but Janek didn't feel like he'd given much in the way of useful answers. He was still struggling to understand exactly what had happened to him when he—

'Hey.'

The plumber turned to see an Asian woman in dirt-caked denims regarding him with a look of ... respect? Could that be right?

'Can I help you?'

The woman held out a hand.

'Lot of people here have never worked a real day's work in their life,' she said. 'Fits this place, I guess. Lazy. Soft. But you know. I can see it.'

'Right. Thank you ...' Janek gingerly shook her hand. It was dry and dusty. 'Janek.'

'Violet.'

Silence hung in the air between them. Violet seemed to feel no urge to fill it and Janek had no idea what to say. Behind them, a man in a tailored black dinner jacket had just begun to complain about their host's absence, when his words were cut off by a piercing scream.

Alvita

She hadn't worn this dress since Tommy had been born. It hadn't fit her for years, but apparently the recent months of insomnia-squashed appetite and Doxatrin had left her thinner than she'd been since she was a teenager. It wasn't a healthy sort of thin, but right now she'd take what small victories she could. She'd even found some pearl earrings in her dusty old jewellery box. They matched the dress perfectly and reminded her faintly of Edith.

In fact, she was in a far better mood than she had any right to be. She knew things here were all wrong. The way the invitation had arrived, the behaviour of the other guests, the fact that she was somehow one of the first people to enter Tobias Fell's penthouse suite in years. None of it made sense and she should have been panicking. Instead, she felt at peace, as though a warm blanket had been wrapped around her. A feeling that had only got stronger once she stepped over the threshold and into the billionaire's home.

'Oh! Sorry!'

Alvita stumbled slightly as little Anna Khan came barrelling into her, closely followed by her strange friend Penny. The blonde girl smiled, a row of razor-sharp teeth curving up her face. Alvita expected that cold, familiar anger to build as she looked at the children who hurt Tommy, but instead she found herself smiling.

'No problem but do be careful. This is a grown-up party, you don't want to—'

At that moment Anna's mother, Prisha, pushed past a heavily ornamented young woman to catch up with her daughter, barely noticing the faint red handprint the woman left on her back.

'I'm so sorry, Mrs Jackson, I hope she hasn't been a bother.'

'Not at all, Prisha,' Alvita replied. 'I'm surprised to see them here.'

'The invite was for them,' Mrs Khan's voice was tight, but her eyes betrayed how confused she was by what was happening. 'I didn't know you would also be—'

Anna's mother stopped dead, her eyes suddenly falling on Penny, still standing at Alvita's side.

'Is this ... I'm sorry, is this child with you?' A weird note of unease had entered Prisha's voice. 'I thought you had a son.'

'Don't be silly, Anna's mummy!' Penny said, waving with her long, sharp little fingers. 'It's me, Penny!'

Prisha's eyes went wide and the blood drained from her face.

'Remember, Mummy?' little Anna said gently. 'I told you she was coming with us.'

Her mother staggered back, paused for just a moment, then let out a scream. Immediately, Alvita was by her side.

'It's OK, hey it's OK.'

Penny just kept on smiling.

Tobias

It was an odd thing to hear a scream through the walls, then half a second later see it on the screen. The delay was slightly disorientating in a way that Tobias found quite pleasant. It was to be expected, of course. He'd been somewhat confused when he'd seen the child's mother in the lift, but on reflection it was obvious. No matter what was influencing the girl, it needed her parent to get her to the party. It had been a bit of a worry at first, given the mother wasn't factored into his dinner plans, but events looked like they were resolving themselves quite neatly.

It was a question, though. The full manifestation of the things his guests had brought with them, the booted thug and the hungry child, was that a function of his penthouse as a locus of the building's energy? Or was the place coming fully awake, giving these projections power enough to be perceived by all around them? Either way, it didn't seem complete quite yet. While the guests were wary of the concierge's brute, it was clear they could not see its rotted face as he did, or they'd all be screaming.

Tobias checked his watch. Still a few minutes until dinner. Plenty of time to see how things progressed. And, of course, there was still the matter of the journalist. But for now, he returned his attention to the mother.

Anna

Anna had never been embarrassed by her parents before but watching as her mother screamed and shouted about Penny, she couldn't help but apologise to her friend. Penny didn't seem to mind, though, in fact she clearly thought it was all a great joke.

The other grown-ups didn't seem to find it quite so funny, however, and Anna could feel their quiet judgement as Mrs Jackson led her mother away.

'You're not real!' her mother shouted back at Penny. 'You're not fucking real!'

Anna gasped at her mother's swearing. She turned to Penny, who was laughing even harder, her mouth so wide it seemed as if her head would split in two.

'It's not funny, Penny,' Anna said seriously. 'She sounds really mad. I think we're in trouble.'

Penny just shrugged. 'I'm hungry,' she said. 'When do we get to eat?'

'It's a grown-up party,' Anna told her, trying to ignore the stares of the other guests. 'There might not be any food.'

'There will be.' Penny had no doubts whatsoever. 'That's why we're here.'

The fancy woman came over, looking worried. Anna thought she was one of the most beautiful people she'd ever seen, with her huge shiny necklace and glittering tiara. She looked like she must be a princess, even if she sometimes touched her jewels in discomfort, and her dress seemed a little bit dirty around the neck.

'Are you girls alright?' she said, kneeling down to look them in the eye.

Anna nodded. She didn't want to cry, not in front of a princess. And Penny would definitely laugh at her if she did.

'Is Mummy alright?'

'She will be, I promise. We'll look after her.'

'When do we eat?'

The sparkling princess turned to look at Penny, taking a moment to hide her surprise at the strange, hissing tone.

'Soon. I think. I'm not sure. Just ... stay here, OK? I'm going to go check on your mummy. I'll keep you both safe.'

She disappeared back into the guests, leaving a few red drips on the floor. The other grown-ups seemed to have moved on and weren't paying Anna and Penny much attention anymore.

'I don't think I want to be safe,' Penny whispered to Anna with a wink. 'I think I want to play.'

Caroline

Cari had rarely gone in for gaudy adornments, generally preferring more understated silver pieces. She had never realised just how heavy gold and gemstone could be, but now she found it weighed her down, slowed her movements and made even lifting her arms a chore. The idea of ballroom dancing in it all seemed almost foolhardy. As she walked away from the girls she tried, once again, to take them off, but her hands shook as she tried to hold them, and her whole body wanted to scream.

She let her arms drop again. The building had chosen her to find them, it wanted her to wear them, and fighting that instinct took energy and willpower that she couldn't spare right now. Damian had taken to calling them 'echoes', the things that had touched them, reflections of the atrocities built into this place. Hers weighed heavy around her neck.

By the time she reached their mother the woman had settled into unsteady sobs. Cari took Alvita by the arm and led her to the side. They both tried to ignore the red smear her hand left.

'Is she going to be alright?'

'I hope so.' Alvita attempted a shrug.

'W-why do you have ... Is that *blood*?' Prisha's voice was small behind them. Cari gave Alvita a look.

'She's not a part of this, is she?'

'I don't know what *this* even is.' Alvita's voice was just a little bit too mellow for the situation and it was setting Cari on edge.

'Neither do I, but it's definitely something, right? And she ...' Her eyes flicked to the weeping mother. 'She shouldn't be here. She wasn't properly invited. Not like us. She might not be safe.'

An expression of guilt passed over Alvita's face, breaking briefly through the calm as she held up a small bottle.

'Yeah. I thought she might be better off if she wasn't ... awake.'

'Doxatrin?' Cari said uncertainly. 'That'll do it, I guess. Odd choice.'

'It was all I had to hand, and she seemed grateful.' Alvita's expression went slightly dreamy again.

'Well, she can't stay out here.'

'I think someone said one of the bedrooms was unlocked.'

'Might be best drop her there, let her rest while ...' Cari gestured broadly to the party.

'Yeah, I'll take care of it. You stay here. Don't want to stain any billion-pound bedsheets.'

The joke was unexpected, but welcome and Cari let out a short laugh. Alvita smiled gently and led the now quiet woman away towards one of the doors on the far edge of the massive room.

She spotted Damian looking over quizzically, so she began to signal him to her, then reconsidered almost immediately, turning it into a wave of dismissal. It felt somehow too early for alarm. Everyone was waiting for something to happen, though no one seemed quite sure what. Until it did, though, panicking just felt a bit premature. She really hoped he actually had that plan he was hinting at earlier. God knows he couldn't make things worse.

'Who is that?' Alvita asked.

'Just a friend.' Cari felt oddly reluctant to give away too much. Damian was being so secretive she didn't want to accidentally expose him.

'He seems nice.' That vagueness had returned. 'He was asking me all sorts of questions about Edith.'

Cari wasn't listening. Something was nagging at her. If the little girl was a part of this, but her mother wasn't, who else here might not belong? She scanned the room, taking in each face, seeing her own fears reflected in their eyes, until her gaze finally settled on David Erikson with a sudden, lurching fear that he was in terrible danger.

Laura

'Look,' the wide-eyed woman persisted, despite Laura desperately trying to ignore her. 'You don't seem to understand how much danger we're in. That's Leon Copeland. In the same room as Carter Dwight.'

Laura tried to place the voice of her new companion. Had she called her about smoke alarms at one point? It had barely even registered among all the weird phone calls, but yes. A very simple query about how many smoke detectors were in her flat.

A normal-sounding question from a normal-sounding tenant.

'You know about the Portman Oil cover-up last year?'

She didn't sound normal anymore.

'Billions of dollars in ecological devastation, and several of the journalists involved in breaking the story have been turning up conveniently falling out of windows.' The woman, who had introduced herself as Gillian, was scrawling out desperate notes on a small pad of paper, apparently oblivious to the fact that her pen had run out of ink minutes ago.

Laura reeled as the stream of information burrowed into her brain like a headache.

'Now, and you may think neither of Copeland nor Dwight were directly implicated, but the director of Copeland's company attended several fundraiser dinners with—'

Finally, Laura couldn't take it anymore. Without a word she turned away to escape the conversation, doubting the woman would even notice. She shouldn't be here. She wasn't like these people, whose voices were so familiar from phone calls begging for floorplans or ranting about stains. They were all unstable, delusional, and the only thing Laura had in common with them was that some weirdo tycoon had invited them all to a party he hadn't even shown up for.

But she was here. Because a ghost had told her to come and she didn't know where her home was anymore. She'd been sleeping in an abandoned flat for two nights now. She caught sight of a man – Jésus somebody? – tapping a hand against his thigh. Her own twitched in response.

Could she really claim to be so different?

'—and obviously I don't have to tell you what those connections to the Tyrona corporation might mean for us.'

Gillian and her stream of nested nonsense had followed her, and Laura all but ran into the sneer of a towering security guard.

She let out a small shriek as he reached for her and roughly shoved her to the side, striding past and towards a nondescript middle-aged man in what looked like his best approximation of a classy outfit.

'David!' A woman's voice shouted from somewhere behind Laura, and the man swivelled to see the figure looming before him.

'Can I see your invite?' the guard said in a voice that promised violence.

'Oh. I—' David began to answer, but he was cut short by a meaty crunch as the heavy club slammed into his stomach.

Laura felt faint as she watched him crumple to the ground, backing quickly away. She couldn't believe what was happening. This wasn't part of what she'd agreed to. The others were standing still, apparently frozen in place, watching the brutality unfold. She raced across the room and grabbed the handle of the door to the old elevators, but it didn't open. Behind her, there was another crunch as the truncheon came down again. She wanted nothing more than to escape, to go home. But she didn't know where that was.

Jason

There was nothing like that noise, the feeling that rippled through the pit of your stomach when you heard the wet impact of real violence. There was no redemption in it, no righteousness. Just some helpless soul whimpering as he heard his own ribs break. After the last week, the sound no longer surprised Jason, but he still felt every blow.

'Max,' he said quietly. 'Max, stop. Please.'

If anyone heard him, they didn't show it. The other guests

gasped as they watched, someone even screamed, but none of them moved to intervene. The baton came down one last time, splitting the journalist's lip and sending him sprawling across the floor. Max addressed the crowd gathered around him.

'Anyone else here uninvited?'

No one said a word. Jason looked to the person who'd called out David's name. She was struggling against the woman in rough denim who was trying to hold her back, helpless hatred spilling from her eyes as her tiara somehow remained in place. Max's gaze lingered momentarily on the tired-looking woman Jason had heard someone call Mrs Jackson, as though trying to see something over her shoulder, but the moment passed.

Then his massive hand closed around the throat of David Erikson, hoisting him effortlessly off the ground. The journalist gurgled something as he faded in and out of consciousness. Max carried him over towards one of the huge glass windows.

'Max!' Jason called out. 'Max, don't do it! Please, he's— You've done enough.'

He looked around wildly, trying to find anyone who might help him stop a murder, but the other guests were all locked tight with fear.

'Max, was it?' The voice that rang out was unfamiliar. Quiet but clear, like one used to being obeyed.

Max stopped instantly, David's feet trailing on the floor as he turned.

'Yes, Mr Fell?'

'No need for that. Take him through to the dining room, if you please. I'm sure we can find him a chair. After all, we wouldn't want him to miss his big story. Not after he came all this way.'

Tobias

He limped slowly out of his office, the door closing behind him. The assembled guests gazed at him with such awe. Tobias Fell himself, in the flesh, the most important person any of them would ever meet. He did his best to smile modestly and ignore the stench of the poor soul from number 15. He was aware it was Banyan Court's doing, of course, but in some ways the rank accompaniment did feel appropriate to meeting the rabble before him.

At least he wouldn't be required to actually converse with these people. They simply needed to listen and, sure enough, they were waiting with bated breath.

'I believe,' Tobias said, 'it is time we retired to dinner.'

Carter

So, this was the famous Tobias Fell, was it? He wasn't exactly what he would have expected. He had always conceived of Fell as a hermit, stooped and awkward with reclusion, turned strange by his self-imposed imprisonment. But the man before them, though impossibly pale, stood tall and trim, with perfect posture and impeccable tailoring. His words carried the easy authority of one who had never had to ask for anything twice.

Two weeks ago, Carter would have considered him a man he could easily work with. Now, as Tobias stepped around a small pool of the journalist's blood, things were significantly more complicated.

Gillian

There he was, the venomous spider at the centre of his web, porcelain-white and smug in his sanctuary. He smiled easily at her in a way that made her blood boil, but she still stepped out of the way as the ogre-ish enforcer 'Max' dragged David's unconscious body past them, the foolish man's limp legs leading the way to whatever grim denouement this evil man had orchestrated. Gillian began to realise very very keenly that as much as she longed for answers, she didn't want to die to get them.

Janek

This was what a billionaire looked like, then? He had met rich people before, of course, but none so incomprehensibly wealthy as the man who now directed them to the dining room. Having his thug beat that man was horrible, of course, but this was not Janek's first experience of such violence and he'd always known that this was what rich people did. He looked over at the bleeding form of the man they'd called David and tried to ignore the shame of his own inaction. Even so, as afraid as he was of a man like Tobias Fell, it was with a sense of dark curiosity that he made his way through the newly unlocked double doors. At least, he hoped, there would be something to drink.

Caroline

Whatever fugue had overtaken her had been thoroughly shattered by watching what happened to David. Concerns about jewellery had vanished from her mind, and she almost collapsed, held up only by the strong arms of the woman who had stopped her throwing herself into the fray. Caroline looked back at her and almost smiled. It was the woman from her video. What was her name? She tried to think, but as they were led through to the dining room it was all swallowed in the mute terror of what had happened to her friend.

The room was not as immense as the one they'd just left, but even so Caroline had never seen a private dining room this large. If she had been told it had once been the feasting hall in some European king's palace, she would have believed it. At the centre was a long table of dark, shining wood, impeccably laid out with twelve place settings, a covered silver platter sat at each one. There were no place cards, so Caroline made her way to a seat far from the head of the table, watching for where Damian sat and trying her best to control her breathing, She tried not to look over as poor David was roughly tied to a chair near the wall. She looked around, searching for any hint of reassurance or resistance in the faces of the other guests, but they all looked away, cowed by the certainty that something even worse was coming. Except for the woman in work clothes, whose eyes shone like garnets, hard and defiant. As Cari sat, she shifted her napkin, smearing it with red.

Alvita

There was a box in the corner. It was made of cheap unworked wood and stood out starkly against the understated elegance of the rest of the room. Alvita sat opposite this box and kept finding that her eyes returned to it. It wasn't quite the right shape for a coffin, but she couldn't help but notice it was easily big enough to fit a body inside.

The warm presence she had felt before was still there, but it had shifted. It felt different. There was no more comfort, but rather an electric sense of anticipation.

Violet

The beautiful woman in blood-stained jewels looked away, searching for a seat. She should hate her for the trophies she wore of slavery and death, but somewhere beneath her new callouses, she found that she couldn't. Something else, deeper than the weariness and dirt, grew brighter at the sight, cutting through her anger. Violet sat down slowly, trying to steady herself. The platters on each table were so brightly polished Violet could see her own face reflected back at her. Hers, and the wordless shadows that stood over her shoulder. She didn't like this place, and she didn't like the man who sat at the head of the table, worm-belly white and relaxed in his power. His was the boot she had felt on their throats, his was the voice that so distantly commanded them to work until they fell. Her work-roughened fingers traced the outline of the domed cover. It was cool and smooth, but she could barely feel it.

Jason

In the corner, the journalist moaned himself awake, the sound muffled by the black tape over his mouth. Jason silently begged him to just sit there and stay quiet, and not to attract any more of Max's attention.

He looked at the place setting in front of his own seat. Wasn't there supposed to be a whole bunch of different cutlery?

That's what it had always been like at weddings – though not his own – or in fancy hotels. Jason remembered seeing pictures of plates surrounded by dozens of different forks and spoons and knives for your bread, meat, fish, soup, whatever the hell else you were having. Well, this was the fanciest place he'd ever been, but for some reason there were only two pieces of cutlery: a posh-looking fork, all smooth sterling silver, and a long, sharp knife. It wasn't even serrated like a steak knife. What exactly were they supposed to be cutting?

Anna

Penny really liked the knife. She kept reaching for it, and Anna had to push her hand away.

'Penny!' she hissed. 'You're going to get us in trouble!'

Anna was very worried that without her mother there the grown-ups would say she couldn't stay at the dinner. She wasn't even sure that she wanted to be here. It was a bit scary and Alvita kept blocking her view of the table or telling her where to look, so she wasn't entirely sure what was going on, but she had promised Penny they'd stay. Penny was desperate to eat and started reaching for the knife again.

Leon

Not too long ago, having a meal with Tobias Fell had been a legitimate dream of his, but now all he could do was worry about getting the tablecloth dirty. He desperately wanted to go and wash his hands, but the glowering stare of 'Max' made the idea of standing up very unappealing indeed. Well, if the smell put Tobias off his dinner, he had no one to blame but himself.

All that said, their smiling host didn't seem to mind. He stood at the head of the table and began to speak in a clear, quiet voice.

'Good evening. I'm sure you all have plenty of questions and, to be perfectly clear, I'm not able to answer all of them. The forces at work here do not lend themselves to clean and simple rules, though they do, in my experience, follow certain patterns. Patterns that can be exploited.

'Let me begin by assuring you that I do not believe in evil. I have no time for ideas of God or hell or any sort of cosmic judgement of our actions. I see morality as a trap, a trick the mind pulls to stop you from fully engaging with the systems our world is built on. Systems designed to enrich a few at the expense of others. All this is obvious, as is the fact that I have, within these systems, won. I have won fairly, as much as is possible, and that necessarily requires perpetuating and causing the suffering of those who have failed to prosper. I have accepted this. All of which is to say that recriminations and accusations that appeal to simplistic ethics are fundamentally going to be a waste of breath. My concerns are entirely practical, and I would hope that you all respond as such.'

Leon listened to this rolling, rehearsed speech in silence. Did he agree? Did he find it abhorrent? Did it matter? He watched as the grey ooze of that familiar stain bubbled from their host's mouth and dropped onto the table in thick wet clumps.

Tobias

He looked over the assembled crowd. A mixed reaction, as expected. Confusion, mostly. He'd had no control over who was here, of course, so it was hardly a handpicked group. But now the power was once again his, he couldn't help but make the most of it. And no one was shouting at him yet, which was promising. Amusingly, he'd felt certain that the next section of his explanation would be met far more warmly than his first. The inevitable realities of a robust economic system were often hard to accept, but by this point everyone in the room definitely believed in ghosts.

'While it is true,' he continued, 'that I reject the idea of any arbitrary eternal judgement of the actions we take in a fundamentally meaningless universe, I have in the last decade or so been forced to reckon with the fact that there is some non-corporeal element to our existence. I hesitate to call it a soul, but we may at least describe it as a shadow. A remnant of the feelings and experiences of the dead. And perhaps the living, though I have little evidence for that.'

A few nods from the room, but most were clearly waiting for the sting.

'I am not a superstitious man. But I have, for many years now, found myself a target, of sorts, for these shadows. At first, there were the days lost to strange dreams, paranoias and awful visions. Then I was nearly killed while visiting a diamond mine in Angola, and again by an equipment failure at a pharmaceutical plant in Michigan.' He touched his leg, absently. 'I do not entirely know why. Obviously, the suffering I have caused, the lives ended because of necessary decisions I have made, are a not insubstantial element of it. And yet such is the burden of any who wield great power, whose decisions affect tens of thousands. So why, you may ask, out of all of them, have I been marked for special *attention*? Simply put, I don't know. It is a question that has long baffled me. But I am a practical man, as I have said, and while identifying the cause of such a situation may satisfy some, picking apart my history and family, trying to dig through the layers of misery calcified around the Fell name … I am more interested in resolving it.

'At first, I tried to outrun the shadows. To hide. When that didn't work, I decided to take action. I spent millions consulting with experts in the field. I spoke to both frauds and true believers, and of the two I believe the frauds had a clearer handle on things. Indeed, their falsehoods did seem to offer some small protection. And in the end, I was certain of what my best chance would be. If there was no use in running, as seemed clear, then I'd make a stand. All the money in the world isn't worth a penny if you're dead, or worse, and the shadows wanted their pound of flesh. So, I designed a trap and I named it Banyan Court.'

Jésus

'This is ridiculous!'

Jésus was used to commanding the attention of a room, but even so, when every person around that table turned to face him, he found himself floundering for a moment.

'You have an objection?' Tobias's voice did not waver.

Jésus felt a flicker of fear, but no one else seemed interested in speaking up.

'I do,' he pressed on. 'You bring us here to talk about ghosts and monsters, you are mad!'

'You have not had some inexplicable experiences of late, Mr Candido?'

Jésus looked around, seeing nothing but credulous, cowed faces staring back at him. No, he would not be so easily dismissed.

'You own this whole building.' His tone became accusatory. 'Who is to say you have not been filling it with hallucinogens in the air, or our water. Your story is absurd.'

Knock knock.

Jésus' whole body went cold. He spun around to see that dreadful little man, Damian, staring at him, while gently rapping his knuckles on the table.

Knock knock.

Jésus' hand began to throb and his head swam. Things his mind was so desperate to forget began bubbling up in his memory. There was no victory in Damian's expression, no enjoyment, he was simply proving a point.

'Is there anything else, Mr Candido?' Tobias's voice remained calm and level.

Shaking his head, Jésus lowered himself back into his seat.

Damian

There should have been some pleasure in humbling an ass like Jésus, but as he watched the shaken man sit back down, Damian felt ashamed. The man hadn't chosen to be a victim any more than the others, but if they were going to find a way out of this then outbursts like that weren't going to help. If they had ever had a chance to walk away that time was past now. The only one who'd actually chosen this was him. Assuming it had actually *been* a real choice. Still, the thought rattled through Damian's head as he looked around the table. Why *had* they been the ones to end up as victims? Unless that wasn't it. He eyes widened slightly at the realisation. They weren't victims of these echoes. They were bait.

'I will not get into the specifics of the building's design. Suffice it to say that I hired more than simple architects to draw it up. It was to be a lightning rod, of sorts, a beacon of what might be called my crimes to all those shadows that might wish me ill. Raised from bricks that saw centuries of pain and degradation, both from my own family and those who inhabited it. Constructed from materials made in the most inhumane deprivation and seeded, where possible, with the human remains of those who died in my name. Exhausted workers, uninsured patients refused treatment, evicted tenants and even one or two betrayed business partners. Powdered bone in the very walls. Such a place that those petty, vindictive shadows that were not strong enough to oppose me in life would be unable to resist its call. And so, they were tied to this place, caught in ropes of symbol and crude metaphor. Every partition, every wire and pipe binding them and keeping them in their place.'

Damian tried to steady his breathing. He had been prepared for some of this, but it was so much more calculated than he had believed. He had assumed what he found in the walls had been some sort of spiritual manifestation, but might it have been real? But the corridor that contained it wasn't really there. Was it? The truth was that it didn't matter. Real or unreal – the end result was the same: a place built on the exploitation and misery of the poor souls trapped within its walls. The living as well as the dead. He looked around for a glass of water to steady himself, something to cut through a mouth dry with fear. There was nothing.

'I admit my original intention was simple. I wished for those who lived in the lower floors of this building to suffer on my behalf. Didn't matter which side. Fed to the shadows I had symbolically bound here, trapped and contained. But it did not exactly manifest as I had believed. Certainly, I seemed safe within my penthouse sanctuary, but the winding passages and dead ends did not channel the shadows as I had hoped, and the touch of my transgressions on those below, on you … It was gentle, even friendly. Unsettling perhaps, but not hostile, brushing past you in forms so subtle as to go almost unnoticed. And certainly not dangerous. And so, a new plan began to form.'

Laura

That Spanish guy had been right, this was all ridiculous. But it was also true, and she didn't feel like she had the strength left in her to disbelieve what was happening. Dead people in the walls. But the old man, he had died here. As the landowner, perhaps the rents were ultimately the fault of Tobias Fell, but she had been the one to try and evict him. Was that why she'd been chosen by these 'shadows'? Why all of them had been? Did they each need something of their own, some sin for the shadows to latch onto? Maybe the old man was her 'crime', assisted by other forces to pursue her for a vengeance of his own. Perhaps he'd been trapped too, the building drawing his soul into it as it had apparently been designed to do. She fought down the urge to raise her hand and ask Tobias about it as he brought his speech towards its climax.

'The dreams returned,' he said. 'I believe given to me by the building itself. They have been getting more and more intense ever since this place was constructed, but in the last weeks they have become almost unbearable. Dreams of this very gathering. Bringing together those most deeply touched by the shadows I have trapped here, bringing them into this sanctum and … Well, I am of the opinion that nothing defuses consequences quite like complicity.'

Tobias smiled again. Deep in Laura's stomach something turned at the sight of that smile.

'My proposal is simple in essence, though I warn you it will be rather gruesome in practice. Tonight, ten years to the day since this building began its life, you will each assume a part of my offences, after which you shall remain a focal point for those spirits that blame me for them. There is no need to concern yourself as to which, they have already chosen you, as I'm sure you're aware. If you accept, they will be bound to you, locked and chained, tormenting you more or less as they do now. Once their attention is focused on you, I shall be free to leave this place. Who knows – you might escape them as well when you leave the building, or perhaps lessen their effects. We shall see, I suppose. In return for this service, I shall pay each of you one billion pounds.' There was a collective intake of breath around the table. Laura hoped she'd caught her own in time. 'I have no interest in haggling about this. Obviously this is not an easy decision and one I cannot afford for many of you to turn down, so to be perfectly clear, if you do not wish to partake, if you refuse my offer, then – I believe it's Max? – one of the nastier manifestations, well, he will beat you to death.'

Nobody breathed a word. Laura suddenly felt entirely alone, despite the full table. She looked over at the smaller concierge, who was deathly pale.

'I suppose the threat alone might work,' Tobias mused. 'But that feels like intimidation, not complicity. And this sort of thing requires a certain thematic consistency to work. I'm sure you understand. It always comes down to money, in the end. The great divider. Funny how it's also what makes us all the same.'

Laura wasn't sure she really understood, but she also knew that she didn't want to die.

Tobias

He gestured for his guests to uncover their platters. No one moved, still stunned. They must have suspected the truth, at the very least, but no doubt the extreme nature of his carrot and stick approach had rattled them. He'd considered going with a lower offer, but he wanted everyone to understand the full extremity of the situation and didn't care to waste time on petty bargaining. The only one who didn't seem surprised was Damian, the young man from the poor side who'd been watching him so intently. Interesting. Given his financial situation it seemed unlikely he'd be in any position to turn down the money.

Surprising him, Gillian spoke up first. 'What if we all say no?' Her voice was working hard to be defiant. 'Together.'

'Then my situation would be unchanged,' Tobias answered pleasantly. 'And you would be dead.'

'He can't kill all of us.' Gillian sounded less certain.

'Yeah.' Jason's voice was flat with terror. 'He can.'

Max's smile spoke of someone not only capable, but eager.

Gillian sat back down.

'Now,' Tobias continued. 'You may reveal your dinner.'

One by one, they lifted up the silver lids. A few clearly expected a billion pounds in cash underneath. Tobias almost chuckled at the ignorance, that such an amount could fit on a serving tray. They really had no idea what wealth truly was.

Instead, they were each confronted with a single, tiny cube of cooked meat, as neat and regular as Tobias had been able to make it. He'd had a lot less to work with than he'd originally hoped, but even a sliver should be enough. His prosthetic leg ached as he looked at the plates arrayed around the table.

Gillian

This couldn't be what she thought it was. It just couldn't. Why would he do this? Had Tobias Fell finally succumbed to the pressures of his long isolation? Gillian glanced around imploringly; some of the other guests shared her expression of horror, but most just looked confused. She reached instinctively for her fork. After all the lies and intrigue, this was apparently the choice before her: death or unthinkable riches and ... this. But she had to be sure.

'Mr Fell,' she asked. 'What is this?'

Caroline

Blood dripped gently from her bracelet, leaving the small chunk of meat swimming in a thin red gravy. Cari swallowed hard, thoughts and connections swimming in her head, ideas of blood and bodies and riches and jewels and the incarnation of misdeeds, but none of the disparate concepts could find purchase. She simply stared at Tobias as he considered how to answer the question.

'I was advised that a partnership of this nature requires a gift. Something of immense personal value to myself. Unfortunately, wealth at the magnitude I possess makes most material possessions essentially meaningless. So, I had to find another way to gift you a ... part of myself.'

A ripple of horror murmured around the table. Cari looked over at Damian, who met her eyes sadly and picked up his fork.

Carter

'I'm sorry, Tobias, but this has gone far enough.' Carter got to his feet with a firm expression and crossed his arms. 'Now, I'm not going to deny I've had an ... unusual experience. If you tell me it's ghosts, at this point I'm not going to argue. But if you're trying to tell me that the answer is ... is *cannibalism*. Then I'm going to say that these ghosts have probably affected your judgement as much as they've clearly affected ours.'

Janek

Janek nodded as the tech guy spoke, seeing others also mumbling agreement, relieved someone else had said it for them.

'Ghosts have made you mad too, Mr Fell. If you think feeding us your flesh will help. But no, I don't think we will be eating.'

From the look that crossed Tobias's face it was clear that the possibility of his own delusion hadn't actually crossed his mind. He stood there in silence for several long moments before answering.

'That is an interesting consideration,' he said, finally. 'But it changes nothing. If this, all of this, is a delusion of my own, then the fact of the matter is I have no way to escape the shadows that want me dead and the result is the same whatever I do. If, however, I am right, then this remains the only way. And, in case I haven't been clear, my survival is my only priority. If I am ... mistaken, well ... My money remains quite real and you will have it as promised. Or, I suppose, we find out whether Max is real enough to kill you.' In response, Max hit the baton against the meaty part of his palm, emitting a very definite *thwack*. 'But it won't come to that, I'm sure.'

366

Anna

It was hard to listen to grown-ups when they got upset with each other, and she didn't really understand what they were talking about. It seemed to be about the dinner, which made sense, as her plate was almost empty. What was there was smaller than a chicken nugget and looked like old bacon. She felt sharp little fingers on her arm.

'Please,' Penny begged. 'You promised.'

Anna pushed the plate towards her, but her friend shook her head.

'No,' Penny said. 'You first. Then I can eat.'

Anna shrugged and picked the morsel up with her fingers. It was tough, and not as salty as she thought it would have been, but that was fine.

Jésus

Should he have stopped the child from eating? It was too late now for such worries. Jésus felt like he was the only one who saw it before it happened. The little girls did not seem like they understood what was going on, and perhaps that was for the best. Tobias had shown himself such a man that Jésus had no doubt he would kill children, and most likely their mother as well.

Though watching her chew the meat slowly, as the long-limbed imitation of an imaginary playmate – how had he ever thought it was simply another child? – nodded eagerly, Jésus felt all his resistance leak away. A billionaire ... what doors would that unlock? What great art of the world could be his?

He stabbed his own piece and ate. Out of the corner of his eye, he saw the rest of the table do the same. Some casting terrified looks at the figure of Max, which seemed to get larger with every bite, flesh sinking with sudden decay. Some salivating for something more precious than meat. The pitiful clothing speaking volumes. And some eating because they couldn't see any other way for this ghoulish party to end.

Leon

He didn't really know what he expected it to taste like. Special, somehow. Like a transgression, maybe. But it was just tough and unpleasant, not unlike over-cooked pork. Then it was gone, and he was, he supposed, now a billion dollars richer. And haunted forever. At least he wasn't going to die, that was something. Did that mean he would never be clean? Filthy rich. Leon tried to smile, but it didn't come.

He looked around to see similar reckonings on the faces of the other guests.

Laura

She was a cannibal. She wanted to throw up. Real people weren't cannibals. Cannibals were something feared by racist Victorian explorers. They were stranded pioneers trapped in the mountains by a fierce winter. They weren't estate agents sitting in a penthouse in Tower Hamlets. She tried to tell herself she did it because she didn't want to die. That was true, of course, but there was some nasty part of her brain that whispered to her that maybe she'd done it for the money. The home she could buy. She'd done it to be rich. And what if she had? Was that so terrible?

Another thought seized her. What about prion disease? Had anybody thought about prion disease? She could feel the panic crawling up through her brain, threatening to overwhelm her, but still Tobias Fell's calm, clear voice cut through.

'Good,' he said. 'That's the easy bit done with. But there is another thing I require before you receive your reward.'

Violet

Something was being dragged across the floor. Violet looked up to see the brute yanking the massive wooden box over towards the table. Somehow, she already knew what was inside it. Part of her recognised Max, knew exactly what he was, recognised the boot that had always stood on the throat of the imprisoned. Another part of her recognised the whole situation from one of her mother's tales, the earned fate of those who accepted invitations from wicked strangers. But mostly, when his bloody hands tore the lid from the box, she recognised the face of the man inside. She remembered his sad eyes as he smoked in the corridor, trying desperately to help her disbelieve her fate.

And she knew exactly what Tobias Fell wanted them to do.

Jason

Jason wondered if anyone else could see how decayed Max was becoming. Their faces were masks of horror, confusion and disgust, but there were so many possible reasons for that he couldn't tell if anyone else had noticed the clinging strands of skin left on nails and splinters as the unresisting body was pulled from the box and laid across the middle of the table. Did the plumber recoil as a sliver of skin slid from Max's skull and dropped onto one of the plates?

Jason knew the man on the table from description: several residents had reported seeing him lurking around the corridors and hallways, smoking. He was alive, at least, his chest gradually rising and falling. Probably drugged from the look of things.

'This man,' Tobias explained gently, 'has been looking for me for some time. I believe one of my oil companies has been destroying the land belonging to his family. Even killed some of them. Some indigenous tribe in Ecuador, I don't keep track.'

Jason stared at the man's face. It would have looked almost peaceful, were it not for the bruises that covered his throat and the rope around his wrists.

'At first, I thought he came here to kill me, but the truth is far more pitiable. I believe he thought me ignorant to the realities of the operation, and that if he could just talk to me face to face then perhaps he could open my eyes, convince me. I don't know exactly where he was hiding as he searched for a way to reach me, but he needn't have bothered. After all, I wanted him here, though obviously I prefer him to be silent.'

Jason looked around, saw the other guests waiting for the next words, knowing they were coming.

'I need each of you to participate in his death.'

Tobias

He paused, considering for a moment how much further explanation was needed. They already knew the choice was between unimaginable wealth or painful death. People are always so surprised at what they are capable of once they've taken a step they deem unforgivable. Would anyone be swayed further by knowing more about the reasoning behind the act? He decided to explain anyway. It had been so long since he'd had the chance to speak in person, he was going to make the most of it.

'We are now connected, and now comes the act of true complicity. This man has unknowingly offered himself up, a symbol of all whom I have harmed. And in harming him you will be a part of that. You each have a knife. I assure you, no violence done here will be prosecuted by the police. I have ensured there is no record of this man's existence here and no one has reason to investigate. Should anyone feel compelled to confess I have more than enough resources to bury such accusations. And accusers.'

He paused.

'Oh,' he remembered with a small laugh. 'Of course, if you attempt to do violence against me, the police *will* be alerted, and arrive within minutes. In case you were considering it. Don't forget what the police would find if they pumped your stomachs.'

Tobias was dimly aware of the reactions around him, the cries of protest, the nervous shaking of heads.

'Bullshit.' The woman in work clothes, Violet, stood up. 'I'm not scared of some fucking thug.'

Max stood up to his full height, which seemed even taller than it had been before. His grin was so wide it tore the skin at the side of his face and his eyes seemed to grow smaller, shrivelling to tiny burning embers. Every bone in his knuckles cracked around his stick as the room grew darker.

'Yeah,' he rumbled. 'You are.'

Violet's body was taut as a bowstring as she stared him down. Then something inside her seemed to falter, and she took a step back, eyes falling bitterly to the floor.

Tobias smiled, but did not get involved in their little confrontation. They knew what the deal was now, they would either do it and be rich or they would die. There was nothing left except to make their choices. Perhaps he would let the child live, it was unlikely she understood enough to meaningfully participate, and he privately wondered why Banyan Court had chosen her at all.

He eyed the tied-up figure on the table. A small flower of disgust blossomed in his gut. Who had this man thought he was, to try and talk to him? He had been given no speaking part in this story, he was a prop, his purpose to suffer and die quietly, far from here. No matter. He could still fulfil his role here. He could still die so that his betters might prosper.

Tobias looked around the table, watching who took up knives and who began to back away.

Gillian

The knife felt wrong in her hand, but even so she poised the tip over the man's chest. She'd eaten because the thought of death terrified her, and of course she needed the money, but that wasn't what moved her towards the bound figure now. More than anything, she realised, she was sick of piecing together awful secrets that kept her up at night. Perhaps this act would tether her forever to this web of cascading conspiracies, but if she must live in a world of terrible truths, let her be the one writing them.

Laura

The old man had told her to come, and she still didn't know fully why. Had it just been revenge? It didn't matter now. Laura picked up her knife. She didn't even have to be the one who actually killed him, she just needed to be involved. It wasn't like she hadn't done that before. And who wouldn't want to be impossibly wealthy? Anyone would take this deal. She was certain of it. Money could buy anything. It could buy this.

Jason

Jason had known Max was going to kill him since the second he'd found that poor kid in the baseball cap, and he was sick of it. He'd eaten, sure he had, maybe one last act of denial, of pretending he could get out of here alive. But no, he was sick of violence and blood on his hands, and he wasn't going to be responsible for any more deaths. This time, he'd step up. He felt a wave of strength flow through him. This had to end.

Janek

Perhaps it would be nice to be able to stand by his principles, to sacrifice his life to keep his hands clean. But he had made many hard choices in his life, and there was no scenario in which given the choices laid out before him, between enough money to provide for his children forever or leaving them grief-stricken and fatherless, well, it hadn't been a difficult decision when it was cannibalism, and it wasn't a hard choice now.

373

Anna

She still didn't understand entirely what was going on, but she didn't want to hurt anyone. She looked to Penny, who just smiled brightly and shrugged. She crawled under the table and began to cry.

Leon

Maybe it should have been Andi standing here, making this decision, but Leon was glad it wasn't. He didn't think she'd have been able to go through with it, and he couldn't stand the thought of losing her. But hadn't he lost her already? If he did this, he'd never be clean. Well, with that amount of money he was certain they could work something out. See the best specialists, like Tobias had. Live somewhere Andi would be happy. As he picked up the knife, Leon considered that perhaps the reward here wasn't simply money, but the opportunity to fully join Tobias in his world as the only ones who understood.

Caroline

Everything had led her here, to this moment. She had come with a desperate trust in Damian and if there was ever a moment to test that, here it was. She had trusted him enough to come here, enough to eat human flesh. Now it was time for him to honour that. Cari looked at him, waiting for guidance, but he gave no sign. She stalled, desperate to not make a choice. Her eyes met with Violet's, and she felt her hand move away from the knife.

Carter

He wanted to be a good person, he did. Whatever torment Donna had put him through, she had been right about Carter's selfishness and ignorance. He wondered for a moment. Would Donna return? Or would his perpetual haunting take another form? But he couldn't ignore the choice at hand. Eating a person's flesh when it had been willingly given didn't harm anyone, he had accepted that. This was murder.

He wanted to be a good person. And he could do so much more good in the world if he was alive. Donna had shown him that, in her own way. Refusing to participate wouldn't save this man. The knife was smooth and cold in his hand.

Jésus

Dying wasn't an option, that much was surely obvious, but there was something else that Jésus felt propelling his hand towards the knife, the same instinct he had felt as he succumbed to fear and devoured the flesh of their host. All of this, the grand table, the sacrificial victim, the twisted last supper, it was ... beautiful. It was the most monumentally grotesque piece of art. And it was only right that he be part of it. Just think, when he finally got home, his painting's embrace would be waiting for him. When he picked up the knife, it felt right.

Violet

At a certain point, beyond all extremity, the only freedom you have left is the freedom to say 'No' and let them do as they will.

She had not exercised it when ordered to eat, choosing instead to live. Perhaps she should have because it turned out to be a trick. They were still trapped in Tobias's sick game. But a life under the heel is no life at all. Violet found herself smiling at the bejewelled woman opposite and as their eyes met, she took a single step back. She would not live in fear. Violet sneered at Tobias. Bosses can hang, she would not do as she was told.

Alvita

She had to look after Tommy, she had to survive. That was all there was to it. It was all there had been when she had eaten, and it was all there was to it now. And yet, as Alvita tried to pick up the knife, she felt a warm hand take hers and guide it away. She looked and saw nothing, but smiled anyway. It was time.

Damian

'No.'

Damian's voice surprised him with how clear it was, how full of confidence and resolve. Everyone turned to him, the would-be killers with knives poised and ready, the nervous ones still looking for a way out, the bruised journalist tied to his chair, even Tobias himself, whose smug expression wavered ever so slightly at how firmly the word was spoken.

For a moment everything was silent expectation.

'You have something to say, Mr ... Simpson, was it?' The shit-eating smile was once again plastered across Tobias's face.

'I don't.' Damian's stomach lurched as he rolled the only dice he had. 'But I think there are a few here who do. Because I've been watching, and I think you've made a mistake. Not every ghost here is contained by your walls.'

Confusion rippled out as Jason and Alvita picked up their knives. This was it. Either he was right, or he was dead.

Alvita

'Her name was Edith Kinney.' The voice was Alvita's, but the words were not. 'She moved here after she lost her husband, and in her loneliness this place reached out to her. But it was too late, she was dying alone and unmourned. Then a stranger knocked on her door, asking for directions to the penthouse.'

Alvita looked down at the bound and unconscious form of Diego and an old woman's fond smile crossed her face.

'He explained his situation and Edith was moved. He seemed like such a nice young man. She let him stay with her, and he kept her company in her last days of life. Even after she passed, he stayed to mourn her. She won't let you harm him, and she is not bound by this awful building that made her final months so miserable.'

Alvita held up her knife, and she moved slowly, dreamlike, towards Diego.

'Max.' Tobias's voice was commanding, but he couldn't quite hide the tinge of panic. 'Stop her.'

Jason

The thing that Jason had once believed to be his friend charged towards Alvita, letting loose a low roar. The baton was raised high, preparing to come down with a force Jason knew would crack the woman's skull like an egg. Max didn't even notice the knife until it slipped into his stomach.

'Boo,' Jason whispered into his ear.

Max turned, the rotten remains of his face still managing to convey a sense baffled betrayal.

'His name was James Andre. He was 16. He was a dumb kid, and made mistakes, but he tried to do right by people and he didn't deserve what we did to him. He's not a prisoner here either.'

Whatever supernatural powers were at work, Jason couldn't say. Certainly the knife wound he had given Max shouldn't have been fatal, but as he watched the brutal thing began to bulge and tear, black and ancient gore gushing out, lashing across the table, the floor, even over the ceiling, until nothing remained but a shrivelled husk of rotten skin and a bloody, splintered nightstick.

Tobias

No. No no no. This wasn't how it was supposed to go. This wasn't how he'd dreamed it. Without Max they could easily turn those knives on him.

'Very well.' His voice betrayed none of his alarm. 'The threat is removed. But the money remains unchanged. Those of you who wish to claim it may still do so.'

He looked across the faces of his guests, trying to gauge their intentions. His hand shook ever so slightly as he reached inside his jacket and activated the panic button app he'd had made especially for this moment.

The police would be here soon, he just needed to explain

that if the others simply put the knives away, he could make all of this disappear. The only person ... No, the only *thing* that had died tonight was just a figment of the building. They had somehow beaten him. That was unexpected, but fairly done. Nobody else needed to die tonight.

He opened his mouth to speak when he noticed Alvita had moved next to Diego and placed the blade against the rope around his wrist. Why? Surely she ... Wait. What had he been told about symbols and their power? About how spirits could use the connections he had made if they weren't properly bound?

'Oh no.' Were Tobias Fell's last words.

Then Alvita cut the rope and set everything free.

Damian

Even if he had known exactly what was going to happen, had more than theory and supposition, Damian could not have imagined how it would feel as the anger trapped in Banyan Court rushed into him. But he was ready, and when the shadows came rushing, he was the first to let them in.

He saw his part in it all so clearly now: Fell's companies liked to make their spaces hostile, keeping away transients and 'encouraging productivity' in their workers. Now he felt those souls, pushed out into the cold by metal spikes and trapped in the glow of harsh fluorescents, rush through him. The space Fell had so carefully constructed, to bind, to keep out, and keep in, was now focused solely on him. As the terrified billionaire rushed for the door out of the dining room, Damian felt himself slam it shut, trapping him inside with a lifetime of righteous hatred.

Carter

The poor fool was trying to call for help, desperately checking his phone, but the data wasn't on his side. The trouble with technology is it all needs to talk to each other. And when Donna's voice emerged from his phone, it was clear that she had no interest in letting his panic button talk to anything else.

'I'm afraid no one is coming to help you, Mr Fell,' she said.

Carter laughed a nasty, synthetic laugh.

Violet

He was flailing wildly now, brandishing one of the knives from the table, keen to harm any who might come close. Violet stretched out her will and the chains of all those he had imprisoned and enslaved and trapped in thankless agonising toil reached out and clasped around him, pulling him to the floor with their weight. She could see tears in his eyes, but it was too late for pity.

Gillian

Tobias was screaming, pleading, begging for his life, offering money and power and all the very real things that were his to give. But he had robbed so many of their voices, silencing them when the words they spoke displeased him. Gillian placed her hand across his lips and felt the white-hot anger pour through her, burning and scorching the skin beneath until the melted, blackened flesh fused together, sealing his mouth shut. He still tried to scream.

Laura

He had exercised such control over property, weaponising people's homes against them, pushing them into squalid conditions or forcing them out entirely for a few extra pennies. Now his own home was turned against him as Laura splintered the floorboards with a sheer force of will and grinding rage. Great spikes of wood erupted, jutting out into his limbs, and vicious nails leapt to impale his back.

Anna

Penny could control herself no longer, and finally leapt onto him with all the hunger of the children starved and poisoned by what Fell's companies had fed them. Her friend giggled in glee as her sharp teeth began to tear chunks from his stomach. She gestured for Anna to join her, and Anna felt her own teeth sharpen as she was pulled to join in the feast.

Alvita

He had sold fake drugs, he'd had his companies refuse people lifesaving care, but Alvita found the spirits flowing through her wanted their revenge in a more visceral form of medicine. She had two hands, hands that had put pill after pill into her own body. And Tobias Fell had two eyes.

Caroline

Gemstones were beautiful and people suffered and died for them. They were also sharp and hard, and as she raked and clawed at the flesh of his torso, Cari found her glittering, bloody hands digging into him with ease. He had burrowed deep into the ground for treasure, at the expense of all else, now she burrowed into him for a very different prize.

Jason

This man had financed death squads to kill union activists, he had hired mercenaries to intimidate and murder those who stepped out of line. So many had lived in fear for their lives because of the brutal regimes he had let run rampant. Now the boot was on *his* face, crunching down again and again, until his jaw and nose were cracked and broken.

Leon

As Tobias's jaw caved beneath Jason's heel, his mouth was torn back open, but he didn't have time to cry out before Leon's face was over his, stretched and distorted as all the pollutants and toxins he had pumped out into the world flowed out and down the throat of the twitching, writhing tycoon.

Janek

So many dead workers. So many lost to cost cutting, unsafe machinery, deliberate negligence. They had died falling or crushed or mangled, and now every one of them reached out, their hands in Janek's as he gripped either side of Tobias's head and squeezed, his grasp like a machine, slowly pressing and pushing and crushing until the bone cracked beneath his grip.

Jésus

So, this was what it was to be truly part of something beautiful. A grand flowing force of revenge. This man had taken land from so many, dispossessed them and stolen what had provided them with life. It only seemed right for the land to take his life back in turn. And as Tobias thrashed his last, Jésus stretched out his hand and felt himself pulling the blood from the many wounds of his victim, down into the floor, into Banyan Court itself, draining the once great man until he was nothing but a dry white corpse.

Tobias

Tobias Fell was dead. His last moments nothing but the purest of agonies. As his guests became themselves again, they could do nothing but stare at the grotesque parody of a human form that had just minutes ago been one of the most powerful men on the planet. None of them said a word, each trying to come to terms with what had happened. There seemed no great satisfaction, no glow of satisfied revenge.

But neither could any one of them bring themselves to regret what they had done.

Epilogue

Burnt Coffee

'I keep telling you, I was concussed.' David Erikson sipped his coffee and gave Cari a knowing look.

'I know. You don't believe the ghost bit.'

'Hey, I believe in ghosts. I mean, I'm subscribed to your channel and everything.'

'It's Damian's channel,' Cari corrected. 'I just help out.'

'My point is, I don't really know what I saw, except maybe that Tobias Fell forced you all to do some really fucked-up things and you, uh, responded poorly to it. You want to say ghosts were involved, who am I to argue?'

Cari tried to smile. She enjoyed her periodic meetings with David, though they had been getting less frequent. Even so, she still wasn't quite ready to joke about that night. In the quiet, she could see he knew he'd gone a bit too far.

'Did you see the article?' he asked, in a more serious tone. Cari nodded.

'Thank you,' she said. 'For keeping us out of it like that. We've been fielding a few anniversary calls from elsewhere and they can get pretty pushy.'

'Tell me about it.'

'Like we would have any idea about forensic evidence from five years ago.'

'Or lack thereof,' David noted. 'To be honest, I still get calls about it too. Wanting to know when I'll write the *real* story. I tell them I was unconscious, concussed, no idea what happened, but ... Well, you remember how the police were. Sometimes it feels like that interview room all over again.'

'Hard to get past something no one else wants to forget.' Cari sighed.

'At least now people aren't afraid to talk about the sort of thing Fell was up to. You read about Insegur going into administration?'

'Yup. The board got a big payday and the CEO now works for a regulator. Justice at last.'

David shifted awkwardly in his seat. They sipped their coffee in silence for a few moments.

'If you did want to tell your side of things,' he probed gently. 'I wouldn't mind doing a more in-depth retrospective on where everyone is now.'

'Not likely.' Cari shook her head. 'I mean, obviously you know where I am. Damian and Violet too.'

'Sure. And congratulations, by the way.' He gestured to her ring. 'I saw the pictures, you both looked beautiful.'

'Thank you.' Cari beamed now. 'Violet was thinking about something a bit more flashy, but obviously gemstones are, uh ... Well.'

'So, what about the others?'

'Well, I don't know about Janek or Laura. She's not at her old firm anymore and didn't keep in touch and he ... well, he specifically said not to contact him. His business is still in the directory, though, so I guess things aren't going too badly. The others, let's see ... Leon's got some new corporate position, don't see him much, and Jésus is still Jésusing up the art world. Used to see Jason quite regularly, but he's moved up to Manchester, working for that charity Carter's been running into the ground as part of his whole "ethical" thing. Oh, and Gill's a teacher now. Primary school, I think. Not sure, been a while since we talked.'

'Whatever happened to Diego?'

'He's still out there, last I heard. Keeps in touch with Violet sometimes, and Alvita I think. He's changed his name. Kind of had to since I think he's still considered a suspect.'

'Oh? What's he going by now?'

'Not my place to say.'

There was a pause.

'So yeah.' Cari shrugged. 'Everyone just … being alive, I guess. Trying to get on as best we can. Not thinking about it too much.'

'Right.' David paused before his next question. 'What about Anna? That sort of thing, at that age…'

'Yeah, it's—' Cari looked uncomfortable. 'Sorry to sound like a broken record, but I'm not sure how much I can tell you. Her parents moved her away, changed their name as well which … fair enough I guess. Didn't want people to associate her with what happened. Alvita's still in touch with them, I think Anna and Tommy see each other sometimes. She says Anna's growing up fine. Eleven now.'

'And Penny?'

'Gone. Like the rest of them.'

'I suppose children can be very resilient,' David said, though he didn't sound convinced.

'I hope so.' Cari's voice was sad. 'That's the part I don't think I could ever forgive. Involving her like that.'

'Yeah.' David considered his next question. 'You still … see anything?'

'I don't dance, if that's what you're asking.' She laughed

hollowly. 'Or wear jewellery. And Violet's part-time. Everyone's got stuff to deal with, David. Even you.'

He said nothing. They sat in silence for a few minutes, drinking their coffee. Cari's phone buzzed on the table.

'Oh, sorry, I've got to go.'

'Sure thing.'

David stood and tried unnecessarily to help her with her coat.

'Did you hear the news, by the way?' he asked as she started towards the door.

She looked back.

'They're pulling it down next year. Might put this whole business to rest.'

'Yeah?' Caroline smiled sadly, silhouette outlined in the doorway. 'And what are they building in its place?'

David didn't reply, though he knew the answer.

'More luxury apartments?' She didn't even feign surprise.

He shrugged, trying a smile. 'Hopefully with fewer ghosts.'

Caroline shook her head.

'The ghosts were never the problem.'

Acknowledgements

I have never created alone, and there are so many people who have helped this book become a reality. I want to say thank you first and foremost to my editor Rachel for taking a chance on me, and for handing me the most timely and inspiring idea. This book is hers as much as it is mine. Thank you to Zoë, my agent, for holding my hand through the strange and unsettling waters of the publishing world. Thanks also to Alex, Lowri, Story, Elizabeth and everyone at Rusty Quill for helping me get here, and my past collaborators and dearest friends Frank, Tim, Jess, Rachel, Kofi, Morgan and Fran. And thanks most of all to Sasha, the centre of my world, without whom I could never create anything a fraction as good. Thanks also to Sir Pouncealot and The Ambassador for occasionally getting off my lap to let me write.

Credits

Jonathan Sims and Gollancz would like to thank everyone at Orion who worked on the publication of *Thirteen Storeys* in the UK.

Editorial
Rachel Winterbottom
Brendan Durkin

Copy editor
Jonathan Oliver

Proof reader
Jane Howard

Audio
Paul Stark
Amber Bates

Contracts
Anne Goddard
Paul Bulos
Jake Alderson

Design
Lucie Stericker
Loulou Clark
Joanna Ridley
Nick May

Editorial Management
Charlie Panayiotou
Jane Hughes
Alice Davis

Finance
Jennifer Muchan
Jasdip Nandra
Afeera Ahmed
Elizabeth Beaumont
Sue Baker

Marketing
Lucy Cameron

Production
Paul Hussey

Publicity
Will O'Mullane

Sales
Jen Wilson
Laura Fletcher

Esther Waters
Victoria Laws
Rachael Hum
Ellie Kyrke-Smith
Frances Doyle
Georgina Cutler

Operations
Jo Jacobs
Sharon Willis
Lisa Pryde
Lucy Brem